With thanks to Annamarie, my Mother Jayne and Father Gordon for your support. Thank you to my husband Colin, for being you. Thank you Kieran for the bears.

 ISBN: 978-1-4461-8492-9

Born This Way:
The Life of Joshua

Prologue

Joshua and his mother didn't often argue, but when a thirteen year old doesn't get his way, he won't take kindly to it. Lynne was shocked that Joshua wanted to go to this party anyway, normally all he wanted to do was sit in his room reading his science fiction novels and watching old recordings of Lost in Space and Star Wars. Joshua knew he had just a few minutes left to convince his mother to allow him out of the house tonight, once the car pulled up outside the school he'd have to explain to his friends why he wouldn't be seeing them tonight.

"Look, I have a headache! I'm trying to concentrate on driving you to school, I've got enough on with your father's childishness without you starting," screamed Lynne. Lynne and her husband Neil were having great marital difficulties and Joshua often felt like a 'go-between', this made Lynne wonder if Joshua's sudden eagerness to spend evenings out were to avoid the atmosphere at home.

"But mum, everyone's gonna' be there, I'll be the only one and they'll all laugh at me," Joshua pleaded.

"For the last time Joshua, no, you are too young to be out 'till the middle of the night, will you just shut up or I'll kill you?!" Lynne replied, tears filling her eyes; life in general had been stressful of late. Of course, she didn't mean what she said, but the stress was making her say things she'd later regret. Joshua could sense his mother's agitation and decided to remain silent for the remainder of the journey to school. Lynne's tears clouded her sight, she had reached breaking point. "I just can't take anymore!" she cried. By this point Lynne had lost her concentration. It all happened so quickly, surely she would see the tree before it was too late.

"Mum!" Joshua screamed, and suddenly darkness.

Joshua awoke in a state of distress. His eyes took a moment to focus on his surroundings. The room appeared to be very regimental and bleak. He sat up in bed hoping for some acknowledgement. A doctor entered the room, aged in his late twenties. Joshua noticed what a clean cut handsome man he was; his presence gave Joshua a sense of calmness.

"Hi matey, I'm Doctor Greg Foster, do you know where you are?"

"I'm not sure," Joshua replied. Doctor Foster explained the accident to Joshua and how they'd hit the tree and made Joshua feel fortunate to not only have survived the crash, but without injury. Joshua attempted to recall the events of that morning and remembered his mother's words "Shut up or I'll kill you!" They were some of the last words Lynne had said to Joshua that day. Of course, he realised Lynne didn't mean it literally, but the irony of the situation alarmed him. "I nearly died?" asked Joshua.

"You could have," replied the handsome doctor, "You were fortunate to be positioned in the safest part of the car". Joshua began putting the pieces together in his mind, if he was in the safest position of the car, did that mean his mother was in the most precarious position? The doctor could see Joshua's anxiety, "Try to get some rest, I'll check in on you later," he recommended. Doctor Foster was avoiding the obvious question of Lynne's condition as Joshua remained in a daze, attempting to gather his thoughts together. Although Joshua's father Neil had asked the sympathetic doctor to break the news of Lynne's death to their son, he was hoping Neil would reconsider for Joshua's sake, he felt it would be better coming from his father. However, Doctor Foster doesn't know Neil, he isn't the best at dealing with difficult situations or with his own grief. Lynne had always seen Neil as weak, which is partly why the marriage had disintegrated. The doctor breathed a sigh of relief as Joshua returned to his previous state of slumber.

In the corridor Neil was sat forward holding his head in his hands, although Doctor Foster faced these types of situations daily, it always 'struck a chord' when children were involved.

"I think you should tell him, and soon," he interrupted Neil's upset, "You need to grieve together." Neil slowly raised his head and declared, "She'd still be here with us now if it wasn't for his devilry."

"He's thirteen years of age, you can't hold him responsible for your wife's departure, it was an accident, just an accident."

"That's easy for you to say, my wife is dead! What would you know about families anyway, I bet you don't even have any kids," Neil began to weep; deep down he knew that if anyone was to be condemned for Lynne's fatality it should be himself, but it was more comfortable to blame Joshua, in order to prevent his own feelings of guilt.

"Actually I do have a child out there somewhere, he'd be about Joshua's age; my girlfriend and I were too young when we had him, we had to give him up for adoption, but there's not a day goes by that I don't wonder about him," Doctor Foster announced, then placed his hand on Neil's shoulder and said "I'm sure you'll do the right thing."

Neil was now alone, stationary, he knew what had to be done, but how could he tell his own son that his mother was dead, and could he refrain from lashing out and distributing blame? Neil entered Joshua's hospital room. Joshua was sleeping, he looked so unscathed, Neil felt this was unjust, his beloved wife, although the marriage had disputes he still loved her with all his heart, and now she was dead and Joshua, who he perceived as the cause of Lynne's death was relaxing, a picture of tranquillity. Neil felt a sense of rage but at the same time he was grieving, he was an emotional rollercoaster, he himself could not have predicted his reaction or upcoming outbursts. Joshua awoke to the sight of his father

standing before him. He had a deranged look on his face, Joshua couldn't fathom it; still piecing together the events of the morning, he said,
"Dad, the car crashed into a tree, it all happened so quickly, I don't know how it happened." Neil wanted to shout and scream but managed to contain his rage, as much as he wanted to announce to Joshua how he'd caused his own mothers death, he remained emotionless.
"It was an accident," Neil proclaimed.
"Is mum ok? The doctor didn't tell me." This was one of the most difficult moments of Neil's life. Although he blamed Joshua for Lynne's death he was trying his best to conceal that and break the news to his son gently. Neil was stalling. "Please tell me dad," Joshua pleaded "Is anything wrong with mum? Is she hurt?"
"Joshua, your mother is dead," Neil announced softly, tears filling his eyes, "She's gone."
"No no no no! She can't be, my mum can't be dead!" Joshua screamed. Neil was cold, he was unable to sympathise with Joshua, he couldn't even face him.
"Doctor says he wants you to stay in overnight for observation," Neil said casually as though he were mentioning he didn't like a record on the radio, and then he departed the room. Joshua was deserted with nothing to see but the dull white walls surrounding him. His own father had abandoned him at the most fragile moment of his life, he felt as though he'd lost both of his parents. He wept through the night, he'd never been so terrified and lonesome in his entire life.

The return home was sterile, conversation between Neil and his son was scarce, the daily routines became conventional, Seven am both alarms sound, eight thirty the silent journey to school, after which Neil would drive on to his workplace, the local printers where he packed boxes, four pm Joshua would catch the bus home and enjoy the hour in which his house was his fortress of solitude, five pm Neil would arrive home, usually with take away food as he was unfamiliar with cookery, six o'clock Neil would perch in front of the television set with a bottle of beer and fall asleep; meanwhile Joshua would be in his room either watching science fiction or reading it. The atmosphere at home however would be deemed acceptable compared to what Joshua faced walking the streets and at school. Neighbours would offer their condolences and confer with each other about "Poor little Joshua, he's only thirteen and that father of his is a waste of space anyway." At school the other juveniles would pause their conversations on Joshua's arrival. Joshua did not attend his mother's funeral, he could not cope with it. Neil saw this as another admission of guilt.

5

Joshua arrived home that day and saw a black tie on the floor, he walked up the stairs and looked in Neil's bedroom, as he passed. His father was sprawled out across the double bed Lynne used to rest in, he was wearing black trousers and a white unbuttoned shirt. Joshua hoped Neil was asleep and continued his journey to his own bedroom.

"Aren't you even gonna' ask me how it went?" a condescending voice came from his fathers bedroom. Joshua reluctantly turned to face his loathsome father, "Well are you going to ask me how the funeral was?" bellowed Neil.

"I was going to….." Joshua replied, "I'm sorry dad."

"Well you know what you are now son, you're a little bastard, a little fuckin' bastard!" At this point Joshua realised his father was intoxicated, Neil had always had a weakness for alcohol but since Lynne's death going out on binges was part of his daily routine.

"Dad please stop."

"You're a disgrace boy! A disgrace!" Neil continued. Joshua could empathise with his father, he too was feeling bewildered and exasperated at the loss of his mother but this he felt was unjust.

"I couldn't face it!" Joshua went on.

"Guilt does that to a person," announced Neil. It was like a light bulb being switched on, Joshua had not realised until this exact moment that Neil saw him as the one to blame for Lynne's death. Joshua cried,

"I did not kill her dad, I didn't." At this point Neil lost his temper, leaped out of bed and struck Joshua across the face.

"Yes you did!"

"It wasn't my fault"

"It was your fault Joshua and I will never forgive you!"

Joshua bolted into his bedroom, he lay on the bed and sobbed deep into the night; his father had never physically harmed him before, he was in a state of distress and shock. Things would never be the same again.

Chapter 1

8

As the months passed by, Joshua tried to return to some kind of normality. His classmates were unsure of how to handle the situation, and, as with most playground gossip, it was forgotten quickly. A death in a thirteen year olds eyes could fall in the same category as 'Jennifer kissed Matt at the school dance', and the latter would most likely be discussed for longer. The one person who supported Joshua was Megan O'Donnelly, an over-achieving, witty, desirable blonde haired thirteen year old. Megan had all a young teenage male could want, the looks, the brains and even a cute Irish accent, she had only moved to Sheffield recently from Dublin and had taken a shine to Joshua. She was wise beyond her years which created jealousy among her classmates, she rode horses, skated and debated, she was adored by the males and cursed by the females. Megan could relate to Joshua as she'd had a similar experience, her father had died six months previously and she had been forced to relocate with her mother, as her career warranted. Megan and Joshua sat beside each other in Maths, French and Geography lessons, they had a connection that their classmates simply could not grasp, they could discuss anything.

Megan and Joshua were on the school bus travelling home on a beautiful summer Friday afternoon.

"What have you planned for the weekend?" Megan asked.

"Dunno,' maybe do some reading" Joshua replied.

"Booooooring, come over to my house, let's do something fun!"

Joshua, go to a girls house! 'Can I really do this?', he mentally pondered. An avalanche of thoughts tumbled through Joshua's head, 'What does she mean by this? Does she have romantic feelings for me? Does she want us to have sex? I'm thirteen, can I really go to a girls house on a Saturday for fun?' "Joshua, what do you say? Are you coming over?" Megan questioned, interrupting his trail of thought.

"Er…well."

"It's ok, If you don't want to….." Joshua could already sense the offence he was causing,

"Sure, what's your address?"

On arrival at home, Joshua's concerns duplicated; he wondered exactly what Megan had planned for their Saturday afternoon together. Was this the point at which he would be forced to decide whether or not he wanted Megan as his girlfriend? He had contemplated this before, however something held him back. Although Megan and Joshua connected intellectually and spiritually, he wasn't sexually attracted to her. He knew this was strange as he appeared to be the only male at his school that didn't use Megan as a masturbatory fantasy, and yet he was her only real male companion. Joshua was confused, he couldn't turn to his father and under normal circumstances he'd talk to Megan, but this time she was the root of his confusion, if she was developing feelings for him, how could he tell her that he was confused about his sexuality? Joshua spent the evening agonising over the upcoming events of the weekend and went to bed at eight thirty.

On this night Joshua had a very significant dream. This dream was a result of his mental torment over the issue of whether or not he and Megan were to have sex the next day. The dream began with Joshua arriving at Megan's house, it was a mansion, a home fit for a billionaire, his imagination was running wild as such a property did not exist in Sheffield. She invited him in,

"So, is your mum home?" Joshua asked,

"No," Megan replied, "We're all alone, we're free to do whatever our hearts desire." Megan was wearing an extremely short skirt and her upper body clothing was little more than a bra. Her breasts were bulging out of her top and in this fantasy were significantly larger than in reality.

"Shall we play a game?" Joshua suggested.

"Yes I have allsorts of toys, come into my room," Megan replied. Megan's room was gloriously spacious and extremely well decorated, and she had an enormous double bed. "Let me show you my toys," Megan went on, she opened the cupboard and revealed a selection of sex toys. Joshua's imagination could only stretch so far, as a thirteen year old the only knowledge of sex toys he possessed he had gained in the school yard. All the basics were there though, whips, dildos, body paints and a selection of condoms. "We can use these later," Megan said seductively. She grabbed Joshua by his shirt and kissed him passionately; they fell backwards onto the bed and continued their embrace. Joshua was feeling overwhelmed, his lack of experience was evident. Unexpectedly, the bedroom door swung open and entered a magnificent figure of a man, blonde wavy hair and blue eyes. Wearing just a pair of tight briefs, his rippling muscles were exhibited for Joshua to see. "My brother's here," Megan cried with delight. She jolted off the bed.

"Can I join in the fun?" asked her handsome brother.

"Course you can!" Megan replied delightedly. The hunk walked over to the bed and climbed on to Joshua.

"Hello there," he said. Feeling overpowered, Joshua replied simply with "Hi." At this point Megan had disappeared; Joshua was alone on Megan's bed with this perfect form of a man. He became excited; the stud ran his hand over the bulge in Joshua's trousers and stated seductively,

"You obviously like what you see." Joshua had no reply; before he could grasp the situation he could feel another man's tongue against his own.

Joshua awoke, he could feel dampness in his bed, he investigated this under the bedclothes and realised he'd just had his first wet dream, something he'd heard so much discussion about in the schoolyard. Joshua felt alarmed by this, the dream had revolved around another male, he had dreamed about embracing another man and it had excited him, Joshua had already been finding other males appealing but this was the first time he had acknowledged these feelings, he had never admitted to himself before that he preferred boys to girls. Joshua attempted to sleep that night but couldn't clear his mind, the dream replayed itself in Joshua's head over and over. A number of questions came to his mind, 'Am I gay?' 'If I'm gay will my friends still like me?' 'Does this mean I can't have children?' 'Can I trust anyone with this information?' Joshua was still yet to reach his fourteenth birthday, this was very puzzling for him. He wished his mother was alive, she'd know what to do.

The next morning Joshua's head was filled with concerns. He wondered how he should interpret the bizarre dream of the previous night and he was bursting with anticipation of the day ahead. What kind of fun was Megan suggesting? Would she even have siblings and if so would she have a brother who looked like the figure in his illusion? What would her abode really look like? Would it be a mansion or a bungalow? Joshua seriously contemplated whether or not to proceed with his plans for the day, but Megan was expecting him and he didn't want to disappoint her, nor did he want to spend the day with his father.

As he approached Megan's house, he was put a little at ease by the size of the property, it was tiny, the opposite of the home he'd seen in his dream. He knocked on the door, waited a few seconds and a figure appeared. 'It's not Megan', Joshua thought, 'Who could it be? Perhaps her handsome brother from the dream?' The door swung open and standing before him was a plain faced woman aged in her mid thirties, she was wearing a white dressing gown and slippers, her hair was blonde but not styled, she had no make-up on.

"You must be Joshua," the woman announced,

"Hi, er……yes I am," he replied nervously.

"Well don't just stand there, come on in. I'm Janice, Megan's mother," she went on. Joshua entered the house and introduced himself to Janice.

"Why don't you take a seat in the living room and I'll tell Megan you're here."

"Ok." Joshua was unsure as to the location of the living room but could only see one exit and concluded that he couldn't be mistaken. He waited in the living room as per Janice's request. As his eyes gazed around the room he noticed many photographs of a beautiful couple. The woman in the photos had long curly blonde hair and the man wore a suit and looked

incredibly handsome. Joshua picked up one of the framed photographs for a closer examination; at this point Megan entered the room and greeted him,
"Hi Joshua."
"Hiya Megan," Joshua replied, a little startled as he was scrutinising the family's belongings.
"Sorry, I didn't mean to….." Joshua panicked.
"It's ok," replied Megan.
"Who are the couple in the photo?" Joshua asked.
"My parents of course," Megan replied, "I know it's hard to believe it now though, mother has really let herself go since then." Joshua remained silent. "We didn't always live like this you know, we used to have a big house when dad was alive," Megan continued.
"It's ok," replied Joshua, "My father works in a factory, he's a drunk and our house is no bigger and …… and ….. and I hate him!" Joshua had surprised himself by confiding in Megan with these private feelings, perhaps he was more comfortable with Megan than he realised. She empathised with him,
"We're such a pair aren't we?" "At least we've got each other." Megan opened her arms, Joshua embraced her, this lasted several minutes, it had been long overdue for both of them. The pair had been deprived of affection in recent months, both their parents had suffered great losses and as a result, their personalities and outlooks on life would never be the same again. Joshua wept in Megan's arms, she continued to comfort him. After several minutes, he stopped and turned away in a state of embarrassment. "It's ok," Megan sympathised, "We all need a shoulder to cry on once in a while." Joshua thanked her, he had never felt this comfortable with anyone, not even his own mother; it was as though they were soul mates, and yet, he couldn't refrain from thinking about his dream. There was nothing physically appealing about Megan to Joshua and yet she was beautiful, but could he contemplate entering into a relationship with her on these terms? "Anyway, I promised you some fun!"Megan announced spontaneously. Oh dear, this was the moment Joshua had feared, was Megan really expecting him to make love to her? Was she about to expose her kinky toys? Megan kneeled on the floor and reached under the settee, she then pulled out a star wars board game. Joshua breathed an internal sigh of relief. "Your favourite,"
said Megan, giving him a cute, cheeky smile he hadn't been exposed to before. The game appeared to be new; Joshua questioned this and Megan replied, "I bought it yesterday, we can play with it today, then it's yours to keep, it's a gift for your fourteenth birthday." Joshua was overwhelmed by his friend's generosity, she was quickly becoming the most important

person in his life, it was also becoming painfully clear that Megan was attracted to him and desired a more intimate relationship. The two companions played for hours. Joshua glanced at his watch, it displayed 'five thirty', and he became agitated. "What's wrong?" Megan asked, "My dad will kill me if I'm late for dinner," he replied. Joshua began compacting the many pieces of the board game into its case.
"Joshua just before you go, I need to talk to you about something," Megan announced, the look in her eyes suggested she was nervous about her upcoming statement. Joshua looked deeply into her eyes, words were not necessary, his look said that he wanted her to continue and ask that inevitable question, he knew he had to deal with this issue sooner or later. Megan continued, "There are a lot of cute guys at school Joshua, but none that I like as much as you, I'm ready for a boyfriend and I want it to be you." There was such maturity in her voice and in her statement, as a result of the tragedies both youngsters had already faced in their short lives, they'd developed rapidly over the last year. Joshua was bewildered, he'd been anticipating this moment for several months now, and yet was still unprepared now that it had come. He couldn't erase the memory of his dream and the man who had featured in it from his mind and he was trying desperately to ignore it. Megan was looking hurt at Joshua's delay in reacting to her statement.
"I'll think about it Megan, I promise I'll think about it," he said in a panic. He bolted away from the house and even neglected to take his gift with him. Megan sat and wept, wondering whether or not she had made the right move.

Joshua was lying awake in bed, monitoring the clock, he saw it change at eleven pm, then midnight and he was still alert at 1 am. He was mentally drained, he wished he could press a pause button on his life and have some breathing space, he was more confused than ever, as well as concerned for Megan's feelings, whom he would have to face on the upcoming Monday morning. Joshua decided to quietly watch the television, he rummaged through the channels and stumbled upon a re-run of Melrose Place. This was extraordinary for Joshua as this was not part of his usual viewing schedule. Something drew him to the programme, he despised this but the attractive semi-naked men on the screen were luring him in. His penis began to stiffen, Joshua was not a compulsive masturbator but he'd made several attempts at it in the past when curiosity overpowered him. He was able to become erect by looking at pictures of women or imagining sexual acts with members of the opposite sex but it required some extra manual stimulation, the sight of a naked man however usually gave him instant excitement, mainly in the most inappropriate, awkward situations, such as the changing rooms following sports at school. He continued to glare at the sun kissed studs on the television before him and began to masturbate, closing his eyes and thinking of Megan, however the temptation was too strong, he had to gaze back at the television to view the muscled bodies which then brought him to orgasm. His feelings changed in an instant, from intense pleasure to extreme guilt. Joshua always felt guilty after masturbating with the aid of a male form, on occasion even to the extent of showering afterwards to clean away the dirty feeling it left him with. He cleaned himself up and dozed off into a deep long sleep, he didn't recall his dream that night and he felt that was for the best.

The next morning, Joshua woke at eleven thirty, prepared for his usual, uneventful Sunday. He strolled down the stairs wearing only his dark blue dressing gown where he found Neil clothed ready for work.
"You'll have to look after yourself today, I'm going in to do some overtime," he said, as though he'd just announced he was attending a funeral.
"Oh ok," Joshua agreed.
"Since I'm the only one who brings any money into this house, we've gotta' make ends meet, we don't all get to do as we please and crawl out of bed in the middle of the day," and on that note Neil departed the house, slamming the door behind him.
"Good fuckin' riddance," Joshua muttered. Just seconds later the doorbell rang, "What did you forget?!" he shouted while pulling open the front door. He was startled to see Megan on the doorstep.
"Hey," she said, reluctantly.
"Er.....Hiya!" Joshua replied while glancing down to confirm that his dressing gown was concealing as much of his body as possible. At this point he noticed Megan was carrying the board game she'd presented to him the previous day.
"You forgot something," she said, smirking in a cute, loving sense. Joshua was puzzled by her attitude, considering the events of Saturday he was preparing himself for a sea of questions, suspicion and bitterness, but it never came; all that had arrived on the doorstep was the same old Megan, smiling sweetly as ever. Joshua gave her a smile in return and was so overwhelmed by the moment that he almost forgot his embarrassment over being seen in his nightwear by a potential love interest. "Are you going to invite me in, or shall I stand on the doorstep all day?" the banter continued.
"Sorry Megan, come in." This was the first time Megan had entered Joshua's house, she noticed the untidy state, a result of an all male occupation. Joshua excused himself and altered his attire, this also gave

him an opportunity to ponder the inevitable conversation he faced with Megan. He knew he could stall no longer, it was decision time, was he to enter into a relationship with Megan? He'd risk destroying the friendship with either decision. Joshua returned to Megan downstairs, she was seated, falsely smiling sweetly. "I really appreciate you bringing the board game to me," he said sincerely. Megan stood and announced,
"I would do anything for you Joshua, anything at all." Joshua felt warm and secure; he had never quite had this feeling since his mother's death. All of a sudden he became relaxed, his inhibitions were no more, the calmness of this beautiful girl put his mind at ease. At this point Joshua realised that rejecting Megan would be foolish, she was the only person in his life that truly adored him and loved him unconditionally; he could feel it, perhaps they were a little young, but the connection was real. Joshua mentally convinced himself he was doing the right thing. He saw this as the 'normal' thing to do. Fourteen year old males are supposed to have a trophy in the form of a female on their arm, or so he had been raised to believe, his mother had always told him he'd be a heartbreaker and that he was the most handsome boy in Sheffield. This was true, Joshua was very attractive physically and many females at his school secretly lusted after him, but he wasn't asked to date often as he seemed unapproachable and because he didn't spend many evenings out it was assumed he wasn't 'cool' and that he listened to classical music. The girls wouldn't admit they found Joshua physically appealing as that would not comply with the image they so desperately sought. Joshua sat beside Megan and took her hand into his own.
"Does this mean…..?" she asked.
"I'd be crazy to say no Megan, you're everything a boy could want." This was music to Megan's ears; at that moment she knew Joshua was 'the one' and they'd be together forever, however thirteen year old girls can often be wrong about these things, she touched Joshua delicately on the shoulder, then pressed her lips against his. Joshua's first kiss, he'd always wondered what it'd be like, and it felt good. Megan felt so fortunate to have this sensitive, caring, attractive boy in her arms.

Chapter 2

18

Joshua was standing, naked, studying himself in the mirror. His sixteenth birthday was rapidly approaching; all of a sudden mischievous acts were to become legal and part of everyday life. Joshua would be able to smoke cigarettes or even have sex if he so wished. It was time to review his life, he was almost sixteen years of age, although having an October birthday made him one of the oldest in his form at school and meant he'd be almost seventeen before he truly became free. As he gazed at the reflection of his body he mentally questioned himself, 'Am I good looking?' 'Should I lose weight?' 'I wonder if my penis is above average size.' The answer to all of those questions when addressed to Megan would be, 'You're fine, I love you just the way you are.' For over two years Megan had been, not just Joshua's girlfriend but also his best friend. He didn't have a lot of close friends, his best male companion was named James Carpenter, they would attend lessons together and occasionally spend time together outside of school, however James resented Megan because of her demands on Joshua's time. Joshua often compared his body to James'. During P.E lessons he observed his friend's toned body and wished he could look the same. However, no amount of flexing his biceps before the mirror was going to improve his body and although he liked to deceive himself, his body hadn't progressed since the last time he examined it.

The next day, at the end of P.E, a crowd of rambunctious teenage boys charged into the changing room. It was the end of school and everyone was anxious to desert the grounds. James and Joshua were removing their sports kit and putting their uniforms back on, as they did so, Joshua once again noticed James' physique. He could feel his penis beginning to stiffen at the sight of this beautiful body. He attempted to pull his shirt down as far as possible to conceal the bulge in his trousers but this was not necessary as James became distracted. Michael Smith had just entered the room. Michael was somewhat a reserved boy, getting to know him was a battle Joshua had given up on several years ago. He was cute in a subtle way, perhaps because in school he made very little effort with his hair and the attire they were all obliged to wear was less than flattering.

"Poofter boy!" James screamed, which then caused a commotion throughout the changing room. Comments about Michael's sexuality were coming from all directions. "You know what we do with poofs Michael?" asked James. Joshua could see the look of terror in Michael's eyes as the immature school boys prepared a punishment. At this point Mr Johnson entered, the tough as nails games tutor,

19

"Alright lads, anyone not showered and changed in two minutes can attend detention tomorrow lunchtime," his voice bellowed across the room. Micheal had been saved by the bell, Joshua could see the look of relief on his face.
"James, why are you being so nasty to Michael?" Joshua asked.
"He's a fuckin' poofter," announced James, "a total Nancy boy!"
"We don't know that," replied Joshua.
"Ask Helen Stevens, he came out to her, the entire school knows." What a discovery, there was a gay student in Joshua's P.E class; he wondered if Michael had similar experiences to his own, his immediate thought was that he simply had to talk to Micheal, he had never been able to tell anyone about his desire for other males, perhaps now he could start to make sense of it. The end of day bell sounded and the boys charged out of the changing room like a herd of elephants.
"Are you coming with me on the bus tonight?" asked James.
"No, I've got plans with Megan," Joshua lied. James departed, leaving only Joshua and Micheal remaining in the room. Michael was peacefully packing away his belongings into his school bag, not as eager to gain those precious extra few seconds of freedom the other students would have by racing out of the door. Michael noticed Joshua's presence, then turned away and continued to compact his belongings into his bag. Joshua shifted slowly towards Michael,
"What do you want Joshua?" he asked bluntly. Joshua took a step backwards, dumbfounded by Michael's reaction to him and at the same time startled that Micheal even knew his name. Joshua realised that Michael was suffering from paranoia, to be expected considering that his most important secret had been discussed throughout the entire school.
"Well, come on Joshua, don't just stand there, do you want to take a good look at the freak too? If you've come to insult me I've had enough for one day thank you," Michael continued. Joshua empathised with his terrified classmate, imagining himself in that position, the entire school pointing, giggling, threatening and all simply because the students feared the unknown. 'What if my own tendencies were to become public knowledge?' he pondered, 'Would James turn against me?' He gave Michael a smile that assured him he'd come in peace.
"I just wanted to apologise for James' outburst," he announced.
"You're not responsible for him Joshua, you have no need to apologise," Michael replied.
"He's my friend, and I feel shame to be seen with him acting this way, he shouldn't discriminate against you for being gay, it's just the way you are, you're not hurting him," Michael smiled and sat on the bench, patting the space beside him,

"I'm not going to bite."
"I know," Joshua sat a comfortable distance away on the bench.
"How did it get out?" he asked.
"My so-called best friend Helen Stevens blabbed to the entire school, I thought she was trustworthy, obviously not," Michael replied, trying his hardest to with-hold the tears falling from his eyes. He then turned his head away and proclaimed, "I don't know why the hell I'm telling you this anyway!"
"You obviously need a shoulder," Joshua replied.
"I don't know you Joshua, I don't know you at all."
"Well you live quite close to me don't you?"
"Yes," Michael reluctantly admitted.
"Let's walk home together," Joshua suggested. The two new found friends strolled home together discussing Helens betrayal and the immature reactions from the school yard. It was clear to Joshua that his sympathetic ear was appreciated. The two teens exchanged mobile phone numbers before departing to different directions home.
"It's been really great to talk to you Joshua," Michael said, "Megan is a lucky girl."
"What makes you say that?" asked Joshua.
"Believe me, she's very lucky to have a boyfriend as mature, understanding and open minded as you are," he replied and gave a look that Joshua couldn't fathom. They parted, promising to speak again soon.

Joshua arrived home to a cold greeting from his father,
"Where have you been? The food is getting cold!" He noticed the fish and chips on Neil's plate and another meal wrapped in paper on the table. 'Fast food again,' he thought, 'Will my father ever learn to cook?'
"Sorry dad," he replied, "A friend needed me."
"I see, one of your queer-boy mates needed you, well next time let me know." Forgetting for a moment that Neil often referred to his friends as 'Queer-boys', Joshua took his fathers statement literally and reacted to it accordingly,
"So what if he's gay?" Neil stared at him in shock,
"I guess I can't tell you who you can be friends with, you'd just do what you wanted as usual, just don't let it rub off onto you."
"You can stick your fish and chips, I hate you dad, I hate you so much!" Joshua yelled and ran to his bedroom in a flood of tears. He positioned himself sideways on the bed, at this point he realised he had foolishly admitted to his father that he'd associated with a homosexual. In Phil's eyes this was sinful; his lack of knowledge led him to believe homosexuality was contagious or something that could be taught, rather than a natural part of life that cannot be changed. Joshua felt a vibration

in his pocket. He reached down and grabbed his mobile phone, it displayed that a new text message had been received. He read through the message, expecting the sender to be Megan, 'Hey Joshua, wanted to say thanks again for your understanding. I wondered if you fancied meeting up again later. Text back please. Michael x.' Fearing the unfamiliar, he was reluctant to accept the invitation, however curiosity and an overwhelming desire to leave the house and his fathers company caused Joshua to respond with a 'Yes'. Two hours later Joshua arrived at the park for his arranged meeting with Michael. The teen was seated on a bench, he looked so fragile, afraid of the entire world, unfortunately this was not entirely paranoia, there were many immature tyrants at the school who feared what they didn't understand. Michael stood and approached Joshua.

"Thank you for coming," he said, "I really appreciate it."

"Don't worry, I was glad of any excuse to escape my father," Joshua replied; his fears and inhibitions about meeting with Michael had already vanished, the two teenagers felt so relaxed together.

"Why did you want to get away from your father?" Michael asked.

"Long story."

"Why don't you tell me all about it over a drink? My round," Michael offered. Joshua was shocked by his new companion's proposal, he didn't even turn sixteen for almost a week and rarely drank alcohol; would he even be served at a bar? Would he become intoxicated and look foolish in front of his new companion? Michael was concerned that Joshua was so reluctant to accompany him, wondering if he was being too forward, "It's ok if you don't want to….." he went on.

"No…..I mean yes, I'll come."

"Great, I know a fab' little place, they never ask for ID."

Michael guided Joshua on the route to his favourite bar, he was unsure of what to expect. A thought suddenly entered Joshua's mind, 'was Michael taking him to a gay bar?'A stereotypical vision came into his mind; he imagined middle aged men in black leather dancing to Y.M.C.A, Lily Savage on the stage, a group of twenty-something's dressed in sailor boy outfits and an orgy of oral and anal sex. 'Oh my god! Am I really ready to go to a place like that?' he pondered. Michael could sense that he was deep in thought as they continued walking.

"Joshua, is something wrong?" he asked.

"You aren't taking me to a gay bar are you?"

"Of course," Michael announced, as though it should have been obvious, "Gay men never go to any other bars you know," he said sarcastically, the comment was followed by a snigger. Joshua realised he was speaking in jest and apologised for his assumption, at the same time quietly impressed by the wit of his new found friend.

They arrived at Michaels chosen watering hole and Joshua realised how idiotic he'd been. Parkers Cocktail Bar was a quaint little establishment with civilised people, all just relaxing after a long, hard day at work. Most of the music being played in the bar was from the 1980's, such songs as, 'Right here waiting,' and 'Tainted love.'

"This place is really nice," Joshua said positively.

"I'm glad you like it. What you drinking?" asked Michael. Joshua instantly replied by requesting a Cola, then mentally kicked himself; sure Michael would think of him as a sissy now.

"You're not drinking?" Micheal asked.

"Well I don't normally," Joshua replied.

"OK that's fine, shame though 'cos they've got some amazing cocktails."

"Go on then, surprise me," Joshua said in a sudden burst of spontaneity. The surroundings were ultra modern and the settees extremely relaxing, the type that make trips to the bar a chore. They seated themselves and quickly slouched down, enjoying the comfort. Joshua had never tasted a cocktail before and was clueless as to the content of his drink. They chatted and giggled about the school, teachers and other students and during the discussion a connection was developing, they discovered many common interests, they both enjoyed science fiction and throughout the evening they both naturally chanted along to the classic records being played in the background. Joshua reached the bottom of his glass and insisted on paying for the next round of cocktails. They were both aware that the issue of Michael's sexuality was looming, it would be raised sooner or later and Joshua was eager to discuss it, while at the same time not wishing to imply that the male sex was another of their common interests. He returned with a jug of cocktail and two glasses.

"Wow, you like this don't you?!" Michael pointed out in astonishment, this being the same boy who'd originally requested a cola.

"It's so nice!" Joshua replied enthusiastically. He then returned to his seat and asked, "So what about Helen? Are you guys still friends?" Michael gave Joshua another unfathomable look; the pair weren't yet accustomed to each others body language. At this point Joshua realised just how extremely attractive his new friend was, he had deep blue eyes, dark hair and an incredibly cute face, his nose was perfectly shaped, as were his lips. Joshua was struggling to find fault in his appearance, and yet he'd never noticed before.

"I can't forgive her Joshua. What she did was so spiteful! You just don't do those sorts of things to your friends," Michael replied, tears filling his eyes. He apologised.

"It's ok, your best friend betrayed you and turned half of the school against you, it's understandable you'd be upset," Joshua sympathised. Michael began to sob. Joshua never liked to see anyone cry, he was himself a sensitive person.
"It's ok." Joshua said, offering his shoulder to Michael. He held him in his arms tightly for several minutes, though it felt like an eternity to them both. "I think you needed that."
"I think you're right, thank you," Michael replied, not want the evening to end. Micheal noticed out of the corner of his eye that they were being monitored by a group of teenagers on another table, "Joshua we're being watched by the lads on that table, I'm not sure who they are, but maybe we should leave. I don't want your life to be made a living hell like mine." Joshua considered Michael's statement for a moment and smiled, he felt so safe with his new companion, as though they were reserved from the rest of the world.
"It's very kind of you Michael, but no. We've got as much right to be here as they have and frankly, their opinion of me doesn't interest me," he replied. Joshua's attitude amazed Michael and made him realise that every cloud does have a silver lining, in this case the teasing and torment at school had resulted in his newly found friendship.
"You're great,"
"I know," Joshua replied in jest. At the end of the night the two teens parted and arranged another get together for the following evening. Joshua carelessly agreed without enquiring as to Megan's plans.

Joshua arrived home to the usual stale reception from Neil he now expected.
"Where the fuck have you been?" asked his repulsive father, then following up his question with, "And you're pissed!"
"Whatever," Joshua replied, and hurried up to his bedroom. He was feeling far too content to allow his father to destroy his mood. Joshua seated himself on the bed and mentally recalled the events of the last few hours. This had been a very significant day of his life; he had made his first gay friend, and to his own surprise had felt more at ease with him than any of his supposed heterosexual classmates. His mobile phone alerted him of the receipt of a text message, he pressed the 'Read,' button and it simply said 'Thank you.' He scrolled down the message and discovered Michael was the sender and replied with 'See you tomorrow,' and added two crosses at the end.

The next morning at 9:00 the school bell rang the way it always did, and as usual hordes of teenagers stampeded through the corridors. Joshua arrived in his form room and seated himself beside James as

normal; however he didn't receive the usual bubbly reception from his best friend.
"Is something wrong?" he enquired.
"You tell me Joshua, you tell me," James replied in a serious manner.
"I don't understand. What's wrong?" pleaded Joshua.
"It's all around the school Joshua, everyone knows, you were seen!" James spoke as though Joshua had been caught robbing a bank or committing a murder. Joshua felt a shiver down his spine,
"Seen where? What are you talking about?"
"It's no use pretending Joshua, we all know about you and Michael," James blurted out; merely saying the words blatantly repulsed him. A lot of people had jumped to conclusions and Joshua was disappointed by James' attitude, but more importantly than that he felt a rush of concern for Megan. Had she heard the rumours? Would she believe them? Joshua hadn't yet felt ready for a sexual relationship with Megan; would she view this as the reason for his reluctance? James continued to glare at Joshua in disgust,
"I can't believe you didn't tell me!"
"There is nothing to tell James, but if we were true friends it wouldn't matter anyway," Joshua said in his defence.
"I don't like fags," James whispered in his ear and proceeded to seat himself on the table in front. Joshua realised he was about to face the same hurtful experience he'd observed Michael tolerate the previous day. The bell rang again and the students began separating into different classes. Joshua was making his way to his science lesson, all the way he could hear sniggers and sarcastic commentary from students passing him in the hallway; he and Michael's so called 'affair' was the gossip of the day. He heard a voice calling his name from behind, anticipating an insult he initially ignored it. He felt a hand on his shoulder and turned to investigate, it was Megan. He embraced her. Having already heard the rumours she could sense Joshua's distress.
"We need to talk," Megan said with concern.

They failed to attend their first lesson of the day; instead they seated themselves on a bench at the nearby park and discussed the conflict of interest that was Joshua and Michael's lives.
"What are they talking about Joshua? I know how Michael's sexuality became public knowledge but why do people think you're involved with him?" Megan questioned Joshua. He had a look of desperation in his eyes. Megan began to feel uneasy; she'd been in a loving relationship with this boy for two years, which to a sixteen year old seems a lifetime,

and now she was uncovering secrets. Joshua was stalling, unsure of how exactly to explain his friendship with Michael and how it had been misinterpreted. "Joshua talk to me," she pleaded, "tell me what's going on."
"Nothing is wrong Megan, I swear, those rumours have begun from nothing," Joshua replied.
"Well then why is the entire school discussing your relationship with Michael?" she continued. He could see the distress in Megan's eyes, those trusting eyes that had supported him during all the difficult periods of his youth. He wanted to put her mind at ease, he would do anything to make the pain disappear and renew the beautiful smile she usually carried around wherever she went.
"Michael and I are friends, his sexuality doesn't bother me, I like him for who he is," Joshua proclaimed. Megan longed to believe her beloved boyfriend, desperate to trust him. "Megan, I love you, I wouldn't want to jeopardise what we have for anyone or anything, so if what people say upsets you I'll stop associating with Michael," he promised. Megan's concerns immediately disappeared, she felt a wave of guilt as she realised that Joshua was only acting the way she expected him to, the way she encouraged him to, this was reason for her respect, affection and admiration of this boy.
"I'm sorry Joshua, I shouldn't have reacted in this way. Michael needs a friend and you're the perfect candidate, you're more mature than the other boys, I should have remembered that," Megan said with pride, "If you can take the torment from the immature boys who assume you and Michael can't be friends without being involved then so can I."
"They can question my sexuality as much as they want, but they don't have a girlfriend as beautiful as you so they don't have a leg to stand on," Joshua replied; he almost believed himself in what he was saying. They embraced for a moment and returned to their designated lessons.

Joshua walked home alone that evening, this gave him an opportunity to reflect on the events of the day; his best friend had turned against him because of a rumour and his girlfriend had almost reacted in the same way. Aware deep down that he did have homosexual tendencies, he pondered over the situation, 'If I did turn out to be gay is this how my life would be? Would everyone hate me?' he wondered.

He arrived home to the customary sight of his overweight father consuming alcohol and deep fried food.
"One of your little pals is in the living room," he informed Joshua, with a hint of sarcasm in his tone. Joshua wandered through the hallway and found Michael seated with his hands clenched together between his knees, he appeared nervous.

"Hey you," Joshua greeted him. Michael stood and gave an apologetic stare.
"Are you ok?" he asked softly, "I feel so guilty, I caused this!"
"No you didn't," replied Joshua, "You have enough worries of your own without adopting mine." Michael felt so fortunate to have such a friend. Most of the other teenage males would have disowned him in these circumstances.
"Why don't we dine out together?" Michael suggested, "It doesn't look as though anything special is on the menu here." Both laughed. Tears began to fall from Joshua's eyes. Michael empathised and approached him, "I needed a hug last night, surely the least I can do is return the favour." Joshua had never been held so tightly, he felt a sense of security he'd never experienced before. "I'll never desert you like the others," Michael reassured him softly. Joshua trusted him, being in his strong arms felt so natural, almost as though it was his destiny.
"Come on then, let's go and have a talk and get some food."

After devouring burgers and fries at the local McDonalds (ironically with a higher fat content than the meal Neil had offered earlier) the pair visited Parkers Cocktail Bar again, it was a comfort zone for Joshua as he was still unfamiliar with bar crawling. As they had done the previous evening, they began with meaningless chit chat, once this dissolved there was silence, it only lasted a matter of seconds but to Joshua it felt like a lifetime.
"We need to talk," Michael announced.
"We are talking," Joshua replied, aware that Michael had meant the comment in a deeper sense than just discussing anything and everything.
"I know we haven't been friends for long but you can trust me with anything," Michael said. Joshua looked concerned and replied,
"What do you mean? I have nothing to tell you." Michael wasn't convinced. He could sense Joshua was in need of a sympathetic ear.
"You can talk to me about anything at all," Michael reassured, his tone implied he was seeking specific information. Joshua was beginning to feel uncomfortable, however Michael persisted, like a dog holding one half of a bone, determined not to let go as though his life depended on it. They were both aware of the underlying point Michael was trying to make but Joshua was hesitant to discuss the matter. "I know how you feel, it helps to talk, I promise you that," Michael continued. Joshua was not prepared for a conversation of this calibre, however Michael persisted, "Please Joshua, use me as a confidant, I can help you."
"Help me with what?" Joshua claimed to be unaware of the point that Michael was struggling to reach. "Coming to terms with it," Michael

replied, “Do you think I can’t tell? It’s so obvious to me Joshua, and it’s ok, it really is, I know you’re gay!” He had the best of intentions but this was too premature for Joshua. “Michael, I am not gay! I have a girlfriend who I love, just because I am your friend doesn’t mean I’m like you in any way.” Michael was unconvinced.
“It’s ok Joshua, I can see the signs and there’s no need to be scared,” Michael said in an attempt to reassure him.
“Look, I know you want a boyfriend but that doesn’t give you the right to try to talk me into being a homo,” Joshua shouted, he was becoming agitated.
“Calm down,” said Michael.
“Oh fuck off queer,” Joshua replied, “The lads at school were right,” and on that note he stormed out of the bar and ran all the way home. Michael attempted to catch up with him but failed, realising his friend needed time alone and he proceeded to his own home.

Joshua arrived home, his eyes were tearful. He was greeted by the sight of his father collapsed on the sofa with empty bottles from various different types of alcohol spread across the coffee table. He dashed up to his bedroom, feeling fortunate to have avoided an insult from Neil and spread himself out on the bed. He removed his mobile phone from his pocket, it displayed ‘2 new messages’. The first text message was from Megan, it read, ‘Hello babe, hope you’re feeling better, sorry I jumped to conclusions earlier, c u 2moro, luv u xxxx’. The second was from Michael, it read, ‘Hi Joshua. I’m really sorry if I upset you tonight, if you’re not ready that’s fine but I’m here when you want to talk. I really hope we can still be friends.’ Joshua replied to the latter of the messages simply with ‘Thanks m8’.

The next morning Joshua was accompanied by James for the first two lessons of the day. Not a word was spoken between them until lunch time, as they were leaving period two’s lesson James shouted,
“Oi gay boy!” Joshua turned to face him. “And who should reply……” James continued, “We all know there are only two fags around here, Michael Smith and Joshua Maguire!” A crowd was forming.
“Fuck off James, I’ve got a girlfriend, you haven’t!” Joshua replied.
“She’s the one I feel sorry for,” James continued.
“You bastard!” Joshua retaliated.
“Don’t call me a fuckin’ bastard!” James demanded and slammed Joshua against the wall, he then pushed his knee between Joshua’s legs causing pain to his testicles. The crowd chanted,
“Fight fight fight……” and Joshua (though struggling to hold back his tears) punched James in the gut.

"I'm not taking that from no poofter!" James announced. At this point Mr Russell, a middle aged balding teacher intervened and escorted them to the head teacher's office where they were forced to shake hands and be friends. Of course this was a charade for the head teachers benefit, it took every bit of thespian talent James could possibly gather together to convince the head teacher of his sincerity. They were both aware that the second they departed the office the tension would resume.

Joshua couldn't face the remaining lessons of the day and quietly escaped to his home where he knew he could spend some time alone, he couldn't bring himself to face the crowds, gossip and scandal in the schoolyard. There were just six weeks of school remaining before GCSE exams would begin and he was counting down the days, wondering where his life was to go from here. He had an idea about being a journalist but was still unsure. Joshua arrived home to an empty house just as he'd anticipated; five hours remained before Neil would charge through the door complaining about his day at work. He seated himself on the sofa, but instead of escaping into fantasy or drifting deep into thought about his life and the people around him he switched on the television where he found the latest episode of an Australian daytime soap opera. This was perfect as it required absolutely no brain power whatsoever. However his lapse of brain power was short lived, within five minutes he was interrupted by the ringing of the doorbell. He panicked,

"Shit I'm not supposed to be here," he muttered to himself.

"Joshua, I know you're in there," came a familiar voice from outside. He opened the door to find Michael standing before him grasping at the latest Star Wars video with both hands. He passed over the gift to and stated,

"A peace offering." Joshua accepted the video, smiled and invited Michael into the house. They stood facing each other. "Are you in any pain?" Michael asked.

"A little," Joshua replied modestly. Michael offered his arms to Joshua who immediately accepted the invitation, he felt so secure being held this way.

Several minutes later they were seated.

"I'm really sorry about yesterday," Michael said apologetically, "I was trying to push you too fast, just as long as you know I'm always here and you can trust me."Joshua interrupted,

"It's ok mate, I know what you were trying to do and I know I can trust you, I was in the wrong. I should have had more faith in you."

"What are you saying?" Michael asked.

"I don't know Michael, I just don't know," Joshua confessed. Michael gave him a puzzled stare and asked,

"What do you mean that you don't know?"
"I know you're trying to help me come to terms with my sexuality but I just don't know what I am," Joshua continued. This was the breakthrough Michael had been anticipating, although his new friend hadn't yet confessed to being a homosexual, he had acknowledged that he was confused about his feelings.
"Go on Joshua, you can tell me anything at all, you know that," Michael reassured him.
"I love Megan, I really do," Joshua declared, "In spite of my feelings, I do love her, but I just don't know what I am. If I'm gay, how can I be gay and in love with a girl at the same time?" Michael sympathised and offered his words of wisdom,
"Don't be so eager to categorise yourself, you may just be a very open minded person. If you love Megan, there's nothing wrong with that."
"But what if I break her heart? What if I'm gay and she has to live with that?" Joshua was begging for his friend to have all the answers but he didn't, all he could do was offer his utmost support. Michael suggested a walk to clear their heads. They continued their discussion as they wandered aimlessly. Joshua felt as though the weight of the world was being lifted from his shoulders, simply by having an outlet for his feelings. The two companions stopped at the children's park. They seated themselves on the swings and the mood of the afternoon began to lighten, they began discussing males they found attractive, beginning with celebrities and moving on to other students,
"What about Nick Peterson?" asked Michael.
"Oh those legs when he's wearing his football kit!" Joshua giggled and nodded in agreement.
"I don't know about you, but I struggle to hide my interest in the changing rooms," Michael proclaimed, they grinned in excitement. This type of banter was a new experience for both of them. Joshua had never confessed his homosexual desires before and Michael hadn't yet acquired any gay associates, until now, or so he hoped. He longed for a group of friends he could relate to, he hadn't yet confronted his parents with the bombshell, and this was made more difficult by the fact that he was an only child. On so many occasions his mother had expressed her desire for grandchildren, this raised feelings of guilt in Michael as he knew he would inevitably shatter her dreams. In spite of this however, he was fortunate, he had two loving parents who would do anything for him and given time would accept their son unconditionally. The gossip continued,
"My god, you don't realise how many attractive lads there are at school until you start to list them do you?!" Joshua had amazed himself. At this point Michael made a risky gesture,

"Well, there's Joey Thompson, Sean Jameson, now he is hot! I could just get lost in those blue eyes of his, and then there's Joshua Maguire." Joshua appeared shocked by this comment. "Don't look so surprised," Michael continued, "Why shouldn't I find you attractive?"
"I'm nothing special," Joshua announced, almost as though he were defending himself.
"How can you say that?" Michael questioned his friend's foolish comment. "You're beautiful, perfect even," he continued, nervously struggling to put a sentence together, he was sincere though and Joshua could sense it in his voice. They gazed into each other's eyes, speechless, neither were quite prepared for this, but would they ever be? They were both inexperienced, although Joshua had been dating Megan for two years they'd only ever got as far as holding hands and petting. Michael glanced around to confirm their solitude. He then leaned across to Joshua who remained stationary besides the slight swaying of the swing. Michael placed his hand around Joshua's head and ran his fingers through his thick mass of hair. Joshua was frozen, unaware of how to react to the situation he had fallen into; he knew that for Megan's sake he should call a halt before he actually had an action to regret. "You're really special Joshua. I can see it, you should too," Michael whispered softly in his ear and then touched Joshua's lips delicately with his finger and caressed his chin before gently pressing their lips together. Both had craved this kiss, it wasn't instigated solely, it was just something that happened, it was the most affectionate kiss either of them had ever experienced initially but soon went on to become the most passionate. Joshua felt Michaels tongue against his own, this was yet another new experience for him; this was indeed a day he'd never forget. The kiss lingered on for what seemed hours, although in reality it was in fact just a few minutes. A wave of guilt swept over Joshua as the reality of the situation became apparent. He had admitted his homosexual tendencies, not only to himself but to a gay man, a man he was attracted to, and in addition they'd just shared the most passionate moment of their lives. Megan's face sprang into his mind; if she were present her heart would be breaking into a million pieces before his very eyes. In the very back of his mind he had always been aware of his attraction to other men but it had only just become a reality. Michael pondered his next move, aware that Joshua was caught in the moment.
"How do you feel?" Michael questioned him, unaware of what his reaction would be. Joshua faced him and gazed blankly,
"How should I feel?" he asked, aware that this was a rhetorical question and therefore didn't await a reply before continuing, "My girlfriend loves me. Megan really loves me! Here I am kissing you! If she knew what I'd

done today she'd be horrified." Michael attempted to offer further advice, "Sexuality is a complicated issue and you have no control over it. Megan is a wonderful person, but she'll just have to deal with it, if you are gay there's nothing you can do about it and it's not wrong, it's just the way you are."
"But Megan loves me, and this will break her heart," Joshua announced while shedding a tear, "And what if I don't know if I'm gay?"
Michael was wise beyond his years and now felt the need to be blunt, "Come on my friend, did what just happened between us feel wrong?" Joshua shook his head. "Be honest with me now, tell me, how often do you have a wank?" Joshua had never been asked such a question and stared at Michael (whom he'd befriended only yesterday) in disbelief. Michael persisted however, "Tell me Joshua, do you masturbate a lot?"
"Sometimes, what the fuck does that matter?" Joshua was clearly becoming agitated as he rarely swore. "All lads do it, it doesn't make you gay." Michael could sense his friend was missing the point entirely, "Of course all lads do it, but tell me the truth please. What makes you do it? What do you look at? What do you think about?" Joshua cast his mind back to recent jerking off sessions and what had instigated them, seeing the naked boys in the changing rooms and later mentally recalling it, the men's underwear section of Littlewoods catalogue and seeing a shirtless actor on television. Michael continued, determined to get his point across, "It's men isn't it? When did you last become aroused by a woman? Are you physically attracted to Megan at all? I know you love her but does she turn you on? Do you see a physical relationship developing between the two of you?" If the truth be known, Joshua never thought of taking his relationship with Megan to a physical level, in fact the fact that they were both soon to be legal worried him.
"No alright? No to everything! I don't fancy Megan! I don't use women as wank aids, only men and no I don't want to shag Megan! Happy now!?" he stood with his back to Michael and took a few steps away from the swings. Michael stood and approached him from behind.
"It'll be ok, I promise," he said reassuringly. Joshua turned to face him, Michael placed his arms around him, both wishing they never had to let go.

The next morning at 7.30 Joshua was preparing himself for the day ahead. Neil had reluctantly left for work early to do some overtime and he was enjoying the peace and quiet, this was until he had an unexpected visitor. James was normally disorganised and if he was at school by 9.00 it was a good day, but here he was over an hour earlier than the time he and Joshua would meet for the journey to school. Weather permitting they would either catch the bus or use their bus fare to buy sweets to eat on the way. Joshua had assumed in light of the events of the previous day that James wouldn't be joining him that morning and had wondered whether or not they would ever engage in conversation again. In the living room they stared at each other, both attempting to fathom what the other was thinking.

"I'm sorry," James muttered spontaneously and gazed at the floor.

"What for exactly?" Joshua questioned his so-called friend, attempting to find the root of his issue with homosexuality.

"I talked to Megan yesterday afternoon…" James began. 'James talked to Megan' Joshua thought, and began to mentally recall the events of the previous day, 'I didn't talk to Megan all afternoon, James did. I didn't. I was off having my first gay kiss. Oh my god, what am I doing?' James could sense that Joshua was deep in thought and blurted out, "I'm trying to apologise! I know you're not gay. You've had a girlfriend for two years, mine never last that long. Megan made me see that you're just being a friend to Michael. I'm sorry I assumed you were one of those people." 'One of those people' thought Joshua, 'For god's sake. Am I from Krypton? Gay people are human beings too; believe it or not mate, got to hold myself back here.'

"Why do you have such a problem with gay people James?" Joshua asked bluntly.

"I don't agree with what they do, it's unnatural, it's sick! Look, I want us to be friends, you can still have Michael as a friend too, but I want things to go back to the way they were for us," James replied. Having been put on the spot, Joshua agreed to this, considering they'd be off to college shortly doing different courses anyway. Joshua was to study journalism and James was to study Sports and fitness, therefore they'd barely see each other anyway, perhaps it was for the best. So as far as James was concerned everything was back to normal.

Chapter 3

The following two years passed by rapidly. In many ways Joshua's life remained the same, he had grown ever closer to Megan, he'd become dependant on her and she was dependant on him, they were each others lifelines. As planned, Joshua was studying journalism, perhaps to be a big shot reporter or maybe just to review the latest releases in science fiction magazines, he didn't really know himself. He had a part time job at the local supermarket which he fitted in between studies and spent each spare minute enjoying his science fiction novels, surfing the internet or seeing Megan or Michael who had become his best friend. James would send the odd text message inviting Joshua out for a 'Catch-up drink' but he was far more concerned with the local football team he was now playing for and his homophobic attitude lessened Joshua's desire for them to remain in regular contact.

On the home front, Neil and Joshua barely conversed. Joshua had now lost count of how many potential step mothers had been present in the house and it wasn't unusual for Neil to be absent for several days at a time and then return without explanation. Neil's behaviour no longer phased Joshua, the relationship had been so distant ever since Lynne's death almost five years ago. Joshua regularly visited his mother's grave, he felt it his duty as if he didn't take care of it, nobody would.

Meanwhile, Michael and Megan had become much closer. Michael was quite unsure of where his life was heading and was working as his father's (who was a council worker) secretary. Megan was studying tourism and marketing and dreamed of travelling the world. She had become a fag-hag to Michael who was now open about his sexuality to his parents and acted promiscuously. What Megan hadn't realised is that she was becoming a fag-hag to her own boyfriend, although she and Joshua had now been a couple for almost four years, they still hadn't been intimate with each other and Megan realised the subject wasn't open for discussion. Although Michael was of course aware of Joshua's confusion over the issue of his sexual preferences he didn't raise the subject with Megan and in fact rarely discussed it with Joshua. Everybody was happy in their own way. Ignorance can be blissful. At present, Megan was using her free time to prepare a surprise party for Joshua's eighteenth birthday.

One thing Joshua had realised is that he needed an outlet for his homosexuality. Well doesn't everybody? Women talk amongst themselves about men and sex, gay men do the same, straight men discuss women, breasts, etc. Joshua found his outlet on the internet. On a daily basis he would visit online chat rooms for harmless discussions of all things gay. Generally the men he would talk to were at least a little older than he and lived miles away. One evening however, just days before his eighteenth birthday, he visited the chat room and was 'whispered' for a private talk by a member named 'Cutegay20'. Everyone on the internet seemed to describe themselves as cute or sexy. The conversation began to flow between them.

Cutegay20: Hello there, a/s/l?
Sheffcutie291: Hi 17 (almost 18) /male/Sheffield.
Cutegay20: 20/male/Sheffield also!

At this point in the conversation Joshua became a little nervous. When talking to a 26 year old in Brighton it was merely a chat, however he knew that this time Cutegay20 would request a meeting.

Sheffcutie291: Cool! Are you near the centre?
Cutegay20: Yes u?
Sheffcutie291: Yes
Cutegay20: Wow! Why don't you have a look at the photos on my profile? www.facefest.co.uk/Cutegay20.

Curiosity overpowered Joshua and insisted he click the link. The man was named Stuart and was incredibly pleasing to the eye.

Sheffcutie291: Very cute!
Cutegay20: Would you like to get together sometime?
Sheffcutie291: Er.....I dunno
Cutegay20: Nothing too heavy, just a drink maybe?

This was so real. Stuart actually lived nearby. A ton of questions landed in Joshua's head, 'Is Stuart really who he claims to be? Will I really be meeting a sixty year old pervert? Can I do this to Megan?' His thoughts were interrupted by the sound of a 'poke' on his computer,

Cutegay20: U there?
Sheffcutie291: Yeh, sorry.
Cutegay20: Don't worry. I won't try to make you do anything you don't want to.

Joshua pondered his decision for a few moments, before making a spontaneous decision to take a chance, though still unsure of whether or not this was a good idea. He asked himself what the worst case scenario was. It had been two years since his kiss with Micheal and almost as long since it was last discussed and Joshua's curiosity of the gay world was getting the better of him.

Sheffcutie291: Ok. Where shall we meet?
Cutegay20: By the burger bar on West Street in 2 hours?
Sheffcutie291: See you there!

As he closed down his computer, reality set in, 'Oh my god' Joshua thought, 'I'm going on a date with a lad tonight!' As nervous and anxious as he was, he knew this was something he had to do. The next decision was what to wear. He spent half an hour pawing through his clothes drawers and wardrobe in an attempt to uncover an item of clothing that at least remotely implied homosexuality; this failed and plan b commenced, to look as smart as possible. He bathed himself and put on his favourite blue shirt and black jeans with freshly polished shoes. He studied himself in the mirror, focussing mainly on a spot he had on his chin.
"Of all the days to have a spot," he muttered to himself. Time was of the essence, he had twenty minutes before he was due to meet Stuart and the burger bar was a fifteen minute walk away. He bolted down the stairs and almost collided with his father.
"You reek like a poofs brothel," Neil commented, his sarcasm knew no boundaries.
"I'm going out," Joshua announced, attempting to appear brave, however his nerves shone through.
"I hope she's worth it," muttered Neil as he trotted off up the stairs. Joshua breathed a sigh of relief at the assumption his father had made.

Whilst walking to the meeting place, he contemplated whether what he was about to do was wrong. Was he betraying Megan? What if someone was to see him tonight? Could he really trust Stuart? His mobile phone rang in his pocket. He stopped to answer it, it was Megan calling. Even before answering it he had an immediate feeling of guilt.
"Hello darling!" She was as bubbly as ever. Joshua felt further awkwardness; talking to his girlfriend when in just minutes he'd be with another man made him feel disloyal, but he knew he couldn't ignore his homosexual feelings, at the very least needed a discussion outside of the internet.
"Hi Megan, how are you?" he replied, attempting to sound as though everything was fine and thanking god for the fact that she couldn't see him shaking as he spoke.
"What are you up to tonight?" Megan asked.
"I'm nipping over to see James for a bit, not seen him for a while," he lied.
"Oh….ok, but I'll definitely see you on your birthday won't I?" Megan asked.

"Of course. We'll spend the evening together, just the two of us," Joshua reassured her. Megan was now satisfied, safe in the knowledge that he didn't suspect a thing about the surprise party she was planning.
"Ok then hun'," she continued, "See you tomorrow, love ya'."
"Bye sweetie," Joshua ended the conversation and glanced at the digital clock on his phone. He had just five minutes left before he was due at his meeting place with Stuart. Joshua was genuinely unaware of Megan's plans for a surprise party, this sweet girl, who loved him so dearly, was spending her time planning it while he was out with another man. He arrived at McDonalds at the arranged time; he could still feel himself physically shaking and perspiring. Although Joshua isn't a shy person, this was un-chartered territory. He wondered how he would appear to Stuart on his arrival. Would Stuart think he was cute? Did his body language suggest he was irritable? Stuart had been delayed and each minute Joshua waited for him seemed like an hour. He pondered every few minutes that perhaps Stuart wasn't coming and he should go home; almost trying to justify to himself why he was contemplating backing out. He leaned by the McDonalds window, then walked forward two paces, glanced to the left, glanced to the right and returned to leaning on the window. He repeated this process for five minutes. Doubts circled in Joshua's mind, 'What are you doing here Joshua?' he asked himself, 'What would Megan say? What would everyone say?' He was becoming restless and attempted to mentally calm his nerves. 'I'm doing nothing wrong. I'm just meeting a new friend for a drink' he convinced himself. Joshua's thoughts were interrupted by the sound of a male voice,
"Hello Joshua, sorry I'm late." He turned to investigate. Stuart was standing just inches away. Joshua had been so distracted with thoughts and concerns that he hadn't noticed the handsome, perfectly groomed man approach him. He looked exactly as Joshua had expected, having seen the photograph online. 'Wow, this guy is hot!' Joshua thought, while simultaneously attempting to manipulate his facial expression in order not to make Stuart aware of how impressive his appearance was.
"Hello St....Stuart?" Joshua stuttered.
"Hi! I'm so sorry I'm late. I really hope you weren't waiting too long. I kept looking at my watch and knew I'd never make it," Stuart apologised for the second time.
"Don't worry about it," Joshua said, and an awkward silence followed.
"So are you hungry?" asked Stuart.
"A little," Joshua replied.
"Well we are outside a McDonalds," Stuart pointed out, displaying a cheeky and extremely cute smile that was already beginning to have an effect on Joshua. He returned the smile and pointed towards the door. As

the two of them queued, Joshua further noted how much effort Stuart had made with his appearance and attire. The outfit appeared to have been very expensive, designer jeans that were full of holes, rips and tears, and a t shirt that gave the illusion he was wearing a plain shirt underneath, after all, it's expensive to look as though you don't care how you look. Stuart didn't have a hair out of place, typical of a gay man, but he had obviously devoted a lot of time to preparing himself for the evening. Joshua was receiving a positive vibe from Stuart. "What'll you have?" Stuart asked, implying that he was offering to pay. 'Should I accept this?' Joshua asked himself, 'Will I seem like a sponger?'

"It's ok, I have my own money," Joshua insisted.

"Come on mate, it's only a McDonalds, you can buy the drinks later if you want." Stuart wasn't intending to accept no as an answer and followed up his statement with another of those smiles Joshua already adored.

"Oh ok then, but I'm definitely buying the drinks," he agreed while mentally listing Stuart's obvious good features, 'cute, generous, seems to have a good sense of humour…..good start' Joshua thought. They seated themselves, now prepared with burgers, French fries, muffins and milkshakes.

"You seem mysterious," Stuart boldly pointed out.

"Mysterious? Nah, I'm boring," Joshua joked.

"I've never seen you on the gay scene," Stuart continued.

"Well I have a girlfriend who probably wouldn't approve," Joshua confessed forcing a smile, though it was obvious that he didn't really find the situation at all humorous.

"I see; you're not out at all then?" Stuart asked.

"Well, I have a gay friend who sort of knows but we don't talk about it. Michael is a friend of my girlfriend," Joshua replied.

"Wow! You know how to weave a tangled web don't you?" Stuart laughed. Joshua enjoyed the meal with Stuart; he talked of his agony over Lynne's death, his relationship with his father, his feelings for Megan and his fears of his sexuality becoming public knowledge (James making the discovery in particular). Stuart offered advice, listened and gave the impression that he genuinely cared. The pair exchanged humorous tales of their pasts, in particular, Stuart told Joshua of how he 'came out' to his ex-girlfriend; at this point Joshua looked sheepish as he was reminded of the reality of the situation.

"Megan will be devastated when she finds out." Stuart began shooting questions, "How long have you been seeing her? Do you think she suspects?"

"No, I don't think she knows. I've been with her for four years! I think she just thinks I'm a frigid Freda," Joshua joked.

"Four years! Wow!" Stuart was amazed, "So you haven't slept with her?"

"No, I can't bring myself to do it," Joshua confessed, "I just can't, I'm not physically attracted to her."

"I understand," Stuart empathised, "You can't force it matey, if you're gay you can't change that, it's just the way you are."

"I learned that the hard way," Joshua admitted.

"Don't we all?" Stuart asked rhetorically and smiled.

"I'm so glad I met you Stuart, I wasn't sure at first, but I feel an instant connection between us, you understand me," Joshua complimented Stuart. Stuart smiled and asked Joshua where he'd like to go for drinks. Joshua took him to his favourite place, Parkers Cocktail Bar, which Michael had introduced him to two years previously. Perhaps it was a tradition as he knew the evening was taking a similar direction as the first outing with Michael. Although it had been so long ago, Joshua often recalled the memory of that night, especially the kiss, his first from another man. Of course, things would have become awkward if Joshua and Michael had taken things any further, since Michael had become so close to Megan. Joshua insisted on buying the drinks and the pair enjoyed some highly alcoholic, expensive and experimental cocktails.

"So what's your girlfriend's name?" Stuart questioned him.

"Megan, why do you ask?" Joshua replied suspiciously. 'Why on earth does he want to discuss Megan?' Joshua wondered, 'Surely she would be the last item on the agenda for an evening between two horny young gay men'.

"Mine was named Kelly," Stuart announced randomly. Joshua passed a look of confusion and he continued, "I broke her heart. I didn't want to, I really didn't. I had no choice, I had to find my true self and unfortunately Kelly was the experiment." The similarity of their situations was becoming painfully obvious to Joshua, who was uncomfortable with the direction this discussion was taking.

"Anyway let's not talk about girls eh….?"

"You've held her back Joshua, for four years you've held her back, to have stayed with you for so long she must have deep feelings for you," Stuart said, unintentionally seeming condescending.

"I know Stuart, I know! Megan means the world to me, she really does," Joshua replied, now becoming defensive.

"You must tell her the truth. It's not fair for her to put her life on hold for you when you know you can't give her what she needs," Stuart said passionately, obviously relating Joshua's predicament to his own circumstances several years previously. It was as though a bolt of

lightning had just struck Joshua. He had known Stuart for ninety minutes and already he was offering good advice and relating to him in a way he'd never experienced before, and his words were so appropriate. Joshua realised that Megan deserved the truth. A tear came to his eye. "What is it? What's wrong?" asked Stuart.
"What if she hates me?"
"I won't sugar coat it; she may do at first, but eventually she'll come around," Stuart said, attempting to reassure him. Joshua was weeping; a crate of bottled up emotions were being released. "I'm so sorry, you've only just met me and already I've reduced you to tears," Stuart apologised light-heartedly.
"No, you've helped me a lot. I wasn't sure if you'd be one of those internet lads who just want a quick shag," Joshua said, struggling to smile. Stuart held Joshua in his arms,
"It's ok darling, it's ok." Although they weren't in a gay bar, no other customers were paying attention to Joshua and Stuart. At this point, Michael entered the bar with his latest conquest, a short but handsome blonde twenty something called David. As they wandered around the bar in search of vacant seating, Michael spotted Joshua in his embrace with Stuart.
"Friend of yours?" asked the blonde hussy.
"You could say that, come on, let's go and sit by them." They approached Joshua who immediately noticed Michael through the corner of his eye and released himself from Stuart's arms.
"Michael!" Joshua used a tone of voice that implied guilt.
"Are you surprised to see me? You know I like this bar," Michael had a hint of sarcasm in his voice, "You've not met my new fella'….this is David." All eyes were not on Michael's latest flame, who then gave a wave that (if anyone had any doubts) confirmed his homosexuality.
"This is Stuart….A friend of mine," Joshua stated, almost defending himself.
"Could we speak in private for a minute Joshua?" Michael asked, rolling his eyes in the direction of the exit.
"Excuse me. Stuart, David, you guys get acquainted for a minute, ok?" Joshua asked nervously.
"If you need me just shout," Stuart said.

"Let's not be a week then, it's cold out here and Stuart and your friend don't know each other," Joshua said bluntly as he and Michael trotted down the steps outside the bar.
"Don't you dare shrug this off!" Michael demanded. Joshua folded his arms in order to emphasize that he was cold and reacted,

"Look Michael, I don't know what the big deal is but it's cold and I don't want to stand out here all night!"

"Who is he?" Michael asked.

"His name is Stuart," Joshua replied, stating the obvious.

"Please don't play games," Michael requested, "Do you know what your girlfriend is doing right now while you're off with that guy?" Joshua looked at Michael blankly.

"She's at home planning your eighteenth birthday party!" Michael continued, "She loves you."

"I know she loves me," Joshua pointed out, "That's not what this is about!"

"I guess I knew anyway, the kiss between us, the signs were all there. I guess I just didn't want to see them because I'm so fond of Megan and I know how much she loves you," Michael blurted out, "How many guys have you been with? How long has this been going on?"

"None!" Joshua insisted, "I haven't done anything, I swear it. This is the first date with Stuart, it's the first time."

"Good, that's something." Michael looked concerned; "I can't believe you didn't confide in me about your gay feelings."

"I did Michael, two years ago. But since then, you and Megan have become so close and it didn't seem right," Joshua replied, "Look, can we go back inside please?"

"Ok, I'm sorry. Let's get together tomorrow and talk some more, ok?" Michael suggested.

"Ok, come over tomorrow," Joshua agreed.

"I am your friend you know, you can trust me," Michael reassured him. Joshua nodded in agreement. "I'll take my fella' to another bar and leave you in peace with Stuart," Michael offered. Joshua thanked him and accepted a hug.

They returned to the bar and the sound of Tina Charles complaining of how she loved to love but her baby just loved to dance. Michael and David excused themselves and departed. Joshua returned to his seat beside a confused Stuart.

"You have a girlfriend ….. And a boyfriend?" he asked.

"No no no," Joshua said, leaping to his own defence, "Michael is just a friend, a friend of me and Megan." Stuart realised the point Joshua was trying to reach and nodded in agreement. "I'm sorry Stuart, I'm so sorry," Joshua apologised.

"What on earth for?" Stuart asked with a puzzled expression on his face.

"Everything," Joshua replied, "We met on the net and ever since you saw

me all I've done is burden you with my problems and place you in awkward situations with my friends."
"I've enjoyed myself," Stuart said in jest, grinning at Joshua's whittling, "It's quite reassuring to see that I'm not the only person whose life feels like a soap opera." The pair laughed hysterically. "Besides, I'm studying to be a social worker so if I can't listen to people's problems, I'd might as well give up now," Stuart added, and then asked, "What are your career aspirations anyway? You never said."
"I'm studying journalism, could be the next Clark Kent," Joshua joked, "If only I looked like the actors who play him."
"Hey, there's nothing wrong with your looks darling, seriously, you're a very cute guy," Stuart promised. Joshua's face reddened with embarrassment as the conversation paused for an awkward moment before he spontaneously added,
"I think you're gorgeous as well." 'I think you're gorgeous. What a stupid thing to say!' Joshua thought, 'He said I was cute, not gorgeous, and I said as well! Aaaaargh, he's going to think I'm so arrogant. Oh my god! Why did I say that? He's probably just being nice anyway. As if someone like him would fancy me.' Stuart smiled, then proceeded to kiss Joshua's cheek and commented,
"It's lovely to finally meet a lad with a little depth; most gay men just want quick shag." 'He likes me, he likes me!' Joshua was mentally overjoyed, while physically still displaying his embarrassment. He could sense another awkward silence was imminent and attempted to stop it before its arrival.
"You can give me a proper kiss if you want to," this was the first statement that landed in Joshua's head and he immediately regretted blurting it out. "I'm sorry, I didn't mean to….." he muttered.
"It's ok……..but not here," Stuart replied, grinning. His body language suggested the time had come for them to leave. Joshua grabbed his coat and they headed for the exit.

Outside, Stuart led the way, "I know the perfect place," he said with a mischievous look on his face. Joshua followed him for several minutes and was led into a dark genal. He was about to discover Stuart's more passionate side. Worried thoughts entered Joshua's mind, 'Have I misjudged this guy? Is he planning to rape me?' At this point he was wishing he could retract his earlier comment about consenting to a 'proper kiss'. The pair were standing in complete darkness in a confined space. "Is this private enough?" Stuart laughed. Unsure of how to react, Joshua laughed along. He felt Stuart's hands firmly clenching his buttocks and froze. It had been so long since his kiss with Michael and he was finally about to repeat the experience. Although he was feeling

nervous, at the same time he also felt rebellious and spontaneous. Here he was, in a dark alley at night with an attractive young man he'd never met before today, about to participate in a passionate embrace. The fact that they'd met online was a risk element in itself. Although Stuart's hands were very busy exploring Joshua's body (as much as one can externally of the clothing), Joshua kept his hands by his sides. Stuart pressed his lips against Joshua's and he could soon feel Stuart's tongue against his own. What an experience. This was the most intense and passionate moment of Joshua's life. He began to feel more and more comfortable in the enjoyment of this and soon his hands were touching Stuart's posterior. Joshua did not care what this was leading to; he was so caught up in the moment. This powerful kissing lasted several minutes before Stuart worked his way down to Joshua's neck. Joshua himself hadn't realised before what a weak spot his neck was, being kissed there was having a unique, unexpected effect on him, he couldn't manage to keep his eyes open, but this made little difference in the dark anyway. However, his eyes quickly opened in a state of shock when he felt an incredible sensation on his neck, more vigorous than before. Unsure of exactly what was happening, he just knew he didn't want it to end. "Sorry about that, perhaps I should have warned you," Stuart apologised, raising his head for air. Reality set in. 'I've just had my first love bite,' Joshua realised, 'What on earth will Megan say when she sees it?'
"How big is it?" he asked.
"Let's go into the light," Stuart suggested. The pair wandered out of the genal and stood underneath a lamp post. Stuart examined his creation on Joshua's neck. "It's a bit of a whopper!" he exclaimed. A look of panic became obvious on Joshua's face.
"What the hell is Megan gonna' say?" Stuart suddenly realised the potential damage he'd caused and apologised profusely.
"I just got carried away!" It was obvious to Joshua that his new friends regret was sincere. Besides, Joshua considered himself as guilty; he'd been caught up in the moment as much as Stuart was.
"It's ok Stuart, you didn't mean any harm. Now, can you give me any advice on how to conceal it please? If Megan sees it it's going to be difficult to explain," Joshua pleaded.
"Concealer for a start, though your father won't have any and the shops will be closed. Oh, and wear a jumper with a tall neck, or a scarf when you're outside," Stuart was desperate to help.
"Ok , I have no concealer and no suitable jumpers!" Joshua announced, his head now being held by his hands.
"Don't panic," Stuart insisted, "Let's go back to my place. I'll arrange it all for you." Was this a ploy? Could Joshua really trust Stuart to take him

back to his flat? Did he have an ulterior motive? In spite of his concerns, Joshua felt somewhat safe with Stuart and his gut instinct was telling him to believe in him.
"Can't go this far and not go further," Joshua said randomly. Stuart looked puzzled. "Sorry, thinking aloud. I can trust you, can't I?" begged Joshua.
"Of course, I'm not going to force you to do anything you're not ready for, we'll just go to the flat and pick out some clothes for you." Joshua decided once again to throw caution to the wind and agreed.

Upon arrival at the student accommodation, they were greeted by a twenty-something female seated on the sofa, legs crossed, almost concealing the rips in the material. She was reading a magazine and appeared to have been doing so for some time considering how many were scattered across the floor.
"Oraight." 'It speaks,' thought Joshua.
"Joshua, this is Becky," Stuart made the introductions, sensing an awkwardness.
"Hi," Joshua said. An attractive, blatantly heterosexual teenage male was wandering around wearing only his boxer shorts, eating a bowl of Shreddies, but he failed to acknowledge anyone as he parked himself on the sofa resting his feet up on the coffee table.
"That's Scott," Stuart added. Scott raised his hand and attempted a sarcastic wave. Anyway, let's go up to my room," Stuart suggested.
"Hey, I'd be careful, once a guy goes up there he rarely comes back down," Becky said. Joshua chose to assume that her comment was meant in jest, even though she hadn't used a tone of voice to suggest so.

Stuart's room was immaculate. The contrast between this and the lounge was unmistakable. It was clean, neat and tidy. A place for everything and everything in its place.
"Very organised," Joshua commented.
"Thanks.....I think," Stuart replied while passing a tube of concealer to Joshua. He thanked him and began examining his neck in the mirror.
"My god, what a Dracula," Joshua muttered to himself.
"Right-i-ho, let's see what would suit you." This was the first time Stuart had sounded camp all evening. Joshua observed him as he opened his wardrobe as though it contained the crown jewels. "I've got some gorgeous outfits," Stuart boasted playfully. Joshua had never seen such a tightly packed wardrobe in his life. Stuart began to explain the organisation of the clothing. "In this corner we have the scene-wear," he explained while pointing to some ultra camp tops that were stretching Joshua's imagination for him to believe they would fit anyone. "They're very snug," Stuart continued, "To wear on the scene only." Joshua

examined the wardrobe further, studying each section in amazement. "Moving down the rail, we have short sleeve t-shirts, long sleeve t-shirts, shirts, zip ups, jeans, trousers, jumpers……" Stuart went on. Joshua watched as his new friend transformed from a straight acting lad to a raging queen before his very eyes. Had he met Stuart earlier that day and been unaware of his homosexuality, he wouldn't have guessed, but meeting him at this moment in time would make it blatantly obvious to anyone. "What about this little number?" Stuart asked as he pulled an expensive looking designer red jumper from the wardrobe. Joshua was dumbfounded by the prospect of wearing an outfit so attractive and extravagant. It was completely different from his normal attire. "Red not your colour?" Stuart asked, attempting to fathom the meaning behind Joshua's facial expression.

"Er….no, it's not that," Joshua replied, struggling to reach his point.

"We haven't got any music on," Stuart randomly pointed out, dashing to the CD player and inserting his 'Ultimate Kylie' disc. "Bit of old school Kylie, can't beat it!" Joshua was finding it a strain to refrain from laughing at that comment. Kylie Minogue songs he didn't recognise blared out from the stereo system. "If you want to choose something else that's fine," Stuart assured him.

"I can't wear this it's too……" Joshua began.

"I know, it's getting a bit old now," Stuart completed his sentence.

"No!" Joshua yelled, "It's gorgeous, I'd just be afraid of spilling something on it or damaging it. It's so expensive and it's gorgeous."

"Oh. Is that all? We can soon sort that, keep it. That way if you damage it, it's yours to damage," Stuart offered. Joshua was tempted to grab the jumper and run.

"I can't, it's too expensive for you to give away."

"Oh don't be silly Joshua. It'd look great on you, try it on!" Stuart insisted enthusiastically. Joshua did genuinely like the appearance of the jumper but realised that he didn't have anything underneath the garment he was currently wearing. If he was to try the jumper Stuart was offering, he'd have to reveal his body, this he was very self conscious about. "Go on darling, try it! I think it'll suit you, and the neck is tall enough to cover the love bite," Stuart encouraged him. Not wishing to appear rude, Joshua removed his jumper. Stuart gave a subtle grin which implied he was pleasantly surprised by what he saw. Joshua quickly concealed his body his body with Stuart's jumper and turned to face the mirror. "That is soooo you!" Stuart said as though he were a TV fashion show presenter or a bonus hungry sales assistant in a boutique.

"You think?" Joshua added positively.

"Absolutely," Stuart continued, "Makes you look even more gorgeous, if that were possible."

"Flattery will get you everywhere," Joshua joked.

"Oh good," Stuart added, "Anyway, I insist you take that jumper. I never want to see it again; it could have been made for you darling!" Joshua considered himself very fortunate to have met such an attractive and kind person, and shockingly it was through the internet. His more daring side desired Stuart and wanted to take things further, but he wasn't sure how to flirt. An opportunity soon presented itself however. "Do I get a thank you kiss?" requested Stuart. Joshua smiled and approached him. Their lips met, as did their tongues shortly after. The spark between them was powerful. Joshua never wanted this embrace to end. As they kissed, he could feel Stuart's hands exploring his body and he liked it. The passion paused for a moment, giving Stuart just enough time to reassure Joshua again, "We won't do anything you're not ready for."

"I'll tell you if I'm not comfortable," Joshua replied and intimacy resumed.

Several minutes later, Stuart pushed Joshua toward the bed, he fell onto it and lay down. Stuart lay on top of him for a short while before moving down the bed and kneeling as he removed Joshua's jeans. Joshua allowed Stuart to explore. His erection was unmistakably obvious through his white fake Calvin Klein boxer shorts. Stuart lay on top of Joshua again and resumed kissing him while at the same time his hand was firmly pressing against the bulge in Joshua's boxer shorts.

"Are you ok? Shall I carry on?" Stuart asked. Joshua nodded in agreement. Stuart returned to the foot of the bed and kneeled to face Joshua's erect penis which he was about to reveal. He slowly pulled the boxer shorts down Joshua's legs and over his socked feet. He began to gently caress Joshua's penis as if to tease him and ease him gently into what was about to happen. Joshua's delight was obvious. Stuart pulled down Joshua's foreskin and licked the shaft of his penis. This was a completely new experience for Joshua and his head was now moving backwards in ecstasy. This felt right. He and Megan had been close mentally, emotionally and spiritually for over four years and yet intimacy between them still felt wrong, and yet on the day of meeting Stuart, already he was allowing him to explore his body and it felt good. His worries of frigidity were flying out of the window. Joshua had never been this aroused in his life. He felt his rigid penis slide between Stuart's lips and his teeth accidentally but delicately caught the front and back of his penis as it slipped into his mouth. Joshua had to cling to the bedposts with his hands and struggled to keep his eyes open, this was enhancing the experience. Stuart was clearly experienced sexually, his tongue was going

places that Joshua had never imagined, he'd never realised before the versatility of oral sex. Although his jaw was strained, Stuart could perceive that Joshua was close to climax and persisted, taking Joshua's penis deeper and deeper into his mouth. As Joshua felt he couldn't take any more pleasure, Stuart contradicted him by rolling his testicles around with his fingers while simultaneously orally pleasing him. Instantaneously Stuart could taste Joshua's semen in his mouth; he then removed his penis but continued to hold it in his hand.
"Sorry, bet that tastes awful," Joshua apologised. Stuart smiled and counteracted Joshua's comment by licking off any remaining seminal fluid from the end of Joshua's penis.
"I've had worse," Stuart commented, then leaned over to kiss Joshua and shared the taste when their tongues met. "See, it's not so bad, just lucky you didn't shoot all over that lovely jumper," Stuart said playfully and they both lay on the bed laughing hysterically. Being his usual fretting self, Joshua began to wonder if Stuart was expecting the same experience in return.
"I don't think I'm ready to do that to you Stuart, not just yet," he said.
"No worries," Stuart replied, now gently stroking Joshua's hair. 'What an understanding guy. What a night!' Joshua thought, 'Just have to face the music with Michael tomorrow is all.' "Let's see how the love bite's doing," Stuart requested. Joshua pulled down the neck on his new jumper to reveal a bruise. "It's a corker!" Stuart pointed out, "Lucky you can conceal it." They smiled and kissed. Joshua then proceeded to re-dress himself. "Shall I walk you home?" Stuart asked.
"Nah it's ok, it's not far. I don't want to put you out," Joshua replied.
"What if I want to?" Stuart enquired in a tone that implied he'd be disappointed if Joshua refused.
"Ok then," Joshua replied.

Without discussion, Stuart led them on the longest route possible to Joshua's home, stopping at several dark spots for a stolen kiss. Joshua felt so giddy and excited; Stuart was now all that was on his mind. Megan was currently at the bottom of his priorities list. As they approached the house, Stuart enquired as to when or if he would see him again. Joshua was bewildered by this question, 'Does Stuart think I'm one of these guys who goes online looking for a quick shag?' he wondered.
"Of course Stuart, I want to see you again as soon as possible. I can't this weekend because it's my eighteenth birthday and I promised to spend time with Megan, but we can talk online and text and I'll see you in the week," he assured him.

"Can't wait!" said Stuart, grinning like a Cheshire cat. The pair had reached Joshua's driveway. "Better not give you a goodnight kiss, someone might see," Stuart pointed out.
"Very true, but text me soon, won't you?" Joshua replied.
"Will do," Stuart said as he delicately tapped Joshua's arm and raced off home.

Joshua entered his house feeling completely satisfied; relieved in a way that at last he had acknowledged his feelings for other males. He glanced at his watch and realised it was now after midnight. Had five hours really just passed by? It was so surreal. In just one evening he'd met Stuart online, then in person, had food and drink, experienced oral sex for the first time and gained a ridiculously expensive looking sweater into the bargain. He tip-toed up the stairs in an effort not to awaken his father before hearing the sound of the front door closing from behind him. 'I'm sure I locked that,' he thought to himself, turning to investigate. Neil had just arrived home, his appearance unusually attractive. For a change he had actually made an effort with his attire.
"Hi son, guess we're both rolling in late tonight!" Neil pointed out, smiling. He'd obviously been drinking, but seemed to be in an unusually good mood. 'Who is this man and what has he done with the ignoramus I call my father?' Joshua wondered. "New sweater? Very nice," Neil commented. Joshua found this strange, but played along,
"You look good too Dad."
"Thanks son," Neil said, patting him on the shoulder as he trotted off up the stairs. Joshua was astonished by Neil's unusually positive attitude towards him. This required investigation. He went into the kitchen and glanced around. Neil's wallet was lying on the side; he opened it and examined the contents. Among his various plastic cards was a yellow post-it note with the name 'Karen' written on it and a telephone number. Joshua had his explanation. Neil, his obnoxious father had met someone new. None of the women he'd dated before had ever made him smile this way. Joshua was unsure of how to feel about his father having another new partner, but if it meant his mood would change so dramatically it had to be a good thing.

Joshua retired to his bed and mulled over the events of the day. He eventually reached the conclusion that Neil's new found romance was a good thing. After all, Neil couldn't be expected to be single forever and he'd had a lot of bad eggs since Lynne. Joshua knew that his father's romance and the love bite that could potentially destroy his life should concern him, but his mood was too positive to allow anything to worry him. Laying in his bed, he saw the clock turn to one, two and three o'clock. His head was buzzing with so much information that he was struggling to sleep.

After eventually managing to sleep, he awoke at eleven thirty, conscious that he was due at the supermarket in an hour. It was just one day until his eighteenth birthday and, as he'd discovered the previous evening, his big party. He hopped out of bed and wrapped himself in his dressing gown.

"Joshua are you up? You have a visitor!" Neil's voice bellowed from downstairs.

"Yeh, I'm up!" Joshua yelled in reply.

"Ok, I'm sending him up!" 'Sending who up?' he wondered. Joshua could recognise the knock on his bedroom door; it was the way Michael always knocked.

"Are you decent?" Michael asked from the other side of the door.

"Do you want me to be?" Joshua asked in jest, then immediately regretting the comment. He realised he was sailing a little close to the wind. Michael didn't react to the comment and remained standing silently. "Wait just a second," Joshua yelled, fumbling around for a pair of jeans and a t-shirt.

"You're not a morning person, are you?" Michael asked as he entered the room to find Joshua pulling the t-shirt over his head. "We need to talk," Michael announced forcefully.

"Ok," Joshua muttered in agreement, "Sit down."

They seated themselves together on the bed.

"Two years ago, you and I had a heart to heart, you told me about your feelings for men and I listened," Michael began.

"Yeah, and I appreciated it," Joshua interrupted.

"Then, you led me to believe that it was just confusion, you were straight and you loved Megan," Michael continued.

"I do love Megan," Joshua insisted, leaping to his own defence.

"Foolishly, I allowed myself to believe you, because I grew so close to Megan, but I suppose deep down I knew we'd end up where we are now. Joshua, tell me honestly. I think you know now. Are you gay?" Michael asked. Joshua could sense Michael's concern was genuine.

"Yes Michael, I'm gay, and it feels so good to finally let it out to people who understand," Joshua confessed.

"You have to tell Megan, you know that don't you?" Michael asked. Joshua realised this and it scared him.

"I don't want to lose her Michael. I don't want her to hate me," Joshua admitted. Tears were beginning to fill his eyes. Michael held him in his arms for a short time. Upon releasing him, Michael's eyes were suddenly drawn to the monstrously sized bruise on Joshua's neck.

"What the fuck is that?!" Michael was astounded. Had he been under-estimating his friend? For years he'd presumed to know him well and had assumed he was frigid, which in a way had been true but mainly because he had been coming to terms with his sexuality and in the recent past even discussing it had been almost impossible, let alone contemplating sexual actions with another male. "Who on earth gave you that?" Michael asked. Joshua hadn't thought about the love bite as he'd been distracted since he'd awoken.

"Shit! Glad you reminded me," Joshua said as he quickly pulled off his shirt and replaced it with his beautiful red jumper. "This covers it up doesn't it?" asked Joshua.

"Er…..yeah. Where did that come from? It looks expensive," Michael commented.

"Tell me about it. Stuart gave it to me 'cos he felt guilty about giving me the love bite," Joshua laughed, still wiping tears from his eyes.

"So this Stuart gave you that bruise then?" Michael enquired, looking somewhat bewildered.

"Yeah," Joshua replied sheepishly.

"What the hell else have you done?!" Michael's tone of voice implied that he disapproved of Joshua's sexual exploration, or perhaps that he was jealous that he hadn't been chosen to participate.

"I let him suck me," Joshua replied, almost sounding as though this was a regular activity. He was struggling to withhold his grin as he recalled the incident.

"You're in a mess Joshua! You can't go on allowing Megan to believe that everything is hunky dory. You need to come clean with her," Michael insisted. Joshua acknowledged this,

"Ok, you're right. But please, let's get tomorrow over with first." "Ok Joshua, enjoy your eighteenth birthday, wear your jumper to conceal the love bite, but you know you have to do it then, you have to tell Megan the truth."

Chapter 4

At 18 you welcome growing a year older, and Joshua was no exception. He awoke at ten o'clock and pondered the day ahead. He wondered who would call during the day, how many people would attend his surprise party and whether or not his father's positive mood would persist long enough to keep him from destroying his special day. He knew his mission would be tough. He had to last the day without Megan or anyone else spotting his love bite. He jumped out of bed and, once showered, immediately dressed himself, including his red jumper. These clothes would last to the end of the day, come hell or high water. Other than the party of the evening, which he was supposed to be unaware of, this was to be a regular Sunday in most ways. He made his way down the stairs, then entered the kitchen to find Neil at the frying pan tossing pancakes.

"What you doing dad?" Joshua enquired.

"It's your eighteenth birthday son, pancakes are your favourite," Neil replied. Shocked by his fathers incredibly high spirit, Joshua commented, "We're not in America dad!" Neil appeared to be slightly upset by his son's unappreciative comment. "I'm only joking dad, I'm really happy you went to all this trouble for me," Joshua attempted to redeem himself, concerned he may have just thrown away the first progress he'd made with Neil in five years. Neil smiled and instructed Joshua to seat himself and eat. Joshua began to enjoy his pancakes and even felt comfortable dining with his father.

"So, what are your plans for the day?" Neil inquired.

"Well, I'm just assuming I'll get loads of visitors bearing gifts!" Joshua replied enthusiastically. Neil was a brand new person. The change in him was so dramatic. Almost overnight he'd changed from what Joshua would have described as an evil bastard to an extremely pleasant individual. He wondered whether the change in his father was temporary, and if so, hoped it would at least last the day. Joshua's plate was soon empty.

"Well you've certainly got the appetite of an adult," his father commented.

"Didn't I always?" joked Joshua. It was time for Joshua to make a bold statement. He was taking a risk by saying this but felt he had nothing to lose, "I'd say Karen's a good influence on you dad, I hope it works out for you. She's obviously making you happy, almost as happy as mum did." Neil gave Joshua a look he'd never seen before. It was a look of pride, and it was followed by a flattering compliment,

"I'm proud of you son. You've grown up into a fine young man. It's quite an achievement considering you pretty much raised yourself." This was music to Joshua's ears. Perhaps at last, he and Neil could have a true

father and son relationship. He wondered what kind of woman Karen must be to cause such a dramatic change in Neil's attitude. "The drawers by the bookshelf," Neil commented.
"What about them?" Joshua asked, looking baffled.
"Take a look in the top one, there's a couple of bits for you," Neil said, grinning like a Cheshire cat. Joshua was intrigued; he opened the drawer to find two small wrapped gifts and an envelope. The envelope contained a typically humorous greeting card.
"Thanks dad, very funny," Joshua laughed and then proceeded to open one of his presents. He removed the wrapping paper and unveiled a small bank book. "Have you been saving for me?" Joshua asked.
"It was your mother's idea," replied Neil, unwilling to confess to too much humanity in the one day. Joshua opened the bank book and discovered the balance was £5000. "We've never had a lot Joshua, but your mother and I did try," Neil commented defensively, unsure of what reaction to expect.
"Dad, I don't know what to say!" Joshua was in shock, this was extremely unexpected, though it was no surprise that their hadn't been any entries into the book except interest in the last five years. "Thank you dad, thank you so much. I wish mum was here so I could thank her too."
"She watches over you son. I promise you that," Neil assured him, then lightened the mood by insisting the second gift be opened. Joshua began to open the remaining present. It felt like a key ring, but why would Neil be buying a key ring for him? He ripped off the wrapping paper to find a Star Wars key ring, but more importantly a car key. "It's an extra key I had made for my car. I've booked fourteen lessons for you starting next Sunday. If you need any more you'll have to pay for them yourself with your wages from the store," Neil said in a vague attempt to be harsh.
"Anyway…." Neil began while piling his breakfast pots into the sink, "I said I'd work overtime today so I'll leave you to it, have fun," and he departed. Joshua shocked himself by actually feeling almost disappointed by Neil's exit. Up until very recently he couldn't have imagined anything nicer than not seeing his father on his eighteenth birthday, but now he was overwhelmed by Neil's kindness, temporary as it may be, and saddened that he had to leave for work.

The doorbell rang. Joshua excitedly dashed to the door to find Michael on the step.
"Just saw your father. He seemed unusually chirpy," Michael pointed out as he invited himself into the house.
"Tell me about it. I just got five grand, driving lessons and access to the car!" Joshua announced, still struggling to believe it himself.
"That will make my gift seem feeble," joked Michael.

"It's the thought that counts," insisted Joshua.
"I'll bring it tonight, I think most people will be bringing a present," said Michael. Joshua's curiosity was getting the better of him as to what was to happen that evening and where it was to take place. He was also longing to see Stuart again. Stuart and Joshua had exchanged several text messages during the weekend and another meeting was inevitable. He tried to coax the details of the party from Michael in order that he could invite Stuart,
"Come on then. I know I'm having a party, so you'd might as well tell me where." Michael resisted, already feeling he'd betrayed Megan's trust enough. Joshua offered a compromise, "Ok then, if I give you Stuart's mobile number, will you invite him?" he asked. Michael was astonished by Joshua's request.
"Are you serious?" he asked, "Do you really want Stuart and Megan in the same room together?"
"It's my eighteenth birthday. I want him there!" Joshua pleaded. Michael reluctantly agreed to invite Stuart to the party and Joshua gave him Stuart's number followed by a hug of gratitude.
"For the record, I think this is a bad idea," Michael commented.
"It'll be fine, he won't tell anyone the truth. Just introduce him to people as our friend," Joshua reassured him. Micheal's face implied he was unconvinced of how the plan was going to work. "Don't worry, it'll be fine," Joshua said, smiling. Micheal couldn't resist Joshua's smile and responded with a smirk of his own. He was considering raising the issue of what Joshua's plans were to bring his homosexuality out into the open, however Megan arrived, accompanied by Joshua's gift which he saw as his cue to exit.

Once Michael had left, Megan instigated heavy petting with Joshua; she'd been wondering recently if her boyfriend's entry to adulthood would make their relationship more physical.
"Calm down Megan," Joshua said, attempting to pry her off his body in the nicest possible way.
"Oh ok," she said backing off, "Hey what's with the new outfit?" Joshua had to think fast,
"Present from dad."
"Blimey, he has changed, the money, driving lessons and clothes!" Megan commented. Joshua nodded in agreement, feeling guilty for partially fibbing. "Anyway…" she began, slapping his knee, "Time to open my present." Joshua eagerly unwrapped Megan's gift.
"Oh my god, this must have been expensive!" Joshua screeched as he revealed Megan's present to be designer jeans and a designer shirt to match.

"You're worth every penny," Megan replied proudly and gave him a peck on the cheek. Joshua was stunned by the outfit; it screamed 'expensive'. He knew he'd look amazing when he wore it and was almost lost for words,
"I don't know what to say Megan."
"Seeing how gorgeous you look in it tonight is all the thanks I need," Megan reassured him. It was time to panic. Joshua's worst nightmare was coming true, there was no way out, if he was to wear the new outfit to the party Megan would inevitably spot the love bite on his neck.
"To....tonight," Joshua stuttered.
"I'm taking you out, remember?!" Megan insisted.
"Yeah...but it's just a quiet drink," Joshua said, playing dumb, "We should save it for a special occasion."
"Don't be silly Joshua. What's more important than your eighteenth birthday?" Megan asked, now wondering whether or not Joshua did indeed like her gift as much as he had implied he did.
"Yeah but we're only going out for a quiet night..." Joshua continued to play dumb in an attempt to justify his reluctance to wear the outfit.
"I don't care; I can't wait to see you in it!" Megan said enthusiastically while throwing her arms around him and sticking her tongue as far into his mouth as it could possibly go. Although he concealed it reasonably well, Joshua was now terrified. The only outfit that would mask the love bite was the jumper he was currently wearing and if he wore that to the party he'd offend Megan, if he wore her outfit she'd notice the bruise on his neck.
"It's not as if we're doing anything special though..." Joshua continued.
"We'll see," Megan said, realising immediately that she's implied there were special plans for the evening. Joshua pretended to be oblivious to this slip of Megan's tongue. They arranged a time to leave for their night out and Megan excused herself. She claimed that she had plans with the family for the daytime, in reality she was off to make the finishing touches to the party. This suited Joshua as he was about to receive an important text message; 'Can I come over and c u? Happy Birthday! Stuart xx' it said. A golden opportunity had just presented itself. Joshua had been eager to spend some more time with his new found friend and now he had the house to himself and wasn't expecting any further visitors. He replied to the text message, giving his address details and encouraging him to arrive as quickly as possible. He merrily skipped along to the mirror to confirm his perfect appearance was unblemished. He pulled the neck of his jumper down slightly to reveal the love bite and smiled to himself. The anticipation of expecting a visit from Stuart had taken Joshua's attention away from his concern of which outfit to wear

later that day. He grabbed the hair gel, which had been left at the top of the sink earlier that morning and began restyling his hair for Stuart's approval. He simply couldn't wait for his arrival.

Just minutes later, Stuart was rattling the door knob as though his life depended on it. Joshua dashed to the door to welcome him. Almost before the door had closed behind him, Stuart's arms were draped around the birthday boy and they were sharing tongues. Eventually Stuart retracted himself and seductively wished Joshua a,

"Happy Birthday big boy."

"I wish I could be angry with you," Joshua began, half joking.

Stuart looked confused. "You've caused me such a dilemma," Joshua continued and went on to explain the implications of the different outfits he was to choose between for his evening wear. Stuart burst into laughter and Joshua reluctantly joined him. "It's not funny," Joshua said, while unsuccessfully making an effort not to laugh. Stuart's laughter paused long enough for him to say,

"I know I know, I'm sorry," then resumed. Joshua playfully slapped his right arm.

"So….you can't get mad at me eh?" Stuart asked, referring to Joshua's earlier comment, "That I can use to my advantage."

"What am I going to do?" Joshua asked, still struggling to contain his laughter.

"Just pretend you didn't realise anything special was happening tonight," Stuart suggested, "and wear the clothes you have on now, which look great on you by the way."

"Sweet talker," Joshua grinned. The Friday evening's rapport was still present and the banter was still bouncing around.

"I got a text message earlier from that friend of yours…Michael," Stuart announced, changing the subject slightly. Joshua immediately knew what Stuart was getting at,

"Oh please say you'll come tonight!"

"Sure, if you want me to," Stuart replied and followed that with, "I'm not supposed to tell you where it is."

"Don't!" Joshua insisted, "at least I can seem a little surprised."

"I'm sorry I don't have a gift for you," Stuart apologised.

"Don't be silly Stuart, you've only known me a couple of days," Joshua reassured him, then began to allure Stuart in, "I can think of a suitable present that wouldn't cost a penny." Stuart gave Joshua a look that said, "Are you sure?" Joshua nodded in agreement for him to proceed, then took his hand and guided him to the sofa. Joshua fell into it and Stuart lay on top of him. Joshua felt almost loved as Stuart affectionately ran his fingers through his hair. Once again he felt Stuart's tongue fiercely

playing with his own. He was becoming excited and interrupted the passion only long enough to say,
"I want you Stuart, I want you now!" Stuart gave him a look of both concern and excitement and asked,
"Are you sure Joshua? It's a big step." Joshua nodded and the passion resumed. Stuart kneeled and began tugging Joshua's jumper off. Joshua followed the routine by doing the same to Stuart, who then pulled a condom from his pocket and unwrapped the packaging with his teeth, the empty wrapper dropped to the floor. Joshua breathed a sigh of relief to see that Stuart planned to take the lead and ensure their frolics would be safe. He could feel Stuart's lips moving further and further down his body. The sensation of being kissed and caressed on his chest was almost unbearable. Stuart suddenly raised his head to the sound of a rattle at the door. "Oh shit!" he said in a panic.
"Who the hell can that be?" Joshua asked rhetorically. They dived off the sofa and re-dressed themselves, then inspected each other to ensure there was no evidence of their activities.
"Is anyone in there? Joshua?!" bellowed James' voice from outside.
"It's James!" shrieked Joshua. Stuart gave a puzzled look as if to enquire about who James was. "I'll tell you later," Joshua responded. He took a deep breath and opened the door.
"What took so long?" James asked while barging into the house.
"We were upstairs. Joshua was showing me some…." Stuart began.
"Videos, Star wars," Joshua finished his sentence, closing the door.
"You've found another fan have you?" James asked in jest.
"Hi, I'm Stuart," Stuart introduced himself, attempting to act as heterosexual as possible. James gave a manly handshake.
"I should come to see you more often, I bet I don't know most of your friends now," James remarked with a hint of sarcasm in his voice.
"Anyway, I'm James," he continued, now acknowledging Stuart again. Joshua gave Stuart a panicked look behind James' back. "Best buddies at school you and I, weren't we Joshua?" James continued with sentiment that almost seemed false.
"So what brings you here today?" Joshua asked, not really focussed on what he was saying. His heart was racing a mile a minute.
"Do you even have to ask? I wouldn't let your eighteenth birthday go by without coming to see you!" exclaimed James. Joshua made a vague attempt to seem appreciative. As the small talk continued, James suddenly noticed through the corner of his eye the empty condom wrapper and the disorderly state of the sofa. Stuart observed James' wandering eyes and gave Joshua a look of unease. James glanced at Joshua with a suspicious look in his eye that almost said, "I know what

you're up to mate." James was unaware of how to react and chose not to at this stage. "Anyway, I'd better be off. I just thought I'd drop in and say happy birthday," he quickly excused himself and departed the house almost as though it were on fire and his life was at risk. Joshua breathed a sigh of relief, but immediately received a look of concern from Stuart.
"What is it?" asked Joshua.
"He knows," murmured Stuart.
"What?!" asked a horrified Joshua.
"He saw the state the sofa was in. He saw the condom wrapper. Trust me Joshua, he knows!" Stuart declared. Joshua began to panic as he mentally recalled the events of the time James had previously suspected his homosexuality.
"How do you think he'll react then? By the look on your face I'd say badly," Stuart commented.
"Put it this way, last time I ended up bruised," Joshua replied.
"Last time?" Stuart gave a stare of confusion, "I don't understand, you told him before?" Joshua went on to explain the events surrounding the fight between he and James at school. "I see, well there's not a lot we can do, just hope for the best I suppose," Stuart said, then added, "The sooner you come out and be honest with people the better. Megan will find out from someone else eventually if you don't tell her."

Joshua spent the afternoon mulling over things. It was all getting very complicated. He wondered whether or not to wear Megan's gift for his party, and if he did so, would he be able to explain the bruise on his neck. He contemplated telephoning James to discuss the situation but decided it was better not to rock the boat as he didn't know for certain that James had fixed the pieces together and reached the correct conclusion. He worried of how awkward the party may be if James wished to make an issue of it. In spite of all his uneasiness though, he did smile as he mentally recalled the passion between he and Stuart, brief as it may have been, and when thinking how surprisingly kind Neil had been. Not every aspect of his birthday had been unwholesome, though he wondered if the best or even the worst was yet to come.

He was staring at the clock almost as though it were a ticking time bomb about to explode. Six thirty came and his father arrived home, still in a vivacious mood. Just half an hour remained before Megan was due to arrive for their evening out and a decision had to be made with regard to his attire. Neil attempted to make small talk, however Joshua's attention was elsewhere; he couldn't take his mind off the looming confrontation ahead. Neil eventually tired of trying to extract

conversation, vacated the room and left Joshua to mentally panic alone. There were just ten minutes longer to dread Megan's reaction to his outfit. The final decision had been made; he couldn't possibly wear Megan's garments and her reaction to this seemed the lesser of the two evils when compared to how she would inevitably react to the sight of his love bite. The clock was ticking. At five minutes before seven o'clock the doorbell rang. "Typical of Megan to be early," Joshua muttered to himself. He answered the door, dreading the lie he was about to tell. He had never seen Megan look so beautiful. She had clearly put a lot of effort into her appearance and she had obviously spent as much on her outfit as she had on his. Although he felt guilty for not making such an effort himself, the decision had been made and it was the best one for all concerned. He knew deep down that the evening would be the end of his dishonesty and he would soon need to confess his true self to Megan in order that they may get on with their lives. This scared him, but he knew it had to be done. Megan had a look of disappointment in her eyes which she was trying to conceal as she entered the living room.
"You're not wearing your new outfit," she pointed out, using the calmest and most delicate tone of voice she could possibly muster up.
"Megan, you look beautiful," Joshua said sincerely. This comment slightly improved Megan's frame of mind, but her concern for Joshua's lack of effort remained.
"Thanks Joshua, but why not wear the outfit I bought for you tonight?" Joshua glanced to ensure his father wasn't within earshot and replied, "My dad thinks I should wear this tonight. It is really nice and I don't want to offend him. Besides, it's not as though we're doing anything special. Just a quiet drink, right?" Although slightly suspicious, Megan smiled and suggested they headed for town. Now all she had to do was guide Joshua to the party.

They walked slowly into the city centre, discussing their activities of the day. Joshua of course neglected to mention his rendezvous with Stuart. He began to subtly tease Megan by making suggestions of where they should spend the evening, knowing perfectly well that she had to somehow guide him to wherever she was holding the party.
"Well we can go round as many bars as you want, since you're legal," Megan laughed, "but first can we nip to my local club 'cos my mother wants to wish you a happy birthday and she'll be there with her friends tonight." Joshua decided not to torture her any further and agreed to visit the club. Megan began to lead him on a detour, attempting to conceal the delight on her face. They arrived at the club within minutes. All the lights appeared to have been dimmed.

"Are you sure it's open?" asked Joshua, continuing to play dumb.
"It has to be," Megan replied, attempting to appear confused. They entered the building and suddenly the lights were all shining and over forty people yelled "Surprise!" The room had been decorated with balloons, banners and various photos of Joshua from his younger years. So many familiar faces were present. Stuart appeared to have latched on to Michael and his date (whom Joshua did not recognise). Neil had not been invited and the majority of the crowd consisted of his old school yard chums, many of which he hadn't seen in years. James was among the crowd, however his facial expression implied he would rather not have been there.
"Happy Birthday!" Megan shouted and threw her arms around Joshua and kissed his cheek. The sounds of the latest dance music bellowed from the speakers which surrounded the room. "Are you surprised?" Megan asked.
"Oh…er….yes!" Joshua replied, attempting to seem genuinely shocked.
"What's up hun'?" Megan asked suspiciously.
"Nothing….I'm just a little overwhelmed. I can't believe you went to all this trouble!" Joshua saved himself by saying exactly what Megan wanted to hear. She looked delighted to see Joshua's gratitude and flung her arms around him again, then dashed to the bar to order a round of drinks. James had been within earshot of the conversation and approached Joshua during his moment of solitude. He tapped him on the shoulder and commented,
"You make me sick you faggot," in Joshua's ear, then escaped into conversation with other guests. The room wasn't small, but not monstrously large either and it was shaped like a perfect square. Nobody could escape the sight of anyone. The DJ was on the stage talking down the microphone and attempting to make the party liven up. The smoke machines were pumping out and creating atmosphere as the bulbs were once again dimmed and replaced by disco lights. Megan's enormous effort in organising this gathering was unmistakable. She quickly returned with a pair of alcoholic soft drinks and passed one to Joshua.
"This is great!" Joshua shouted, trying to overpower the sound of the music pumping from the speakers. Stuart was pondering whether or not to approach Joshua, but then he himself was taken away from his view by Michael.
"Give them some time, she's been planning this for so long," begged Michael. Stuart nodded in agreement and promised to be discreet. Meanwhile, at the other side of the room, James was muttering to several other guests of how he couldn't stand Joshua and how much he despised being there, without giving a reason. Megan was oblivious to any bad feeling in the room and to the pouring rain outside; she was engrossed in

physical contact with Joshua, who was glancing at Stuart through the corner of his eye. Michael's date was becoming lonely as his pet talk with Stuart continued.
"Just try not to hurt Megan."
"That's not my intention. I promise tonight won't be the night, in fact I'm going to make sure of that," Stuart said as he wandered away from Michael and towards James. "Hello James, I'm Stuart. We met earlier today."
"I remember," James answered with a look of contempt on his face. Stuart persisted with his attempt to be pleasant in spite of James' attitude.
"Was there something else?" James asked sarcastically, as though he wouldn't contemplate wasting his time on Stuart without a specific purpose.
"Just wanting to get to know Joshua's friends," Stuart said defensively.
"Oh I bet you do. I bet you want to get to know me really well. Look I'm not into that, ok? You make me sick," James stated rudely and walked away in disgust. Stuart caught up with him and tapped him on the shoulder. James turned to face him and said, "Touch me again and I'll floor you!" Stuart could sense that he was deadly serious.
"Ok, feel how you want about me. But please don't spoil tonight," Stuart pleaded. James shrugged him off and escaped to the toilet. The guests were now starting to nibble on the buffet and dance. Megan didn't appear to have any intentions of leaving Joshua's sight for the rest of the evening. They were now seated eating and chattering with several of Megan's girlfriends. Stuart was almost jealous as he observed Megan affectionately touching her boyfriend. Joshua could feel a vibration in his pocket and reached for his mobile phone. A text message from Stuart awaited him. He read the message, trying hard to conceal it from Megan and her friends. It read 'I wish I could kiss you'.
"Anything exciting," asked Megan in her usual innocent yet bubbly manner.
"Oh, just another Happy Birthday message. I've been getting them all day," Joshua replied and quickly sent a text message back to Stuart who was grinning at the other side of the room. The message read, 'Me 2 x'. As the night wore on, the patrons (many of whom were underage) were becoming intoxicated further and had formed a series of groups around the room. The dance floor was full and included Megan, Joshua, Michael and Michael's floozy. James was seated alone drinking pint after pint, barely acknowledging anyone. Joshua excused himself to the toilet and Stuart proceeded to follow him.

The toilets were empty. Joshua entered and was heading for the urinals when Stuart arrived.

"Joshua, I have to talk to you," he demanded in a panic. Joshua felt agitated by Stuart's presence.
"For gods sake be careful! What if someone catches us?!"
"It's not that," Stuart insisted, "I have to warn you about James." Joshua looked puzzled,
"Wasn't it me that warned you?"
"He's on the warpath Joshua. I think he may cause a scene if he gets anymore drunk!"
"Yeah, he made a vicious comment to me earlier," agreed Joshua.
"Just be careful," Stuart said lovingly before returning to the party.

Megan was having a rest from dancing and noticed Stuart leave the toilets, then rejoin Michael and his date. Joshua returned to the room and joined Megan.
"Looks like he's got two on the go now, bless him," Megan commented randomly and laughed. Joshua was beginning to feel more and more uncomfortable, though this was being partly rectified by his high level of alcohol consumption. James appeared to be even more intoxicated and looked as though he resented the world at this moment in time, this was making Stuart very concerned, he could sense that James would do something vicious at any moment to put a dampener on the event.

The music was unexpectedly interrupted and a dance floor of youngsters were gazing around in search of an explanation for the silence. Had the police discovered there were so many underage drinkers present? The panic ended as the DJ took to the stage.
"How you all doing tonight? You having fun?" he yelled down the microphone in a patronising tone of voice. The audience didn't react.
"We've got a couple of people who want to say a few words," the DJ continued. The crowd all turned to face Joshua and began chanting,
"Speech, speech!" Joshua covered his face with his hands to demonstrate his objection. Megan took Joshua's hand and guided him to the stage.
"Ok, I'm gonna' do my best to embarrass him now," Megan began, speaking down the microphone. The audience laughed and cheered. "I won't get too sappy, but this is a very special day," Megan continued, "…and we all love Joshua. I just want to thank him for being the best boyfriend a girl could ever want for four years now and wish him a happy birthday." She was so sweet and innocent. Joshua knew he would soon be breaking her precious, trusting and fragile heart. He was about to speak down the microphone when a voice interrupted from the audience.
"Wait. I want to say something," James shouted, stumbling across the dance floor.

"He's pissed as a fart," Stuart intervened, attempting to salvage the situation he'd earlier predicted, "I'll take him home." Stuart placed his hand on James' arm but was shrugged away.
"Fuck off!" James marched on to the stage and grabbed the microphone. "Joshua and I were best friends all through school…" James slurred, luring Megan into a false sense of security, "….and it surprises me that his girlfriend came up here to say such kind words, and yet his boyfriend is just standing in the crowd. You see, I didn't know until today that Joshua was a fag. Come on Stuart, don't be shy, come up here!" Megan looked mortified; her heart was ripped into a million pieces by James' statement. She looked Joshua directly in the eye and asked,
"Is it true?" Joshua gazed into her eyes, unable to find the appropriate words to say. "It's ok, don't bother. It's written all over your face," Megan said with a hint of both disgust and disappointment in her voice, then bolted out of the room in a flood of tears.
"How could you?!" Joshua demanded. James (who was struggling to stand up) failed to reply. His facial expression dictated that he felt no remorse and he appeared to be very satisfied.
"You never deserved her," he said eventually. Joshua raised his fist to James. Stuart intervened again attempting to de-fuse the situation,
"He's not worth it, go and find Megan. She needs you." Joshua nodded in agreement and quietly departed. As he walked across the dance floor, he could sense that all eyes were on him. Everyone was glaring at the freak show. Things were going from bad to worse and he couldn't wait to leave. The DJ began to quietly pack away his equipment, attempting to avoid any looming trouble. James had now given up on any hope of remaining upright and was sitting on the edge of the stage. The crowd were gossiping amongst themselves. Michael's date left and so he approached Stuart.
"What a mess," he pointed out.
"I'm so sorry," Stuart apologised, "I'd never have come if I'd known…."
"It's ok," Michael assured him, "It's not your fault….This wanker here is to blame."
"Don't you call me names you fuckin' arse bandit!" James butted in. Michael gave him a look of hatred and continued his conversation with Stuart,
"I just hope he finds her and that she's ok. She was a wreck."

Joshua was drenched in water from head to toe. He'd been bolting around the streets of Sheffield in the pouring rain with no umbrella. Several times already he'd risked his life darting across busy main roads, determined to locate Megan and offer some kind of condolence. If truth be known, he didn't have a clue what he was planning to say to Megan when he did eventually catch up with her, but he couldn't bare the thought of her experiencing so much pain. The rain was getting faster and the sound of thunder was overpowering. He prayed for an end to the storm. Joshua realised he was achieving absolutely nothing and headed for a bus shelter to temporarily escape the rain and gather his thoughts together. He wondered where Megan would go at a time such as this. He guessed that she wouldn't have headed for home because her mother would have returned by this time and, being the independent person that Megan was, she wouldn't want to face the interrogation that would await her if she was to arrive home early. All of Megan's friends had been at the party, which eliminated any possibility of her hiding at any of their homes as well. He had an idea, recalling their days as young teenagers, Joshua remembered that he and Megan often visited the park on the way home from school, not to use the facilities for the purpose for which they'd been designed, just simply to sit on the swings and chat. They'd had a lot of meaningful conversations on those swings and both of them had fond memories of the park. Joshua ran as fast as possible through the persisting rain.

The party had now been abandoned by the DJ and all the guests with the exceptions of Michael and Stuart who were now seated in the almost silent room. Michael was smoking a cigarette.

"I feel terrible," Stuart confessed.

"It's not your fault," Michael said in an attempt to comfort him, then added out of curiosity, "So are you serious about Joshua? Do you genuinely like him or is it just sex?"

"I haven't known him for long, but we've got a real connection. I like him a lot.........I'd like him to be my boyfriend.....If it's what he wants," Stuart replied truthfully.

"I think he likes you, just be patient with him," were Michaels words of advice. Stuart appreciated the support that Michael was offering, in spite of his friendship with Megan. Michael held out his arms in an offer of comfort to Stuart, sensing that Stuart had deep feelings of guilt and understood his predicament.

Joshua arrived at the park. Sure enough, his hunch had been correct. There she was, this beautiful girl, seated on a swing. She seemed to be oblivious to the rain that was ruining not only her hair and make up, but also her outfit. She obviously had the weight of the world on her shoulders. Joshua didn't know what he would say to Megan. He felt he had destroyed her hopes and dreams in just a split second. There was nothing he could say or do to retract what had happened. In spite of his sexual preferences, Megan was the most important person in his life. He valued his friendship with her above anything else, and the thought of

losing that terrified him. He slowly approached her, almost as though he were a hunter attempting to catch his prey. He didn't want her to be conscious of his presence until it was absolutely necessary. Her head was facing downwards as she stared at her soaking shoes. The swing was swaying slightly but not enough for her to lose her grip on the floor. It was difficult to tell, but Joshua assumed tears were rolling down her face as well as the raindrops. Her name was being called. She tilted her head to investigate. There he was, standing just inches away; the boy who'd demolished her heart in under a minute. The rain began to calm. Megan pulled away the hair that was blocking her view. They stared at each other for just a few seconds, though it seemed like an eternity.
"Well, the rain's stopping, that's something," Joshua said light-heartedly. Megan made no attempt to produce a smile. "May I sit down?" Joshua asked.
"It's a free country," Megan replied bluntly, wiping her face in an attempt to hide the evidence of her tears. Joshua sat on the swing closest to hers; the small amount of air between them could have been cut with a knife. Neither could muster up the right words to say. Joshua was the first to break the silence,
"You'll catch pneumonia if you're not careful."
"So will you," Megan replied bluntly, still staring at the floor.
"Touché," Joshua pointed out, attempting to lighten the mood. This was not working. After another long silence, Megan eventually turned to face the man who'd been the most important person in her life.
"What do you want Joshua? Why are you here?"
"Because I care," Joshua replied sincerely.
"I believe you, even now I believe you. Maybe I'm just a fool….or a glutton for punishment," Megan said, displaying no emotion whatsoever.
"Don't say that, please," Joshua begged, "I don't want to lose you."
Megan stared at him for a moment with a look of contempt. She stood and began to walk away.
"Please……" Joshua pleaded. Megan turned to face him and asked,
"In what way don't you want to lose me Joshua?" He looked confused.
"Do you not want to lose me as a girlfriend, a friend, a lover or is it that you don't want to lose me as a mug? A doormat? A lapdog?! Someone who'll stand by you no matter what and foolishly believe in you and expect the feelings to be reciprocated." Joshua was speechless.
"Well?....Well?!" Megan demanded. He stood and grabbed hold of her arms.
"I don't want to lose you because you're the most important person in my life," he insisted.

"Let go of me!" yelled Megan, releasing herself from Joshua's clutches.
"Why Joshua? Why did you lead me on for all these years?" Megan asked calmly.
"It's not easy Megan, it's complicated" Joshua began, in attempt to make her understand, although heterosexuals can never and will never truly understand what gay people face when coming to terms with being different. Joshua had learned this already. "I was so lucky that someone as special as you wanted to be with me…"
"Well I thought you were special too," Megan interrupted sarcastically.
"Ok. I deserved that. Please try to understand how difficult it is to come to terms with it Megan," Joshua pleaded.
"It's all about you, isn't it Joshua?" Megan replied, still taunting him, "You were having a tough time so it's ok to put my life on hold for four years!"
"It's not like that Megan and you know it," Joshua insisted, "I love you Megan. I really truly love you."
"Just not in the way that a man should love his girlfriend," Megan ended his sentence. Joshua replied with a simple,
"Yes." He then followed it up with, "I'm really sorry I didn't confide in you about the confusion of my sexuality, it was just so hard." Megan gave Joshua a look of disappointment that he hadn't seen on a woman's face since his late mother had read his school report cards.
"Goodbye Joshua," she said, giving no indication of how final this statement was. She turned and walked away. Joshua re-seated himself on the swing, alone with his thoughts, where he remained for over an hour.

Joshua didn't stir until eleven o'clock the next morning. He'd intended to take the day off as he was expecting a hangover; however, in spite of not having one, he felt the need for time to mull things over. He switched on his mobile phone. Messages were waiting for him from Michael and Stuart but Megan hadn't made an attempt to contact him. After showering, he put on his red jumper again (as it was the closest item of clothing available) and slowly made his way down the stairs. He seated himself for a moment, debating with himself whether or not it would be wise to telephone Megan. He decided against it and made his way to the kitchen in search of food. His scavenging was interrupted by a knock at the door.
"Who can that be at this time?" he muttered to himself, and then yelled, "Coming!" He answered the door to find Megan on the step looking surprisingly cheerful. "Megan, I didn't expect to see you today," Joshua said.
"Can I come in?" Megan asked. They went through to the living room and parked themselves on separate seats.

"What can I do for you?" Joshua asked, intrigued by her visit.

"I came to apologise Joshua. I want to say I'm sorry for my behaviour last night," she replied. Joshua was bewildered by this statement.

"You have nothing to be sorry for!" he assured her.

"You're wrong Joshua. I do. This is my fault, I've nobody else to blame," she said, tears filling her eyes. Joshua was confused.

"You didn't cause my homosexuality. This is no implication on you as a girlfriend. Please, please don't think that!" he pleaded.

"Listen to me!" Megan demanded assertively. Joshua stopped talking. Megan looked into his eyes. "Do you honestly think I didn't know you were gay?" she asked, "or at least suspect it."

"You knew?" Joshua said, almost dumbfounded.

"Somewhere deep down. I wouldn't admit it to myself. You can't get to know someone as well as I know you and miss something like that," Megan replied.

"But if you knew, then why did you stay with me?" Joshua asked.

"It was selfishness Joshua, pure and simple. I'm selfish. I love you and I didn't want to lose you, so I ignored the signs. I suppose I hoped it was a phase you'd get over in time. I didn't want to believe it was true," Megan said as she seated herself, then buried her head in her hands and began to weep. "I'm so sorry. I'm so so sorry, if I'd dumped you, you would have been free to explore your sexuality and live your own life. It's my fault it all turned out this way, I should have let you go instead of selfishly clinging to you," she apologised in a state of distress that Joshua had never witnessed before. He seated himself beside her and put his arm around her.

"It's ok. It's not your fault. I promise, and I don't regret a minute of our time together." Megan gazed at him as if attempting to visually decide whether or not he was being sincere. "Besides, being with you has made me the man I am today. I wouldn't trade the time I've had with you for anything. I love you. You're my best friend," Joshua said and they hugged each other tightly.

"Best friends forever," Megan demanded.

"I wouldn't have it any other way," Joshua replied.

"Just one thing…" began Megan, "Is Stuart really your boyfriend?" She asked, genuinely interested.

"We only just met, but I'd say this is a good sign," Joshua replied, pulling down the neck on his jumper to reveal his trophy from his favourite hunk. Megan laughed and slapped his leg, just the way a best friend does.

Chapter 5

It was a new beginning for Joshua; it seemed as though the weight of the world had been lifted from his shoulders. James' intentions had been so wicked, and yet the end result had become a positive one. It was eleven thirty pm and Joshua was lying in bed imagining the possibilities that lay ahead. Megan would stay in his life, he could now be open and honest with everyone except his father about his sexuality and with regard to Stuart, well, Joshua daren't even allow his mind to explore the potential in that area. Stuart had had a major impact on Joshua's life in a very short space of time; in a way he was a role model. Joshua wasn't sure if he was falling in love or not, but what he did know was that he wanted Stuart physically and emotionally, there was no doubt about that. Little more than twenty four hours ago in the park Joshua had just wanted the earth to open up and swallow him whole, but now life couldn't look rosier.

Joshua awoke the next morning and gradually made his way down the stairs in just his underwear. He entered the kitchen and was astounded by the sight of a forty-something female placing bread into the toaster.

"Morning love, you must be Joshua," the mysterious lady said as she turned to face him. Her smile was beaming, as though she'd just been told she had the weeks winning lottery ticket. Joshua froze. Not only was he wondering who this strange woman was, but he was also highly embarrassed by the fact that she had already seen him in his underwear.

"I am Joshua…Who are you?" he stuttered.

"My name's Karen," the mysterious lady replied cheerfully. Suddenly it became so clear, Karen was Neil's new girlfriend and it appeared as though she was settling in quickly.

"Your dad's at work. I thought you and I could have breakfast together and get to know each other," she offered. Joshua was unsure of how to react to this invasion of his personal space and excused himself.

"Sure….let me just pop some clothes on first," he muttered as he left the room. Joshua was unsure of what opinion to form of Karen at this stage; she was pleasant, but he felt it was too soon for him to be wandering into the kitchen to discover her casually making breakfast, as though she'd resided there for years.

Several minutes later he returned to the kitchen and was immediately questioned as to how he preferred his toast. He answered and was requested insistently to be seated whilst Karen prepared it. It was as though she was already his step-mother. Although he felt a little uncomfortable, Joshua realised that Karen was making a genuine attempt to be nice and she obviously longed for him to like her.

"So how was your birthday?" here began the small talk.

"It was good," Joshua replied. After another several minutes of meaningless chatter, Joshua made a bold statement, "Karen, you don't have to try so hard. My dad is the happiest I've seen him in years." Karen smiled.
"I'm so glad you feel that way. I don't want you to think I'm trying to replace your mum, no-one could," she insisted.
"Damn right," Joshua said bluntly, "We're all adults here. I think your relationship with my father is a good thing and we'll get on great I'm sure!" Karen grinned and put her arms around Joshua. She had obviously been apprehensive about meeting Joshua and her relief was obvious.
"Right, I have to dash to college. See you later."

Joshua was wandering to college feeling quite satisfied by his unexpected start to the day. He realised that Karen's intentions were obviously good; his mood however was threatened when he spotted James approaching him with a look on his face that implied he was a cross between shocked and angry. "What do you want?" Joshua asked sternly.
"Tell your boyfriend that if he wants to remain in one piece to stay away from me!" James demanded fiercely. While still angry, Joshua was also confused by this statement.
"What the fuck are you on about?" he asked, genuinely unaware of what point James was trying to reach.
"You know what I'm talking about; sending your boyfriend round to threaten me! Like I'm gonna' be scared of that poof." Suddenly the pieces fell into place. Joshua smiled discreetly as he realised that Stuart had obviously visited James to warn him to stay away from him.
"Bless him," he said, almost forgetting to whom he was speaking. James was unimpressed by Joshua's reaction and carefree attitude.
"Any more visits from your poofter boyfriend and I'll fuckin' knock him out," James threatened. Joshua decided he wasn't going to tolerate this and retaliated.
"You tried to ruin my life on Sunday. I'm just thankful that not everyone in my life is as mean and spiteful as you are. I've known Stuart less than a week and already he's proving to be a better friend than you've turned out to be in years."
"Well you should have told me that you were a poof then shouldn't you?" James asked rhetorically, a rather pathetic tone to his voice. He could sense he was losing the argument and followed his last comment up with a demand, "Just tell your boyfriend to keep away from me…..and that goes for you too!"
"Suits me," Joshua said firmly, "If I never see you again it's too soon, now get out of my way so I can get to college." James reluctantly

dislodged himself from Joshua's space. Joshua bluntly thanked him and strolled off to college. James grunted and headed off in the opposite direction.

Joshua's mobile phone began ringing. He reached into his pocket and pulled it out. Stuart was calling.
"Hey babe," he said enthusiastically as he answered it, still continuing his journey to college, "How's it going?"
"I'm fine darling. How are you?" Stuart replied cheerfully.
"All the better for hearing your voice…thank you for what you did last night."
"Last night?" Stuart said, claiming to be unaware of the reason for Joshua's gratitude.
"You know what I'm talking about, warning James off. It was very sweet of you," Joshua continued.
"Has he been bothering you again?!" Stuart asked angrily.
"Calm down. I sorted him out. He won't be bothering us again," Joshua assured him.
"Oh good. People like James we can do without….Hey listen, I get out of uni' at three today, why don't I meet you from college?" Stuart suggested. Joshua was delighted at the thought of spending the evening with him, however it dawned on him that Karen may find his absence from the evening meal to be rude.
"I'm not sure Stuart 'cos I think my dad's girlfriend might be staying for tea today. She was a bit wary about meeting me this morning and I don't want her to think I'm avoiding her," Joshua replied truthfully.
"Ok," Stuart replied with a subtle sigh, unsure of whether or not Joshua was making excuses. "Well….how about we meet up later then…after tea?" he suggested, clutching at straws but trying his hardest not to sound desperate. Joshua immediately agreed without hesitation to meet Stuart at eight o'clock. This would give him enough time after eating to make himself look as gorgeous as possible. He later received a text message from Megan which read, 'Hey best friend! What you up to tonight?' Joshua replied stating he had made plans for the evening and that he'd telephone her when he was available. Already she was being neglected.

After a day at college full of stares and whispers from the other students, Joshua arrived home to discover his father looking unusually well groomed and Karen was cooking a steak dinner. This was the first time in five years that a real meal had been cooked in the house. The normality had been microwavable snacks and take away for so long that the smell of a home cooked meal was unfamiliar.
"Is that Joshua?" Karen asked, her head still buried in the oven, not yet realising that he was now in the same room.

"Hey Karen," Joshua said, still not entirely comfortable with her presence in the house. She closed the oven door and confidently informed them that dinner would be ready in half an hour. It almost seemed as though she'd been living in the house for years by her manner and familiarity with the kitchen, Lynne's kitchen. Joshua followed the implied orders by leaving the room to change his clothes and prepare for dinner. Neil remained chatting to Karen as she prepared the meal.
"You're trying so hard," he pointed out.
"I just want him to like me," Karen replied. Her tone of voice almost demanded sympathy.
"He will like you, just be yourself," Neil suggested lovingly. Karen smiled and Neil placed his arms around her.

Joshua was upstairs deciding on an outfit to make him look as sexy as possible for Stuart later that night. Neil knocked on the door and entered.
"Can I talk to you for a minute son?" Neil asked. It had been so long since he'd referred to him as 'son' that Joshua had almost forgotten how their relationship was supposed to be.
"Sure dad, what's up?" Joshua replied while burying through the wardrobe. Neil seated himself on the bed.
"It'll only take a minute," he said, implying that Joshua should pay attention to the conversation and put his clothing decision on hold for a moment.
"OK," Joshua agreed, turning to face him. Neil patted the bed to indicate that he'd like Joshua to sit beside him. He did so.
"It's about Karen…" Neil began. Joshua looked at him in anticipation of where this was leading. Surely she wasn't moving in already?! "She's really a nice person. I know she'll never replace your mother, but I'd like you to at least be friends. She's trying so hard." Joshua cracked a smile, "Yes, she's definitely trying." They both laughed.
"Don't worry. I like Karen," Joshua assured him, "I think she's been a positive influence on you. She's made you happy and she'll be nice to have around. There really is no problem." Neil breathed a sigh of relief and briefly hugged Joshua, who was now becoming accustomed to Neil's change of attitude and was feeling optimistic about its potential permanence. Neil went on to tell Joshua the ins and outs of how he'd met Karen at a party. His excitement was almost that of a school boy on his first date. Joshua could relate to his fathers excitation. He longed to be able to tell Neil of how he met Stuart and how he was himself falling in love, but the time wasn't right, Neil was happy for the first time in years and Joshua was genuinely glad about this, in spite of the way Neil had treated him. If he were to find out now that his son was gay, the news

probably wouldn't have a positive affect. He knew that he had to tell him sooner or later, but he had enough to deal with facing all of his friends with the revelation at this time.
"I'm really happy for you dad. I mean it."
"You're one in a million," Neil said, "I'm really sorry that our relationship has suffered so much, and I hope we can get back on track." Neil didn't face Joshua as he said this and afterwards immediately turned to face the door, it was as though he didn't want to give Joshua an opportunity to respond. It had obviously been a very difficult apology for Neil to make. Making up for five years of mistreatment with one statement is a tough thing to do. Joshua had to quickly make the decision of whether or not he was able to write off the tension of the last five years in those few seconds. He saw no point in dwelling on it and this was the breakthrough he'd prayed for.
"Dad," he said, stopping Neil in his tracks. Neil turned back to face him. "Apology accepted." They both smiled and embraced each other.
"Right, you'd better get ready for dinner, Karen's going to a lot of trouble," Neil said, quickly resuming his masculinity and at that point family life began again.

At Parkers Cocktail Bar, Joshua was slouched on a sofa in the corner enjoying a vodka and coke, awaiting the arrival of Stuart. He wondered what outfit this handsome young man would be wearing tonight and where the evening would take them. The possibilities were endless now. No more hiding, no more secrets. To most people, Joshua was now 'out' and it was as though the weight of the world had been lifted from his shoulders. Stuart arrived looking exquisite as ever. He hadn't a hair out of place; his outfit matched perfectly and the shape of his bubble butt was nicely on view through his skin-tight drainpipe jeans. He leaned over and pecked Joshua on the cheek, then sat beside him.
"So how was your day?" Stuart asked. Joshua smiled and told him of the discussion he'd had with Neil earlier in the day. "I can see such a change in you already," Stuart pointed out. There was a sense of awkwardness about the situation, it was as though something had been left unsaid. Stuart and Joshua were becoming extremely close and had even been intimate, yet their status was yet to be clarified. Were they a couple or just friends? Joshua was almost certain he was falling in love but feared raising the issue in case he and Stuart weren't thinking alike. What he failed to realise was that Stuart's thoughts were in sync with his own; however raising the issue was easier said than done. Stuart strolled over to the bar to collect two cocktails for himself and Joshua. As he seated himself beside Joshua a silence loomed. Neither knew quite what to say. A succulent young man wandered past who caught both Joshua and

Stuart's eye. This gave a chance for Joshua to end the quietude,
"I saw you looking." They laughed.
"I wouldn't kick his arse out of bed," Stuart giggled. Joshua had been on a roll this week and decided to test the limits of it.
"We need to talk," he said, dipping his big toe into the water, almost ready to take a dive.
"We are talking babe," Stuart replied, afraid that what Joshua was about to say would be negative.
"I'm being serious Stuart, things are different now…." Joshua began. A look of terror appeared in Stuart's eyes.
"Yeah….but….."
"Let me finish," Joshua interrupted.
"I don't want to lose you," Stuart blurted out randomly. Joshua smirked, now feeling more confident about the statement he had to make.
"I don't want to lose you either, that's the last thing I'd want," Joshua replied. Stuart was obviously experiencing a feeling of relief at the sound of those words.
"I'm so glad…." Stuart began.
"Let me finish," Joshua interrupted once again. "Now that Megan isn't an issue, we need to decide where to go from here." Stuart remained silent signalling for Joshua to continue, he was intrigued to know what point Joshua was struggling to reach. "I want us to be a couple……Officially I mean," Joshua stuttered. Stuart's facial expression implied that all his Christmas's had just arrived at once. It was easy to see that they'd been thinking alike. "So what do you think?" Joshua asked, almost sure of what the reply would be already, judging by the Cheshire cat seated beside him.
"I thought you were going to say that you just wanted to be friends," Stuart said, wiping a tear from his eye.
"I'll take that as a yes then," Joshua said, stating the obvious.
"I really wanna' kiss you right about now," Stuart declared. Joshua glanced around to judge whether or not this was a feasible suggestion.
"What would people say?"
"I know, I also don't like the look of that gang in the corner. Don't fancy having my face re-arranged. Let's go back to my place," Stuart suggested.

Stuart's room was as ship shape as ever. It almost seemed a shame to crease the bedclothes.
"So we're a proper couple then?" Stuart said, hunting for confirmation as they both stood awkwardly gazing at each other. Joshua nodded in agreement. They edged closer to each other and kissed slowly and passionately. This time it was a kiss based on love, not lust. "What did I do to deserve you?" Stuart asked light heartedly as they took a brief break

from their moment of passion. The heat began to rise as their tongues once again met and whilst kissing they both gradually stepped towards the bed. Soon they were both lying on the bed enjoying the intimacy. This was quite a slick manoeuvre considering that neither had released their tongues or opened their eyes. It wasn't long before both had banished their clothing into a heap on the floor. Stuart orally pleasured Joshua once again. It felt even better than the first time. This time there was trust, and Joshua knew what to expect. He relaxed and allowed Stuart to explore his body without hesitation or reservation. Joshua returned the favour by pleasing Stuart; he worried over how he would fit Stuart's impressive love tool into his modestly sized mouth and that his lack of experience he wouldn't be able to satisfy his man. It was obvious however by Stuart's facial expression that he was entirely satisfied which put Joshua at ease until the warm love juice shot into his mouth, causing Stuart to switch from orgasm to hysterical laughter in seconds. Joshua's face began to crack and he joined in with the giggling. They held each other on the bed, as if to confirm that this had been an act of love and to recover from a tiring experience. Joshua felt a great sense of achievement and satisfaction.

"Do you think you're ready to go all the way?" Stuart asked randomly in Joshua's ear. Joshua released himself from Stuart's arms and nodded excitedly. Stuart reached into a drawer and pulled out a sachet of lubrication. Joshua looked at him in a state of bewilderment. "It'll make it easier," Stuart promised.

Stuart was as gentle and delicate as he could possibly be. Joshua felt pain at first. He imagined this experience must be similar to what women tolerate during childbirth. Gradually the pain became less intense and the pleasure began to set in. It was difficult to determine why he was enjoying something so uncomfortable, but he knew he didn't want it to end. This was so powerful. Joshua had never shared anything so intimate with anyone else before. He hadn't imagined just a fortnight ago that by this point his life would have endured so many dramatic changes and that he'd have had so many new experiences.

Both exhausted by the intensity of the evening, they lay silently on the bed. Stuart was slowly running his hand through Joshua's hair, twisting the various strands around his fingers; it was so tender. Although Megan had often done this during their courtship, it somehow felt different with Stuart. It felt natural, almost as though fate had brought them together and at that very moment it really felt as though they'd never be apart again. They both eventually drifted off into a deep sleep, no longer conscious of the time.

"Oh shit!" yelped Joshua as he glanced at the clock face displaying '6:30'. "Oh hell," he shouted as he jumped out of the bed and fumbled around for the clothes he'd so hastily shed the night before. Stuart also began to stir. His eyes opened to the sight of Joshua frantically dressing. "Stuart, it's half past six, I've been here all night!"

"Oh, morning hun" Stuart replied nonchalantly while rubbing his eyes and stretching his arms. His reaction was too calm for Joshua's mood.

"I've gotta' go!" he screamed, frantically putting on his trainers.

"I can't see the point of rushing now, the damage has been done," Stuart commented whilst almost returning to his state of slumber. Stuart's laid back attitude was beginning to annoy Joshua. He sighed and reached for his mobile phone. It displayed '6 missed calls'. Upon further investigation he discovered that five of the calls had been from Neil. He glanced at Stuart and began to calm himself. He smiled as he gazed lovingly at Stuart in his dormant state. He pecked him on the cheek as he departed, but Stuart didn't notice as he had now returned to his deep sleep.

Joshua was almost trembling as he made his way across town to his house. He wanted to arrive home before Neil left for work, but at the same time wasn't prepared for the line of questioning he'd inevitably face. The last thing he wanted at this stage was to rock the boat and demolish all the progress he'd achieved with his father in recent weeks. "Brace yourself," he said under his breath as he opened the front door. Karen and Neil were seated eating toast as he entered the house. Neil heard the sound of the door slamming and darted to greet him.

"I've been very worried," Neil said with a balance of annoyance and genuine concern.

"I'm sorry dad," Joshua apologised.

"I'm just glad you're ok," Neil said as he threw his arms around him. "I know you're an adult and if you want to stay over at Megan's that's fine.....just let me know." Almost overwhelmed by Neil's intimacy and sincere concern, Joshua felt he couldn't lie,

"Megan and I have broken up dad. I fell asleep at a friend's house." Neil's facial expression implied that he didn't entirely believe Joshua's story. He immediately leaped to the conclusion that his son had just enjoyed a passionate one night stand, with a random woman he'd met just hours ago. He grinned with male pride.

"Anyway, I'd best get to work tiger!" Neil laughed, and then left the house. Joshua wandered across to join Karen at the breakfast table, wondering whether Neil knew him at all. Even if Joshua was heterosexual, he wasn't the type of person to sleep with strangers."Would you like some toast?" Karen asked. Joshua smiled and nodded as he seated himself and poured a glass of orange juice. Karen placed two slices of bread in the toaster and returned to the table. “So what’s his name then?” she asked randomly. Joshua raised his head to make eye contact with Karen, almost as if to ask, “Did you really just say that?” Both Karen and Joshua were silent for a moment. He didn’t have a clue what to say. The silence was broken by the sound of the bread popping out from the toaster. Karen collected the two slices and asked “Butter or jam?” Joshua didn’t answer immediately, causing Karen to turn to face him to investigate. “Well?” she asked. Joshua had a glazed look on his face. “Butter or jam?”

“Er….butter please,” Joshua answered eventually. Karen spread the butter onto the toast, handed it to Joshua and returned to her seat. After quietly eating the first triangle, he plucked up the courage to ask, “How did you know?” Karen laughed,

“I assure you Joshua. I can see the signs. I have a lot of gay friends, although you’re not blatantly obvious, not to most anyway.”

“Oh,” Joshua said with a look of terror on his face.

“Don’t worry, I won’t tell your father. I know how men can be,” Karen assured him, as though they were discussing the breakage of a china cup. Joshua couldn’t believe how casual Karen was on the issue. “So, you still haven’t answered my original question,” she pointed out. “What’s his name?”

“It’s Stuart,” Joshua replied, a hint of a trusting grin now beginning to show.

“Bless, what a lovely name,” Karen said, and then proceeded to attempt to extract further information.

“You definitely won’t tell dad….” Joshua insisted, still uncertain of Karen’s credibility.

“No, but I don’t think he’d react too badly anyway. His male pride might be affected but that’s all,” replied Karen.

“No offence Karen…” Joshua began delicately, “but you clearly don’t know my father all that well. You’re a good influence on him. He hasn’t always been this way.” Karen displayed a genuine look of disappointment and surprise. “I’m hoping the bad times are over now, thanks to you,” Joshua said in an attempt to redeem the situation. Karen smiled and returned to her state of delusion.

“I’m sure everything will be ok from now on.”

“You won’t tell him I said that will you?” Joshua pleaded. He almost felt uneasy now, knowing that he and Karen shared secrets.

“Course not, so how many people know about your sexuality?” Karen asked, changing the subject.

"Well….pretty much everyone except dad." Karen frowned.
"Maybe you should tell him before someone else does," she suggested, attempting to sound as casual as possible whilst she began to wash the breakfast pots.
"Not yet Karen," Joshua insisted firmly and excused himself in order to prepare for college.

The conversation with Karen played on Joshua's mind all day. If she had so easily leaped to the conclusion that he was gay, was it really obvious? Was he deluding himself by thinking that people had been unaware prior to James' declaration? The conversation repeated itself over and over in Joshua's head. How could Karen be so casual about holding information that could potentially ruin his life or at least his new found harmony with Neil?

Joshua was dumbfounded during the evening meal. What do you say to someone after a conversation such as the one they'd shared that morning? His bitchy side was now wondering whether or not Karen actually had a home to go to or not.
"Bloody Travers was in a mood today," Neil ranted, referring to his boss. He was passing looks across the table that implied concern over the silence.
"Weather the storm," joked Karen, then she enquired as to Joshua's day, who wasn't paying attention and required a nudge from Neil in order to initiate a response. "How was your day?" Karen repeated herself. In Joshua's slight lack of concentration he thought he heard Karen say, "Are you still gay?" and stared at her.
"Christ almighty, how hard is the question?! Did you have a good day or not?" Neil asked, half joking, although his day at work had put a strain on his sense of humour.
"Oh fine," Joshua replied eventually.
"You're just not on this planet are you love?" Karen replied, using her new found maternal attitude. She'd developed this in spite of having no children herself and Joshua was still wary. The ringing of his mobile phone saved Joshua from an awkward situation by excusing him from the dinner table.

"Hey sexy, what's happening tonight?" Stuart asked excitedly down the phone.
"What do you fancy?" Joshua asked, having already guessed by Stuart's tone that he had something in mind.
"Well…." Stuart hesitated, "It is karaoke night at Dream." Joshua was reluctant to respond."We don't have to go there if you don't want," Stuart frantically added, ending the moment of silence.

"Er…" Joshua stuttered.
"It'd be fun. Your first night on the gay scene will be an experience you'll never forget." This was what Joshua was afraid of. It was obvious that Stuart was keen to introduce him to the gay scene.
"I suppose we could," Joshua answered vaguely.
"Honestly, if you're not ready we don't have to," Stuart assured him, although he clearly didn't want Joshua to feel uncomfortable, it was also quite blatant that he wanted to go to 'Dream'. Another pause lingered in the conversation. "It's ok darling, we'll give it a miss for tonight," Stuart said, now feeling almost guilty for raising the issue.
"No…" Joshua began, interrupting his ramblings, "I have to go sooner or later, may as well be tonight, as long as you're going to look after me." Joshua's tone of voice was becoming softer and gentler, almost childlike.
"Fantastic! You won't regret it, we'll have a great night," Stuart promised and left Joshua wondering whether or not he'd just made a mistake. His state of mind was quickly rectified by reminding himself how valuable any time spent with Stuart was to him. This then led to a panic, as his next consideration was what to wear. He frantically rummaged through his drawers and wardrobes, desperate to find something appropriate. Although, he'd most likely have had more success had he known what would be suitable. Having never had any experience of such places, he was clueless as to the dress codes. He contemplated telephoning Stuart for advice but decided against it through fear of embarrassment.

"You're going to a gay bar?!" Michael said in shock.
"I had to call you, I couldn't think of anyone else," Joshua said in a panic.
"Calm down darling, I'll help," Michael assured him, "tell you what, I'll pop over with some t shirts, you can choose one to borrow." Joshua thanked him, ended the call and awaited his arrival. His nerves were not helped by an interruption from Karen. She knocked on his bedroom door and requested permission to enter. Joshua reluctantly granted it.
"Have you got a minute?" Karen asked in her usual sickly sweet, 'butter wouldn't melt in my mouth' type of voice.
"Only one, I have to get ready to go out," Joshua replied sharply while pretending to rummage through a drawer.
"Are you off anywhere nice?" asked Karen, showing a genuine interest but feeling that her efforts were being thrown back in her face. Joshua turned to face her, almost judging the situation in an attempt to decide whether or not Karen was worthy of the truth. Eventually he threw caution to the wind,
"I'm going to Dream bar."
"Oooh nice place," Karen replied, astounding Joshua.

"You've been?!"
"Yes. I told you already that I have gay friends. In fact I'm quite well known in there from escorting good old Trevor." Karen was wandering too far off the subject at hand for Joshua's liking.
"Wait, you're a regular? I don't believe it....So what's it like then?" he asked eagerly.
"It's your first time?" Karen appeared surprised.
"I've not been out on the scene before," Joshua confessed sheepishly.
"Bless you," Karen grinned, "It's not a bad place really, you'll have fun."
A rush of questions arrived in Joshua's mind.
"What music do they play? What sort of people go there? What do they wear?" he blurted out. Karen answered all of his questions with one simple word, "Anything."
Joshua looked puzzled.
"You can wear anything and get away with it. You can even wear nothing! The music, well....you get cheese, dance, hardcore....... Anything goes. As far as the people, well, I'll let you find that one out for yourself," Karen elaborated. Joshua's trust in Karen was growing and the potential of a relationship with her was becoming clearer. He was now feeling far more relaxed about the evening ahead. "I'm sure Stuart will look after you," Karen teased. Joshua laughed and nodded.
"Michael, another friend of mine is coming any minute with some outfits for me to choose from," Joshua explained. Karen giggled.
"Well in that case, why don't I suggest that your father and I go for a walk? We're still at the point in our relationship where he listens to me." Joshua eagerly agreed. "Right, better go get rid of him for you then," she said, smiling as she headed for the door.
"Karen..." Joshua began, stopping her in her tracks. She turned around.
"Thank you. Your help means a lot," Joshua said truthfully.
"You're welcome," Karen replied and wandered down the stairs. Things were beginning to come together. Soon Michael would solve the issue of the evening's attire, Karen was disposing of Neil and all that was left to do was to survive this new experience.

Neil and Karen had barely left the driveway when Michael arrived, armed with a satchel bag crammed with fashionable clothes and accessories.
"We are going to make you look sensational!" he promised as he parked his bag of goodies down on the bed and began to empty it, talking in great detail about each item. "This little number I bought on holiday in Spain. It would go really well with some blue jeans, perhaps faded and a little ripped..." he went on. Joshua laughed. This was definitely helping his nerves.

"You missed your calling; you should have been a salesperson for QVC channel or one of those guys that describes outfits on the catwalk." Michael interrupted his jabbering long enough to offer some words of sentiment,
"Aww babe, you're gonna' have a fab' time at Dream! If only I could re-live my first night on the scene. What a wild one that was." He then began laughing to himself. Joshua eventually coaxed the story of Michael's first gay night out, but soon regretted it as it made him more uneasy. Realising this, Michael added, "It'll be different for you though, 'cos you've got a boyfriend," almost in a teasing manner. "Anyway…." he began, changing the subject, "Which of these outfits would you like?" Joshua glanced blankly at the various items of clothing Michael had presented. "Ooh calm down, we don't want you getting too excited," Michael added sarcastically. Joshua apologised and explained that he was overwhelmed by everything and didn't know what the most suitable outfit would be. Michael took it upon himself to settle this by making the decision for him. "OK, let's get that top off," Michael demanded. Joshua followed the instructions and removed his shirt. Michael passed him an extra small sky blue t shirt.
"Are you sure?" Joshua asked reluctantly.
"Just get it on," Michael demanded humorously. No sooner was Joshua gasping for air by the compact clothing, than he'd a pair of jeans full of rips handed to him.
"These aren't my size," he protested. Michael laughed.
"There's no way that you're going to a gay bar wearing baggy jeans!" Joshua replaced his jeans with Michael's. "Perfect," Michael commented enthusiastically. Joshua gave a look of uncertainty. Michael however was too preoccupied rummaging through his bag to notice. Joshua wondered what on earth would be next to leave the bag. Michael produced a cream belt and began to force it around Joshua's waist.
"I think these jeans are tight enough," Joshua commented uncomfortably.
"The belt is fashionable dear; it's not to tighten you up. You're thinking too logically darling, think hot!" Michael replied in the campest tone of voice Joshua had ever heard him use. Michael glanced up and down Joshua's body. "Finishing touches….." he said to himself while touching his lower lip. He seemed as though he were planning a photo shoot. "Of course!" he gasped as though he'd just realised a cure for cancer had been staring him in the face for years and he returned to his rummaging. This time it was a tub of hair wax that he removed from the bag. Joshua waited patiently as Michael performed 'a miracle' as he put it, on his hair. Joshua slipped on his trainers as Michael washed his hands. "Are you ready to look in the mirror?" Michael asked.

"No," Joshua replied, half seriously.
"You're right, one more thing….." Out came a pair of what appeared to be ludicrously expensive sunglasses.
"Why?" Joshua asked bluntly.
"Image dear, image!" He slipped them on and they wandered over to the mirror. "You look sensational," Michael remarked, "Good enough to eat." Joshua smiled. It was true. Joshua had never looked better in his life and reluctant as he was to admit it, he knew it himself. He grinned away like a Cheshire cat as he admired his new appearance in the mirror. Joshua quickly kissed Michael on the lips.
"Thank you so much, you've made me so much more confident for tonight."
"I'm glad," Michael said genuinely. It was almost as though the kiss was from Joshua had sent him into a trance, a parallel universe perhaps. He was present with Joshua in body but not in mind. His mind was miles and miles away.
"Hellooooo," Joshua said, attempting to revive his friend. "You were a million miles away!"
"I'm here, I'm ok," Michael said as he landed back on planet earth.
"Anyway I'd better be off soon," Joshua commented, subtly informing Michael that his services were no longer required. "You're right, I hope you have the time of your life," Michael said as he wandered into the bedroom and packed his bag. He put it on his shoulder and they trotted to the bottom of the stairs.
"Thanks again, I don't know what I'd have done without you," Joshua attempted to conclude the conversation. Michael leaned toward him in search of a goodbye kiss and received a peck on the cheek. Michael was about to open the door to leave when he turned and softly asked,
"You really like him a lot don't you?"
"I do Michael….and I think he likes me too. No offence, but I can't be like you.." Michael quickly dived to his own defence,
"What's that mean?"
"No offence babe…" Joshua repeated himself, "But I can't fritter from one guy to another in the way you do. I want something to last."
"I understand," Michael said in a tone that Joshua couldn't fathom.
"Anyway, see you soon babe," Michael said as he departed. Joshua spent a few moments deliberating over whether or not Michael's odd behaviour was anything that should be of concern to him. However his attention quickly returned to focussing on the evening ahead.

After half an hour of remaining as stationary as possible, attempting to keep his hair in tact, his shirt unruffled and his general appearance pristine, Joshua ventured out. Stuart was immaculate as ever,

not a hair out of place and of course, wearing a new outfit. McDonalds had become a traditional meeting place for them now. Stuart gave Joshua a confused look as he approached him.
"I wondered who that amazing looking guy was, then realised it's my boyfriend!" Stuart sweet-talked Joshua.
"Don't make me blush!" Joshua joined in with the 'camping it up'.
"The hair, the shades, the outfit….What happened?"
"Michael happened," Joshua replied. Stuart pointed and commented,
"I like that guy more by the day." Joshua smiled.
"Listen hun', are you sure you're ready for Dream?" Stuart asked while caressing Joshua's shoulder.
"Ready as I'll ever be," Joshua was unconvincing.
"We don't have to do this you know. If you need more time that's fine," Stuart assured him.
"And waste this magnificent look? Not a chance, lead the way….."

'Dream' was a very discreetly positioned bar, however once the building was located, the lilac exterior made its target clientele obvious. They entered the extremely cosy hallway that led to the bar, where they were greeted by a pair of butch lesbians in a booth.
"Hey Stewey," one of them said, her speech slurred by the gum she was chewing. She leaned to the front of the booth (where you'd normally expect to find a glass screen) and hugged and kissed him on the cheek. Joshua mentally noted that the Sheffield Wednesday T Shirt she was wearing was greatly over-sized. At this point, Joshua was still unsure as to the gender of the other member of staff in the booth. The familiarity between Stuart and the girl he was hugging was causing him to wonder just how often he visited this place.
"Who's the cutey?" she asked once returning to her seat.
"This is Joshua….My new fella'," Stuart began the introductions.
"Is he wanting to join?" the other prune faced member of staff butted in.
"This is Jen," Stuart said, referring to the girl he'd embraced and disregarding her colleague's attitude.
"Tell you what. See what you think tonight and join next time," Jen suggested in an almost patronising tone of voice. Joshua forgave this as she was so genuinely nice. And with that, they trundled off. Two huge doors with handles the size of coat hangers enclosed the bar. The sound of eighties hits could be heard quite clearly, perhaps even miles away.
"Are you ready?" Stuart asked, as he began to open one of the doors. Before he had a chance to do so, the doors swung open from the inside and out stormed a paper-thin, beautiful form of a man. He was aged only around twenty years old and was followed by two less attractive cronies.
"He's a bastard!" yelled the leader as he flung his arms in the air.

"He is, he is… He's not good enough for you," one of the followers said.

"What a sucker," Joshua muttered to Stuart.

"That's Nathan, I don't think I've ever once been in here and not seen him around. The ultimate scene queen," Stuart replied.

"You're right, you're right," Nathan exclaimed arrogantly as he turned to face his followers.

"I can have anyone I want, I don't need him," he added flamboyantly. And with that they headed back to the bar, barging past Stuart and Joshua as though they didn't exist. The doors slammed behind them.

"Please tell me they're not all like that," Joshua pleaded. Stuart gave a look of uncertainty, then opened one of the doors and signalled for Joshua to enter ahead of him. He entered the bar, closely followed by Stuart. 'I used to think that the day would never come, that my life would depend on the morning sun' appropriately bellowed from the speakers. The bar was dark. There was a very limited amount of tables and chairs, and the ones provided weren't being used. Lots of groups of people were scattered around. There were people of all ages, shapes and sizes. Young, slim, blatantly arrogant lads, middle aged overweight men who seemed to think they were still teenagers, transsexuals, transvestites, butch lesbians of various ages wearing baggy outfits and modelling gents hairstyles, heterosexual females, even the odd heterosexual couple. In spite of the variety of breeds, everyone in the bar had one thing in common, when someone entered, everyone glared. Joshua was particularly noticed as it was his first visit. The opinions across the room varied. Some envied Joshua's look, some of the more confident (or perhaps more appropriately the more supercilious) lads pitied him, the older generation wanted him and some of them even deluded themselves into believing they were in his league. Joshua was desperate to leave the spotlight. All eyes were on him.

"Do you want to stay down here or go upstairs?" Stuart whispered in his ear.

"Let's get a drink down here first. I can't face another crowd just yet." Joshua felt as though he was moving in slow motion, as he attempted to avoid all the watchful eyes. They eventually reached the bar where Stuart was greeted by a kiss on the lips from an attractive bar man in his mid twenties. Joshua was taken aback by the familiarity of his boyfriend and the barman.

"Who's this then?" the handsome member of staff asked in an unintentionally false tone, referring to Joshua.

"Patrick, meet Joshua," Stuart replied.

"Ooh, not seen you in here before," Patrick said as he forced his lips against Joshua's.

"Hi," he said wearily. Stuart ordered the drinks. While he and Patrick chatted away, Joshua glanced around and noticed another barman. The second barman had the figure of an elderly man before his time. He looked so frail, as though he'd been under-fed and living on the streets. Stuart turned to face Joshua, passed him a drink and suggested they be seated.
"Who was the other barman?" Joshua asked curiously.
"You mean Anorexic-Andy?" Stuart asked in reply. They placed their drinks on the table and parked themselves down.
"He looks like he's about to drop dead," Joshua commented naively.
"Well I don't think he's quite that bad just yet...." Stuart replied.
"The scene can do that to you. You mustn't try to be as paper-thin as the raving queens." Joshua's attention was wandering. He was mesmerised by the wonders of the gay scene. It was as though he'd just stepped through the door into a whole new culture.
"Is it what you expected?" Stuart asked, gulping down his rather odd looking drink.
"I don't know what I expected," Joshua confessed vaguely, continuing to observe the various posses around the room. All of a sudden a plastic folder was descended onto the table by a passing queen.
"Oh, it's karaoke night," Stuart remembered. Joshua stared at Stuart as he began fumbling through the various pages of songs in the file, as if to say "I'd rather die than go up there."
"What shall we sing?" Stuart asked casually.
"You ARE joking!" Joshua insisted.
"I love to sing," Stuart boasted.
"It's not quite my forte," Joshua laughed.
"Why don't you choose a song for me then?" Stuart suggested.
"Are you sure?" Joshua asked. Stuart nodded and passed the folder to Joshua, who then struggled to suggest a song. He wondered what Stuart's opinion would be and feared ridicule if he was to make a choice that was too soppy. Several minutes later, Stuart snatched back the selection of songs in jest and assured Joshua that he'd thought of the perfect one to sing. He quickly and discreetly noted his choice and passed it to the DJ. Upon returning to his seat, Joshua enquired as to what he'd decided to sing, but Stuart insisted on surprising him. The first karaoke contestant took to the stage. It was a male in drag wear.
"I need a hero, I'm holding out for a hero till the end of the night...." his voice reverberated from the walls. It was perfect.
"That guy has to be a professional," Joshua whispered. Stuart nodded. The performer received minimal applause. "He was magnificent. He was hardly clapped!?" Joshua commented in amazement.

"They've all seen him perform that one a million times," Stuart replied.
"Well I wouldn't like to think I was to follow him," Joshua said as he relaxed into his chair and swigged his drink.
"They're all yours Stuart," the DJ called over.
"Guess that would be me then…" Stuart whispered to Joshua. They kissed briefly and Joshua wished him luck.
"Stuart's going to give us a change tonight. He's singing Hero!" the camp DJ yelped down the microphone.
"You're not doing the same song?" Joshua was confused. Stuart smiled suspiciously as he left the table and approached the stage.

"Well, this is a little different for me, let's just say I've been inspired," Stuart announced as he gazed at a red faced Joshua in the crowd before him. The music began and it was soon obvious that Stuart was not about to repeat 'Holding out for a hero'.
"Let me be your hero…" Stuart whispered softly down the microphone.
"Would you dance, if I asked you to dance? Or would you run and never look back?...." Stuart began to sing. He didn't sing a note out of place. Joshua had been unaware before of what an exquisite voice Stuart had. The audience were enjoying the performance and had begun to wave their arms in the air. Stuart displayed amazing stage presence and encouraged audience participation during verse one, until he reached the chorus. At the beginning of the chorus, the lights were dimmed (Stuart having requested this to the DJ earlier that evening). As Stuart began the chorus his movement ceased, he stood perfectly still and gazed directly into Joshua's eyes. "I can be your hero baby. I can kiss away the pain, and I will stand by you forever. You can take my breath away…." In Joshua's mind, the room had emptied. He was no longer aware of anyone else's presence. It didn't matter. At this moment, he and Stuart were the only people who mattered. All of Joshua's fears and insecurities were flying out of the window. He listened so carefully and cherished every word. This may have been a karaoke night, and the song may have belonged to a Latino heart-throb, but as far as Joshua was concerned, these were Stuart's words, based on his affection and they came straight from his heart. "I can be…. Your h-e-r-o." The lights gradually brightened again and the audience cheered. This seemed to be a rarity at this particular bar. Joshua remained seated, gazing at Stuart. "Wow, never had an applause like that before," Stuart said, almost casually as he reclaimed his seat. A passing customer stopped and commented,
"That was really different for you, well done," then glanced at Joshua and said, "You wanna' hang on to this one darling!" before mincing away towards the bar.

"I intend to," Joshua announced, aiming the remark solely at Stuart. He blushed with embarrassment. "You were amazing. Don't be modest," Joshua insisted, bursting with pride. He then followed that comment with, "No-one's ever done anything like that for me before."
"Lucky for me that I found you first then," Stuart replied. He always seemed to say the right thing. Joshua couldn't recall a single moment of his life in which he'd felt happier or more contented. At this point the conversation almost became awkward. They had just shared a special moment and a new peak in their relationship, which made it difficult to then begin talking about something mundane, such as the weather or the latest UK top 40. Luckily several interruptions from the bars regulars broke the silence. The entire clientele appeared to be intrigued by the fresh meat that was on display. It was however clear to all that this meat was not for sale on the market. It wasn't long before Stuart's tongue was lodged firmly in place in Joshua's throat.
"Are you ready to go upstairs?" Stuart asked eventually, interrupting the flow of furious passion.
"Sure!" By this time, Joshua felt he could tackle anything and was welcoming new experiences.

The upper dance floor was dim, with the exception of a fast moving white illumination that appeared to display people's features in an ever-so flattering light. Stuart followed as Joshua glanced around. The music lacked words or any sort of message. The dance floor was packed with beautiful boys, each of them obviously under the impression they were better than the last. There were discreet, dimly lit corners, obviously designed for couples (or pairs who had met that evening and become very intimate very rapidly) and another bar. They seated themselves in a secluded corner and Joshua gazed at the dancers.
"You're intrigued aren't you?" Stuart asked.
"Who do they all think they are?" Joshua asked rhetorically, "They're like.....Kylie's backing dancers or something."
"They'd like to be," Stuart laughed.
"They've sucked all the fun out of it. All they care about is how they look," Joshua observed.
"You've caught on quickly, I'll give you that," Stuart complimented Joshua, now almost hysterical himself. "So do you like this place at all?" Stuart asked in jest.
"Yeah, it's ok as long as you ignore everyone around you," Joshua replied, now giggling himself.
"At least we're having fun," Stuart pointed out. Joshua nodded in agreement, genuinely enjoying the experience. He pecked Stuart on the

cheek and thanked him; this began another intense session of petting and touching. Joshua excused himself to the toilet.

On arrival at the lavatories he was greeted by a pair of topless twenty-something's who separated their tongues just long enough to indiscreetly give Joshua a thorough examination. Groaning sounds could be heard coming from one of the cubicles and this was making Joshua uneasy. He then gazed in bewilderment as a butch lesbian passed him, heading for a cubicle. The two men he'd been ogled by on the way in caught his attention and one said,

"It's all unisex in here boy. She aint bothered about looking at our bits, I promise!" They then laughed amongst themselves before re-joining tongues. Joshua felt mocked and chose to disregard the rude couple. Joshua approached the urinals, but spotted a middle aged, balding man who appeared to be stalling in an effort to get a sighting of Joshua's penis. He gave a look as if to say, "I know your game you dirty old pervert," and made a b line for the privacy of a cubicle. Once finished, he washed his hands and headed for the door. "I think he has a little willy," one of the rude lads (whom Joshua was beginning to severely dislike) commented. He turned to face them, then decided against commenting and exited.

When returning to his seat, Stuart could sense some disturbance in Joshua's mood.

"Are you ok?" he enquired.

"Yeah I'm fine. I don't think I was quite prepared for the toilets," Joshua replied bluntly.

"You get used to it," Stuart commented sympathetically. Joshua glanced at his watch.

"We'd better go; my father will wonder where I am. I'm hoping he'll be in bed when I arrive home so that he doesn't see my outfit, but he'll hear what time I arrive." Stuart agreed and they departed.

Outside the bar, Stuart and Joshua shared a kiss. "Thanks a lot Stuart, I've really enjoyed myself." Stuart smiled and they hugged.

"Listen, you know a lot of people in there.... If you want to stay a little longer, don't go home just because I am," Joshua said selflessly.

"Are you sure?" Stuart asked.

"Of course," Joshua replied, "Go have fun and I'll call you tomorrow."

"You're the best!" exclaimed Stuart, and they kissed before he returned to the bar.

Joshua began strolling home, feeling happy and satisfied with the events of the evening. The words from the song 'Hero' were now firmly implanted in his mind and were replaying over and over in his head as he recalled Stuart's gesture.

“I can be your hero baby..” he began to sing quietly to himself as he walked. All of a sudden he could feel a presence behind him that was moving faster and faster. He began to increase his own pace through concern for his safety. He heard a male voice shout “Faggot!” coming from behind, then felt a blow to the back of his head. He fell to the floor and blacked out.

Chapter 6

Joshua was dancing beautifully on the 'Dream' dance floor. Everyone was watching him in amazement. He was the centre of attention. All eyes were on this beautiful boy. He could have any man he wanted in the bar. He was gorgeous and he knew it. The dance floor was pumping with other amazingly handsome young men. Joshua spotted his prey, a young man, no older than he, blonde hair, blue eyes and a perfect form of a body; and there for the taking. He was gagging for it. All it would take would be for him to approach this fine young specimen, give off the correct vibe and he'd be eating from the palm of his hand. And off he went,

"Hello there," Joshua said, giving a seductive stare and lightly touching the boy's hips. He immediately responded by kissing Joshua and placing his hands on his anus. They danced together, the two most beautiful boys on the floor; the envy of all the other dancers. The stranger took Joshua's hand and guided him to a secluded corner where they could be intimate. Their fun had barely begun when his new found friend began to guide him to the toilets for a sexual encounter. This is the done thing after all, so off Joshua went with the flow.

The toilet cubicle was somewhat shabby and uncomfortable, but who cares? Joshua and his mystery man were horny as hell. Nothing mattered but being penetrated. Joshua's shirt fell to the floor and he began to unbuckle the belt of the blonde stud standing before him, ready to take that succulent piece of man meat into his mouth, when, all of a sudden the door swung open. There he was, Stuart, standing before him, a look of utter contempt on his face. What had Joshua done? He had become one of those; a stereotype. How could this have happened?

"I can explain!" Joshua cried. But he couldn't, there was nothing he could say to justify his actions. Stuart simply stood before him, not angry, just disappointed. All he could say was

"Joshua, Joshua, Joshua," over and over while shaking his head. "Joshua, Joshua, Joshua….."

"Joshua, Joshua…" Dr Greg Foster repeated as Joshua's eyes were slowly beginning to open. "Can you hear me Joshua?" Joshua was bewildered, it seemed he'd been with Stuart at 'Dream', then back at the bar with another man and now he was in a strange place with a strange man all in the space of a few minutes.

"Yes. Who are you? Where am I?" Joshua asked.

"You're in the hospital," Greg replied. Joshua attempted to sit up in bed.

"Don't strain yourself," Greg insisted. The pieces began to fit together, of course, it had been a dream. After all, he couldn't have undergone a personality transplant in a matter of hours. "My head hurts," he whinged, "I ache all over."

"That doesn't surprise me," Greg commented, "You've got a fracture to the skull and two broken ribs, not to mention extensive bruising to your arms and legs."
"Oh god!" Joshua gasped.
"What the hell happened to you?" Greg asked. Joshua mentally recalled the events of the previous evening. "You were found lying in the street like this! Who did it to you?" Greg demanded.
"I don't know," Joshua replied honestly. "There was someone behind me, and then I remember feeling a bang on the head," he continued, purposely leaving out the 'faggot' comment. "Well the police are waiting outside, as is your father. Do you feel up to talking to them?" Greg asked.
"Well I…..I suppose so," Joshua hesitated.
"Do you remember me Joshua?" Greg enquired curiously. Joshua stared at him for a moment.
"You're familiar."
"I remember you very well. When your mother died, I took care of you; you've grown up a lot now though." Joshua attempted a smile. Without giving him a chance to respond Greg departed the room, warning that he'd be sending Neil and the police in shortly to have a discussion with him. Joshua glanced under the bedclothes at his injured assemblage. His arms were so bruised, as were his legs. He flinched and immediately experienced the throbbing of his broken ribs. At this point, he decided it was wise to remain motionless. He was alone, stationary, with only his thoughts for company. He wondered who had removed his clothing, whether or not Neil had seen them and whether people had already reached the conclusion that this had been a homophobic attack or if they'd assumed it was a mugging. After all, he had strayed several streets away from 'Dream'.

Joshua's deliberation of the various issues surrounding his assault was soon interrupted by his father's arrival.
"Knock knock," Neil said as he invited himself in.
"Hey Dad," Joshua mumbled, reminding himself not to say anything incriminating until he'd fathomed precisely what his father knew about the previous evening.
"What on earth happened?" Neil asked as he seated himself at the foot of the bed.
"It's so hazy, didn't the doctor tell you?" Joshua asked, stalling the situation, unwilling to disclose any additional information.
"Just said it looked like a mugging, but the doc' reckoned your wallet and mobile phone were still in your pockets, so I guess they were interrupted or something." Perfect. Neil was jumping to his own conclusions. There was no implication towards the bar or his sexual orientation whatsoever,

and he evidently hadn't seen the outfit he'd been wearing. This was damage control at its very best, now all he had to do was concentrate on healing, easier said than done, but in the grand scheme of things his health was being relegated to the bottom of his list of priorities. Karen tip-toed into the room as though she was expecting him to be sound asleep. And then it dawned on him, Karen knew everything. She was aware of Joshua's sexuality and she even knew where he'd planned to spend the evening. It wouldn't take a genius to put the pieces together with all the information available.

"How's the patient?" she asked in an even more irritating tone than usual; a manner perhaps she saved for serious occasions. Joshua was tense. He had recently begun to develop a trust with Karen, but he didn't know her well enough to predict her actions under this type of circumstance. Would the fact that he'd been injured over-ride the promises she'd made and make her feel that she needed to disclose the truth to Greg, and even worse to Neil?

"He's a really brave lad," Neil whispered with a strange sense of pride.

"Course he is," Karen replied as she placed her hand on Neil's shoulder. Joshua began to close and re-open his eyes, endeavouring to make himself appear less vigilant than he actually was. "He's exhausted, bless him," Karen continued, her tone becoming ever more patronising.

"Listen, I'm sorry to do this but I'm gonna' have to get to work, I'm late as it is," Neil apologised, then stood and affectionately ruffled Joshua's hair. "You'll be OK son. We'll get the bastards that did this to you," Neil said assertively, "I'll be back later," and he left. A look passed between Karen and Joshua, it was a stare that implied Karen had fathomed exactly what had really happened but was reluctant to release the words from her mouth. She seated herself beside Joshua and gently caressed his cheek. He remained cautious. They both knew what had really transpired the night before, but if Joshua didn't state it he could always deny it.

"These people need to be stopped," Karen blurted out, looking deadly serious. She meant what she was saying. It was clear that she was not going to be messed with. Joshua remained silent. "I've been through all this before," Karen continued, "My friend Jim was attacked by homophobes and they nearly killed him. You must tell the police the truth," she pleaded. Joshua shrugged Karen's hand away from his face.

"I was mugged. End of story," he insisted, and turned away, closing his eyes in an attempt to claim he was sleeping.

"Joshua…." Karen said sternly. Her tone reminded him of events in his childhood in which Lynne would say something indisputable. Joshua wondered what right Karen thought she had to address him in this way. He turned to face her and demanded to be left alone. Tears began to

trickle down Karen's face. Joshua found this difficult to comprehend. How could this make her shed tears? She hardly knew him. Perhaps he was being too callous, after all she clearly cared very deeply for him. However, regardless of Karen's motives, he couldn't allow the details of the attack to be unearthed, as this would reveal his true sexuality to Neil.
"I'm sorry," Joshua apologised, now beginning to feel guilty. There was no point in denying anything to Karen, after all she already knew the most important fact.
"Please, please tell the police the truth," Karen begged.
"What difference will it really make?" Joshua asked, "All I care about is that my father doesn't find out why I was attacked." Karen gave a look of frustration as she headed for the door. Before leaving, she turned to face him.
"I won't tell anyone. I want to, but I won't," she promised.
"Wait, could I ask a favour?" Joshua asked, postponing her exit. Karen gave a glance requesting him to continue. "Could you ask Stuart to visit me?" Karen nodded dotingly and departed.

Joshua was isolated once again, deserted and unable to move because of the various pains throughout his body. At this point the seriousness of what had happened began to dawn on him. Someone, who obviously had major issues of his own had violated him. Joshua had done nothing to provoke his attacker, it had been completely random. He recalled the saying 'If you hate gays, you are gay' he'd once heard. He'd never been in such a predicament. If he was to tell the truth he'd be out-ed to his father and most likely destroy the positive relationship he'd recently developed with him.
"The police are ready to talk if you feel up to it," Dr Greg said as he poked his head through the doorway. Joshua nodded and two policemen in their mid-thirties entered. One of them was mildly attractive, in an 'older guy' sort of way, Joshua thought. The policemen were treating Joshua with kid gloves.
"I'm Terry, this is Martin," began the less attractive officer. Joshua nodded, trying not to stare excessively at Martin.
"Do you feel up to telling us what happened?" Martin asked delicately.
"Well yes, but there's not much I can tell you really," replied Joshua while attempting to sit up in bed.
"What were your movements of the evening?" Terry asked.
"Well…" Joshua began, stalling whilst he concocted a story.
"We need to know your whereabouts," Terry added.
"I went to a few bars with my friend Stuart," he lied.
"Which ones?" Martin asked, now almost interrogating him.
"What does it matter?" Joshua asked, moving his head around to imply he

was drowsy.
"We need to know what happened in order to find the culprit," Terry insisted. "But nothing did happen," Joshua persevered, now becoming agitated. "I went round a few bars with a friend, we split to walk home and then it happened." "What happened exactly?" Terry asked.
"I was mugged I suppose," Joshua replied vaguely.
"How much money was in your wallet last night when you went home?" Martin enquired. "About a tenner I suppose."
"Eleven pounds, sixty four pence, an ipod, a mobile phone and several bank cards. Not usually the contents of someone's pocket after a mugging," Terry announced, almost sternly.
"Perhaps they were interrupted," Joshua suggested, now feeling as though he was being cross-examined. "Stop talking to me as though I'm a criminal!" Joshua demanded, turning his head ignorantly to face himself away from the policemen, signalling the end of the conversation. Joshua was uneasy and it showed.
"Joshua, we need you to be honest with us," Martin said softly as he seated himself beside Joshua on the bed. Joshua turned to face him and gazed into his eyes. For a thirty-something he was pretty damned hot, Joshua thought, or perhaps he had a fetish for uniforms he was just now discovering.
"Homophobic attacks are very serious," Terry declared hesitantly. Joshua appeared horrified by this statement. Was it really that obvious? Was it in scrawled on his forehead? "There were seven assaults near Dream last year alone," Terry announced.
"Tell us the truth, I promise we'll be discreet," Martin said honestly. Joshua sensed almost instantly that Martin was trustworthy. His manner was almost like that of a doctor.
"I can't let my father find out," Joshua insisted.
"Fair enough Joshua, so, the truth please....Were you at Dream last night?" Joshua nodded. By admitting the truth, he felt fear for the consequences, but simultaneously it was a relief to be honest and feel that there would at least be a glimmer of hope of tracking down the culprit. Dr Greg returned and announced that Joshua had been harassed enough. The police thanked Joshua and left, promising to stay in contact, and once again Joshua found himself with only his thoughts and fear to keep him occupied. 'Perhaps the night before had been a huge mistake,' Joshua pondered over the events of the previous evening. He realised that being gay definitely wouldn't be without its negatives. After all, over the past few weeks he'd thrown caution to the wind and transformed himself from a closeted homosexual with a girlfriend to an openly gay man (to most) with a boyfriend who went out on 'The Scene'. The transition had clearly

taken place too rapidly. Joshua's naivety was flying quickly out of the window. How could a complete stranger hate him so much to want to hurt him so severely? That is, assuming of course that it had been a stranger that'd attacked him. He'd read about racist and homophobic attacks before, but had never in his wildest dreams imagined he'd ever be a victim of one.

"Are you up to more visitors?" Dr Greg asked as he entered.

"Hello Greg," Joshua said invitingly.

"Well, there's a lovely young lady and two very nice young men," Greg replied enthusiastically. Megan followed Greg into the room. Her natural beauty was impaired by her look of concern.

"Don't look so glum," begged Joshua, "I need you to cheer me up!" Megan exerted herself and almost managed a smile.

"I'll do my best," she muttered, trying to sound positive. Michael and Stuart followed closely behind. Stuart appeared tense.

"I'll leave you with your friends, call me if you need anything," Greg said tenderly as he wandered off.

"Thanks doc'," Joshua shouted as he left.

"He seems lovely," Megan commented, unsure of what to say.

"He's great. He seems to like me, even remembers me from when mum died," Joshua replied. Stuart and Michael remained sheepish and silent.

"We came the second we heard," Michael eventually blurted out, almost as though he had to justify their actions.

"I'm so so sorry Joshua, this is all my fault," Stuart apologised, tears forming in his eyes. "I didn't mean for any of this," he continued. Joshua was startled by Stuart's reaction to the situation.

"Stuart, I don't blame you, this is not your fault," he insisted.

"I was the one who took you to that bar. If it hadn't been for me.....you wouldn't be here," Stuart replied, distressed. Michael handed him a tissue to wipe his eyes with.

"You weren't to know," said Joshua.

"I said this to him," Megan interrupted, "But would he listen?" she asked playfully. Hearing Megan's 'Mother knows best' routine made Michael smirk. "Come on, a smile please Michael, in fact, all of you!" Joshua demanded, and then announced, "I'm not dead, and I have no regrets."

"Oh Joshua, you know how much I care for you, don't you?" Stuart asked while holding and kissing him on the cheek. This was difficult for Megan to observe, after all just weeks ago she'd have been the one reacting in that way. Now, although she wanted to hold him, she couldn't. Megan was no longer Joshua's partner. She still loved him though. She was in love with him, not feeling the brotherly/sisterly type of love that Joshua felt for her. She concealed her envy well and let her anxiety over Joshua's

condition overshadow it. Stuart's grip was so tight that he was almost strangling Joshua. "I don't know what I'd have done if you'd died," Stuart shrieked out of the blue.
"Hey, hey calm down babe, it's not that serious," Joshua assured him. A glance passed between Michael and Megan that said, "Whoa!"
"It was me that wanted to go to that damn bar!" Stuart reiterated. "I should have walked you home too," he continued, almost as though he was striving to find as many faults in himself he possibly could. Joshua was taken aback by the intensity of Stuart's reaction.
"Stuart calm down!" Joshua demanded. Stuart detached himself from Joshua's body and looked him in the eye. "I don't blame you or anyone else….. Except of course the mongrel that did this to me, and that's the last word I want to hear on the subject of blame," Joshua insisted, obviously still tired and weary and struggling to raise his voice. Stuart nodded in half hearted agreement.
"You must let us know what you want us to bring to make you more comfortable," Megan butted in.
"Yes, I'll go to yours later and get some books for you," Stuart intercepted, as though staking his claim. Michael wondered whether to keep records of the points scored between Stuart and Megan as they both attempted to kill Joshua with kindness.
"I'm sure my father will take care of all that," Joshua said, now becoming agitated.
"I heard raised voices, is everything ok?" came a voice from behind. Greg looked stern. He wasn't about to tolerate his patient being unduly stressed.
"It's ok thanks Greg. I'm very tired though," Joshua replied, implying that his friends should be escorted out. "Ok, I think he's had enough excitement, he needs his rest," Dr Greg hinted for the party of friends to leave. Megan kissed Joshua on the forehead and said, "We all love you."
"I know," Joshua replied, smirking. Michael smiled and he and Stuart discreetly blew a kiss. They all departed and Greg briefly entered the room.
"You get some sleep." Joshua turned over and within seconds was out like a light.

Joshua slept for several hours before being awoken by Megan shaking his shoulders. She had a look of panic on her face.
"Joshua, wake up, it's important!" Joshua was disoriented.
"Are you still here?" he asked, under the impression only minutes had gone by since they'd last spoken.
"It's six o'clock in the evening Joshua, I've been to college!" she yelped.
"Ok, ok," Joshua said calmly, lowering his hands in an attempt to calm

Megan down.
"Joshua, listen to me, this is very important," she demanded. It was clear from her tone that she was deadly serious. "It's the paper, if your father sees it…." Megan began, but was interrupted by Neil clearing his throat behind her. "Megan, could you give Joshua and me some privacy for a moment please," Neil requested profoundly. He was not going to be messed with. The look on his face was like thunder. He was clearly on the verge of explosion. Megan complied with Neil's wishes and headed for the exit, noticing that a newspaper was poking out from the back pocket of Neil's jeans. She waited in the corridor. If ever there was a time that Joshua needed her, this was it.

Meanwhile, at the hospital news agency, Stuart was selecting some treats to deliver to Joshua's hospital bed. He glanced over at the newspapers and spotted the local 'Star' newspaper.
"Oh shit!" he screamed, dropping the bag of sherbet lemons he'd had in his grasp. The other customers in the shop all turned to investigate the disturbance in their otherwise peaceful shopping. Stuart made a vague attempt at an apology before dashing off out of the shop and heading down the hospital corridor.

Megan was attempting to eavesdrop into the inevitable conversation between Joshua and his father. She felt a tap on her shoulder and turned to face Greg, whose annoyance was obvious.
"Don't you think Joshua and his father deserve any privacy?" he asked.
"Doctor, this is so important. Joshua needs me," Megan pleaded. Greg could sense her sincerity and sheer desperation. As he was about to question her, he was almost knocked flying out of the way by Stuart.
"No running! This is a hospital," Greg yelled.
"I have to see Joshua. It's important!" Stuart broadcasted as though his life depended on it.
"It's too late Stuart, Neil knows and he's in there now. He's seen the newspaper," Megan sobbed.
"Right, you two are coming with me and you're going to tell me exactly what's going on," Greg said, holding out his arm to lead the way. Megan and Stuart shared a look of panic.

Neil was silent for several minutes before approaching Joshua's bed. This made Joshua feel uncomfortable.
"Is there anything you want to tell me Joshua? If there is, now is the time," Neil said eventually. Joshua pondered his next move. Neil had clearly made a discovery about him. The immediate conclusion to jump to was that his worst fear was happening, but how? He asked himself how Neil could possibly have discovered his sexuality. Karen immediately sprang to mind. Perhaps she couldn't be trusted after all. "Well?!" Neil

demanded, interrupting Joshua's trail of thought. "Is there anything you want to tell me or not?" he re-iterated.
"No I can't think of anything," Joshua muttered in a vague hope that the point Neil was trying to reach was in no way connected to the topic Joshua had so feared would be raised.
"Are you absolutely sure?" Neil asked again. He was like a dog with a bone, he was not about to let this drop. "Do you know how embarrassing this is for me?" Neil asked, his voice rising higher and higher in volume.
"What dad?" Joshua asked, now almost cowering like a school boy.
"Don't play fucking dumb with me kid," Neil continued aggressively. His tone was fierce. He pulled a newspaper from the back pocket of his jeans. Joshua shielded his face, expecting to be struck by it. Instead, Neil opened it out and slammed it down on the bed. Joshua lowered his arms and glanced at it. The headline read 'HOMOPHOBIC ATTACK IN CITY CENTRE'. Joshua raised his head to make direct eye contact with his father. "Well, what have you to say for yourself?" Neil asked calmly, and yet still furiously.
"What the hell do you expect?" Joshua yelled, answering a question with a question once again. "For the majority of my life you've been a complete and utter bastard!" Joshua continued, "And now you want to know why I couldn't confide in you about my sexuality," he went on after taking a break for a gasp of breath. "You're a joke of a man dad. I'm a queer and I'm more of a man now than you'll ever be!" Joshua wasn't sure what had possessed him, but it felt good to release years of pent up anger. Neil raised his fist in a sudden surge of rage.
"Hold it right there!" Greg said sternly from the doorway. Neil turned to face him and lowered his hand. Joshua gave Greg a look of despair. "Did he touch you?" Greg asked, now addressing Joshua.
"I didn't lay a fuckin' finger on him!" Neil interrupted, as though he feared Joshua was about to be economical with the truth out of spite.
"Joshua?" Greg said, making a point of ignoring Neil's disruption.
"I'm fine Greg, he didn't hit me." Greg attempted to escort Neil out of the room when Joshua stopped them. "Wait, I want my dad to stay."
"Are you sure?" Greg seemed bewildered.
"Just give us ten minutes alone, we have things to discuss," Joshua requested. "You heard him doc'," Neil butted in, self-righteously. Greg gave Neil a look that insisted he wasn't to be messed with.
"I'll be back in ten minutes," he declared as he reluctantly walked out of the door. Neil's smug face turned back to face Joshua.
"Glad you still know what side your bread's buttered on," he commented.
"I'm not coming home dad," Joshua announced spontaneously. Neil was taken aback by his son's display of independence.

"Why?"

"I can't believe you would even need to ask that," Joshua stated, now becoming agitated. Neil's look of surprise soon became that familiar one of resentment and bitterness.

"You are coming home. You, Karen and I are going to be a family….Soon as you get these silly queer ideas out of your head," Neil insisted. Joshua sighed as he realised that his father had absolutely no idea of what he'd gone through and hadn't a clue what he was talking about. The change in his attitude had been enjoyable, but Joshua's fears of it being temporary had just been confirmed. Neil's display of anger had already proven that.

"Stop this silly talk now," Neil said, clearly struggling to find the right words.

"There's no silly talk dad, I can't live with you any longer. Soon as I leave the hospital I'll arrange for someone to collect my things." Joshua sounded very final.

"Very well, if that's the way you want it…." Neil began as he approached the door. He opened it then turned to face his son, "Just don't think that once you've moved out you'll ever be welcome back." He stormed out into the hallway, where he received a look of disgust from Stuart who was propped up against the wall. Stuart contemplated making a comment but somehow refrained. He achieved personal satisfaction by sticking two fingers up at Neil behind his back as he headed for the exit. It didn't matter that Neil didn't see, the glare had said all that Stuart wanted to say. He wandered over to the door of Joshua's room and peered through the window. Joshua was now lying on his side, facing away from him. Stuart sensed that his friend needed some time alone.

Neil angrily barged into the house, slamming every door behind him. Karen paused her stirring of the rice she'd planned to present for his evening meal.

"Have you seen this?" Neil asked, throwing the newspaper onto the dinner table. Karen noticed the headline and the pieces suddenly fitted together. She contemplated admitting her previous knowledge of Joshua's sexuality and companions, but decided against it as she observed the tempestuous look in Neil's eyes.

"Is that referring to Joshua's attack?" Karen asked, playing dumb.

"Can you believe it?" Neil asked, nodding his head in despair. His face was a fiery red. He looked as though he could collapse from exhaustion at any moment. Karen attempted to console him by putting her arms around him, but was quickly shrugged away. "Don't crowd me, I need to think!" he yelled. Karen hadn't seen this side of her new partner before and was cautious, unaware of how to handle his temperament. She returned to the pan of rice that had now been unattended for several minutes. Neil remained facing away from her, his anger now lessening as the reality of the situation set in. "He's not coming home Karen," he said calmly and solemnly. They turned to face each other and Karen spotted a tear rolling down Neil's face; it was a dramatically quick change of mood for him. Karen had never witnessed a display of this type of emotion from Neil and it was a rare lapse in the masculine image he normally portrayed to perfection.

"Perhaps he didn't mean it Neil, he was probably just angry and emotional, he's been through a lot," Karen said compassionately. Neil wiped the tears from his eyes.

"I'm supposed to be a man."

"Crying doesn't make you any less of a man Neil, it just makes you human. Just like being gay doesn't make Joshua any less of a man either. He's a fine young man, regardless of his sexual orientation," Karen proclaimed. Neil listened carefully to her words of wisdom and nodded in agreement.

"I've made a lot of mistakes," he confessed. Karen approached him and held him in her arms.

"You're a good man too Neil. It takes a real man to admit his flaws," she said, comforting him. "I love you Neil."

"I love you too Karen," Neil replied. Karen could sense the honesty in his voice. "Give it a week or two," she suggested, "He might calm down and be ready to come back then."

Megan wondered what Joshua was dreaming about as she gazed at him. He looked so peaceful as he slept that it was hard to believe that he was the same person who'd just been through such an ordeal. She ran her fingers through his hair, just the way she used to. She didn't require any more amusement than this. Just watching Joshua in this quiescent state was all the entertainment she would ever hope for. Greg entered quietly behind her.

"He's having a long nap isn't he?" he commented.

"He's been out for hours," Megan replied, smiling.

"Well I have news, not sure if it's good or bad." This sounded ominous. Greg all of a sudden had Megan's full attention. "Joshua can go home tomorrow…..As long as he takes it easy," Greg said, seeming almost disappointed. Megan smiled delightedly.

"That's great news!" she cheered.

"Are you sure? I would have thought he was better off here than with that father of his," Neil said, expressing genuine concern.

"Don't worry, I'm hoping that won't be an issue," Megan assured him.

"I'll leave you to tell him the good news," Greg said, now grinning and he left the room. Megan smiled as she noticed Joshua beginning to stir.

His eyes opened and he focussed in on Megan staring adoringly at him. "Did I wake you?" she asked, lightly stroking his cheek as though he were a sick little boy. She kissed him on the forehead. He propped himself up and leaned on the pillows.

"How long have you been here?" he asked.

"I'm not sure really. I've been waiting to give you the news!" she excitedly exclaimed.

"News?" Joshua was intrigued and began to seat himself, resting on his pillows. "You can go home tomorrow!" she announced, becoming flustered by her own words.

"Oh……I haven't much time then," Joshua mumbled to himself. Megan was confused by Joshua's apparent lack of excitement. He read her facial expression and divulged, "I told my father I wasn't going home. So now I only have 'till tomorrow' to arrange something."

"Perfect," exclaimed Megan as she began to stand. Another deranged look arrived on Joshua's face. "I don't have to talk you into it now!" Megan cheered. "Talk me into what?" Joshua asked vaguely.

"Moving into our spare room!" Joshua hadn't seen Megan so passionate about anything in a long time. The prospect of him moving in was obviously pleasing to her. Joshua could see the logic but was dubious in light of recent events.

"Are you sure?" he asked.

"Absolutely! Mother loves the idea. Hell…she loves you!" Megan was not intending to accept 'no' for an answer. "We've got a huge house going to waste with just mother and I. Having my best friend living with me would be great, and Stuart could come go as he pleased." Joshua grinned. "Is that a yes?" Megan asked, judging his facial expression. Joshua nodded and Megan immediately wrapped her arms around him. "Thank you so much!" Joshua yelped, now becoming excited himself by the idea. "You're amazing Megan," he stated.

"I know," she agreed playfully. "Not many girls would be so kind after such a blow being dealt to them. I appreciate it Megan, and I love you in my own special way. Nobody could ever replace you," Joshua said honestly. Unsure of how to respond, Megan announced that she was going to prepare for what she described as 'the royal arrival' and quickly excused herself. Joshua relaxed and smiled at the thought of how fortunate he was to have such a great friend in Megan.

Megan and her mother were washing the dishes from the evening meal, Janice being as careful as possible not to crack one of her new false nails. She had recently turned forty and was fast realising that life was too short for the life she'd been leading. She'd had an extreme makeover for her birthday and hadn't looked back.

"So you're sure that you can handle living under the same roof as Joshua? Considering all that's happened…" Janice asked, genuinely concerned.
"It'll be fine," Megan insisted, "In fact, it'll be more than fine, it'll be great!" Janice gave a brief glance that unmistakably showed she was not convinced by what her daughter was saying. The pots were now dripping on the draining board. "Honestly, it'll be fine," Megan re-iterated, sensing her mother's lack of faith.
"Ok, ok," Janice said defensively, lifting her hand to form a 'stop' signal. She glanced at her watch and noticed the time. "Crikey, Is that the time? Vera will be waiting for me!" She hurriedly slipped on her coat and shoes, kissed Megan on the cheek and dashed out of the door.
"I can handle this," Megan said to herself. She spent a few moments reminiscing about happy times she'd spent with Joshua in their teenage years. Although she wouldn't admit it to herself, she longed for things to be the way they were again. Although on the surface she was completely at ease with the reality of the situation, deep down she still had visions of she and Joshua as an old married couple with children. She'd always imagined twin boys wearing matching outfits and a little girl. She'd painted a picture in her mind of how they would look. The boys would have Joshua's eyes, Megan's nose and Joshua's cute smile. As much as she deluded herself into thinking she'd come to terms with the fact that this could never happen, deep down she wanted it more than ever.

Megan's trail of thought was disturbed by several moments of constant banging on the front door. She awoke from her trance.
"Coming!" Megan opened the door slowly and was almost knocked flying as Stuart barged into the house. "Won't you come in Stuart?" she asked mockingly. Stuart appeared to be so full of rage that Megan was half expecting him to begin foaming at the mouth. She closed the door and they stood, facing each other. "Stuart, what on earth is the matter?" Megan asked.
"Who the hell do you think you are?!" bellowed Stuart. Then, without giving Megan an opportunity to respond, he followed that up with, "Face reality Megan, it's over between you and Joshua. He's a gay man! He wants to be with me now."
"I know that," Megan added defensively.
"Then why the hell are you asking him to move in with you?" Stuart continued, remaining firmly on his soapbox, his anger developing further.
"Because he's my best friend and he needs to get away from his father!" Megan yelled, attempting to overpower, or at least match the volume of Stuart's voice. "I'm his boyfriend, he should be moving in with me," Stuart declared in an infantile way. "I know what your game is," he continued, "You think that you can get him back. You think you can turn

him straight. It doesn't work like that sweetheart….."
"Don't patronise me!" Megan screamed. She was an incredibly placid person but once she became angry she was uncontrollable, and her buttons were being firmly pushed.
"Joshua's been the most important person in my life for five years. Yes he may be gay…….." Stuart attempted to interrupt at this point but Megan raised her voice and continued, "But we love each other in our own special way; obviously a way that you can't comprehend."
"But I'm his boyfriend now!" Stuart reminded her.
"That doesn't give you exclusive rights to him, and it doesn't make me any less important to him. Don't think that you mean more to him just because you've shagged him!" she said bluntly. Stuart was speechless. Never had he witnessed such feistiness from Megan, but she was in no mood to be messed with. "I think you should leave," she suggested after a moment of silence. It dawned on Stuart that he had acted unfairly towards Megan. Perhaps she did still harbour some romantic feelings for Joshua, but her head had obviously faced the reality of the situation and it wasn't right for Stuart to expect her to give him up.
"I'm sorry Megan," Stuart apologised. She stared at him, judging his sincerity. "You're right. I'm a jealous pot. I always get like this when I meet someone I really care about. I get so paranoid. I know I can trust Joshua, I guess I just need a lot of reassurance." Stuart was humble; his manner almost begged for pity. Without saying it, Megan had learned that Stuart's past relationships obviously hadn't been positive experiences. This was the first time the normally over-confident Stuart had shown any signs of weakness and insecurity, and Megan could now understand the reasoning behind his outburst. Megan held out her arms, inviting Stuart into them.
"I'll look after him, I promise," Megan said softly as she gripped Stuart tightly. "I'm sorry," Stuart apologised, now feeling rather foolish. Megan assured him that he'd be welcome there anytime and Stuart became contented with this knowledge. "I feel so stupid," Stuart said as he withdrew himself from Megan's arms and shamefully looked away. Megan smiled and touched his arm. He turned to face her.
"Just don't hurt him and we'll get along great," Megan promised.

"All ready for the off?" Greg asked as he entered the ward to find Joshua packing his satchel bag.
"Definitely!" Joshua replied, his smile beaming.
"Someone's pleased to be going home," Greg laughed. Joshua explained that he was relocating and his reasoning behind the move. Greg moved closer to him and listened attentively. A tear arrived in his eye as he heard of Joshua's agony through the years with his father. "I'm glad you're

finally getting away from that fiend," Greg commented harshly.
"I'm sorry, I didn't mean to upset you with my story," Joshua commented, a little shocked by Greg's reaction.
"It's ok, it wasn't meant to be this way Joshua. Your life was supposed to be different. I swear it was. You were meant to be with two loving, considerate parents." Greg's statement seemed to be very irregular, but Joshua chose to shrug it off.
"Aren't we all?" The bizarre conversation was disturbed by the arrival of Karen. She knocked on the open door and caught Joshua's eye.
"Can I come in?" she asked. Greg looked weary, but Joshua nodded for her to proceed. "I won't take up much of your time," Karen promised, "I just need to talk to you."
"Ok, what do you have to say?" Joshua asked bluntly. He was in no frame of mind for niceties or brushing things under the carpet. His bag was now packed and he was ready to depart, and not heading for his father's house. Greg made himself scarce for the inevitable awkwardness of Karen's visit. Once they were alone, Karen opened her arms, inviting Joshua to embrace her. He contemplated it for a moment, but quickly caved in. He'd needed this. Tears were filling his eyes.
"It's ok," Karen said, "I promise it'll all be ok." Joshua released himself and wiped his eyes. "Your dad wants you to come home, you know."
"Karen, I like you a lot……but you really don't know my father as well as you might think you do. He will not accept my sexuality, and I won't go on living a lie." Joshua was being assertive and Karen admired this.
"Just promise you'll visit plenty," she pleaded. Her voice was soft and motherly, so difficult to disappoint. Joshua agreed to the promise and embraced her once more. "He is trying," she added, clutching at straws. Joshua smiled vaguely. "Megan's waiting outside for you." They departed to the corridor where Megan appeared excited to be taking home her best friend. As they headed towards the car park, Greg's voice bellowed from behind them,
"You take care Joshua. Nothing strenuous!" Joshua nodded and waved as he and Megan stepped into her mother's car and Karen headed off to her own.

Joshua was sprawled out across the couch watching a marathon of Star Wars movies, fully equipped with chocolates and crisps, all the calories that were the bane of every gay man's life. He now felt more relaxed after just a few short weeks of living with Megan and Janice than he ever had in the previous five years with his father. Stuart was also by this time making the home his own; he would regularly arrive unannounced. Janice had begun to see Joshua as the son she never had, and Megan was trying to convince herself that she now saw Joshua in a

brotherly sense.
"Joshua hun', you've got a visitor!" Janice yelled from the kitchen.
"Send him through," Joshua shouted back, assuming that Stuart had arrived for another unscheduled visit to eat her out of house and home. Anticipating his boyfriend's arrival, Joshua moved into a provocative position. He began rubbing his penis through his jeans in an attempt to seduce Stuart on his entry to the room. He was startled by the sight of Greg wandering into the room. Greg was stopped in his tracks by the sight of Joshua's almost masturbatory activity. Joshua glanced at Greg, unsure of how to explain his activities.
"Maybe I should come back later," Greg said in jest. He could clearly see the humorous aspect of the situation. Joshua laughed.
"I thought you were my boyfriend, I was just being playful!" he blurted out in between spurts of uncontrollable giggling. "You are the last person I was expecting," Joshua said, now catching his breath.
"Clearly," uttered Greg, still smirking. Joshua's rudeness dawned on him and he sat upright, offering Greg the seat beside him. Greg was out of uniform and looking very casual and somewhat impressive. He parked himself on the sofa.
"I didn't know I was due a visit."
"You weren't Joshua, this is a social call. It's not an official visit. I just wanted to know how you were," Greg said proudly. Joshua was puzzled by this statement. Since when do doctors have the time or the desire to make random house calls to former patients? Joshua already felt he'd exhausted the potential for conversation merely by saying hello. Greg had been with-holding his laughter up to this point but couldn't refrain any longer. Joshua smiled. "I'm sorry," Greg apologised, wiping tears from his eyes. "I've not had anyone try to entice me in that way before." Joshua playfully punched his arm. "So seriously, how are you?" Greg asked, pulling himself together.
"I'm doing great. I'm really on the mend," Joshua said positively.
"How are things with your father?" Greg asked randomly. The line of questioning was now becoming very personal and Joshua was uncomfortable. Something just wasn't quite right about Greg's excessive interest in Joshua. It went far beyond the parameters of the doctor-patient relationship.
"I don't really see him," Joshua replied eventually.
"Probably for the best," Greg commented inappropriately. Joshua stood. "I'm sorry to cut this short but I have to get ready to go out," he announced abruptly and turned off the Star Wars video that had been little more than background noise since Greg's arrival.
"You're not overly straining yourself are you?" Greg asked, following his

cue to stand.
"No I'm fine," Joshua insisted. Greg gazed at Joshua, who was itching to head for the door to escort him out.
"I really admire your attitude," Greg said, "A lot of lads your age would have been after revenge. In my experience, they've been angry and sometimes an ordeal such as this can change their entire character. I'm glad you stayed the sweet young man that you are." As he said this, Greg touched Joshua's shoulder. Joshua saw this as an invasion of his personal space and subtly shrugged him away.
"Anyway, I'll see you again," Joshua said half-heartedly as they approached the door.
"Definitely. I'll be keeping an eye on you!" Greg joked. Joshua could sense that this comment was partly serious in spite of Greg's tone. He knew he hadn't seen the last of this doctor.

"What a lovely man that Greg," Janice commented as she tidied the cushions around where Joshua was relaxing. "There's not many doctors would visit you in their own time. Is he single?" she continued. Joshua laughed hysterically.
"Hey, he's only a few years younger than me you know!" Janice yelled, offended by the humour Joshua had found in her statement.
"Well I never thought you were that naïve," Joshua said, turning his attention to the TV.
"Hey you, don't start something and then leave me dangling. What makes me naïve?" Janice asked. Joshua's attention returned to her.
"Do you want me to spell it out?" he asked.
"Yes," Janice replied bluntly.
"Fair enough….He fancies me, it's obvious. Look at all the attention he gave me in hospital, and now he visits me at home! It's the only explanation." Janice glared in disbelief.
"No, he's not gay….No chance!" she insisted. Joshua gave a look of scepticism. "Fine, I'll get a date with him then," Janice announced. Joshua's face gave away that he was struggling to hide his amusement. Janice playfully threw a cushion at his face. "You wait and see," she said sarcastically as she glided back to the kitchen. Joshua wondered what tricks Janice had up her sleeve.

Stuart joined the newly formed family unit for their evening meal. Stuart and Joshua were seated opposite Megan and Janice. Although Janice spent little time seated as she was so busy dashing around, catering to everyone's needs. The conversation always flowed well during these meals. Joshua was truly experiencing how a pleasant, happy home life could feel. "Thanks for feeding me," Stuart said as he shovelled mashed potato into his mouth. Janice replied with,

"You're very welcome hun'," she was very fond of Stuart. She then followed that up with, "You might want to come for tea tomorrow to see me prove a point to Joshy." Stuart glanced at Joshua in search of an explanation; he was intrigued by Janice's comment.
"Here we go again!" Megan moaned playfully, tired of the ongoing argument. "You still haven't given us your input," Janice reminded her.
"That's because I don't know. He doesn't seem gay but he shows a lot of interest in Joshua," Megan replied. Stuart was now becoming paranoid and glancing around the table looking puzzled.
"Well, we'll find out at dinner tomorrow," Janice announced, wandering over to collect the desserts from the kitchen.
"You've invited him here?" Joshua asked loudly.
"Yes, we'll get to the bottom of it soon," Janice replied from the kitchen. The entire conversation was flying straight over Stuart's head. Megan attempted to explain,
"You see, mother fancies Greg Foster….You know, Joshua's doctor, but Joshua thinks he's gay because of all the attention he's shown him." Stuart glared at Joshua, seeking confirmation.
"Don't exaggerate," Joshua demanded.
"That's what you said when he came here to visit you," Megan reminded him, putting her foot in it even further.
"He visited you?!" Stuart asked, almost angrily.
"Look, it's not an issue…." Janice butted in, defusing the situation, "….because he's not gay. I can tell, and I'd put money on the fact that I'm going to land a date with him!" Her mix of confidence and sarcasm made for a convincing argument; however it wasn't enough to relieve Stuart of his paranoia.
"He's practically old enough to be your father," Stuart bitched.
"Hey, come on, he's a nice man and we're jumping to all sorts of conclusions here," Janice said defensively.
"Well I'll be here for dinner again tomorrow night just to make sure," insisted Stuart. He had a stern look on his face. Heaven help Greg if he was attracted to Joshua. A look passed between Janice and Megan that suggested they disapproved of Stuart's over-protective behaviour. Megan was beginning to notice a pattern here as she recalled the argument she'd had with him over Joshua's change of residency.

"How about some sort of oriental dish?" Janice asked, her face buried a cook book.
"Hmmm, bit risky," Joshua replied as he opened the refrigerator and began to drink milk straight from the bottle. "What if he doesn't like it or has an allergy?"
"Very true. Something a little more standard then," Janice continued

rambling. “But elegant,” Joshua butted in playfully. Janice turned to face him and lost her place in the book as a result.
“I want to make a good impression Joshua. It’s a long time since I’ve chased a man, and tonight I want everything to be perfect.” She was deadly serious. It wasn’t until this moment that Joshua had realised just how fond of Greg she was and this made him feel guiltier, as he was so certain that Greg was homosexual and indeed was attracted to him.
“I hope it all goes to plan for you,” Joshua said sincerely.
“Thanks hun’,” Janice replied fondly. The clock was ticking. It was just three hours until Greg was to receive the grilling of his life.

Stuart arrived considerably earlier than he normally would for a meal at the O’Donnelly’s. His subtlety was non-existent. It was clear to everyone that he was frightened to death of missing anything. He seated himself on the sofa, just millimetres away from Joshua. Megan could sense his agitation, but Janice was far too busy flapping around, changing out of outfits and constantly checking the oven.
“If he starts coming on to you…….” Stuart muttered, addressing Joshua.
“Stuart, stop panicking, he’s not like that. He takes an interest but he’s not sleazy,” Joshua said in an attempt to calm his boyfriend.
“Not yet,” Stuart replied firmly.
“Well, you’ve nothing to worry about because I have you and I wouldn’t let some thirty-something get in our way,” Joshua said light-heartedly. Megan was eavesdropping into the conversation as she applied her mascara in front of the mirror. She rolled her eyes at Stuart’s comments as she was between strokes. Joshua was sensing this but ignoring it for Stuart’s sake.
“Ok then,” Stuart responded, smiling at Joshua’s sweet comment.
“Besides, Janice seems certain that she’s going to bag a date with the good doctor,” Joshua laughed. Stuart excused himself to the toilet. Megan interrupted her primping and turned to face Joshua.
“How obsessive is he getting?” she asked sarcastically.
“I know, he’s a little paranoid…” Joshua began.
“Just a bit!” Megan said strongly.
“He’s a great guy,” Joshua insisted. “We all have our flaws.” Megan was partly convinced by what Joshua was saying and returned her attention to the mirror. Stuart re-entered the room holding out his left arm.
“Presenting, the beautiful, outrageous………” he said in a camp tone of voice, as though he were on stage introducing a drag queen. “Janice O’Donnelly!”
Janice entered the room. She was wearing a beautiful red dress that was just right; it knocked years from her age and made her appearance sassy enough to be on the cover of ‘Vogue’ magazine. The boys had never

witnessed Janice make such effort, nor had Megan since her father's death. Everyone realised at this point that the bet between Janice and Joshua was more important to her than she'd exhibited. She was finally ready to return to the dating world and she had her eyes on a prize. Megan hoped for her mother's sake that Joshua was wrong in his presumption of Greg's sexuality.
"How do I look?" Janice asked humbly.
"You look amazing mother," Megan said, hugging her whilst trying to avoid creasing her outfit.
"I feel so under-dressed," Stuart said, giggling. "Do you think I'll get his attention?" Janice asked, addressing the question to Joshua.
"If I'm wrong, and I hope I am, you'll knock him dead," Joshua replied. Janice smiled, then dashed to the kitchen, realising she hadn't checked the oven in over a minute. "She looks amazing!" Joshua commented honestly.
"I've not seen her look so great since...........well, since dad," Megan said. Janice returned to the room.
"Dinner's almost ready," she announced with pride. The doorbell rang.
"Well, this is it," Janice said as she headed for the door.
"I hope she's not setting herself up for a fall," Stuart said insincerely. Megan crossed her fingers for all to see. Joshua gave that cute smile she remembered so fondly. Greg entered the room carrying a bottle of what appeared to be very expensive wine.
"Hello guys," he said, attempting to appear hip. His attire was more impressive than anyone had anticipated. Stuart wondered who Greg was trying to impress. Greg seated himself on a chair, as Stuart remained firmly in his place beside Joshua on the sofa. The tension was mounting already. Megan seated herself beside Stuart and broke the silence.
"It was really great of you to come."
"I was glad to be invited," Greg said politely. "It's not often I become so fond of my patients." This comment made Stuart's blood boil. Megan wondered in what context to read it. After all, if Greg was a gay thirty-something that preyed on teenage boys, would he really be so blatant about it? Stuart was giving Greg the 'dead eye' and this made him try his best to look anywhere but in Stuart's direction.
"Mother's a great cook," Megan boasted, attempting to lighten the mood.
"Oh good, I can't wait. I've been on a long shift at the hospital and I'm ravenous!" Greg said playfully.
"It's ready!" Janice yelled joyfully from the dining room. Megan smiled and led the way.
"What you think?" Stuart whispered to Joshua. He shrugged his shoulders, unsure of how to comprehend Greg's actions.

The table had been set very carefully. Girls on one side, boys on the other. Janice had ensured she was facing Greg during the meal, whilst Megan was opposite Joshua and Stuart. Joshua had been placed beside Greg, intentionally splitting up he and Stuart.

"This looks fabulous," Greg complimented Janice. She became embarrassed and insisted the meal had been thrown together in minutes which caused Megan and Joshua to struggle to retain their laughter. Stuart however kept a straight face and remained vigilant of Greg, closely monitoring every word he uttered and every slight move he made. Various topics of conversation were covered during the meal, including Janice's past and the emphasis on her current availability. As interested as Greg seemed, the conversation still drifted on to Joshua every so often. Greg was fishing for information and prying into Joshua's past, in particular, his relationship with Neil. Each time the subject of Joshua arose, Stuart became more flustered. Megan could sense this and was making attempts to divert any potential outbursts from him. Janice was oblivious to the situation, as her focus was gazing at Greg's handsome face and fretting over her own appearance. Stuart was in no mood to be messed with. Joshua failed to comprehend the reasoning of Stuart's concern, after all, he'd never choose a man in his mid-thirties over his boyfriend, but Stuart wasn't secure enough to see that and every ounce of interest that Greg expressed in Joshua just wound him up further and further.

"I could definitely see you as a journalist," Greg complimented Joshua.

"Well thank you," Joshua replied, secretly enjoying the attention. Stuart once again glared at Greg, as though he were a dog that was jealous of his owner giving attention to the neighbour's baby during a walk.

"So how come you're not married Greg?" Stuart blurted out. Janice gave a look of disapproval, but at the same time was eager to hear Greg's response. Greg suddenly had the attention of the entire table. Greg looked uncomfortable. Stuart immediately jumped to the conclusion that this was because he was reluctant to confess his homosexuality.

"There was someone very special once. We were engaged to be married," Greg began. Megan could sense this was difficult for him.

"You don't have to tell us Greg," she assured him.

"No it's ok. It was a long time ago," he continued.

"What happened?" Janice asked softly.

"She died." The words were obviously tough to find. The word 'she' was now making Stuart feel extremely foolish. Janice placed her hands on Greg's.

"I'm sorry. I know what it's like," she empathised. Greg nodded. He acknowledged that Janice had experienced firsthand all of the pain he'd

suffered. This was a turning point for Stuart as well. All of a sudden, instead of seeing Greg as the big bad doctor who was out to steal his boyfriend, he saw the real Greg. He was kind, caring and fragile. Above all, he was straight; therefore Stuart was now allowed to like him.
"Anyway, we'd best be off, hadn't we guys?" Megan announced randomly, glancing at her watch without allowing herself enough time to read what it displayed. She winked discreetly at Joshua who then proceeded to play along. "You're right, we'll miss the start of the film if we're not careful."
"Are you up to going out?" Greg asked, showing genuine concern.
"I'll be fine," Joshua assured him while tucking his chair under the table. Megan read Janice's lips as she silently thanked her. They both smiled. Stuart and Joshua held hands as they said their goodbyes and followed Megan out of the door.

"I wonder how it went," Megan speculated while pouring milk on her corn flakes.
"Well something's tired your mother out, she doesn't usually sleep in this late," Joshua replied playfully. They both laughed.
"What's so funny?" Janice asked from the doorway.
"Nothing mother, we were just talking about last night," Megan replied, turning to inspect the state of her mother's appearance. She was wearing her new dressing gown that she'd been saving for the winter. She looked so contented. Megan struggled to recall the last time she'd seen Janice in this light.
"So how'd it go after we left last night?" Joshua asked, now impatient from awaiting the gossip. Before Janice could respond, the sound of footsteps moving down the staircase could be heard. Megan and Joshua stared at each other as though they were children who'd just heard Santa arrive, and then they both stared at Janice. Greg entered, straightening his tie.
"I need to get to work. I'll call you later," he said surprisingly casually.
"OK love, see you later," Janice replied, and then received a peck on the cheek. Greg waved goodbye to Megan and Joshua and left for work. Janice approached the breakfast table in a cavalier fashion. She was being stared at as she poured her bowl of corn flakes.
"Well?!" Megan demanded, holding out her arms.
"We connected, we really did…..In a way I haven't experienced in a long time." "I'm glad mother, I'm so happy for you." Megan hugged her mother. Joshua felt excluded and was nodded in by Janice. The group hug went on for what felt like minutes. They split and Janice proceeded with preparing her breakfast. The mood began to lighten.
"Well Joshua….." Janice began, attempting not to giggle, "Looks like I

won the bet!” Joshua grabbed a damp wash cloth from the side and threw it at her in jest.

Chapter 7

"Oh what shall I get for him?" Joshua asked in a camp tone of voice as he minced around Janice's bedroom.
"You know him better than I do," Janice replied as she struggled to concentrate on applying her mascara in front of the mirror.
"But a one year anniversary is really special," Joshua droned on.
"I'm sure that Stuart will be more than happy with any gift you buy," Janice said, being rather unhelpful. It was just days before the first anniversary since Stuart and Joshua's relationship had begun.
"You're no help. It'll be a different story when it's yours and Greg's anniversary," moaned Joshua. He had a valid point. It was only a couple of months before Janice and Greg would be celebrating their first anniversary as a couple and she knew deep down that she was going to irritate Joshua right back when the time came.
"You're right babe," Janice acknowledged and turned to face him. "Get him a new outfit," she suggested.
"Oooh I dunno, what if he doesn't like it? He'll feel obliged to wear it…" Joshua whittled on. Several ideas later, Janice had tired of the conversation and resumed her attempts to make herself look beautiful before the mirror for her beloved 'Greggy' as she now affectionately called him. Joshua trotted off to badger Megan instead.

"Just shag him, I'm sure he'll be satisfied," Megan proposed, engrossed in her romance novel.
"Ha ha," Joshua laughed falsely.
"I'm sure he'll be happy with anything that's from you. You know what the soppy sod's like," Megan said, briefly extracting her head from her book. "Anyway, he's more annoying than you right now…." Megan commented.
"Why?" Joshua asked curiously.
"He's looking for a birthday present as well as an anniversary gift."
"Really?!" Joshua became excited.
"Yes," Megan replied sternly. "Don't tell him that I told you but he's been nagging for ideas too." She had now given up on any concentration towards her book and folded the page. Joshua pestered for further information but Megan refused. "He also asked where he should take you. I just said that as long as it's not as eventful as your eighteenth birthday you'll be fine," she laughed. Joshua now knew that Stuart was agonising over his gifts. This information comforted him to a degree but also made him fear that the gift he bought may be outshined by the one he was to receive.
"You've still not opened this post!" Janice yelled from downstairs. She was now awaiting a lift from Greg.

"Coming!" Joshua shouted in reply and headed downstairs. Megan was now thankful for some peace and quiet.

"It could be your first birthday card," Janice commented as she passed him a stylish looking envelope.

"That's not for weeks," Joshua said, brushing off her suggestion. Janice began to reminisce.

"I can't believe you'll be nineteen in a few short weeks. It seems not five minutes since I first met you all those years ago." Joshua was disinterested in Janice's stroll down Memory Lane and eagerly opened the envelope. His face became white as a ghost as he examined the contents. It was a card, but not a birthday card as Janice had suspected.

"What's wrong Joshua?" Janice asked seriously. He gazed at her and passed her the card. She began to read it out loud, "You're invited to the wedding of Neil Maguire and Karen Thompson…."

"Have you seen the date?!" Joshua shrieked.

"Two weeks!" Janice declared with astonishment. "But they've been together less than a year…." She continued.

"I haven't seen him since I moved in here, but I doubt he's changed all that much. I hope Karen knows what she's letting herself in for," Joshua said. He was frightened for Karen. Mentally recalling the emotional and at times even physical torture he had endured from his father for so many years made him fear for what Karen was to face as Neil's wife; his new step-mother. The fact that it had all been so rushed panicked Joshua too. It was almost as though Neil had purposely speeded things along in order to trap Karen into a marriage before she had a chance to realise what a mistake she was making.

"Joshua…." Janice said, waving her hand in his face in an attempt to grasp his attention. He was so deep in thought and staring into space. He gave his attention. "What are you going to do?" she asked. What could Joshua do? It had been almost a year since he'd seen or heard from his father or Karen, mainly through his own choice; he didn't feel he had the right to meddle in their affairs now.

"I really don't know Janice," he replied and seated himself, re-reading the invitation over and over again.

"Maybe you should go. He is your father after all," Janice suggested. Her well-meaning chatter was not helping Joshua's trail thought. Could he possibly just arrive at the wedding after all this time? "Why don't you pay your father and Karen a visit first? Clear the air…" Janice suggested. This seemed a good idea to Joshua, but he soon had a better one.

"I wonder if I could get hold of Karen's address…." Joshua thought out loud.

"You're going to visit Karen and not your father?" Janice asked in surprise.
"Good idea or bad idea?" Joshua asked.
"She's probably already living with your father now anyway," Janice pointed out. This seemed logical. Joshua decided to visit home shortly after Neil was due at work.

"I'm coming with you!" Stuart insisted in his usually over-protective fashion.
"That's not necessary. Besides if my father happens to be there we'll just alienate him further."
"Ok, but be careful, remember he almost hit you the last time you saw him," Stuart continued. Conscious of how much this was all costing on his mobile phone bill, Joshua began to wrap up the conversation.
"Thanks for worrying babe but I'll be fine. I'm just gonna' go there in the morning and talk to Karen, that's all. Anyways I gotta' go. See you tomorrow….."
"Ok, love you," Stuart declared for the seventh time that day.
"Love you to," Joshua replied, ending the call. It gave Joshua a warm feeling inside when Stuart announced his love for him; such feelings he had been denied through his teenage years. Stuart and Joshua had now grown very attached to each other. The bond was strong, and Joshua hoped it would be eternal. For the first time since his mother's death when he heard the words 'I love you' it was the truth.
"Are you ok?" asked Megan's voice from behind him in the lounge.
"I'm fine," Joshua replied unconvincingly.
"Has mother gone out with Greg?" she asked. Joshua nodded. "Ok so from what I overheard, it sounds as though you're going to visit Karen. Why would you be doing that?" Megan asked looking puzzled. Joshua passed the wedding invitation for her to read.
"Want me to come with you to see Karen? If Neil's there he'd be a bit more susceptible to me than Stuart." Joshua wanted to be strong and face this alone, but the thought of having Megan's support was encouraging. It had been almost a year since he'd set foot inside his childhood home and the bad memories definitely outweighed the good. He swallowed his pride and agreed she should accompany him.

They arrived at Neil's house just minutes after he'd left for work. This was in the hope of catching Karen in the short space between his departure to work and hers.
"Are you sure you want to do this?" Megan asked. Joshua nodded.
"I think I've put it off long enough. I can't stay away forever." Megan held Joshua's hand tightly for a moment in a gesture of friendship. Joshua was still one of the most important people in her life. She'd only ever had

the one boyfriend and since the discovery of his homosexuality she hadn't moved on at all. She'd refused any requests for a date and hadn't contemplated making any effort to find someone new.
"Let's do it," she suggested positively. Joshua rang the doorbell. Although he had a key it seemed somehow impolite to use it now.
"Door's open!" came Karen's familiar voice from upstairs. Joshua glanced at Megan as though seeking approval.
"Let's go in then," she said. Joshua opened the door and they entered the house. The hallway was barely recognisable. There was new carpeting, new wallpaper and even a new book case. Granted, these changes had been long overdue but it was startling for Joshua to observe how dramatically it had changed. It was as though the memories of his mother had been ripped away and she'd never existed.
"I'll be down in a minute!" Karen yelled from upstairs. She was clearly expecting someone else. They headed through to the lounge. It was as though Joshua had stepped into the wrong house. There was a new cabinet and TV, a new sofa, new carpeting, new wallpaper, lamps and light shades. Even the frame that used to contain a photograph of Joshua as a toddler had been replaced by one of Neil and Karen. There was no sign of anything that had ever belonged to Lynne in the lounge either. Joshua wandered into the kitchen leaving Megan seated on the sofa. Even the colour scheme of the kitchen utensils had changed. Lynne had always obsessively had everything red: the teapot, the biscuit barrel, the crockery, the cutlery; all red. It was now a variety of junk that looked as though it had been acquired at a car boot sale.
"She's certainly made her mark on this place. It's barely recognisable," Joshua remarked as he re-entered the lounge.
"You know what women are like," Megan commented, attempting to comfort him and lighten the mood.
"Sorry I'm taking so long. You're a little early," came Karen's voice again. She was now making her way down the stairs. As she trotted into the lounge expecting to find a work colleague she was startled to discover Joshua and Megan had made themselves at home.
"Joshua….. What a surprise!" Karen screeched, vaguely attempting to sound positive. Karen had dyed her hair red; this distracted Joshua and Megan's attention away from the bruise below her eye on the right side of her face for a moment but it soon came into focus.
"Your hair looks great," Megan complimented her.
"What the hell happened to your face?!" Joshua asked bluntly and without reservation. Karen had obviously attempted to conceal the bruise with make-up which was presumably the reason she'd been so busy upstairs, but it was still clear to see.

"Oh that's nothing.....I...bumped into a door," Karen lied, smiling falsely. "Listen, I'm sorry but I have to get to work. Brenda will be picking me up any minute now." It was as though she couldn't rid herself of them fast enough. A car horn beeped outside. "That'll be Brenda," announced Karen, obviously thankful for the opportunity to escape.
"I'll be back Karen, I need to talk to you about the wedding," Joshua insisted.
"Looking forward to it," Karen replied unconvincingly as she ushered them out of the door and escaped into her friend's car.

"Let's not jump to conclusions," proposed Megan as she slurped her coffee and parked herself on the very edge of the sofa. Joshua gave her a look that said, 'Oh come on Megan, get a grip!'
"It is so obvious what's going on!" Joshua yelled in anger, running his hand through his hair and almost ripping it out as he paced the room. His movements were almost making Megan dizzy.
"We don't know," Megan said in an almost maternal tone of voice. As placid as she was, and as much as she was striving to have a calming affect on Joshua, deep down she knew his theory was almost certain to be correct.
"He's beating her Megan, the bastard's beating her!" exclaimed Joshua. Megan sighed, realising that nothing she could say would change the facts. The visit to Joshua's old home had complicated matters further. It had been difficult enough for him to decide whether or not to attend the wedding, but now he knew for certain that the marriage was inevitably going to be unwholesome. Karen faced the same fate his mother had suffered, perhaps it wouldn't be the death of her the way it had been for Lynne, but she faced the same miserable existence that Lynne had endured for so many years. Joshua simply couldn't allow this to happen. He was fond of Karen after all, she'd been a trustworthy friend at a time when he'd needed it the most and he couldn't stand to watch as she faced the same fate as his poor mother. "I'm going over there to talk some sense into her tomorrow morning!" he announced aggressively. He was pacing up and down the kitchen; he simply didn't know what to do with himself.
"Are you sure?" Megan asked, "It might not be such a great idea.....If Neil found out...."
"Fuck Neil!" yelled Joshua, then quickly apologised for his behaviour. Megan held Joshua in her arms the way she'd always used to. "I can't bear for Karen to have the same sort of life my mother suffered for all those years," Joshua said while holding back the tears in his eyes. Joshua's childhood memories were flooding back to him. The sight of Karen's bruise had forced him to recall the events he'd repressed in his

mind for so many years. Megan insisted they be seated and Joshua complied, "I always tried not to think about it but.........there were so many times when mum had those so-called accidents and she and dad were always arguing," Joshua confessed.
"I didn't realise their marriage had been so terrible. I always knew that you didn't like your father and that they'd had a rocky marriage, but I didn't realise things were that bad," Megan stated in shock. Joshua stared into space and replied coldly,
"Neither did I until today." He was reliving memories that were painful. The reality of the torture his mother had faced in her final years was becoming apparent. "I was too little to understand before, but it's so clear now. He beat her. My bastard of a father beat my mother senseless." Tears were streaming down Joshua's face as he relived the pain of the past. He stood. Something had just dawned on him.
"What is it?" Megan asked sensing he'd just recalled something of importance. She was fascinated by this. It was almost like watching someone with amnesia regaining a lifetime of memories. He turned to face her. She stood.
"It was his fault," uttered Joshua, contempt in his voice. Megan looked puzzled.
"What are you talking about?" she asked.
"It's his fault that my mother is dead. For years he's blamed me, but it wasn't my fault. He killed her, he might as well have put a knife through her heart," Joshua announced, now becoming exasperated. "I hate him!" he yelled.
"I know you're angry at Neil's behaviour but your mother's death was an accident..." Megan attempted to offer the voice of reason.
"No Megan. I remember it so clearly now. That week, it'd been particularly bad. The fights had been constant. When we entered the car, mum was riled up. She couldn't concentrate on the road. He did that to her. He put her into that state! I remember she was wound up because of him just before the crash. He killed her!" exclaimed Joshua. His emotions were taking over. Megan attempted to calm him but it was no good. He had a mission; there was no way Joshua would allow another person to undergo the lifestyle that Lynne had tolerated. "I'm going back over there and I'm going to bring her to her senses!" Megan knew he meant what he said and offered her full support.

Joshua and Megan monitored Neil's house, awaiting his departure to work.
"I feel like an undercover cop," joked Megan, attempting to keep Joshua's spirits up. He smiled vaguely while keeping his eyes on Neil's car. As soon as it pulled away they'd be banging on the door. This would

give them the maximum amount of time possible to talk things over with Karen before she'd leave for work herself. "She may not listen you know, you should prepare yourself for that," Megan pondered out loud.
"She has to listen," Joshua replied in his aggressive but caring manner. He was now becoming irritable from sitting on an uncomfortable wall.
"All I'm saying is that when you're in love with someone you don't always want to believe the truth about them. You bury your head in the sand," Megan said, offering her words of wisdom. She sounded as though she was speaking from personal experience. She then went one step further, from implying her point to bluntly blurting it out. "Look at me and you. If anyone had tried to tell me that you were gay a couple of years ago I'd have told them to fuck off. I would have accused them of being jealous. I'd have said anything to justify to myself that they were wrong. And Karen will be the same." Joshua looked Megan directly in the eye.
"I'm sorry Megan. I wish I'd been able to be more open to you, and to myself."
"I'm not looking for an apology Joshua. I just want you to realise that it might not be so easy to convince Karen that she shouldn't marry your father." Neil's car pulled away.
"You're right, I'm going to give it a damned good try though," Joshua said with determination in his tone.

Joshua banged loudly on the door, his heart was beating fast, he meant business.
"Don't go in there with all guns blazing," warned Megan. There was no answer. "Maybe she already left," Megan suggested. It was obvious that Karen knew who was at the door and was avoiding them through embarrassment and fear of the inevitable lecture she'd be subjected to. Joshua continued to pound loudly on the door. If Karen was in, there was no way she could avoid him. Eventually the door slowly opened and a natural looking Karen stood before them in her red robe. She hadn't yet applied any make-up to her face, which further emphasised the bruise.
"Can we come in?" Joshua asked softly. He wondered what other injuries were being concealed by her robe.
"Can't keep you out of your own home," Karen remarked almost defensively as she opened the door wider. She seemed depressed. It was just weeks before her wedding day, supposedly the happiest time of her life, and yet here she was moping miserably and looking dreadful.
"We wanted to catch you before work," Megan said cheerfully.
"I'm not going to work today, I don't feel well," Karen announced matter- of-factly as she closed the front door. She guided them into the lounge and politely offered them a beverage.

"Why don't I make the tea? You guys need to talk," Megan suggested, excusing herself to the kitchen. Karen insisted she and Joshua be seated, crossed her legs and placed her hands on her knees.
"What is it that we need to discuss then Joshy?" Her tone of voice was patronising, but not motherly or caring, not at all the way he'd remembered it. She'd lost her sparkle. It was as though her entire personality had disappeared and something had come along and sucked all the life out of her. It didn't take a genius to realise who was responsible.
"I think you know what we need to talk about," Joshua replied. He wasn't giving an inch. Karen stood and began to pace the room, tapping the fingers of one hand against the fingers of her other.
"We don't need to debate whether or not you should come to the wedding. We both want you there, but it's your decision to make. Either turn up or don't. It's up to you," Karen said coldly. She was purposely avoiding eye contact with Joshua as she spoke.
"Please sit down, you're making me nervous," Joshua begged. Karen hesitated, and then returned to her seat. "The bruise looks even worse today," Joshua pointed out tactlessly.
"Thanks, you're a real charmer," Karen joked dryly. Joshua made no attempt to smile.
"He's a bastard, pure and simple. My father is a horrible, sorry excuse for a human being," Joshua said seriously.
"Come on lovey, that's a bit much," Karen attempted to reduce the seriousness of the discussion.
"It's true," Joshua insisted. "He doesn't appreciate anything or anyone. I hate him." Karen glared at Joshua. She couldn't find any words inside herself to defend Neil. She knew deep down that he didn't deserve any defence. She made one final attempt to convince Joshua that the black eye was the result of an accident, this fell upon stony ground. "Did you bump into his fist?" Joshua asked sarcastically. Karen stood again, turned away and folded her arms.
"Please Joshua, don't meddle. Just leave us be. I love you father, and he loves me ….. In his own way. He just has a lot of stress in his life at the moment…." Karen said weakly. Joshua stood.
"So that's been his excuse for twenty years has it?" Karen remained silent. "Look at me!" Joshua demanded. He grabbed her by the arms and glared directly into her eyes.
"Mum made those sorts of excuses for thirteen years. I'd forgotten how bad it was. I'd repressed so much, so many memories. It wasn't until yesterday when I saw your face that it all came flooding back. For

thirteen years he made excuses; stress, alcohol, you name it….I used to hear the screams from downstairs when I was in bed….Shouting and screaming." Joshua paused to wipe away the tears that were streaming down his face. Karen was glaring at him sympathetically, unsure of what to say.
"You…You don't have to go on," she stuttered.
"It's the only way I can think of to make you see what he's like!" She began to turn away sheepishly. Joshua grabbed her arms, again forcing her to face him. "You're going to hear me out damn it!" Karen took a step backwards. She looked afraid. "Oh my god, has he made you that nervous? I'm not going to hit you Karen; he's made you a nervous wreck!"
"I'm sorry," Karen apologised.
"Listen to me Karen, you have to hear this." Joshua's past was coming back to him as he spoke. The memories were painful, but he knew he had to share them for Karen's sake. "I remember every Monday night, dad used to go out with his work-mates. He'd come home completely pissed and lay into mum. She always had an injury of some sort on a Tuesday. I just came to expect it. I used to lay in bed watching my science fiction films on high volume to drown out the noise. It was escapism I suppose. I was off in a fantasy world, not in the room next to my mother who was having the crap beaten out of her by the man who called himself my father. But in the morning I always had to face reality again." Karen wiped the tears from Joshua's cheek. It was obvious to her that he was being brutally honest. Megan was standing by the door eavesdropping. "I remember when it all went quiet; sometimes I'd go and listen in to their conversation. Mum would always be crying. Usually dad would be sorry. He'd blame something and say it'd never happen again and that he loved her, but it always would, it never ended." Karen's facial expression implied that the scene being described was familiar to her. "Until, of course mum died… It was his fault you know. He's the reason she was in such a state that day. He's the reason she couldn't concentrate on the road. He killed my mother. Don't allow him to do the same to you Karen, please." Karen was speechless. What could she say in reply to a statement like that? Joshua was asking her to do the most difficult thing she'd ever contemplated. All of her life she'd waited to find Mr Right, and now this nineteen year old boy was asking her to give him up. He was asking her to give up her life. It was difficult for Karen to come to terms with, but deep down she knew that Joshua was right. She'd been lured into a false sense of security by Neil, but recently the reality had set in. Neil wasn't the wonderful man that Karen had fooled herself into believing he was and there was no future for them, at least not a happy one. What

Karen knew deep down however and what she was willing to face were not necessarily the same.
“You don’t know how long I’ve waited for love,” she uttered, her tone of voice was like that of a disappointed child, her eyes begged for Joshua to wave a magic wand and make everything ok, but he couldn’t and she knew that. “You’re asking me to give up my life,” she whimpered.
“I’m asking you to save yourself,” Joshua said firmly. Megan entered the room carrying a tray of hot drinks.
“Is everything ok?”
“I think Karen sees my point,” Joshua replied.
“Shall we all sit down and have a cup of tea?” Megan suggested, passing around the drinks. They seated themselves. A silence loomed for a moment until Joshua made a suggestion,
“If we all mucked in we could get your things packed, we’ve got all day. You could be gone forever by the time dad gets home.” Karen appeared astounded by this remark. Thinking about leaving Neil and starting a new life was one thing, but going upstairs and packing suitcases now was quite another.
“I can’t Joshua; I have to think about this. My house is being rented out now. I can’t just throw the tenants out. Besides I’ve got plants to water….” The excuses poured out.
“You can stay with us for a while,” Megan offered, eliminating her main excuse. Karen stood abruptly. Her tea spilled all over the floor.
“Stop badgering me like this!” she yelled and then calmly added,
“You’ve said your piece and I appreciate it, but now respect my right to choose.” Karen clearly couldn’t take any more torment. Joshua stood and Megan followed his lead. “I need to think about it,” Karen said weakly. Joshua held her hand and gently replied,
“Ok but please think very carefully and make the right decision. I’d hate for you to end up with the kind of miserable life that my mother was subjected to.” Karen held Joshua tightly.
“Thank you for caring,” she whispered in his ear. Megan saw this as her cue to exit and took the used cups to the kitchen. Karen held on to Joshua firmly for several minutes. Joshua allowed this; he could sense that she’d been starved of genuine affection.
“I’m lucky, I have a new family now with Janice and Megan. It will happen for you too,” Joshua assured her as he loosened his grip. Karen nodded as she wiped the tears from her eyes. Megan returned and they headed for the front door.
“Thank you,” Karen said. They turned to face her. “For caring I mean…” Karen continued, repeating her earlier statement. Joshua smiled and

departed with Megan.
"What do you think?" Megan asked as they walked up the driveway.
"I don't know. I just hope she sees sense and takes our advice. Otherwise I dread to think what the future holds for her," Joshua replied with sincere concern in his eyes.

"I knew he was a bastard, but I didn't realise he was that bad!" Michael declared while sipping on his margarita. 'Dream' was quiet that night, so the boys had decided to remain downstairs drinking and chatting.
"Are you sure you're ok hun'?" Stuart asked.
"Yeh, I'll be fine, it's just been a stressful couple of days," Joshua replied, putting on a brave face.
"I know what's going to cheer you up anyway…." Stuart teased. Joshua looked intrigued. "Your surprise for our first anniversary," Stuart announced. Joshua smiled.
"I still haven't arranged yours," he uttered worriedly. "Don't worry. Just having you is all the gift I need," Stuart said. Joshua could sense his sincerity and the knowledge of being loved filled him with a warm sense of security. In spite of Stuart's attitude, Joshua had every intention of surprising him with something special.
"So have you guys seen that new film with Johnny Depp in?" Michael asked, desperate to change the subject.
"No," they each replied in turn, both seeming disinterested in Michael's new topic of conversation.
"Come on then, what have you planned?" Joshua was intrigued.
"You'll have to wait," Stuart teased. Stuart kissed Joshua, this led to a marathon tonguing session with nothing for Michael to do but watch. This was not helping in his attempts to conceal his envy. Deep down Michael wanted what Stuart and Joshua had. Although his actions suggested that he was just out for a good time, he longed to be loved and still harboured feelings for Joshua. His fondness for Joshua had been developing ever since they'd shared secrets with each other the day he'd approached him in the changing rooms at school. Stuart raised his head for air and noticed Michael's stern facial expression as he sipped his margarita. "Sorry," Stuart muttered. Joshua latched on to the situation and apologised as well. Michael gave a false smile and excused himself by complaining of tiredness.
"Ooops," Joshua giggled, and the passion resumed.
"Do you think we'll still be as horny as this next year?" Stuart asked in jest. Joshua began to frown, somehow he wasn't in the mood. "Why so glum hun'?" Stuart asked.

“I was just thinking about Karen,” Joshua replied sadly. “I feel almost guilty for being here, laughing and enjoying myself with you whilst she could be over there getting the thrashing of a lifetime.”
“Hey, you did all you could, and I’m so proud of you,” Stuart reassured him, “You’ve no need to feel guilty. You’ve had your share of that bastard’s torture.” Stuart was becoming fired up at the thought of the emotional pain Neil had inflicted on this man he doted on. Joshua smiled contently, feeling safe in the knowledge that Stuart cared so deeply for him. Joshua was in love for the first time. He had given Stuart his body and his soul and trusted him completely with them. “I love you,” Stuart reminded him. Joshua couldn’t help but grin when he heard those words, regardless of what sort of mood he was in or his frame of mind. Stuart could sense that Joshua was anxious to get home and offered to escort him.

Upon their arrival at Janice’s house, Joshua invited Stuart in to greet everyone. When they opened the door, they almost tripped over the variety of suitcases and carrier bags in the hallway.
“We’re in here,” came Megan’s voice from the living room. They stepped over the suitcases and entered the living room. Megan, Greg and Janice were all seated around an emotional Karen.
“I had nowhere else to go,” she murmured as she wiped a tear from her eye. Joshua smiled in a way the others had never witnessed before. It was beaming. The weight of the world had just been lifted from his shoulders. He’d been so concerned for Karen’s safety, and now he could relax, safe in the knowledge that his father couldn’t harm her the way he’d harmed his mother. He opened his arms out, inviting Karen to embrace him. She stood, directly facing him and managed a smile herself. It was infectious. She approached him slowly and he held her in his arms. “Thank you Joshua. You truly are a wonderful person,” Karen complimented him, sniffling between her words. “He sure is,” Janice motioned, bursting with pride for the young man she now considered one of her own.
“The bastard ought to be shot for what he put you and your mother through,” Greg said, exhibiting an aggressive streak he’d never revealed before.
“You must be tired,” Janice said lovingly. Karen released herself from Joshua’s grasp and nodded.
“I’ll show you to the spare room,” Joshua said.

“She’ll be ok, she was out like a light,” Joshua said to Megan as he closed the door of the spare room. She had followed him up the stairs and awaited an opportunity to talk to him alone. “Looks like my little pet talk worked,” Joshua bragged playfully. He felt both a sense of pride and relief to have separated Karen from his father. Megan was eager to make

a point whilst she had Joshua alone.
“Listen a minute….” She pleaded.
“What’s up hun’?” Joshua asked, sensing some concern.
“When Karen arrived, I told them all about the memories you’d repressed from your childhood and about how your dad was treating Karen…” Megan began, rushing to get her point across. Joshua had a glazed look on his face which itself said, “What on earth are you getting at you silly bitch?”
“And…?” Joshua asked.
“Greg got really angry. He was furious, positively fierce!” Megan went on, she sounded as though she’d just looked up the word ‘Anger’ in a thesaurus and found as many ways she possibly could to express it.
“I get the point,” Joshua said sarcastically, not quite grasping the severity of Megan’s news.
“Joshua, he was so angry he could have punched someone. My god, if Greg and your dad ever came face to face…”
“He was that angry?” Joshua asked. Although they’d now been close friends for over a year, he couldn’t help but feel that Greg’s reaction was over the top. There was something worrying about Greg’s protectiveness over him. Megan had obviously been thinking along the same lines to bring it to his attention. “We’d better get downstairs or they’ll wonder where we are,” he said, leaving the conversation unfinished. They headed back to the living room where Greg and Janice were still seated. “It’ll only be until she gets rid of her tenants,” Joshua assured them.
“It’s ok darling, I’m happy to help,” Janice replied in her usual caring manner.
“Anything to keep her away from that bastard is fine with me!” Greg added angrily. Joshua glanced at Megan as her point was being proven. He could now sense Greg’s fury and realised that Megan hadn’t been exaggerating the severity of his rage.
“Calm down babe,” Janice said whilst patting Greg’s shoulder. She was obviously concerned.
“When I think about the treatment you’ve endured from that man…..Oh it makes my blood boil!” he exclaimed, his hands flying up into the air. Everyone in the room was pondering what the reason could be behind Neil’s exasperation. Of course, nobody with any human decency would condone Neil’s behaviour, but Greg appeared to be over-reacting to the situation considering that it didn’t concern him to any great extent. He had been Joshua’s doctor, now his friend and role model, but never close enough to be this upset by events in his life. They each jumped to similar conclusions as to the reason for Greg’s reaction. They assumed that either he was relating this to past experience in his life or to others he’d dealt

with in his career. Megan, Janice and Joshua were indeed all far too polite to ask. "People like Neil just make me want to be physically sick!" Greg continued. His raving was interrupted by a loud banging on the front door.
"Who the hell can that be at this time?" Janice grumbled as she headed for the hallway.

The banging continued and Janice's voice could be heard from the living room saying "I'm coming, I'm coming!"
"Well done son, for talking Karen out of that house. I'm proud of you," Greg complimented Joshua, now beginning to act more calmly.
"Yeh, he's a hero," Megan joined in, rubbing Joshua's arm affectionately.
"Where is she?" Neil's voice could be heard bellowing from the hallway.
"Oh god, Dad's here!" exclaimed Joshua, with genuine fear in his eyes.
Greg's temper was about to flare up again as he stormed out of the room.
"Come on, he'll kill him!" Megan yelled to Joshua, and they chased after him.

In the hallway, Janice was bravely attempting to hold back a screaming Neil when Greg charged through, out for blood and closely followed by Megan and Joshua.
"Just tell me where my fuckin' woman is!" Neil demanded, referring to Karen as though she were a possession that had been stolen.
"Leave now Neil or so help me I'll.........." Greg threatened, barging Janice out of the way to reach Neil.
"You'll what?" Neil enquired angrily.
"Stop it Greg, he's not worth it!" Janice yelled.
"I'm not leaving here without Karen," Neil insisted, his face red with rage. "It's not enough for you people to take my son is it? Now you want to take my fiancé too!" Neil exclaimed in a desperate attempt to appear the victim of the situation.
"You lost your son because you're a bad parent, pure and simple. And now you've lost Karen because she sees you for what you really are," Greg announced, now beginning to calm down again. Joshua grabbed Greg's arm from behind.
"This is between my father and me, let me handle it." Joshua's eyes were calm and trustworthy. Greg could sense that he had the maturity to fight his own battles and this filled him with pride.
"Are you sure?" Janice asked. Joshua nodded.
"You lay one finger on him....." Greg muttered and was reluctantly escorted back to the living room by Megan and Janice. The time had finally come. Neil and Joshua were alone at last. This confrontation had been overdue for years. It wasn't only about Karen, it was about

everything, his sexuality, the way Neil had treated Lynne, the years of shabby parenting and now the abuse of yet another person he'd grown close to.

Joshua was trembling with fear as this pathetic excuse for a man he called a father stood before him. He was expecting more yelling, but it didn't come. Instead all he could see was fear in Neil's eyes. Perhaps it was fear of loneliness.

"She's all I've got Joshua. Please don't take her away from me," he pleaded. He was like a child. It would have been the easiest thing in the world to feel sympathy for this man. He was weak, even though he was violent, at the same time he was weak and pitiful.

"You should have thought of that before you beat her," Joshua replied coldly, remaining strong and unemotional.

"I didn't mean to do it, I swear I didn't," Neil murmured feebly.

"Just like you didn't mean to do it to mum?" Joshua asked sharply. Neil didn't react. How could he possibly respond? For all of these years they'd never discussed the beatings Lynne had suffered, and Neil had assumed that Joshua was unaware of them. "You're pathetic, look at you. Pa-the-tic," Joshua announced.

"Hey, I'm still your father!" Neil reminded him, trying his hardest to scrape together any remains of his manhood he possibly could.

"He's right, you are pathetic," came Karen's voice from the head of the staircase.

"Karen, please….. We can work this out. I swear we can," Neil begged, turning his attention to Karen. Karen slowly worked her way down the stairs. She had no fear, and Neil could sense this. "Come on home," he pleaded. Karen glared at him in disgust. "Not if you were the last man on earth," she replied confidently. Neil's facial expression almost demanded sympathy, but Joshua and Karen had passed the point of feeling any kind of tenderness for him. Having eavesdropped into the entire conversation, Greg now returned from the living room. Neil was now emotionally drained, his anger had become sorrow. He didn't have the energy to flare up again, no matter what Greg was to say. Besides, what Joshua and Greg were saying was the cold harsh truth, and Neil knew it.

"Yesterday you loved me. How does that change so quickly?" Neil asked Karen.

"How can she love someone who abuses her?" Greg butted in.

"It's ok Greg," Karen assured him. She had suddenly gained such an independent nature, simply by making the decision to leave this bully. "I was in love with the person I deluded myself into thinking you were. But I could never love the despicable excuse for a man that you are," Karen announced boldly. A tear trickled down Neil's face. Joshua hadn't seen

his father cry in such a long time, not even during the period of time surrounding his mother's death. The only emotion he'd ever observed from Neil was anger, but here he was, his world falling apart, and he was sobbing before his estranged son, fiancé and the man who was shaping up to be an enemy.
"I think you should go, crocodile tears won't help you now," Greg insisted. Karen and Joshua could sense that Neil's tears were genuine, however this display of remorse was too little too late. Neil glanced at Karen who stared him directly in the eyes, coldly. He then faced Joshua who turned away. He wasn't going to allow his emotions to cloud his judgement.
"I love you both. I know you don't believe me, but I do," Neil muttered feebly. He opened the door and took a step outside. He turned to face them once more, but before he had a chance to state another word of manipulation Greg had slammed the door in his face. Neil's life was over, and he knew it. Karen was afraid, she had to pick up the pieces of her life and move on, but she knew it was for the best.
"I have no father," Joshua said with contempt in his voice. He was deadly serious. Greg placed his arm around him and comforted him, "You have us, and we're your family now." Janice and Megan returned to the hallway smiling. They'd obviously overheard everything that had transpired. Joshua believed Greg, it was true, this did now seem like a family unit to him. It was a little unorthodox, his former doctor, his former girlfriend whom he'd dated before realising he was homosexual and her mother, but the combination worked and there was great love and mutual admiration and respect within the household. With Neil now out of his life, all that remained for Joshua to focus his attention on was wondering what plans Stuart had for their one year anniversary celebrations.

"Oh my god! That's the one! It's fab'!" exclaimed Joshua, thrilled by the sight of a silver bracelet he was sure would suit Stuart's wrist.
"It's a bit expensive," Michael pointed out, but Joshua wasn't interested in the price, he was in love and didn't care about the cost. The sales assistant could sense the sale was imminent and was very obliging when Joshua requested the cabinet be opened for him to give the bracelet a closer inspection.
"He's gonna' love it," Joshua said giddily. Michael was attempting to appear vaguely interested but failed to convince. Joshua put his attitude down to jealousy.
"Do you do inscriptions?"

"Yes," the sales assistant eagerly replied. "In fact there's a special offer at the moment, buy the bracelet and the inscription is free of charge." He was obviously commission driven.
"Ok I'll take it then," Joshua instantly decided. Michael pulled him away for a quiet word whilst the sales assistant locked the cupboard.
"I really don't think you should spend all this money." Joshua ignored Michael's opinion and approached the sales assistant with his ideas for the inscription.
"Ok, I want it to say….." He paused and pondered for a moment, then decided, "Dear Stuart, thank you for a wonderful year. My love always, Joshua." The assistant didn't even flinch at the discovery that this gift was being given to one male from another. He was either very open minded or just couldn't care less as long as his sale was made. This was slightly disappointing for Joshua as he was by this time finding reactions to these situations somewhat amusing. Michael was obviously uncomfortable, although Joshua was unable to grasp as to why. His attention however was far more focussed on the task at hand. "He's gonna' love it!" he shrieked ecstatically. Michael gave a false smile and claimed to agree.

"Well I hope that Greg makes this much effort for me!" Janice screamed with glee, "It's gorgeous!" Finally, he was receiving some genuinely positive feedback. Joshua now felt far more confident to unveil the gift to Stuart.
"You really like it?" he asked, desperate for reassurance.
"Hell yes! And if he doesn't appreciate it then bin him!" Janice joked as she passed the bracelet back to Joshua and began tying her hair back in front of the mirror. "Can't wait to see what he has for you!" It was just two days now until Stuart and Joshua would celebrate one year as partners and Joshua felt a great sense of achievement, after all, in the gay world a two week long relationship can seem like a lifetime and even getting as far as a second date can seem a commitment. Janice's usual supportive nature was exactly what Joshua needed, having tolerated Michael's negative attitude in the earlier part of the day. Although Michael was a very important friend of Joshua's, he couldn't help but become annoyed by his jealous nature and the streak he had inside him that didn't wish others well if his life wasn't going exactly as he'd like. Joshua's mobile phone rang. "Speak of the devil," Janice commented, correctly predicting the caller's identity as she applied her eyeliner. Joshua dashed to his room to answer the call.
"Hiya babe…" came Stuart's sweet voice from the other end of the line. Even after a year, Joshua still became excited by Stuart's calls and even slightly nervous. "Just two days," he continued. Joshua was bursting with

anticipation over what was planned for the big day, but Stuart remained tight-lipped. It seemed he hadn't breathed a word to anyone else either, so badgering their friends would be pointless.
"Please give me a hint," Joshua begged.
"Wait and see," Stuart insisted.
"Fine!" Joshua said in a vague attempt to sound annoyed.
"You'll find out on Saturday," Stuart teased. "Come over to my flat at three o'clock."
"Maybe I will……" Joshua tormented.
"Ok don't then….." Stuart laughed.
"No….no, I'll come," Joshua screeched in a panic. Stuart was in hysterics on the other end of the phone line.
"I love you," he announced seriously.
"I love you too," Joshua replied.

Joshua awoke early that Saturday morning. He wanted to look absolutely perfect in case Stuart was planning to take him to a swanky restaurant or an up-market bar that night. Even after a year he was still making an effort with his attire for Stuart, a trait he'd originally learned from Michael.
"Its ten o'clock, you're not meeting him until three," came Megan's voice from outside the bathroom. Her Irish accent was so cute when she was slightly annoyed.
"I need to look perfect," Joshua laughed as he applied his moisturisers.
"Shout me when you're done," Megan grunted. She was about to walk away when the door swung open.
"I'm done!" Joshua declared. He was five hours early and would now have to be careful not to ruffle his hair or crease his outfit, but better early than late.
"How do I look?"
"Amazing Joshua, I've never seen you look better," Megan replied honestly. He knew that Megan could always be relied upon to tell him the truth, far more so than Stuart. If he wore an outfit that didn't look right, Megan would be the first to verbalise her thoughts. At least that way he was getting an honest response, and if he did on this occasion, he could be confident of his appearance.
"Thanks Megan!" exclaimed Joshua, throwing his arms around her. Megan was genuinely happy for Joshua, but he hadn't stopped to consider for a moment that this wasn't easy for her. After all, it was still only just over a year since she had lost him as her boyfriend and she was still yet to move on with her life. Joshua however had become a completely different person in a very short space of time. While she encouraged him and helped him as best she could, she still had a very strong longing deep

down inside. She wouldn't admit it at this stage, not even to herself, but if Joshua was to suddenly announce he wasn't gay and wanted Megan back, she'd throw her arms around him and never let go.

At twelve thirty, Joshua banged loudly on the door of the student house at which Stuart resided. Ok, yes he was two and a half hours early, but he just simply couldn't wait any longer. The anticipation of his surprise gift from Stuart was too much for him to take. He knew that this was breaking every rule of the dating game but he thought 'bollocks to it', after a year the games are over and if they aren't then the relationship might as well be.

"It'll be for you Becky. I'm not expecting anyone!" Scott yelled from upstairs. Becky's voice could be heard from the kitchen,

"Ok, Ok. I'll get it.......Becky do this, Becky do that..." she sighed. The door opened abruptly and Becky took one look at Joshua, then left the door wide open and headed back to the kitchen.

"Don't know if he's up yet," she muttered. 'He must be' Joshua thought, 'surely he's preparing whatever he has planned for us.' "Go on up though," she continued in her disinterested tone. Joshua closed the front door behind him, not that Becky would have noticed if he hadn't done so.

"Has he said anything about my surprise?" She turned and looked at Joshua as though he'd just spoken in a foreign language she didn't understand and was awaiting a translation. "It's our one year anniversary today, I wondered if Stuart had mentioned what he had planned for me."

"Why would he tell me?" Becky asked matter-of-factly, "I don't see him from one day to the next." She plugged in the kettle and switched it on, then began rubbing her eyes. "Too much fuckin' vodka last night I think," she laughed. Was Becky actually making conversation? In an entire year this was the most substantial discussion the two of them had shared.

"Want a cuppa'?" she asked. Realising that he was far too early and that Stuart would almost certainly not be ready, Joshua decided to accept the drink and parked himself on the seat beside her. He was on a roll, now making progress with the ignorant students, or one of them at least. Becky prepared two cups of tea and then lit a cigarette.

"So it's been a year then has it?" she asked. Joshua nodded proudly. "I don't know Stuart THAT well. We keep ourselves to ourselves in this house," Becky went on. 'No kidding,' Joshua thought. "He seems a good guy though, shame he's gay. Bet he's a good shag!" This topic of conversation was making Joshua uncomfortable and his face was becoming red as a beetroot. "Relax, I'm just messing with you," she redeemed herself, slapping Joshua's arm as she slurred her words. "It surprises me that a couple of gay guys your age have stayed together. Do you sleep around as well then?" she asked ever so casually, just as though

she was asking whether or not he shopped at Tesco. Joshua however was horrified by the suggestion.
"Certainly not!" he insisted.
"Alright, don't get your knickers in a knot," Becky went on as she puffed away on her cigarette. It was obvious to Joshua that diplomacy was not this girl's strong point. In short, she was common as horse manure and didn't know the meaning of the word tact let alone practise it. "It's just that all the gay men I know in your age group like to sleep around."
"Good for them," Joshua muttered sarcastically as he sipped his tea.
"You're cute," Becky laughed.
"We love each other," Joshua said assertively.
"Bless," Becky teased, and then pinched Joshua's cheek. He couldn't recall ever feeling this patronised in his life.
"Look, you might be a slut but Stuart and I only have eyes for each other!" Joshua was now tiring of the topic of conversation. Becky had touched a nerve. Joshua was aware that a lot of young gay men are indeed very promiscuous and considered himself to be fortunate to be in a committed relationship. Becky's line of questioning was touching on his insecurities, which he preferred not to discuss, particularly with strangers. He was relieved to finish his tea as this meant he could politely excuse himself from Becky's company.

It was now one o'clock. Joshua was trotting up the stairs towards Stuart's room. He wondered if he should knock on the door or enter unannounced and surprise him. If Becky had been correct and Stuart was still in bed, he planned to quietly enter and join him as he'd done several times before. He took the plunge and opened the door, wondering what would be awaiting him on the other side, jewellery, a surprise party or maybe he'd be going on a trip. It seemed that Becky had been correct as the room was completely still. The only sound that could be heard was Stuart's light snoring.
"Lazy sod," Joshua said to himself and began to approach the bed. 'He must have been up very late studying last night,' Joshua thought. He gazed at his beloved as he slept peacefully. He contemplated whether or not waking him was a good idea and decided to proceed. He lifted the covers of the bed from the bottom with the intention of tickling Stuart's feet. At this point he made a horrifying discovery; there were two pairs of feet at the end of the bed. He placed the covers back down and stood in a state of shock. There were two men in the bed. Was this to be his surprise? On the first anniversary of their relationship, Joshua was to discover that Stuart was a cheating rat. The other man in the bed was entirely concealed by the duvet. Joshua contemplated whether or not to

pull it off and reveal his identity, but before he had a chance to make the decision Stuart's alarm clock sounded. He began to stir. Joshua was standing, staring at him. He didn't know how to react to the situation. Stuart's eyes opened and he became aware of Joshua's presence. The situation dawned on him and he sat up on the bed. The mystery man was still yet to stir.
"Joshua, I can explain," Stuart pleaded. They stared at each other silently. A tear finally reached the surface of Joshua's eye. He slowly wiped it away. No way was Stuart going to enjoy the satisfaction of observing Joshua's tears.
"How could you?" Joshua asked eventually. Stuart continued to glare at him from the bed. He couldn't find the appropriate words to say except, "I'm sorry Joshua." Joshua was furious, and yet at the same time he was calm, his is rage still yet to reach the surface.
"Don't sorry me you bastard," he said as he struggled to hold back his tears. He didn't know what to do, so he walked away. He closed the door behind him and walked down the stairs. He walked slowly, feeling disoriented by the situation, he simply didn't know what to do with himself. Becky was standing in the hallway reading a text message on her mobile phone.
"Couldn't you get him up?" she asked casually, and then noticed he was crying. "What's up?" she asked, almost sounding as though she actually cared. Joshua was in no mood to confide in this girl that he'd struggled to tolerate for as long as he'd known her. Normally he'd head for Stuart's room without even acknowledging the other students if at all possible.
"Nothing, I'm fine," Joshua answered her coldly, continuing his journey down the stairs.
"Fair enough," she said, sounding slightly annoyed. Joshua wasn't paying full attention to the gangway as he approached the door and almost tripped over a pair of trainers. He kicked them out of the way and glanced at them as he did so. They were red 'Nike Air Max' trainers. He instantly recognised them.
"Whose trainers are they?" he asked.
"God knows, don't think they're Stuart or Scott's," Becky replied, now once again engrossed in her text message. Joshua inspected them more closely and said to himself,
"Please god no…" He dashed back up the stairs where he ran into Stuart who was heading downwards. He'd thrown some clothes on and had intended to chase after Joshua. Joshua glared at Stuart for a moment, then ran past him up the stairs.
"Joshua…No!" Stuart yelled and chased after him. Joshua re-entered Stuart's room and approached the bed once again.

"Joshua, wait…" Stuart said from the doorway. Joshua had a suspicion of who was under the duvet. He had seen those trainers so many times before. "Joshua, let's go downstairs and talk about this," Stuart suggested, attempting to prevent Joshua from removing the bedclothes and revealing the mystery man.
"Fuck off Stuart. I've got a right to know!" Joshua yelled. His fury had now surfaced. "Please let me be wrong," he prayed. He pulled the duvet down just far enough to reveal the identity of the man lying in the bed. Incidentally this man had remained asleep and unaware of what was happening. "Just as I suspected," Joshua muttered and hurried for the door. Stuart grabbed his shoulder.
"Please, don't let's leave things this way," he begged.
"Don't touch me!" Joshua yelled as he turned to face Stuart and pushed his hand away. Joshua ran wildly down the stairs and out of the house as fast as he possibly could.
"Damn it!" Stuart yelled, slamming his fist against the wall.

Betrayal was something Joshua had been accustomed to in his past, and developing a trust with Stuart had not been easy. He had however managed it, but now here he was again, right back at square one. He felt violated, used and above all foolish. For so long he'd believed that he and Stuart were exclusive, he'd believed that they were in love. Now he realised it had been an illusion. He wondered how many men Stuart had betrayed him with, and how many times his sexual health had been put at risk as a result of Stuart's infidelity and selfishness. As he wandered aimlessly through the streets of Sheffield he attempted to analyze where he'd gone wrong and why Stuart had done this to him. He had wanted to have his cake and eat it. He'd always seemed proud of the relationship that he and Joshua shared and had always insisted that he wanted exclusivity.

Megan answered the door to a panicked Stuart.
"Is he here?" Stuart asked. Megan glared at Stuart as if to ask, "What the hell are you talking about?" "Is Joshua here?" Stuart asked again.
"No he isn't. Is something wrong?" Megan asked.
"No," Stuart lied.
"Come in," Megan suggested adamantly, "I want to know what's going on."

"You bastard!" Megan screeched, having just heard the entire story from Stuart. "How could you do that to him?" she asked. "He loves you!"
"And I love him," Stuart dived to his own defence. Megan gave a look of disbelief. "Have you any idea where he may have gone?" Stuart asked.
"No," Megan lied. She knew exactly where Joshua would be. He would

be where he always was when he was distraught over an event and needed time to think things over. However, she felt Stuart didn't deserve the information of his whereabouts.
"If he comes home, call me…..please," Stuart requested. He looked desperate, but Megan wasn't feeling any sympathy for him.
"I'll do as Joshua wishes," Megan replied bluntly. Stuart sheepishly departed and Megan immediately set off to track down her friend.

Legs in, legs out, legs in, legs out, "Higher mummy higher," those were the words Joshua would scream when his mother pushed him on the swings. The park was such a special place for Joshua, it held so many memories. He felt closer to Lynne by being there because of the many times she'd taken him during his childhood. It also brought back so many fond memories of visits to the park after school for he and Megan during their teenage years. Today he wasn't swinging high, just seated on an old tyre swing and gathering his thoughts together, mulling over the events of the day and the last year. He wondered just how much of his relationship with Stuart had in fact been real.
"You feel like some company?" Megan's voice came from behind him. He glanced over at her, then patted the tyre beside his. She seated herself and said, "I talked to Stuart, he told me everything."
"How could they?" Joshua asked.
"I don't know Joshua, I really can't understand them."
"I thought he loved me…" Joshua began, his words clouded by his sniffling, "...And I thought Michael was my friend."
"Well it didn't take a genius to see that Michael was jealous of your relationship but I never thought he'd stoop so low," Megan said, now becoming wound up herself. Joshua could sense her frustration and smiled at her.
"You've always been there for me," he pointed out.
"What's a best friend for?" she asked, returning the smile. "Oh god!" Megan exclaimed as she noticed Stuart approaching them. "I'll get rid of him," she said as she stood.
"No, I'll talk to him, I've got plenty to say," Joshua said, standing assertively.
"I followed you Megan, I'm sorry I had to do that," Stuart apologised. His maturity shone through, although it was too little too late for Megan.
"Very well Stuart, let's go for a walk shall we?" Joshua suggested, then added sarcastically, "You can give me your wonderful explanation as to how you and Michael ended up in bed together." Megan remained seated on her swing as Joshua and Stuart wandered across the park. "I just don't understand," Joshua said, "I thought everything was great. I thought we were in love."

"We are Joshua, we are," Stuart promised, "It was just sex with Michael, that's all." Joshua was amazed by Stuart's casual attitude towards sex.
"Well I'm sorry if I take things more seriously than that…" Joshua began.
"It honestly meant nothing," Stuart interrupted. He didn't seem to be truly able to comprehend the reason Joshua was hurt.
"I wanted all of you Stuart," Joshua said as he pulled the gift he'd intended to give to Stuart for their anniversary from his pocket. He passed it to Stuart. They stopped walking. "Read it," Joshua demanded.
"Thank you for a wonderful year. My love always…." Stuart read aloud. Stuart reached into his satchel and pulled out two plane tickets. He passed them to Joshua who read them, "Paris."
"We can still go," Stuart said, "I do love you."
"I love you too Stuart………More fool me," Joshua said negatively as he passed back the plane tickets. "I'll never understand you. You became so jealous of anyone who ever came close to me and yet all the time you were sleeping with one of my best friends," Joshua said. His eyes were filled with disappointment. Stuart could feel him slipping slowly away from him.
"I do love you," Stuart persisted.
"I believe you," Joshua replied honestly, "That's what's so sad about this. We could have had it all Stuart." Stuart's eyes became watery.
"Please Joshua, I won't let it happen again, I swear," he pleaded.
"It's no good Stuart. I can never trust you again. You want to have your cake and eat it and Michael can't stand anyone having anything that he doesn't. You're not the sort of people I want in my life," Joshua said calmly. He was suddenly seeing everything so clearly. "Just look at her," he said, pointing to Megan, "She'd do anything for me. I probably don't even deserve her, but I'd never want to lose her from my life. As for you and Michael, I never want to see you again. You're both dead to me." Stuart could sense that Joshua was deadly serious. He'd never heard him speak so solemnly before. He didn't know how to react. Begging clearly wasn't going to help. Joshua wanted him and Michael out of his life and they had no choice but to respect his wishes. As they stood in the middle of the park, Stuart knew he'd made the biggest mistake of his life, and it was too late to redeem himself. "Thank you Stuart," Joshua said seriously. Stuart was puzzled by this statement for a moment, until Joshua elaborated, "You've taught me not to give my heart so easily. I'll be more careful next time." Stuart couldn't help but feel guilt and sorrow, but Joshua had made it clear that this was the end of the line and now they'd both have to move on with their lives separately. "Goodbye Stuart, and good luck," Joshua said sincerely. He returned to Megan who was now standing beside the swings. Stuart watched as Megan held him in her

arms for a moment and they walked away holding hands. Out of his life they went. He gazed at the bracelet he still held in his hand. “My love always…” he reread it over and over. He realised he’d just lost the best thing in his life and at the same time that he didn’t deserve it to begin with.

Chapter 8

"You wash, I'll dry," Joshua cheekily suggested as he and Janice approached the dreaded dishes in the sink.

"Go on then." Janice rolled her eyes as if to acknowledge that Joshua had once again used his charm to wrap her around his little finger. Although they claimed to hate it, Joshua and Janice would often use washing the pots as an excuse for a 'mothers meeting'. They'd gossip about the events of the day in various people's lives, 'who got off with who at what bar', real girl talk sessions. It had been two years since Joshua had shunned Stuart and Michael from his life and his twenty first birthday now loomed. During this time Karen had returned to her home after disposing of the tenants and Neil hadn't made any attempt to contact her or Joshua. He and Karen would often catch up and boogie together when their paths met at 'Dream'. "Can we talk confidentially for a minute?" Janice asked as she began dipping a dirty plate into the soapy water. Joshua glanced at her, attempting to determine whether or not she was being serious. She clearly was. "It's about Megan," she began.

"O…K," Joshua acknowledged her.

"All she ever does is go to Dream with you. Don't you think it's time she found a boyfriend? It's been three years since you and she….well…you know." Janice was struggling to find the appropriate words, but Joshua could sense what point she was trying to reach. He agreed that Megan should move on with her life and find a new man, but at the same time Joshua himself hadn't dated anyone since Stuart. He had been burned quite severely and as a result had shied away from anything more meaningful than a snog on the dance floor. "I do worry about that girl," Janice continued, "She should be working her way through a queue of men that want to date her. She's such a beautiful girl, and the only guy she's ever dated is…..well….you." Janice was striving to be tactful. Joshua knew where Janice was coming from; he saw her almost as a mother now and Megan was like a sister to him, but perhaps even all these years later Megan still saw Joshua quite differently. "Don't you know any straight guys at uni' that you could set her up with?" Janice asked. Joshua could think of a hundred, and he'd only been at university for a matter of months, but Megan wouldn't willingly go along with a set up and Joshua knew that.

"She will not go on a date I set up for her," he protested. Janice pondered this for a moment; the dish she was wiping was getting an incredibly thorough clean as her mind focussed on her daughter.

"Take her somewhere then that she's likely to meet someone. Take her to a straight club, please Joshua," Janice pleaded. "All she ever does is tag along with you to that Dream place. Take her to a straight night club."

"Ok, ok," Joshua said, raising his hands in defence, "I'll do my best."
"I knew you wouldn't let me down," Janice said as she wrapped her arms around him, covering his expensive jumper with soap suds. Not many people would get away with that, nor the affectionate ruffling of his hair that followed.

"What time are we going to Dream tonight?!" Megan yelled from the bathroom as she applied her eyeliner in front of the mirror. Joshua wandered in, as he was allowed to.
"I thought maybe we'd go somewhere different for a change tonight, maybe to Club Z."
"Club Z?" Megan repeated, looking as puzzled as though he'd just suggested they join a nunnery.
"Well, we always go to Dream, don't you feel like a change?" Joshua asked. Megan was silent for a moment. Perhaps she hadn't admitted it, even to herself, but the reason she enjoyed visiting 'Dream' so often was because it provided a safety net. While ever she was there, she had no worries of being harassed and sleazed on by the males. This of course is the reason many heterosexual females attend gay bars and events, but the majority of those have a husband or boyfriend waiting at home for them. In Megan's case, she was safe and secure and didn't have to face her fears of becoming involved with a new man. "Who knows, you might meet a fella'!" Joshua teased. Megan smiled falsely. She couldn't quite take this at face value. Joshua had enjoyed 'Dream' for so long and now all of a sudden he wanted to go clubbing off the gay scene. She wondered if he had an ulterior motive, then more optimistically pondered the possibility that he was turning straight. The fact that Joshua had been single for so long was just enough to feed the delusion and allow Megan to believe that this was a possibility. "What on earth am I going to wear to a straight club?" came Joshua's voice from the next room. Megan grinned. Perhaps this was something to look forward to after all.

"Hmmm," muttered Joshua as he admired himself in the mirror. He was wearing a blue shirt, black jeans and black shoes. This was vastly different from the usual tight t-shirt, drainpipe jeans and trainers he'd wear on the gay scene. "Well I look straight," he said to himself.
"And very handsome," Janice commented from the doorway. "Thanks for doing this babe," she said as she approached him. Joshua smiled. "She needs a man, don't allow her to leave the club without one," Janice demanded, laughing but at the same time deadly serious. It was obvious that the next morning he'd be in for a grilling whether Megan pulled a man or not. Joshua began playing with his hair, testing out different styles.

"Well you can lead the horse to water….." he began.
"If anyone can make her drink you can," Janice said in jest.
"Hmmm, yeah…vodka maybe," Joshua replied.
"She seems really excited now. I know you'll show her a good time," Janice said and tapped him lovingly on the shoulder as she left the room.
"Perfect!" Joshua said to himself as he completed his exploration of every possible style he could apply to his hair. Megan entered the room. She was wearing a beautiful outfit that only came out of the wardrobe for special occasions. Her top was ruby red and just a little revealing and it complimented her black skirt beautifully. Her hair was curly and free. This was the first time Joshua had seen Megan's hair curled and not tied back in months.
"Will I pass?" she asked, appearing as though she dreaded the answer.
"You look amazing," Joshua replied honestly. Megan's face lit up like a Christmas tree at the sound of this compliment. Joshua, having seen the effort she'd made was beginning to wonder if he'd been selfish in not varying their evenings enough, but Megan's effort was not intended for the single males of 'Club Z', she had her eye on one prize and one prize only, the man she'd always loved. She was however concealing her delusion well. As they headed off out, Joshua had no idea of the type of thoughts that were running through Megan's head and he had every intention of assisting her to meet an attractive young man.

"You got any ID mate?" asked the overweight bouncer who was guarding the entrance to the club, having already allowed Megan and several other attractive females to enter irrespective of their age.
"I'm nearly twenty one," Joshua protested.
"Take it as a compliment darling," the bouncer said sarcastically. Perhaps the outfit wasn't concealing Joshua's homosexuality after all. Joshua gave the bouncer a look of annoyance as he fumbled around for his wallet, hindered by the flurry of teens barging past him. Out came the student card. "There you are, that proves I'm over eighteen," he boasted, now adopting the bouncer's attitude problem. Megan gazed from inside the doorway, attempting a smile.
"We only take passports and drivers licenses," the bouncer lay down the law, still allowing others into the club as they talked.
"Look, I don't drive or travel, this has my photo and bloody date of birth on!" Joshua raised his voice to compete with the sound of the crowd clambering to reach the entrance. The bouncer rudely snatched Joshua's student card from his hand and began judging its authenticity. He then turned to his equally obese colleague to consult him. Joshua had almost forgotten what straight clubs were like. The gay bars he usually attended were far more lenient about proving peoples ages and if there were a

category of being allowed in because the bouncer found you appealing, he'd usually fall into it. Joshua naturally reacted by placing his hands on his hips. A passing twenty-something male gave a brief stare and Joshua glared back, making him turn away. He'd been embarrassed enough and was in no mood to be messed with.
"Alright you can go in, but next time we need a passport or drivers license," the bouncer said as he handed back Joshua's student card. His tone of voice implied that he should be thankful. He immediately turned his head away and dived for the entrance.
"Don't have a bloody passport or drivers licence….wouldn't wanna' come back anyway," he muttered under his breath.
"At last," uttered Megan as she was reunited with Joshua.
"Tossers," he exclaimed. The music from the main room of the club was bellowing through the hallway, 'Holding on to one another's hands, trying to get away into the night and then you put your arms around me….' "At least the tunes are good," Joshua cheered, now perking up. Megan grabbed his hand and they followed the sound of the music.

"We should come here more often," Joshua slurred as he gulped down his seventh alco-pop. "I don't know why we never come, it's great music!" Megan however, wanting to cling on to some degree of sanity had taken it easy with just a pair of Bacardi and cokes.
"I'm enjoying it too," she shouted, her voice competing with the volume of the music. She gazed affectionately at Joshua as he held on to the bar, struggling to stand by himself. She giggled as he stumbled and he joined her in laughter at the situation.
"Come on hun', don't let me be the only drunk one, let's get another round in," Joshua suggested, pulling another ten pound note from his wallet. His attention was distracted by the sight of a blonde twenty-something passing him on his way to the dance floor. The superbly stunning creature joined a mixed sex group of friends dancing to Abba.
"He is hot, you should get in there!" Joshua screeched as though he'd just had the idea of a lifetime.
"Don't be silly, one of those girls is probably his girlfriend," Megan replied, shying away from the situation.
"Doesn't look that way to me," Joshua observed. "Come on, let's go and dance near him!" Giving Megan no choice in the matter, Joshua grabbed her hand and dragged her to the dance floor. He parked them just inches away from the man they'd just been observing and they began to dance.
"You should talk to him!" Joshua yelled in Megan's ear, struggling to overpower Bjorn.
"Joshua, I'm not so sure," Megan protested. The group consisted of three females and two males, none of which appeared to be coupled. One of the

females began to glance at Joshua and Megan regularly, this went on for several minutes. Megan was beginning to feel uncomfortable, but Joshua continued to dance completely oblivious of the attention they were receiving. One of the females from the group tapped Megan on the shoulder. She was somewhat attractive, with strawberry blonde hair, aged in her late teens.

"My friend likes your friend," she commented rather childishly in Megan's ear. Megan was unsure of how to handle this. At last she thought she could sense that Joshua may be open to the idea of a heterosexual relationship and now it seemed she had competition. Megan was mentally panicked; all she wanted to do was get herself and Joshua out of the bar as quickly as possible in order to hold on to her territory.

"He is gay…right? Brad thinks he's really hot," the girl continued in Megan's ear. Megan turned her head to glare at her new alleged friend. Was Joshua's gaydar faulty? Only she could be unfortunate enough to have her gay best friend recommend that she chase a man and then he end up being gay himself and the situation backfiring. 'Perhaps this could be the ultimate test,' Megan pondered. She couldn't keep from Joshua that he had an admirer. She decided that this would be the way in which she'd determine whether or not Joshua was still completely homosexual. The experiment didn't take long. "Oooh, looks like he does like him!" the girl giggled in Megan's ear. Megan turned to face Joshua who had all of a sudden attached his lips to Brad's. What a fool she had been. Was it not enough for Megan to come to terms with the love of her life being homosexual once? No, she had to foolishly convince herself that the 'phase' was over and put herself through the heartache all over again. The passion was becoming more and more intense between Brad and Joshua. Megan watched them for a moment, realising how absurd her recent thoughts had been. Joshua reclaimed his lips just long enough to pass Megan a smile. She falsely returned the gesture, and then gave a signal informing him that she needed to use the toilet. Joshua quickly resumed his exploration of Brad's mouth. This was very daring for him as he wasn't in a gay environment and not all nightclubs are gay friendly, however the people around didn't seem to be at all phased by what was happening.

The sounds of laughter, drunken frolicking and bitching were all that could be heard from Megan's toilet cubicle. Who got off with who, who slapped who, who was fit, who was so intoxicated that they were on the verge of collapsing, these were all the subjects of gossip as the girls adjusted themselves in front of the mirrors. Megan was perched on the toilet with the seat down, having given it a thorough wipe with tissue first. Tears streamed down her face as she realised how absurd her recent thoughts had been. She pulled her mobile phone from her pocket and glanced through the photos that had been saved on to it. Some of them had been taken with other phones and transferred over. It was filled with treasured memories of she and Joshua.

"She's takin' fuckin' ages! I need a piss!" came a loud voice from outside the cubicle. Megan didn't care. She needed some alone time, and the drunk girl on the other side of the door would have to wait for her relief.

"Have you seen them two gay boys on the dance floor?" Megan's ears pricked up at the sound of a common girl discussing Joshua and Brad with her friends.

"Fittest lads in the place if you ask me," another girl butted in as she awaited a free cubicle. She then screeched with laughter.

"Fuckin' typical," another girl commented.

"I bet I could turn them, just give me five minutes alone with them," came a voice of vast experience. Following that remark, all Megan could hear was the sound of roaring laughter. Even here she couldn't escape her foolishness.

"Ok Megan, pull yourself together now," she whispered to herself quietly as she prepared to face the other clubbers. She put away her phone, stood and wiped her eyes. She opened the cubicle door to receive glares from various pairs of impatient eyes.

"Better not reek in there," the common girl muttered. Megan blatantly disregarded the girls as she headed for the mirror. She had far more important matters to concern herself with than the strain she'd caused the various intoxicated women's bladders. Mainly, how she would make it all the way home with Joshua without him realising how upsetting his frolics of the evening had been. She glared at herself, unable to see the beautiful girl who could have almost any man she desired. All she could see was the dunce who'd not only deluded herself into thinking she could have a gay man once, but twice.

"He's not worth it you know," came the voice of an observant girl beside her. "They're never worth your tears and when you find the right one he won't make you cry."

"It's a bit complicated," Megan said, attempting to shun her newly found acquaintance.

"Isn't it always," she commented as she left.

"I've been looking everywhere for you!" Joshua yelled excitedly, "I got Brad's mobile number!"

"That's great babe," Megan replied, forcing a smile.

"He's so nice…" Joshua continued. Each word was like a dagger in Megan's heart. She focussed her effort on fooling Joshua into thinking she was happy. This wasn't a difficult task as Joshua's attention to detail was somewhat swayed by the excessive alcohol consumption of the evening and the happiness he was feeling as a result of meeting Brad. His romantic entanglement had given him a much needed confidence boost. After such a long stay in 'Singles-Ville' and having received very little male attention in some time, Joshua was excited by the possibilities of having Brad's mobile number. Megan was attempting to appear as though she was happy for him, in reality however she was just determined for him to remain oblivious to the crazy notion she'd had buzzing around in her head. She simply couldn't believe she was feeling this way. When she recalled how things had been with Stuart in the past, it seemed ridiculous for her to feel jealous of Brad now. Stuart had ended up being like one of the family and Megan had accepted him as Joshua's partner, but now, having had him all to herself for so long since the demise of their relationship, Megan didn't want to give him up again. The relationship between a gay man and his heterosexual female best friend is a complicated one, and in Megan and Joshua's case, it only differed from a heterosexual couple's relationship by the fact that they didn't have sex.

The streets of Sheffield were cold and deserted that night as Megan and Joshua desperately sought a taxi to avoid having to walk home. All that Megan could think about was how desperate she was to be alone with her thoughts. She longed to be able to stop pretending, but as they walked, her nose was constantly being rubbed in it. Joshua's mobile phone was bleeping away with text messages after text message, each of them would then be read out several times, analysed and replied to. For Megan on this particular night, this was hell on earth.

"Only you could pull at a straight bar Joshua," laughed Greg as he chewed on his toast. Joshua was walking the kitchen like a zombie holding his head in his hands.

"Have we got any paracetamol?" he asked.

"Oooh someone had a heavy night," Janice commented as she was passing through.

"Just the one too many," Joshua defended himself.

"And the rest…. My sober daughter told us everything. She's already out and about," Janice pointed out. In reality, Megan had in fact awoken early intentionally to avoid facing Joshua and to give herself an opportunity to clear her head. "What was he like then?" Janice asked, emphasizing her already vast knowledge of the previous evening.

"Gorgeous!" exclaimed Joshua, suddenly perking up.

"Tell me more…" Janice continued nosily.

"Blonde hair, blue eyes…. ooh just a dream. He seemed so nice too."

"How old?"

"About my age, maybe a little older." Joshua's mobile phone bleeped signalling a text message. He almost fell on his face as he dashed to read it.
"What's he say?" Janice asked, peering over Joshua's shoulder. He attempted to pull away but Janice read enough of the text message to tease him about it. "Fancy a drink tonight eh? Someone's got a da-ate." Greg chuckled at the sight of Joshua's torment.
"Leave him alone, you'll embarrass the poor lad," Greg said, only partly seriously.
"That's the idea," Janice stated. now almost in a fit of laughter.
"Fine, if you're going to be like this I'll go to my own room and send a reply," Joshua pouted, aware that he was teasing the gossipmongers.
"Mardy git!" Janice yelled in jest as Joshua headed up the stairs.
"It's good to see him getting excited over a lad. It's been too long," Janice commented as she passed a fresh cup of tea to Greg. "I wish Megan would though." Greg nodded in agreement as he swallowed his tea but his inevitable words of wisdom were interrupted by Megan's return. "Hey honey," Janice greeted her cheerily. Megan quickly threw down her coat and scarf and dashed upstairs to her room.
"Just got some stuff to do," she said briefly as she departed. Janice could immediately sense Megan's upset and followed her to her room.

Janice attempted turning the handle on the door of Megan's room but was surprised to find it was locked. It was rare for Megan to lock her door. Normally she'd welcome anyone into her room without even expecting them to knock.
"Are you ok in there love?" Janice asked.
"Fine mother, just trying on some clothes and having a clearout," Megan lied. Janice saw straight through this untruth, as normally Megan wouldn't be disturbed by anyone seeing her body, she'd even walk around half naked in front of Greg.
"Listen Megan, I can tell something's wrong so why don't you just let me in and we can discuss it without the boys finding out," Janice suggested softly. Both Megan and her mother remained silent for a moment. Eventually the key turned in the lock but the door didn't open. Janice waited for several seconds before turning the handle and entering. Once inside she locked the door behind her. Megan was seated on the bed facing the wall. There were no clothes in sight. Anticipating tears and wanting to spare her daughter any unnecessary embarrassment, Janice seated herself behind Megan. "It helps to talk," she pointed out softly as she lightly caressed her daughter's shoulder. "Won't stop me being an idiot," Megan said harshly. Janice was confused by Megan's behaviour. She couldn't understand why she was so troubled all of a sudden. "Please

let me help you. You know you can trust me," Janice said, now lightly rubbing Megan's arm. Megan quickly turned around and grabbed her mother tightly as though she never wanted to let go. Janice patted her back lovingly.
"I'm such a fool," Megan declared, her voice impaired by her tears and sniffling.
"I don't understand Megan. What's happened?" Janice asked.
"It's Joshua…." Megan began reluctantly. This comment made no sense whatsoever to Janice as she'd just passed Joshua a moment ago on cloud nine.
"Joshua's happy as a pig in mud," Janice pointed out.
"I know. He's happy…. But I'm not," Megan continued. "I love hum mum, I love Joshua," she declared between bursts of tears. Janice gently pushed Megan away slightly to look her in the eye.
"I thought you were past all that," she said sympathetically.
"So did I mum. I'm an idiot. I was so stupid to even think there'd be a chance," Megan continued harshly, tears rushing down her cheeks. Janice pulled a tissue from her pocket and wiped Megan's face dry.
"Megan!….. Janice! You in there?!" came Joshua's voice from the other side of the door.
"Don't let him in. I don't want him to see me like this." Megan was panicking. Not many excuses would be convincing to Joshua as to why he was being refused entry so Janice had to think fast. After all, the girls were usually comfortable talking to him about everything.
"I need a shopping partner. I've got to get a new outfit. I have a date with Brad tonight!" Joshua broadcasted excitedly, not just rubbing, but stamping salt into Megan's wounds with his size twelves.
"We're going to be a little while, we've got rubbish everywhere. We're having a bit of a clearout," Janice yelled in reply.
"OK, see you later then," Joshua shouted as he bellowed down the stairs. If he hadn't been so preoccupied with thoughts of Brad he would have certainly required further convincing of what was happening. And with that they were alone again. Janice took Megan's hand into her own and gazed lovingly into her eyes.
"Let it all out," she said as she used her free hand to stroke Megan's hair. She could sense that her daughter was in desperate need of this talk.
"It had been so long Mum," Megan's confession resumed. "He'd gone so long without a boyfriend and then all of a sudden he wanted to go to a straight bar…. I got this silly idea in my head that he'd started liking girls again."
"That's my fault darling, I convinced him to take you to that club. I did it because I wanted you to find a boyfriend. How ironic," Janice confessed.

Megan smiled.

"I love you for what you were trying to do," she said with genuine appreciation.

"I didn't realise you didn't have a boyfriend because you still loved your gay best friend," Janice said bluntly. Megan began to giggle, then stopped herself feeling that she shouldn't be finding this humorous. Janice suddenly burst into a fit of laughter and Megan joined in. Her tears of sorrow had almost become tears of joy in an instant.

"How silly have I been?" Megan asked rhetorically. Janice nodded in agreement.

"The heart wants what it wants," she said sympathetically.

"Don't worry. Joshua need never know." Megan smiled and thanked Janice for her support.

"It's what mothers are for," Janice reminded her. "He may not be in love with you but he loves you in a very special way and bet you're still around long after all these fella's have disappeared from his life," Janice pointed out logically. Megan smiled as she grasped just how true that statement was. After all, statistically as Joshua's girlfriend she'd only last a few years at the most but their special relationship could potentially last forever.

"I missed the last bus. Are you sure I can't tempt anyone any one into shopping with me?!" Joshua yelled from the foot of the staircase. A special smile passed between Janice and Megan that only they could understand. Megan's smile was one of a sense of achievement and Janice's was one of maternal pride.

"Give me five minutes!" Megan shouted back to Joshua.

"OK, Brad seems fashionable, so we need to find something extra special to make me look fabulous!" Joshua announced as he and Megan entered the shopping precinct, his hands in the air with excitement. Of course, Joshua was insistent on purchasing a new outfit for his date with Brad. Even though Brad hadn't seen the majority of his clothes and he already owned various outfits that would make him look as nice as, if not better than anything he could find in the stores, but Joshua didn't feel himself that they made him look as good as something new would. He also didn't realise that Brad would most likely be fretting too much over his own appearance to even worry about Joshua's. They had both definitely decided that they liked the look of each other. Megan felt almost dizzy as she was being dragged around every clothing store the city had to offer as Joshua raced around as though his life depended upon it.

"Fabulous!" exclaimed Megan as Joshua modelled his new outfit before her. She smiled as joyfully as she possibly could while watching

as the man she loved prepared for a date with someone else. Joshua himself was far too pre-occupied to notice what was bubbling under Megan's surface.
"You sure it's ok? I want to look hot!" Joshua said, attempting to appear as though he was oozing with confidence. Megan however could sense his nerves. After all, it had been a long time since Joshua had dated or trusted a man. Stuart had a lot to answer for. "Do you think he's going to like me?" Joshua asked, changing his tone and displaying his insecurities. Megan patted the bed signalling for Joshua to sit beside her.
"How could he not like you?" Megan asked lovingly.
"Well, I'm boring," Joshua replied harshly. Megan gave a puzzled stare.
"It's true," Joshua protested, "That's what went wrong with Stuart. Even if Brad likes me he'll get bored of me."
"You don't know that. Not all men are like Stuart," Megan said in an attempt to comfort him. Her wisdom however was only based on watching soap operas and reading romance novels as personally she'd only ever dated Joshua himself.
"You're right, let's do something fab' with my hair!" Joshua suggested, his excitement returning.

Outer McDonalds was almost becoming a traditional meeting place for Joshua's dates. As he awaited Brad's arrival he recalled his first date with Stuart, although this wasn't a good omen. Joshua was on tenterhooks as he anticipated how the evening ahead would pan out. He didn't want his apprehension to show but planned to remain cautious of Brad's intentions. Having forgotten his watch, Joshua was continuously reaching for his mobile phone to check the time. Although Brad was only three minutes late, Joshua's paranoia began to set in. What if he had been stood up? Had it all been a joke? Was Brad in the bushes across the road giggling to himself? A group of three females and two males were heading towards him. He looked away in order to avoid giving the impression that he was staring. Looking in the other direction he reached for his mobile phone to check the time again.
"Boo!" came a female voice from behind. Joshua turned to investigate. The group of five were Brad and his friends whom he'd spotted on the dance floor the previous evening.
"You not brought that Megan?" asked Brad's fiery ginger haired friend.
"Er…no," Joshua stuttered. This was possibly the most embarrassing moment of Joshua's life. Had he misread all the signals? How could he have confused a friendly drink in a group for a date? He cast his mind back to the text message in question. 'Fancy a drink tonight?' Could this have just been a casual friendly invitation? It was so blatantly obvious to

everyone that Joshua had arrived alone under the impression that he was to attend a date with Brad.
"Hi Joshua, I'm Matthew," Brad's male friend introduced himself. "We didn't get a chance to talk last night," he continued. He was a pleasant, mildly attractive, seemingly heterosexual twenty something. Joshua held out his hand though it was obvious to everyone present that he didn't want to be there. Inside he was wishing that the ground beneath him would open up and swallow him whole.
"Where we going then?" asked another female from the group appearing impatient as she folded her arms signalling how low the temperature was.
"It's not cold Ruth," teased Matthew while imitating her actions. Joshua falsely laughed along with the crowd. Brad was still yet to speak.
"We eating at Maccy D's?" asked the rather common sounding redhead. Everyone was anxious to get inside away from the cold.
"Yeh sure, I can't stay too long though," Joshua added having deliberated how he was going to quickly remove himself from the awkwardness of the evening.

Several minutes into the meal Joshua had established the fiery red-head's name as being Jenna and the remaining quieter girl as Jessica. Brad was still relatively quiet and had barely acknowledged Joshua's presence within the group. Matthew could sense Joshua's discomfort and was questioning him in an attempt to find some common ground. Joshua felt as though he was being given the third degree. Brad quickly and quietly excused himself to the toilet.
"Joshua, I'm sorry about Brad," Jessica began the second Brad was out of earshot. She was obviously the quiet and sensible member of the group, the type you confide in with your troubles.
"What do you mean?" Joshua asked, giving his full attention.
"This should have been a date for you and Brad…" Jessica began, "But at the last minute he got cold feet and invited us along. He's extremely nervous and shy. Always has been since he was a teenager." She made it sound as though his teens had been so long ago.
"How old is he?" Joshua asked. Jessica revealed that Brad was in fact twenty six years of age which was surprising to Joshua but not off putting.
"Come on ladies, let's go and leave them to it," Jessica suggested to the crew, referring to Matthew and the girls as ladies.
"Good idea, quickly before he gets back," Matthew added. Joshua hurriedly received a peck on the cheek and good luck wishes from Jessica and Matthew and suddenly found himself alone. Brad slowly approached the table, having noticed Joshua's solitude. He seated himself opposite Joshua.

"Shy eh?" Joshua asked light heartedly. Brad's face turned red with embarrassment.
"I'm sorry I've put you through this. I don't know what you must think of me," Brad apologised.
"You didn't seem at all shy on the dance floor," Joshua pointed out. Brad smiled vaguely but his embarrassment was still apparent.
"I don't do this often," he added. There was an innocence about Brad that Joshua found quite charming. "The alcohol helps my confidence," Brad muttered. Joshua struggled to understand how one so attractive could lack confidence. Joshua steered the conversation to one about their favourite bars. Brad revealed that he had never visited a gay bar. Initially this was surprising to Joshua but he quickly realised the advantages of this. Although Brad was older, at the same time he was fresh and yet mature, he hadn't yet been corrupted by the gay scene and had his value system converted to one that had the importance of a person's facial appearance only second to the shape of their body. Joshua grinned at Brad approvingly. "You think it's funny don't you?" Brad asked timidly.
"No," Joshua protested, "I think it's really sweet, a breath of fresh air in fact." He then discreetly held Brad's hand in his own under the table.

As the evening continued the pair visited several quiet bars where they shared intellectual conversation. Brad expressed genuine interest in Joshua's aspirations of becoming a journalist while Joshua listened attentively to the details of Brad's career in accounting. This was unlike any date Joshua had ever had. There was no innuendo, just maturity and mutual respect. Joshua also found Brad's timid nature to be rather cute. He seemed to be the type of lad that could be relied upon, and his incredibly good looks were the icing on the cake. Joshua was intrigued by how a catch such as Brad had been left on the shelf for so long.

"I'm sorry for how this date started out," Brad apologised as they walked through the city centre about to part, showing his insecurities. "Most lads wouldn't want to know me after the way I brought my friends with me tonight," he rambled on, convincing himself of his inadequacy. "You don't have to see me again…." he continued. Joshua stopped in his tracks. Brad quickly realised and halted in line. Joshua glanced to confirm their solitude. There was nobody around, they were completely alone. "I will totally understand, I'd rather that you be honest than leave me hanging…" Brad babbled on. Joshua placed his finger on Brad's lips signalling for him to be quiet.
"What if I do want to see you again?" Joshua whispered in his ear. Brad was dumbfounded and had a look of bewilderment on his face. The small amount of alcohol he'd consumed in the evening clearly hadn't had the same confidence boosting effect he'd experienced the night before.

Joshua placed his arms on Brad's shoulders and kissed him gently. Brad was correct in stating that many lads wouldn't appreciate him the way he was, but having been severely burned by Stuart whom he'd naively considered the love of his life, Brad's maturity, good looks and charm were very appealing. It was almost a sixth sense that told Joshua that Brad could be trusted. Many lads would view Brad's lack of experience with men as negative but Joshua looked at it from a different perspective, at least by lacking experience with men he'd be less inclined to stray should they enter into a relationship. This was the first time since his betrayal by Stuart that he'd felt open to the idea of putting his trust in another man. The kiss lingered on for several minutes. Sheffield City Centre is by no means the ideal place for passion between two homosexual men, but they didn't care. At that moment the world was only the size of the paving stone on which they stood. They had both lost touch with reality outside of their embrace. The kiss of the previous evening had been far more intense but somehow this was more enjoyable; it was a kiss based on a blooming friendship, not on a sexual attraction with a stranger on a dance floor. The embrace was uninterrupted until they could both hear the sound of a group of loud youths approaching, most likely heavily alcohol induced judging by the chatter. It was time for them to part. Joshua had leaped to the conclusion that Brad lived alone, based solely on his age and wondered whether or not he would receive an invitation to spend the night with him. He wasn't entirely sure how he'd feel or react if such an offer was presented to him. They stood facing each other in the street, both smiling and feeling slightly embarrassed.
"I'd better get going, I have to be up for work in the morning," Brad announced honestly.
"Yes I've got quite an early lecture too," Joshua agreed.
"I had a great time and I really want to see you again," Brad said with a little more confidence. His honesty was a breath of fresh air to Joshua. He recalled the way he'd felt after his first date with Stuart and this was very different but somehow just as special. In a way it was like a Galaxy bar and a Dairy Milk, both tasted great to Joshua but are very different.
"I want to see you again too," Joshua stated as the gang of highly intoxicated, loud young men passed and staggered off into the distance.
"I think we're alone again," Brad pointed out and reached in for a kiss, this time accompanied by mutual exploration of each other's bodies. They said their goodbyes and headed off in different directions. Joshua pondered for a moment as to whether it was a good or bad thing that Brad hadn't attempted to instigate the sharing of a bed that night. He quickly reached the conclusion that Brad's lack of expectations was a positive and that he obviously liked Joshua for who he was, not what he was.

"I wondered if I'd see you tonight," Janice said light-heartedly as she sipped her coffee. She was sprawled on the sofa pretending to watch a late night movie.

"You know me better than that, otherwise you wouldn't have waited up for me," Joshua replied, outsmarting her original quip.

"Touché," she responded and held out her arms.

"You're very nosey," Joshua commented.

"Just looking out for my family," Janice replied. Those words were so kind and welcoming. Almost without any of them realising it, Janice, Greg, Megan and Joshua had become a family unit. "There's some coffee in the jug," Janice announced and patted the seat beside her on the sofa as she began to sit upright, inviting Joshua for a girly chat. Joshua pretended to be reluctant in joining her and revealing all the juicy details of the evening but in reality he was bursting to discuss it with someone. He made a coffee and seated himself beside Janice. "So what's Brad like then?" she asked, touching Joshua's leg with excitement. Before Joshua could even have a chance to speak his mobile phone alerted him of a received text message. The smile across his face as he read it made it obvious to Janice that Brad was the sender. "It obviously went well then, he can't leave you alone," Janice teased.

"The fact that he's texting already is a good sign isn't it?" Joshua asked.

"It certainly isn't a bad one," Janice remarked, then followed the comment with, "Oh to be young again, I remember my first date with Trevor…" At that point she drifted off into a fantasy. It was as though her body was still present but her mind and spirit were miles away. She so rarely spoke of her late husband, even now eight years later and with a new partner it was still difficult for her. Joshua was almost oblivious to Janice's mental absence as he focussed his attention on replying to Brad's text message. After all, at this crucial, fragile stage in a relationship it's important to think very carefully about what you type. Having sent the message, Joshua put down the phone and slurped his coffee, ready to explode with information for Janice.

"Janice," he said loudly, sensing her lack of concentration. Janice returned to reality. "You were miles away," Joshua commented before delving into graphic details of Brad and the evening.

"He sounds adorable," Janice commented.

"He is, it's so refreshing to meet someone that's not become an arrogant sluttish scene queen, he's cute and loyal and smart……." Joshua went on, listing Brad's strengths as though he were making a sales pitch to Janice. He was focussing purely on positives, just as everyone does when they first meet a potential partner.

"He sounds terrific," Janice responded. "So when are you going to see him again?"
"Tomorrow according to the text message!" Joshua replied eagerly. They both agreed that it was time they ought to be in bed. Joshua needed his beauty sleep ready for his next date after all.

Joshua awoke at seven o'clock to the sound of his mobile phone vibrating over and over, reminding him constantly that a text message awaited him. Normally this would have irritated him during his state of slumber, but anticipating who the sender of the message would be, he quickly dashed out of the bed to grab the phone. It read: 'Morning sexy. Had a gr8 night. Looking 4ward 2 seeing u again.' Joshua's smile beamed as he read the message over and over again. He was receiving a positive vibe from Brad. He quickly replied to the message with similar niceties, but not actually saying anything. He then slowly made his way down the stairs, still in the process of becoming fully awake and alert. He approached the kitchen in search of a coffee, although it only seemed like a couple of hours since his last caffeine fix. He halted his steps upon hearing the mention of his name as he approached the door to the kitchen. He focussed his attention on the conversation from outside the door.
"I am happy for him, really I am," Megan said. Joshua was confused by this comment. He wondered why Megan would need to defend herself in this way.
"We're not disputing that my darling," Greg assured her.
"Mother, why did you tell HIM anyway?" Megan asked rudely.
"I thought Greg could help you to feel better," Janice said softly. Megan realised the harshness of her previous remark and apologised. Joshua wondered what the three of them were discussing. The conversation was intriguing him.
"Don't feel guilty, you can't help who you love," Greg said softly.
"But I shouldn't have these feelings for Joshua anymore. I should have come to terms with this years ago," Megan replied emotionally.
"It's obvious why you're feeling this way. Joshua hasn't had a boyfriend for a long time and you've had him all to yourself. I guess you became very attached again," Janice said, offering logic to the discussion. All the pieces immediately fell into place for Joshua. He almost felt foolish for not realising before that Megan still harboured feelings for him. He needed time to ponder his next move and decided it would be for the best if Megan were to remain unaware of his newly found knowledge.

He tip-toed back up the stairs into his room where a vibrating phone and a fresh text message awaited him. 'Can't wait for tonight! What u wanna do?' the message read. Joshua was excited by this but his attention was consumed by what he'd just overheard in the kitchen. He

placed his mobile phone down making Brad wait for a response and he lay on the bed, hands behind his head, gathering his thoughts together. He wondered how long Megan had been harbouring these feelings for him. For years he'd been under the impression that Megan was completely over him and he'd trusted her with his inner most secrets and thoughts. This discovery changed the goalposts of their friendship. The trust had been broken. Joshua wasn't sure how to feel exactly but he knew that Megan's dishonesty would have a negative impact on their friendship and he felt so foolish not to have realised before how she was still feeling. After all, she'd not had a boyfriend since they'd split and how many beautiful young girls spend so many years without a boyfriend? Greg peered his head through the crack in the doorway prompting Joshua to turn his head to face him.
"Morning son," Greg said, he was becoming more paternal with Joshua and Megan as time went on. Joshua could sense that Greg was eager to confide in him but was being held back by a sense of loyalty to Megan. The context of the conversation he'd overheard was playing over and over in Joshua's mind. He simply couldn't contain it any longer.
"I heard you in the kitchen," he muttered.
"I know, I could see you through the crack in the doorway," Greg revealed, "that's why I came up to see you."
"How long have you kept this from me?" Joshua asked, now sitting up on the bed. Greg seated himself beside Joshua.
"You can't choose who to love. What would have been the point of me telling you?" Greg's words made a lot of sense and Joshua knew that he was right but he now felt unable to enjoy his newfound romance through fear of hurting Megan. He explained his feelings to Greg who smiled and placed his hand on Joshua's forehead, he seemed as though he was bursting with pride. "How could one with such an upbringing have turned out so well?" Greg asked rhetorically. Joshua was unsure of how to react to this but was barely given a chance to before Greg followed the comment with, "Don't tell Megan that you know how she still feels for you. It will only damage your relationship." Joshua nodded his head in agreement. The last thing he wanted was for his friendship with Megan to be damaged, he valued that in some ways more than anything a man could offer. Joshua's mobile phone began to bleep once again. "You've got a keen one there," Greg commented as he ruffled Joshua's hair and exited the room.

Chapter 9

"Happy Valentines Day," Brad said as he passed a beautifully decorated gift bag to Joshua. "Our second valentines together," he pointed out as he reached for a kiss. They enjoyed a long, lingering kiss and both said the words "I love you," as though it were expected of them to do so. Brad's flat was now well stocked with Joshua's belongings, although he didn't officially reside there, he would sleep there more often than not and only tended to use his own bed at Janice's home when he and Megan had a girly night in that took them into the early hours of the morning. At twenty-three years of age, and with a partner of almost thirty, Joshua was finding himself to be very mature of late. It would appear that he had it all, he was nearing the end of his university course and on the way to his degree and the career in journalism of his dreams and he had a boyfriend who worshipped the ground he walked on, and had now done so for two years. Joshua opened the bag to find a silver watch.

"This must have cost a fortune," Joshua said, mesmerized by the extravagance of the gift. "You really shouldn't have!"

"Nothing's too good for my Joshy," Brad insisted honestly. Joshua had never been so well treated by a man. Brad was deeply in love with him and he showed it everyday in everyway. Joshua placed the watch on his wrist and admired it. "Do you like it?" Brad asked timidly.

"It's amazing," Joshua replied, "Makes my gift to you look so pathetic." Brad smiled and excused Joshua's lower spending,

"You're a poor student after all babe." Joshua passed Brad a neatly wrapped t-shirt which had obviously cost only a fraction of the amount that Brad had spent. Even so, Brad was perfectly satisfied with the offering.

"Sorry it's not much," Joshua apologised, feeling guilty for Brad's overspending.

"Don't worry, it's fab' hun'," Brad replied, meaning every word. Material possessions were unimportant to Brad, he had Joshua and that was enough to make him happy.

"We should go out to Dream tonight for a change, I'm sure they'll have some sort of Valentines Day special event going on," Joshua suggested. It wasn't often that they ventured out on to the gay scene these days. Brad had accompanied Joshua to gay bars on a couple of occasions but had never become fond of them. What was the point anyway? Neither of them were 'on the pull' and therefore it wasn't necessary. They tended to prefer quiet nights in, visits to the cinema or quiet nights at the local pub. As usual, Brad agreed to Joshua's suggestion without hesitation. What made Joshua happy made Brad happy. Joshua had become accustomed to having his own way, and Brad's easygoing nature meant that they never

argued. Joshua raced up the stairs excitedly, already mentally deciding what he would wear. He flung the wardrobe open and reached for a tight black vest which he would wear over the top of a plain white shirt with blue ripped jeans and trainers; his old favourite. Normally he hated to wear the same outfit more than once but it had been such a long time since he'd spent an evening at 'Dream' bar that by now nobody would recall it. He felt stunning. He looked stunning. He had it all, he was twenty-three years of age, he had the looks, the body and a boyfriend who'd do anything for him. Joshua was feeling more stability in his life than ever before. "How do I look?" he asked, modelling his outfit.
"I can see I'm going to have to be careful tonight if I want to hang on to my valentine," Brad said light-heartedly as he reached out to grab Joshua by his hips. They kissed passionately as Brad's hands explored Joshua's body. Although he had the body to be able to, Brad chose not to wear tight outfits and had thrown on a pair of baggy jeans and a loose t-shirt. He looked nice but wouldn't come across as being blatantly gay to an unsuspecting passer by in the street. Joshua wondered who would be present in the nightclub that evening. On previous occasions as it was one of the very few gay bars in the area, it had tended to attract a lot of regular patrons. "I love you," Brad reminded Joshua once again, instigating another passionate embrace.

"So what did you get for valentines day?" Megan asked eagerly from the other end of the phone line. The call was interrupting Joshua and Brad as they were preparing for their evening out but Joshua didn't mind as he wasn't able to spend as much quality time with Megan anymore.
"Bless him…." Megan said as she heard of Brad's extravagant gift. At this point the real reason for Megan's call became apparent.
"What about you then? Any valentines cards from those lads who sit gawping at you at uni?" Joshua asked.
"I got twelve red roses delivered to the house and the hugest card you've ever seen in your life…." Megan blurted out, "You know one of those that comes in a cardboard box…."
"Oooh, did the sender leave a name?" Joshua was intrigued; he wondered if perhaps Megan was finally ready to move on with her life. After five years of being in love with a man she couldn't have, it was about time.
"They were from Owen," she revealed.
"He's nice!" exclaimed Joshua, having met her attractive fellow student.
"Yeah, he is," Megan agreed unconvincingly.
"He must like you a lot to go to all that trouble, not to mention expense!" Megan was clearly overwhelmed and unsure of what she wanted, but recalling the conversation he'd shared with Greg with regard to Megan, Joshua decided not to push the matter any further.

It was cabaret night at 'Dream' and the sounds of the show could be heard all the way down the road. "Life is a cabaret…." was the introduction to the show.

"It's just starting," Joshua said to Brad as they dashed in. They paid little attention to the butch lesbians at the entrance and hurried for a seat. There were three drag queens all of very different ages and builds. It was difficult to determine exactly how old they were but one clearly stood out as being very much younger than the others, most likely around Joshua's age. The drag queens would take it in turns at performing and whilst one was entertaining the crowd the others were applying their various different costumes and make up. They imitated various celebrities including a rendition of Tina Turner performing 'Simply the best', a medley of Dolly Parton numbers and a tribute to Dusty Springfield. Brad and Joshua clapped and sang along during the performance and were even forced to participate in some of the riskier activities. Joshua had endured Dolly's balloon breasts in his face and had Tina pretending to have sex with him. He wondered if his outfit had attracted them to single him out. Next on the stage came the youngest drag queen. He was wearing a big blonde wig, falsely over-sized breasts and extremely tight lycra leggings. He was obviously very slim in his natural form. He wandered up and down the stage singing 'All that jazz' and making eye contact with each member of the audience in turn. He obviously wasn't as experienced as the others, but his performance was impressing the crowd who were singing along and cheering (by this point most of the audience had consumed vast amounts of alcohol). He walked across the stage continuing to make eye contact with various members of the audience. Upon reaching Brad he gave a little wink.

"Oooh he likes me," Brad commented in Joshua's ear. The drag queen glanced at Joshua and lost his beaming smile for a moment. He looked as though he'd seen a ghost and almost missed a line of the song. Joshua wondered what it was about him that had caused such a reaction, after all he didn't appear at all threatening. He looked into the eyes of the young entertainer and sensed a familiarity he couldn't quite understand. He knew those eyes, he'd seen them somewhere before, a vision from his past. Of course the rest of the drag queens face was heavily concealed by makeup but Joshua knew he'd seen this person somewhere before.

As the entertainment drew to a close the crowd returned to their usual activities. Nothing had changed in this bar. Up went the volume of the music and the dance floor began to fill. The arrogant yet eternally single slim and perfect men headed for the stage to display their moves foolishly under the illusion that they were being viewed, admired and envied. Brad and Joshua seated themselves at the side of the dance floor;

Joshua had his head rested lovingly on Brad's shoulder.
"Look at those two," Brad said while pointing at a pair of older men who were obviously on the prowl and in search of a good time. They were the type of gay men who'd never matured or found a partner, and never wanted to until it was too late.
"Old queens," Joshua giggled, his hand now stroking Brad's leg.
"I'm so glad we're away from all that," Brad said, "I'd hate to have to go out on the pull again." They wanted as a variety of men of all ages, shapes and sizes sought out a 'lay' for the night or at least a little affection. This all seemed almost foreign to Joshua now as he'd been settled with Brad for so long and he'd been settled with Brad for so long and had never had any need or desire to behave this way or to go in search of a man. They continued to chuckle to each other as they ridiculed the various moves of the people on the dance floor as well as some of the outfits and hairstyles. Brad would light heartedly christen them with nicknames that usually involved comparing them to television characters and Joshua would find it highly amusing. He cringed as he spotted a group of the bar's regulars approaching them.
"Here we go," he muttered in Brad's ear. There were three in the group, Chris was tall, Martin was extremely short and Damien was average height but very obese and the butt of everyone's jokes.
"Not seen you in here for a while," Damien remarked, giggling falsely. A look passed between Brad and Joshua that displayed their irritation. Fortunately the gang were far too busy prying to notice.
"Don't think I've ever seen you here," Chris remarked as he glanced at Brad as though he were a piece of meat and judging his tenderness. Brad gave an unimpressed look and quickly replied,
"No I'm not part of the furniture like some," then laughed just as falsely. Martin remained silent but stared at Joshua, making his attraction to him blatantly obvious. "Excuse me, I need the toilet," Brad said bluntly and whispered for Joshua to disburden them in time for his return.
"He's a bit of alright," Chris commented, leering over Joshua. Joshua's forced smile was beginning to infuriate him. As the trio of bores continued their ramblings Joshua noticed the youngest drag queen was at the bar chatting to a member of staff. His eyes were regularly wandering to Joshua the way they had been during the show. Joshua was now wondering whether or not he was suffering from paranoia but at the same time he couldn't dismiss the familiarity of this person. The more he glared at the bubbly entertainer the more certain he was that he'd seen him somewhere before. If only he could remove the makeup and reveal his true identity. "Anyway, we're getting off," Chris said, "I'm up early

in the morning." Joshua was paying no attention to the pitiful threesome. The drag queen was now blatantly and constantly staring.
"Wakey wakey, earth to Joshua," Damien said as he waved his hand in front of Joshua's face and laughed goofily. This blocked his view of the drag queen and forced his attention to return to his acquaintances.
"Sorry, what did you say?" Chris glanced to the bar, unsure of what had distracted Joshua's attention.
"I said we're off," he repeated himself.
"Oh, ok bye," Joshua replied, seemingly disinterested. And with that Joshua was alone at the table awaiting Brad's return. He couldn't help but return his eyes to the bar. But now the drag queen was nowhere to be seen. A barman approached the table holding a piece of paper.
"Madame Minge sent this," he said as he passed the note to Joshua. It read, 'Please call me Joshua. I know I don't deserve it but please call me.' A mobile number was scrawled on the reverse of the sheet. Joshua was intrigued. The writing on the paper implied that the drag queen was under the impression that Joshua was aware of his identity. He glanced around in hope of spotting the mystery man and noticed the drag queens dressing room. It was the obvious place. If he'd left the bar he'd need to go to the dressing room first to return to his masculine identity. Joshua noticed a window of opportunity; if he quickly headed for the lair now he wouldn't be spotted. Joshua was not the most spontaneous of people but his curiosity was getting the better of him.

The room was like none he'd ever seen before. The hallway was covered with photographs of drag shows from top to bottom; so much so that wallpaper was pointless. At the end of the corridor Madame Minge was crouched over the sink removing his make-up and washing his face. This was it; if Madame Minge turned to investigate he'd reveal his true identity. Joshua gazed at him for a moment, mesmerised by the effort that had obviously been put into his costume. The drag queen's wig accidentally fell to the floor revealing a modern hairstyle. His face was wet in the sink and he reached for a towel, unable to open his eyes. The towel was a little out of reach for him and Joshua boldly passed it to him from behind. Madame Minge accepted the towel and dried his face, then lifted his head. In the mirror he saw his own reflection and Joshua standing behind him, completely still. Joshua was horrified to discover Madame Minge's true identity. He couldn't fathom what to do or say. The shock of seeing this demon from his past had him completely stunned. The drag queen continued to glare at Joshua's reflection in the mirror. He was trying to pluck up the courage to turn and face the man he'd caused so much pain to in the past.

"You…." Joshua said, finally locating his tongue.
"Yes Joshua, it's me," said the man who'd once meant so much to him as he turned to face him.
"I don't…..I don't believe it," stuttered Joshua.
"I know this is a shock for you…" Madame Minge began.
"That doesn't even begin to describe it," Joshua replied with utter contempt in his voice. At this point, he realised that although so much time had passed he was no closer to forgiving him for the pain he'd caused.
"I really am sorry for what I've done to you in the past. If I could turn the clock back I would," he pleaded.
"Well you can't," Joshua replied bluntly. He was completely defensive, in a way his former friend had never witnessed before. It was obvious that Joshua by this time was a stronger person. He was not about to be messed with again. "Anyway, I'd better be off, my boyfriend's waiting for me. He doesn't stab me in the back," Joshua said as he began to turn away.
"Wait," Madame Minge replied, stopping Joshua in his tracks. "I'd like to talk this through."
"There's no point," Joshua insisted, his back still turned on his estranged companion.
"Please," he begged, but Joshua continued to walk away.

Brad was now seated, glancing around in search of Joshua.
"I'm here darling," Joshua said as he scuttled back to the table.
"Where'd you get to?" Brad asked. Joshua hesitated as he contemplated whether or not to be truthful in his reply. He wasn't quite sure why he lied for the same reason that he was unsure of why he'd held on to the note he'd passed earlier that evening with Madame Minge's mobile number. Curiosity of how his friend had changed was getting the better of him.
"Bloody Damien wanted to show me his new car didn't he?" Joshua replied. He hated to lie to Brad but everything inside of him was telling him to do so.
"At least they've gone now," Brad laughed, completely trusting his beloved partner. He drifted on to another topic of conversation, but Joshua wasn't paying attention; he couldn't focus on anything, his mind was completely preoccupied with the blast from the past he'd just faced. He wondered how he'd gained the identity of 'Madame Minge' and what had possessed him to do it. He also wondered whether or not he'd really changed since the day he'd hurt him so badly. "Are you alright?" Brad asked, sensing that Joshua was preoccupied.

"I don't feel too well," Joshua lied; he needed an excuse to be alone, to give himself time to think. He needed to ponder whether or not to allow someone back into his life who'd caused so much pain in the past.
"Do you want to go back to mine?" Brad asked.
"I think I'll go home tonight if that's ok. You'll be out all day tomorrow and it'd be nice to spend some time with Megan," Joshua replied. Brad agreed, completely oblivious to any ulterior motives.

Joshua entered his bedroom and seated himself on his bed. He immediately pulled the note from his pocket and read it over and over again. The handwriting was so familiar. What seemed like a million memories came flooding back. The way the note read seemed so sincere, as though the writer felt genuine guilt for his actions. Joshua turned over the note where the telephone number was displayed. Temptation was beating him. He reached for his mobile phone and began to dial the number but pressed the red button to end the call before it had a chance to connect.
"No," he said to himself, "I'm not letting him back into my life." He placed the mobile phone on to his bedside table and ripped the note into several pieces which were disposed of in the waste paper bin within seconds. A text message arrived; it was from Brad, it read, 'Hope you're feeling better in the morning my darling xxxx.' Joshua smiled and said to himself, "I've got everything I need." Something inside him was pushing him to make the call, but his head was telling him to resist, and having made the mistake of following his heart throughout his life so far, Joshua was finally learning.

"A drag queen!" Megan said in astonishment. Joshua nodded slowly. Megan tilted her head and glared at him with a look of disbelief.
"It's true," he said, slightly laughing. Megan was a rational person and always saw the best in everyone. Joshua knew that he could rely on her rational judgement of the situation.
"And he wants you to call him?" Megan repeated Joshua's words in disbelief.
"Yes, he claims he's sorry for everything," Joshua continued.
"Wow. What'll you do?" Megan asked.
"I don't think I'm going to do anything," Joshua declared unconvincingly as he seated himself beside her on the sofa.
"I can tell you're tempted to contact him," Megan teased.
"What do you think I should do?" Joshua asked, and then proceeded to answer his own question, "It doesn't matter anyway, I've binned the note with the number on it."
"That's that then," Megan said finally.

"So you think I should keep away from him?" Joshua asked, putting words into Megan's mouth. She laughed as she observed Joshua's actions; she knew him so well, she could sense that what he really wanted was for her to say that it would be a good idea to pursue a friendship with his estranged companion. His curiosity was obvious.

"Only you can make the decision, on the one hand he may have turned over a new leaf and by not contacting him you could be missing out on something special. On the other hand, he hurt you badly in the past and he probably isn't worth risking your relationship with Brad for." Megan was wise beyond her years and although she was attempting to appear as though she was giving an unbiased viewpoint, it was obvious that she was subtly manipulating him, with the best of intentions. She clearly did not want Joshua to do anything that would put him at risk of losing Brad.

"You're right darling, thanks! I'm going to call Brad and arrange our plans for tonight," Joshua said as he skipped out of the room.

"Anytime," Megan said to herself, wishing she faced these types of predicaments herself.

In the hallway, Joshua reached for his mobile phone and pressed the green button in order to select Brad from the list of recently called numbers. At the top of the list was the number that had been written on the note. It had completely slipped his mind that he'd dialled the number the previous evening. He entered his own room and scrolled down the list of numbers to Brad's. He knew that was the number he ought to dial. He knew that Brad was the purest and most genuine man he'd ever find, but the allure of what might be was too strong. He scrolled back up to the top of the list of numbers and pressed the green button to instigate the call. Joshua was shaking and perspiring as he heard the dial tone. His heart was climbing up his throat and into his mouth, ready to jump out.

"Hello," a familiar voice answered. It was surreal. They'd shared so many telephone conversations in the past and yet this was the most difficult call he'd ever had to make. "Hello," a familiar voice answered. It was surreal. They'd shared so many telephone conversations in the past and yet this was the most difficult call he'd ever had to make.

"Hello, it's me…Joshua."

"I'm really glad you called." Joshua sensed sincerity in his voice and was tempted to trust him, or maybe he just wanted to trust him.

"This is a little awkward, do you want meet tonight?" Joshua asked.

"I'd love to." His eagerness was obvious. Unaware of what to say next, Joshua made arrangements for a meet that evening and hurried off the phone. At this point a text message arrived, 'Hi baby. Are you feeling better? Do you want me to come over tonight?' it read. Joshua hated to be dishonest to Brad, especially considering all he'd done for him and the

happiness he'd brought into his life, but he saw no other way. 'Sorry darling. Going to have an early night. I'll definitely see you tomorrow,' Joshua's reply read. Joshua's feelings of guilt were quickly were quickly replaced by ones of anxiety over his pending meeting with his estranged friend. He wondered what he should wear, what would be discussed during the evening, and how the time passed since they'd parted would be explained. One thing he was sure of was that there was much to discuss.
"I take it you're going then?" Megan said from the doorway. Joshua glanced at her with a sinful look on his face. He was fully expecting her to disapprove. "Good. I can't wait to hear his explanation!" she said gleefully, her sense of curiosity was stronger than her sense of disapproval. She was eager to learn the truth about this bizarre turn of events.

It was a frosty evening, but this didn't stop Joshua sweating as he approached Parkers Cocktail Bar, preparing to face one of the demons of his past. There had been a mutual decision not to meet at Dream through fear of who they may be spotted by. Joshua arrived, with fifteen minutes to spare; his body was trembling with fear, he wasn't sure why as he ought to have the upper hand in this situation. After all, the two of them shared a lot of history but that's just what it was and so much had happened to change Joshua's life since they'd parted that in theory this blast from the past shouldn't have a major affect on Joshua's life. For some reason however, it did. Joshua could see a figure in the distance. It was a perfect form of a man, just the way Joshua remembered him. He'd aged so well. His body was more defined than ever and he hadn't lost his youthful good looks.
"Hello Joshua."
"Well hello there Madame Minge," Joshua replied in jest.
"I'm not on stage now." They both laughed and entered the bar. There was a strong sexual between them that neither could ignore. As they seated themselves, Joshua hurled a mountain of questions in the direction of his estranged friend. His fear had disappeared in an instant and replaced by a thirst for information.
"So at what point did you become Madame Minge?" he asked and quickly followed up the question with, "At what point did you realise you were gay?"
"Whoah, calm down; Madame Minge is my stage name, here I'm still plain old James," James insisted. Joshua stared attentively, awaiting the answers to an endless series of questions. "I've had a lot of time to reflect in the last five years," James began; his tone was serious and obviously heartfelt. "I'm so truly sorry for the way I treated you. If I could change the past I would. I suppose it's the old cliché, if you hate gays then you

are gay. I just wasn't willing to admit it, not even to myself. I'd always hated the concept of it, and by bullying you and outing you….I made myself feel better. It was wrong Joshua; it was so very wrong of me. There's not a day goes by that I don't regret the way I treated you. Please believe that." At some stage during that powerful speech, without Joshua realising it, James's hand had firmly grasped his.
"I do believe you," Joshua said as he gazed into James's powerful brown eyes. He was taking in every word and storing them away in his mind like valuable jewels. The bitterness that Joshua had been holding in the back of his mind for so long was being replaced by the sweet words he was now hearing. Back in his teenage days, he'd fantasised about the prospect of James sharing his homosexual desires; he'd dreamed of touching every inch of his body, a body that was still as attractive to Joshua as ever.
"Do you forgive me?" James asked sheepishly, tightening his grip on Joshua's hand. Joshua nodded. "So your other question, well, I just made some friends who were drag queens, gave it a go and the rest is history," James blurted out, lightening the mood. This was all so surreal to Joshua. It had never even crossed his mind that James may be gay, let alone working as a drag queen, but here he was and he was remorseful.
"Anyway, enough about me. Tell me about what's been happening to you in the last five years," James insisted.
"Crikey, where do I start?" Joshua asked, then immediately summarised his absence from James's life, "Broke up with Stuart when I realised he'd been sleeping with Michael…"
"Not Michael Smith?!" James interrupted. Joshua nodded his head and continued,
"Left my father after he found out I was gay…."
"How did he find out?" James interrupted again, listening attentively.
"There was an incident…" Joshua was struggling as he mentally recalled his attack but James unwittingly pursued the subject. "
What do you mean, an incident?" he asked.
"I was attacked," Joshua uttered. James's face displayed a look of concern. "But I lived to tell the tale," Joshua continued, shrugging it off. "Anyway, it was reported as a homophobic attack in the newspaper. My father and I fought and I left. I also convinced Karen, his latest partner to do the same."
"Wow," James said in amazement, "I've missed so much. It hasn't been easy for you has it?"
"It's not all been bad," Joshua replied more cheerfully, "I met Brad a couple of years ago and he's been wonderful to me."
"That's nice," James commented, though his words of support seemed somewhat insincere. "Where are you living these days?"

"Well, officially I live at Megan's house, but I spend most of my time at Brad's," Joshua replied. "How about you?"
"Student accommodation," James said with a cheeky grin, then quickly followed it up with, "It's only just down the road if you want to view the pig sty." This was not a good idea, and Joshua knew it. His head was acknowledging that this was a bad idea but his heart was saying something quite different.
"OK, Can't hurt to come and have a glance."

James's apartment brought back memories of Stuart's student accommodation, the main difference being a more feminine feel to the place. There was a mirror as tall as James, surrounded by different varieties of make-up. The décor was mainly pink and the surroundings delicate and gentle. "This is very different from your old room," Joshua commented, noting that James's implications of the untidiness of the place had either been modesty or blatant lies.
"Well a lot has changed," James laughed. He opened the wardrobe and revealed a variety of dresses that he obviously wore during his drag shows.
"Very colourful," Joshua said as he struggled to with-hold his laughter. The contrast between the James of five years ago and the present James was difficult to digest. "Nice duvet," Joshua commented as he glanced at the frills.
"Hey, it's bloody comfy!" James said, hurrying to the duvet's defence, then dashed over to the bed and seated himself on it. "Come and test it for yourself," he suggested. Joshua hesitated for a moment, then joined James on the bed, ensuring a small space remained between them. "See, aren't I right?" James asked light-heartedly. The mood then changed in an instant as James placed his hand on Joshua's knee and said, "I'm really glad you're back in my life. I never thought it would be possible to have you here like this, laughing and joking with me again like old times." They gazed into each other's eyes and Joshua could sense the power James had over him. As teenagers, Joshua had been so sexually attracted to James that he'd often been ready to burst by the end of PE lessons after observing him in the changing rooms wearing his skimpy sports outfits. Joshua knew that he should remove James's hand from his leg, but deep down he didn't want to. James leaned in for a kiss. This was wrong; Joshua knew it was wrong, but every fibre in his body cried proceed. He'd waited ten years for this. Throughout his teenage years, he'd dreamed and fantasised so many times about this very moment, how James's touch would feel, the way he would taste. He turned his face away, rejecting James's lips. "I'm sorry," James apologised. Joshua

turned to face him once again. He simply couldn't resist this opportunity. James gazed at him, unsure of what to say. Joshua placed his hand over the top of James's, which was still placed on his leg, but he didn't remove it; instead he clinched it tightly. James used his free hand to caress Joshua's neck. They both leaned in for a kiss. James's kiss was soft and passionate; it exceeded even Joshua's wildest expectations. It was as though they'd practised for years to achieve this perfect embrace. After several minutes, their lips parted and they remained seated on the bed staring into each other's eyes. It was as though time was standing still, nothing else in the world mattered. Joshua's feelings of guilt were being replaced by ones of contentment. It was as though he'd been trying to squeeze two pieces of a jigsaw together that didn't quite fit for so many years and now they slotted together perfectly. "You're so perfect," James said as he stroked Joshua's hair. The sincerity in his voice gave Joshua no doubts of his honesty.

"You don't know how long I've waited to hear that," Joshua laughed.

"About as long as I have I think," James replied, grinning like the cat with the cream. He reached in for another kiss, but this time it was more vigorous. Joshua could feel James's tongue at the back of his throat; the passion was intense. Without stopping, James unbuttoned Joshua's shirt and pulled it off his back, then interrupted the kiss for a moment to remove his own shirt. James lay on top of Joshua forcefully and yet at the same time passionately. As they continued their intense petting, James began to rub his hand over the bulge that had now formed in Joshua's jeans. Joshua could already sense moistness in his underwear. "Joshy," James muttered between kisses. This one word triggered a flood of memories of Brad, "Nothing's too good for my Joshy….Happy Valentines day Joshy…..I love you Joshy," came Brad's voice inside Joshua's head. These were happy memories; memories of being loved and secure, the way he always felt in Brad's presence. Joshua knew that what he was doing wasn't morally right. He pushed James away from him and stood up, facing the door. "What's wrong babe?" James asked from behind, seductively placing his finger down the top of Joshua's jeans. Joshua turned around and put his shirt back on. "Did I do something wrong?" James asked.

"No, but I definitely did," Joshua replied.

"I understand," James said sincerely.

"I need some time to think, I'll call you," Joshua said and hurried out of the door. James lay down on the bed feeling discontented; he was so near and yet so far from what he'd wanted for so long.

As he slowly walked home in the cold and dark of the night, Joshua could feel his mobile phone vibrating in his pocket. 'How are you feeling babe?' the text message read. At this point the last thing Joshua needed was a reminder of the lie he'd told to add to his sins for which he was already experiencing feelings of guilt.

"What's the story then?" Megan asked excitedly. She'd obviously been anticipating the gossip all day. Joshua seated himself on his bed staring blankly at the wall. Megan seated herself beside him; her concern was obvious. "Tell me what happened," she demanded coldly.

"We came close Megan." Megan was confused. She gave a puzzled stare.

"James and I came close to having sex tonight," Joshua elaborated bluntly.

"What stopped you?" Megan asked. Her tone was non-judgemental.

"I stopped it. I wanted it so badly, but I stopped it. I just couldn't do that to Brad," Joshua replied. "Well, this is a turn up for the books after the way he behaved at your eighteenth birthday party. So he's not only gay, but he wants you too," Megan said, absorbing the situation. It was obvious as she spoke that she hadn't even come close to forgiving James for his actions of the past, even though Joshua clearly had. "Where does this leave you and Brad?" Megan asked. Joshua hesitated for a moment. Without allowing him to reply, Megan followed it up with "He's a great guy you know. Think very carefully before giving him up, especially for someone who's treated you so badly in the past." Joshua nodded in agreement but remained silent. Megan left the room. Joshua lay on the bed, clutching his pillow tightly. Having to decide between staying with Brad or pursuing his former bully was not a decision he'd anticipated. His mobile phone rang; it was James. Initially he ignored the call but James persisted. He answered the phone. James sounded worried on the other end of the line.

"I'm so sorry if I went too far," he apologised. Joshua accepted his share of the blame and insisted he wasn't angry. "Can we meet tomorrow please, just to talk?" James pleaded. Joshua agreed, although unsure of whether or not he'd made the right decision.

Joshua awoke the following morning and could feel a pleasant stroking sensation in his hair. His eyes adjusted to the light of a new day and he turned to investigate. Brad was laying beside him, gazing lovingly and slowly running his fingers through Joshua's hair.

"Morning sweetness," he said affectionately.

"How long have you been here?" Joshua asked.

"A couple of hours or so, Megan snuck me in," Brad replied, "How are you feeling?"

"Much better now," Joshua said, his feelings of guilt increasing by the minute. The fact that Brad had made such a lovely gesture made Joshua feel even more ashamed than he already did for the events of the night

before.
"If you don't feel up to going to uni' we could have a nice quiet day in," Brad suggested. Joshua contemplated this for a moment, then quickly remembered that he'd agreed to visit James. He knew what he had to do; he just needed to tell one more white lie to excuse himself and then he'd visit James and tell him that he couldn't see him anymore.
"No, I'm ok, I really should go to uni' today."
"OK, I'll drive you then," Brad offered and proceeded to kiss Joshua's forehead. His kindness only made Joshua feel worse.

After being escorted to university, Joshua quickly headed for James's flat. As he approached the door he reminded himself of what he planned to say, "I can't see you anymore James, it's not right." Joshua was late, and James had obviously been eagerly anticipating his visit. As soon as he knocked on the door it opened. James stood before him, he'd made an effort with his attire even though he had no plans to leave the house.
"Thanks for coming, come on up."

James seated himself on the bed and invited Joshua to join him. He did so, but intentionally left as much space between them as possible. "I'm not going to bite," joked James. His appearance was as stunning as ever. To Joshua, James was completely flawless. Joshua moved in a little closer and James did the same. "I was worried I'd done something wrong when you dashed off last night," James said innocently.
"I did something wrong, not you," Joshua replied. James gazed at Joshua requesting elaboration. "It's not fair on Brad; he's such a nice guy. I had to leave because I didn't trust myself, I knew what was going to happen," Joshua confessed.
"If you're so happy with Brad, then why would you be so easily tempted?" James asked seriously. Joshua was uncomfortable with this line of questioning, and James could sense he'd touched a raw nerve.
"Brad is a lovely person. He'd do anything for me……He loves me," Joshua uttered reluctantly.
"Do you love him?" James asked.
"Yes; he's the most genuine person I've ever met," Joshua said in his own defence.
"I'm sure that Brad is everything you say he is, but if you were truly happy with him, we wouldn't have been ripping each others clothes off here last night," James pointed out.
"Stop, I feel bad enough!" Joshua yelled, the conversation was clearly bothering him. "Brad gives me security, love…"

"You're bored Joshua, it's obvious." James was right. This hadn't dawned on Joshua until he'd just heard it said out loud. He wanted to be in love with Brad because he was the perfect man, kind and caring, but it wasn't enough. James was exciting, and that was something that Brad couldn't compete with. Joshua stared at James for a moment. The look he gave said more than words ever could, it confirmed that what James was saying was right. He wanted James in a way he'd never wanted anything before in his life, but he knew that before he gave in to these feelings he had to be honest with Brad.

Joshua waited outside the grounds of the university for his lift to arrive. He was an hour early but he didn't care. It was an unseasonably pleasant February day, and Joshua needed time to think. He watched as happy heterosexual couples passed by the entrance to the university, hand in hand, laughing and joking. He wished that society would allow him to have such a relaxed relationship in which public displays of affection were acceptable. He watched one particular couple that were seated on a bench. They were aged in their early twenties. The male was seated straight and his girlfriend beside him leaning her head on to his chest. The male was stroking the female's strawberry blonde hair affectionately. The love between them was unmistakable to any passer by. They appeared to be in a little world of their own. The female was particularly oblivious to anything that was happening around her; she was safe in her boyfriend's arms; she had everything she wanted or needed right there on that bench. Watching the romance between the couple reminded Joshua of all the special moments he'd shared with Brad. He recalled the way Brad so often held him in his strong arms and how secure and loved it made him feel. What James was offering was something quite different, he offered passion and excitement, but Joshua wondered if that was really what he wanted. He contemplated the worth of excitement and fun in comparison with the love, affection and thoughtfulness he received from Brad. Joshua was so deep in thought that he couldn't hear Brad calling his name from the open car window. Brad stepped out of the car, approached Joshua and tapped him on the shoulder. Joshua quickly looked up.

"You were miles away," Brad said with a smile.

"Brad, you're early," Joshua said as he returned to earth.

"I thought better to be early than late," Brad replied, "Come on, let's go, we can spend a quiet evening together." They entered the car and Brad placed his hand on Joshua's knee. He could sense that Joshua's mind was still elsewhere. "Are you feeling ok?" Brad asked, and then, without allowing time for a reply, he said, "I love you." Joshua hesitated for a moment, then placed his hand on Brad's and replied,

"I'm ok now. I love you too," and smiled sweetly. At that moment the decision had been made.

"How about a horror film tonight?" Brad suggested as he loaded the DVD player.

"Only if I have you to protect me if I get scared," joked Joshua. They giggled as they curled up together on the sofa.

"I'm glad my Joshy's feeling well again," Brad commented affectionately. Just as they became settled in each other's arms, Joshua's mobile phone began to ring. The phone had been placed on the coffee table.

"Shall I grab it for you?" Brad offered. Joshua panicked for a moment, fearing who the caller may be and insisted on answering the call himself. He dashed to grab it and saw the name 'James' on the screen. Brad glanced at him with curiosity. "Expecting a call?"

"Nah," Joshua lied, "It's just Megan." He rejected the call and immediately switched off the phone. "It's our night tonight, let's have no interruptions," he said with a smile. Brad grinned as he returned to his content state of delusion. Joshua felt satisfied that he'd made the right decision as he realised how easily he'd almost let go of what he'd longed for for so many years.

The next morning, Joshua awoke on the sofa and realised that he and Brad had spent the night there. He glanced around for signs of life but could only spot a 'post it' note. It read, 'Had to leave early babe. Didn't want to wake you. Love and hugs, Brad xxxx.' Joshua smiled as he read the note and said, "Bless him," to himself. He picked up his mobile phone and switched it on. A text message from James awaited him. 'Please answer the phone babe.' Joshua had to put an end to this situation. He realised that the only way was to cut all ties with James; as difficult as it would inevitably be. The phone had barely located a signal when it began to ring. Joshua was hesitant to accept the call but realised he couldn't delay this any longer.

"Hello," he answered the call, as though he had no idea who the called would be.

"Joshua, I've been so worried. Did you tell Brad about me? What did he say?" James fired questions without giving any opportunity for Joshua to respond.

"We need to talk. I'll come and see you later," Joshua said, squeezing a statement in. His tone was cold and to the point. James could immediately sense that things had changed and his tone altered in line with Joshua's.

"What's wrong Joshua? Have you changed your mind?" James persisted. Not wanting to have this conversation by telephone, Joshua re-iterated that he'd visit James later that day. He ended the call, then sprawled himself back on to the sofa. He noticed a framed photograph of he and Brad and picked it up. At that moment he knew he was doing the right thing.

James answered his door within seconds of Joshua's first knock. He'd obviously been preparing for his visit since the earlier telephone conversation. He looked as perfect as ever with no hair out of place. They remained standing once James had closed the door. Joshua was unsure of what to say, and James could sense that he hadn't visited to consummate their relationship, the sort of visit he'd been hoping for the previous day.

"What's wrong Joshua? What's changed?" James asked bravely. His heart was residing in his throat.

"Can we sit down?" Joshua requested. They did so. James placed his hand on Joshua's.

"I don't understand what's happening. Yesterday you seemed sure that it was me you wanted and now I can sense that's changed," James said, feebly struggling to cling on to Joshua for dear life.

"James…You're exciting, you're gorgeous, and I've wanted you for as long as I can remember…" Joshua began.

"And I'm all yours, you can have me," James interrupted.

"It's not that simple," Joshua explained, "I realised last night that Brad gives me everything I've always wanted…"

"But it's me that you want. The connection with me is stronger than what you feel for Brad and you can't deny that," argued James. Joshua looked downwards and became silent. "You're in a rut, let me bring you out of it," James pleaded. Joshua made eye contact with James once again. James leaned in to initiate a kiss and the temptation was too strong. Joshua couldn't even attempt to stop it happening. Their tongues met and the kiss became more passionate. James pushed Joshua down onto his bed and began kissing his neck; he then felt James's teeth sinking into him. The excitement reminded him of the very first love bite he'd received from Stuart in his teenage years. Joshua assisted as James pulled off his shirt, closely followed by his own. Their erections were apparent as James orally explored Joshua's upper body. Sensibility and loyalty were forgotten. This is exactly what they both truly wanted. James vigorously yanked Joshua's jeans down to his ankles and took his firm penis deeply into his mouth. His tongue explored Joshua's shaft first of all, then lightly stretched all the way down. Joshua could feel enough sensation to lose any kind of concentration, but at the same time wasn't receiving quite enough stimulation to cause an ejaculation. James released Joshua's penis from his mouth and licked his way down to his scrotum. He took Joshua's testicles into his mouth one at a time and sucked on them vigorously.

Joshua panted, feeling as though he were about to explode. Sensing that ejaculation was imminent, James pulled off Joshua's jeans completely, turned him over and lay him face down on the bed. He caressed Joshua's buttocks for a moment, admiring their shape. He reached for a tube of lubrication from his desk drawer and smothered Joshua's anus hole in it. As he cushioned his anus with lubricant, he placed two fingers inside him. Joshua squirmed with delight.
"This is what you want, isn't it Joshua?" James confirmed.
"Yes, I want you James," Joshua whispered. He felt a sense of both pain and pleasure as James entered his body. His penis was the thickest he'd ever taken. Joshua was unable to move as he lay face down on the bed, James's body pushing against his own. He'd never before experienced such excitement. At this point any feelings of guilt had evaporated and thoughts of Brad couldn't be further from his mind. Although James's actions were robust and powerful, at the same time he had a gentle nature and asked Joshua as to whether or not he was comfortable. Just when Joshua felt he couldn't take any more, he received a final thrust against his G spot followed by a warm feeling inside him as James reached a climax. Joshua could sense that he was perspiring but nothing mattered at this time. James slowly withdrew his penis from Joshua's body, then lay beside him and placed his arms around his chest.
"You don't know how long I've waited for that," James said as his head affectionately rested on Joshua's shoulder. This made Joshua feel so special, as though he were the sexiest man alive. Neither of them knew quite what to say next, having just shared such an intense experience, and yet both not knowing what the other was feeling. But no words were necessary. James lay beside Joshua lightly caressing his chest and occasionally kissing him. Although the gas fire was generating some heat, the room was slightly cold, giving Joshua a sensation as he was being touched. They lay silently for almost an hour before James had the courage to ask, "What happens next?" Their actions had completely contradicted Joshua's reason for visiting James. Although, if the truth be known, although he didn't like to admit it even to himself, what he visited James to say could have been done by telephone. He made the visit because he was still at that point severely tempted by James. He hesitated to respond to James's question for a moment. What could he say? His actions that day were completely against his own morals. He'd dismissed Stuart from his life for a similar offence and now he'd been unfaithful himself, and to someone who definitely didn't deserve this kind of betrayal. Noticing Joshua's hesitance to answer, James excused him from the question. "Don't worry. You don't have to answer that right now."

"No James, it's ok, I have to be honest with Brad. I'll tell him the truth about what happened between us."
"Will you stay with him if he'll allow you to?" James asked.
"No," Joshua replied with no reluctance. "What happened today proves to me that I'm not truly happy with Brad." James kneeled up on the bed in order to look Joshua in the eye.
"Are you sure it's over then?" James asked. Joshua nodded. "I don't mean to rush you or anything….but this wasn't just a bit of fun for me. I really want to be with you," James declared.
"I feel the same way," Joshua replied.

Brad arrived home later that day to find the living room floor populated with bags full of clothes and Joshua's personal belongings. His heart sank without a trace. Joshua trotted down the stairs, unaware of Brad's presence. He immediately noticed his facial expression and the look he gave in return confirmed Brad's worst fears. "I'm sorry," Joshua said as he placed another bag on the floor. "If I'd known you'd be home so soon I wouldn't have done this now. I was going to take these to Megan's and come back to talk to you later."
"I don't understand," Brad said feebly, his lips beginning to tremble.
"I'm really sorry Brad," Joshua continued.
"Please Joshua, we can work it out, whatever the problem is," Brad pleaded.
"Let's talk." Joshua agreed, forcing a vague smile. They seated themselves and Brad immediately held Joshua's hand as though it would stop him from leaving. "I'm going to be totally honest….even if it means you'll hate me," Joshua said.
"I could never hate you," Brad declared.
"I hope not," Joshua said as he released his hand from Brad's. Joshua went on to explain the events of the evening he'd met James in his alias of Madame Minge. Brad glared blankly, wondering where this story was going. "I met up with James for old times sake," Joshua went on.
"Well that's ok, you're allowed your friends," Brad interrupted innocently, killing Joshua with kindness to the bitter end.
"I know, I know," Joshua continued, realising again how adorable Brad was. Brad clearly wasn't putting the pieces together using the information he'd been given. Perhaps this was because he didn't want to face the obvious truth. It was time for Joshua to be blunt. "I slept with him Brad, I slept with James," he blurted out. Brad's face had never looked so pale; Joshua's guilt multiplied by ten at the sight of it. He couldn't stand to see such a harmless person so disappointed.
"Why?" he asked calmly.

"I'm sorry. It wasn't planned," Joshua apologised honestly. Almost as though he hadn't heard Joshua's reply, Brad went on to say,
"I love you." His tone of voice resembled that of a child, stunned by what he'd heard. He stared blankly at Joshua, not lovingly, the way he usually did, but not with contempt either, there was nothing.
"I'm sorry," Joshua repeated.
"So you keep saying," Brad said; his tone of voice was so cold but yet not loathsome. Joshua had never heard him speak in such a way. "Don't you love me anymore then?" he asked sharply.
"Not in the way you want me to," Joshua replied gently.
"Did you ever?" Brad continued. The interrogation was beginning to make Joshua uncomfortable but he realised that answering Brad's questions was the least he could do, considering what he'd done and he couldn't bare to be anything but completely honest, even though this wasn't what Brad wanted to hear.
"I don't know." At this moment Brad wanted to crawl into a hole and die. He'd deluded himself for so long that he and Joshua would be together forever, and Joshua had made no effort to discourage him. Now here he was, his world crumbling around him.
"I'm not exciting enough for you, am I? I'm boring," he muttered. Brad had just hit the nail on the head, but Joshua couldn't possibly confirm this. He didn't need to. His expression said it all. "It's ok," Brad continued, "I know I'm right, you don't have to say it. I'm going for a walk. You've got an hour to finish packing and be gone." Brad walked out. Joshua wanted to say something to make things right, but there were no words that would mend a broken heart. Joshua seated himself for a moment. He had a feeling of emptiness in the pit of his stomach, almost the same way as if someone close to him had died. Although guilt ridden, he knew he had to pack his belongings and leave as soon as possible, for Brad's sake as well as his own.

"What's going on?" Megan asked as she entered Joshua's room to discover a sea of filled carrier bags and a suitcase. Joshua was filling drawers with his belongings. He turned to face her. The expression on his face said it all. "You've left him," Megan announced to herself. Joshua nodded neither sadly nor happily. "Was it….?"
"Yes I'm with James now," declared Joshua. Megan was shocked.
"You're a couple. Just like that it's over with Brad!?"
"Brad was everything I thought I wanted in a man," explained Joshua, "But with James there's this spark."
"I understand," Megan said, though Joshua wasn't convinced. "So do I get to meet him again soon?" she asked cheerfully.

“That’d be great,” Joshua replied, and she embraced him, giving him the same love and support she’d never failed to provide before.

Chapter 10

Joshua arrived at James's flat after a long day of studying at University and entered using the key James had cut for him. As soon as the pair laid eyes on each other, James dashed over to Joshua's arms to tell him of how he'd missed and loved him and to share a kiss. Even after a year of togetherness the passion was as strong as ever.

"Joshua…" James began, using his manipulative tone and puppy dog eyes. "Why don't you just move in once and for all?" Joshua pondered James's suggestion for a moment as he gazed into his eyes. He'd held back from moving in with James because Janice's house was a convenient safety net in the event that his relationship failed. Perhaps after a year of bliss though, it was time to take the plunge. At 24 years of age Joshua finally felt he belonged and there wasn't a doubt in his mind that James was 'the one' and they were destined to be together.

"I think you're right James. Let's do it!" Joshua agreed. James threw his arms gleefully around him.

"I love you so much," he declared.

"I'll start bringing my belongings over tomorrow," Joshua said in between the flurry of kisses he was being inundated with.

No sooner had Joshua's new residency been decided when his mobile phone sounded. The number calling was unrecognised.

"Ooh, is this a secret lover?" James asked playfully as he prepared for the evening ahead.

"Hello," Joshua said as he answered the call.

"Joshua, can you come over please? It's very important," came Neil's voice from the other end of the line; he'd obviously shot straight to the point through fear of Joshua hanging up the phone.

"Dad, is that you?"

"Yes," Neil replied, "It's important. Please come to see me."

"Why should I?" Joshua asked. James glared at him with concern.

"Because we're family," was Neil's reply as he attempted to cling to any sense of loyalty that remained in Joshua. "I need you," he uttered. His tone of voice demanded sympathy. It was like that of a child who'd just broken the neighbour's window and wanted to be forgiven.

"I'll be over in a couple of hours," Joshua said with no affection in his voice; he was simply stating his intentions. He immediately ended the call and faced James's worried facial expression.

"You can't seriously be going over there?!" he said in disbelief, having picked up the key points of the conversation.

"He's my dad," Joshua pointed out.

"But he's dangerous!" James argued.

"I'll be ok, he sounds as though he needs me," Joshua said with

uncertainty in his voice. James approached him and took his hand.
"You're a big softy.... I guess that's why I love you." He held him tightly and begged him to be cautious.
"I'll be fine, Joshua reassured him. "I'll be back before you get home from work, safe and sound, I promise."

Joshua arrived at Neil's house; the house that had been his own home for so long. The garden looked as though it hadn't been touched in years. He slowly approached the door, still wondering whether or not he'd made the right decision to come. As he reached for the doorbell, an avalanche of memories came pouring into his head. He recalled living in this home as a child with his mother, the beatings from Neil, the good times and bad. Before he had a chance to press the button to activate the bell, the door swung open.
"I watched you walk up the driveway," Neil said as he stood in the doorway before him. Neil's appearance was untidy; his hair was long and hippy-like and it was obvious he hadn't shaved in weeks. He looked completely pathetic, but Joshua was reserving judgment. He wasn't about to allow Neil to play on his sympathies. "Hello Dad," uttered Joshua dutifully.
"Come in son," Neil said as he cleared the hallway.

Karen's presence was still strong throughout the house. Her absence however was abundantly clear by the lack of cleanliness. "I'm sorry the house is in such a mess," Neil apologised.
"Not my problem," Joshua said harshly.
"Do you want a drink or anything?" Neil asked.
"Tea would be nice," Joshua replied reluctantly, wondering if his father would remember how he liked his tea and whether or not the mug would be clean. Neil trotted off to the kitchen, giving Joshua an opportunity to be nosey. He glanced at some post that had been left on the coffee table. Several of the envelopes contained reminder bills and final notices.
"I've no tea. How about a cold can of lager?!" Neil yelled from the kitchen. Joshua sighed.
"It's ok Dad, I'm not that thirsty." Neil returned to the living room holding a can of lager in one hand and an unlit cigarette in the other. He placed the can down in order to light the cigarette.
"Thank you for coming Joshua," he said as he seated himself and instructed Joshua to follow suit.
"I still don't understand why you wanted to see me," remarked Joshua, making it clear that he had no intentions of being manipulated.
"This isn't easy for me son," said Neil. He realised that attempting to gain Joshua's sympathy was not an option given his son's current attitude.
"Get to the point please," requested Joshua. His bluntness was a side of

him that Neil had never seen before. While it didn't suit his current beg for sympathy, Neil couldn't help but feel pride for the strength of character his son was now displaying.
"Joshua. I don't like the man I used to be…" Neil began. Joshua was intrigued by this statement and gave a stare of disbelief. "I've been trying to change; I'm drinking less and I'm attending anger management classes. I really want to get my life on track," he continued, as though attempting to sell an unpopular product. "And…." Joshua said in a tone that implied he couldn't care less.
"I've learned at the classes that family support is essential. I need help to get my life on track, to turn over a new leaf," Neil begged. Even Joshua couldn't doubt the obvious sincerity in his voice, although he found it ironic that his father was slurping lager from a can as he said these words. He did however struggle to find a possible ulterior motive Neil may have had.
"What exactly are you asking of me?" Joshua asked.
"I want you to move back home son. Come home where you belong." Neil's statement was laughable. Joshua had never felt he belonged with his father since the day Lynne had died, however even after all that had happened, Joshua wasn't cruel enough to point that out. He gazed at Neil, judging his sincerity. Neil looked pathetic, like a lost soul. "Please Joshua," he begged. Joshua could feel himself becoming sympathetic towards his father which forced him to question his own strength of character. 'Am I a pushover?' he wondered. He was almost angry at himself for the compassion he was beginning to feel. "I need some support if I'm to get my life back on track," Neil re-iterated. This was the man who'd beaten his mother, beaten, teased and tormented him; but he was still Joshua's father, and he longed so desperately to believe that he wanted to change.
"OK, I'll move back in on a trial basis," Joshua agreed reluctantly. "But I come and go as I please. I have my boyfriend here whenever I want, and you have no say in how I live my life whatsoever," he announced forcefully. Neil nodded in half-hearted agreement to his son's terms.
"I love you son," Neil said with a tear in his eye. He was so convincing. Joshua hesitated for a moment before replying with,
"I love you too Dad. I just don't always like what you do." Neil stood and held his arms open. Joshua wanted to throw himself into them and forget everything that had happened, but taking things one step at a time seemed the sensible thing to do. "I'll be back later with my things," Joshua said, ignoring Neil's gesture, and departed.
"Joshua," Neil called from behind him. He turned to face his father.
"Thank you son. You don't know what this means to me," Neil said.

Joshua nodded and closed the door behind him.

At Janice's house just minutes later, Joshua was gathering his personal belongings together and packing them into suitcases and bags.
"So it's finally happening is it?" Megan said as she entered the room, carrying two cups of tea. "Can't say I wasn't expecting it. You and James belong together."
"I'm not actually moving in with James," Joshua said casually as he threw various pairs of boxer shorts into a carrier bag. Megan placed the two cups down and her hands on her hips.
"What's going on then?" she asked. The doorbell rang.
"You'd better get that," Joshua pointed out, feeling glad to be able to pause the conversation. Megan left the room and Joshua continued frantically packing. It was as though he felt that the more items he packed, the less likely he was to be talked out of the move. Megan quickly returned accompanied by James, who darted to Joshua for a passionate embrace the way he always did. Megan watched in confusion as their lips locked together. She wondered what the excitement was for if they weren't moving in together.
"Thought you could use a hand with the packing," James said.
"James…." Joshua began, attempting to explain the situation. Without allowing Joshua a chance to speak, James turned to Megan and joked,
"I hope you don't mind me taking him off your hands." Megan glared vaguely at him but all he could think of was how much he was looking forward to living with Joshua. "It's going to be so fab' living together!" James screeched, turning back to face Joshua; his camp tone of voice reflected his excitement. "And you can come over whenever you want," James said, turning back to Megan.
"Joshua, I'm confused," Megan began, "You said you weren't moving in with James." James glared at Joshua in search of an explanation.
"Please wait outside Megan. James and I need a word alone," said Joshua. Megan nodded and left the room.
"What's going on?" James asked. The expression on his face had changed so suddenly from one of anticipation and joy to one of disappointment. He gazed at Joshua, longing for him to deny what Megan had just unwittingly announced.
"My dad needs me," Joshua began. James's face now displayed a look of anger. "After all he's done…."
"He's still my father, and he wants to turn his life around. He needs my help," Joshua explained.
"But does he deserve it?" James asked.
"I gave you a second chance," Joshua reminded him. James was silenced by this statement. "We'll still see plenty of each other, and it won't be

forever. As soon as dad's sorted I'll move in with you as planned." James smiled vaguely and they hugged.
"You're too nice for your own good sometimes," James said as he rested his head on Joshua's shoulder.
"I agree," Megan commented as she returned to the room, accompanied by a forced smile.
"At least you've saved me the trouble of making another announcement," Joshua said in jest.
"Have you room in there for a little one?" Megan asked. Joshua and James smiled and welcomed her into their embrace.

"You are joking! After all the bastard's done!" Greg yelled fiercely in response to the news of Joshua's new residence. Neither Janice, Megan nor Joshua had seen Greg this exasperated before.
"I'm sorry Greg. This is my decision and I've made it," Joshua said firmly and returned to his packing upstairs. Greg grabbed hold of a plate and threw it at the wall. Megan and Janice glared as it shattered into a thousand pieces. Megan excused herself awkwardly, leaving Janice and Greg alone together.
"I'm sorry," Greg said as he began to calm down.
"What on earth got into you?" Janice asked in amazement.
"It winds me up the way that the bastard treats him and Joshua runs back for more. I really thought that he'd learned better than this now!"
"I agree Greg. What I can't understand is why you're so worked up about this," Janice said in search of an explanation for Greg's seemingly excessive concern. "He's not even…." Greg began and interrupted himself.
"Not even what?" asked Janice.
"It doesn't matter," Greg said and grabbed his car keys.
"Where are you going?" asked Janice. Greg left without answering.

Neil was seated, slowly smoking a cigarette in his dimly lit living room. He placed it down on the ash tray for a moment and poured himself a glass of whiskey. He took a sip and savored the taste; this was a celebration after all. There was a loud banging on the front door. Anticipating Joshua's arrival, he put out the cigarette and hid the drink. He turned the light switch to its maximum brightness and glanced around to confirm the tidiness of the room. He fluffed the cushions on the sofa and headed for the door. As he opened it, he expected to find Joshua on the doorstep surrounded by a sea of luggage.
"Hello Neil," Greg greeted him sarcastically as he barged his way into the house. "Who are you?" Neil asked. He vaguely recognised him, having met him at the hospital at the time of his wife's death but couldn't immediately recall where they'd met before.

"I'm the man who knows what's best for your son. And that's not you!" Greg yelled. "You don't remember me do you?"
"No I don't and you don't know me, so how the hell would you know if I'm good for my son?" Neil replied angrily.
"Let's just say that your first impression was a lasting one," Greg commented. Neil glared at him attempting to put the pieces together. "Ten years ago I tried to save your wife's life, and all you could do was blame your teenage son," Greg announced. Suddenly it all became clear in Neil's mind. He became humble for a moment.
"I was grieving. It was a difficult time for both of us."
"If only that were all. I know everything. I know about the beatings. I also know about Karen. You haven't changed and you never will!" Greg was losing his temper. Neil was speechless. He had no idea how Greg could have all of this information. All of a sudden he remembered that he'd seen Greg at Janice's house the day he'd begged Karen to return.
"You're knocking off that Janice," he said insultingly.
"I love her!" Greg said, rushing to his own defense, "I know it's an emotion you're unfamiliar with."
"I bet you don't have kids do you?" Neil asked. Greg's facial expression gave his reply without the need for words. "Well you're not having mine!" Neil continued. "Stop it Dad!" Joshua shouted from the doorway, "Greg's been good to me and I want you to respect him. As for you Greg, this is my decision and it's none of your business." They both glanced sheepishly at the man they considered a son. "Well are you going to help me with my bags then?" Joshua asked; instantly dismissing the situation he'd just interrupted. Both Greg and Neil dashed to assist him by relieving him of a suitcase each. "See, teamwork!" Joshua said in a patronising manner that wouldn't normally be tolerated by either recipient. However, on this occasion Joshua held all the cards and took full advantage of the upper hand. "Is my room just the way I left it?" he asked as he marched up the staircase.
"Exactly," Neil replied promptly as though trying to score bonus points.

Neil was absolutely correct. The room didn't appear to have been seen by human eyes in years. Not a single item had moved. Perhaps it had been kept as a shrine to the estranged Joshua, or perhaps Neil just wasn't one for cleaning. All of the belongings Joshua hadn't felt the need to take with him were firmly in place. Dust had gathered but it was clear that a spring clean had happened somewhere along the line, probably by Karen, Joshua thought. It was almost like stepping into a time warp back to his teenage years and this made Joshua feel uneasy. Not all of the memories kept in this room were happy ones. He recalled his mother tucking him into his bed at nights during his childhood; he remembered how she kissed him on the forehead and sang to him in an effort to lull him off to sleep before the inevitable sounds of shouting of the night ahead. He recalled having friends over and putting on a brave face. There was still a framed family photo more than ten years old sitting by the bed. Joshua picked it up. Whoever said that the camera never lies should have their own honesty questioned. This photograph displayed a happy family unit, Lynne's arms securely around both her son and her husband. Three smiles that looked so real, but it wasn't, the photo was a lie; it had never been that way. Joshua's reminiscing was cut short by the vibration and sound of his mobile phone ringing.

"Is everything ok? Is your dad being nice?" James asked without even a greeting. "I've been here about three minutes and already you're whittling," Joshua laughed. "Sorry, just wanted to make sure you were ok," James replied genuinely. Joshua smiled. It felt good to know how much he was loved. Although James's call was very welcome, it reminded Joshua of just how much he'd rather be moving in with him. He reminded himself why he was doing this. It was to assist Neil in turning over a new leaf, and he'd longed for that for so many years. "If he starts playing up get in a taxi and come straight over," James continued using dominance he applied so rarely that Joshua secretly adored.

"It'll be fine, I promise," Joshua assured him. He quickly ended the call and returned downstairs to break up the potential feud.

He proceeded slowly down the staircase in apprehension of the atmosphere he'd inevitably be about to endure. He could hear the faint sound of laughter. Surely not; what could either of them possibly have to chortle about? Before reaching the living room, Joshua parked himself on the staircase and began to eavesdrop into the conversation.

"He really used to do that as a child?" Greg asked.

"Sci-fi mad he was!" Neil declared. Joshua was willing to overlook the reason behind the laughter being embarrassing tales of his childhood if it meant Greg and Neil could hold a civil conversation. "He's a good lad for helping me like this, considering all that I've done to him," Neil continued. The sincerity in his manner even appeared to be convincing Greg.

"He's one in a million," Greg commented. As Joshua listened to them, it gave him a warm feeling inside to know how deeply these two men obviously cared for him. They were two of the most unlikely people to ever be having this discussion, but here they were. At one point Joshua hadn't intended to speak to his father again and he'd once considered Greg to be just his doctor. He picked himself up off the staircase and joined his father and Greg.

"Don't worry about me Greg. I'll be fine," he said. Greg nodded and

excused himself. "I'm proud of you dad. I never thought you'd get Greg on side," Joshua said as he grinned like a Cheshire cat.
"The good doctor's not daft, he knows I'm trying," Neil replied. There was an awkward pause in which Joshua contemplated embracing his father for a moment. He'd kept an open mind about Neil although he'd taken a big step by moving in with him. At this stage however, he wasn't quite ready to completely let his guard down.
"I'm really tired, goodnight," Joshua said, removing himself from the situation. Neil's face looked slightly disappointed as he replied simply with "Goodnight," and Joshua returned to his room.

"I can't believe we've reached a stage where I can feel comfortable here like this," James said as he leaned across Joshua's bed in search of a kiss which became several kissed.
"The past few weeks have been great, my dad's really changed. I never thought I'd see the day." Joshua's smile beamed as he said these words. For so long he'd have given anything for a genuine closeness with his father, and now he finally had it, along with acceptance of his sexuality. In addition to this he had what he perceived to be an amazing boyfriend and many special people in his life, his studies were successful and it seemed as though nothing could happen to jeopardise this.
"I love you," James reminded Joshua yet again. Joshua smiled with contentment and leaned in for a further embrace. Joshua's mobile phone began to ring as it often did at intimate moments much to James's annoyance. "Ignore it," James suggested, interrupting the kiss.
"Let me just check who it is," Joshua replied as he reached for his phone on the bedside table. He glanced at the mobile phone and then immediately at James in a state of shock. "Who is it?" James asked, curiously concerned. Joshua glared at him, failing to respond. James grabbed his hand and glanced at the phone.
"Stuart! What the hell does he want?" James blurted out. He was feeling slightly insecure and angry to discover that Joshua was still in contact with his former partner. "Since when do you and Stuart chat on the phone?" James asked. His tone of voice suggested a hint of annoyance.
"We don't," Joshua protested, "I haven't heard from him in years." James gave a look of mistrust. "Don't you believe me?" Joshua asked, showing a rare display of aggression and annoyance. The phone stopped ringing, leaving James and Joshua in silence. "I don't know why he's calling. We haven't spoken in years," Joshua said more calmly. James looked into his eyes. It was obvious that he had issues with trust and yet he'd never mistrusted Joshua before. The phone began to ring again. James snatched it from Joshua's clutched and answered it.
"Hello," he said abruptly.

"Is that you Joshua?" asked a confused Stuart on the other end of the line.
"No it's his boyfriend," James replied. Joshua glared at James in disbelief and grabbed the phone back.
"Hello Stuart it's me. What can I do for you?" Joshua asked.
"It's been a long time," Stuart pointed out, "How are you?"
"Fine," Joshua replied bluntly. "What do you want?"
"I need to see you Joshua," Stuart insisted. Joshua was in no mood for niceties or strolls down Memory Lane. After all, he was currently the recipient of a dirty look from James.
"What do you want Stuart? I thought I made it clear that I wanted you out of my life a long time ago," Joshua said, refusing to give an inch.
"It's very important Joshua. I have some news that could affect you." Stuart's tone of voice was serious. Joshua could sense that he meant what he was saying.
"Are you in Sheffield?" Joshua asked, feeling himself backing down after such a successful attempt at being forceful.
"Yes. Can you meet me tomorrow lunch time? How about Pizza Hut?" Stuart suggested. Joshua reluctantly agreed and speedily ended the phone conversation. James looked sheepish as it dawned on him how his lack of trust had been so apparent.
"I'm sorry," James quickly apologised, while still curious to learn of the outcome of the call.
"Don't you trust me?" Joshua asked. James hated to see the look of disappointment on his lovers face and began to feel very guilty.
"I do trust you. It just scared me for a moment to see that Stuart was calling," James explained, attempting to escape from the hole he'd dug for himself.
"I haven't seen him in years," Joshua clarified.
"I know that," James admitted sheepishly.
"He desperately wants to see me tomorrow. God knows what for. So I said we'd meet him for lunch at Pizza Hut," Joshua said. His subtle invitation reassured James further of the innocence of his intentions. James opened his arms in search of a hug. Joshua obliged. Never before had Joshua witnessed this insecure side of James's personality. While on the one hand it brought into question the level of trust James had for him, at the same time Joshua couldn't help being grateful that James cared enough to become jealous.

The Pizza Hut was so crowded that Joshua and James were struggling to spot whether or not Stuart was among the crowds. The restaurant was mainly populated by families enjoying their Sunday lunchtime treat.
"Perhaps this wasn't the best idea for a meeting place," James whispered

in Joshua's ear as they waited to be seated.
"Table for two?" a waiter asked.
"There's one more joining us," Joshua replied and the waiter guided them to a table.
"Why are we even giving Stuart the time of day?" James asked viciously.
"I'll ask him what he wants and then he can fuck off," Joshua replied, putting James's insecurities to rest. Joshua noticed Stuart arrive at the doorway.
"Ooh someone's gained a few pounds," James bitched.
"Don't be a cow," Joshua said, half joking. He waved Stuart over, then quickly realised he wasn't alone.
"Who else do we have here?" James asked sarcastically. As Stuart walked closer to the table his companion showed his face. It was Michael. "You are joking. Bloody Michael too!" exclaimed James.
"Hello," Stuart greeted them. Michael remained silent. Both were obviously confused by the presence of James whom they remembered as a homophobic bully. The group silently glared at each other. Everyone was in disbelief over the combination of people present. There were so many questions in everyone's minds and yet everyone was so reluctant to speak. Both James and Joshua were confused by Michael's presence. Did this mean they were now a couple? Had they been a couple ever since the demise of Stuart and Joshua's relationship? Meanwhile Stuart and Michael were finding themselves even more astonished by James's attendance to this luncheon. Had Joshua now forgiven him? Are they a couple? Is the most notorious homophobe of the city now actually gay himself? A waiter interrupted the silence by asking if an extra seat was required for the unexpected fourth diner. Once everyone was seated, the many questions were deferred for a moment as Stuart began to make small talk. "I think I might have the pepperoni. How about you guys?"
"Why don't we just get on with discussing whatever it is we're here for?" James suggested fiercely. Joshua glared at James in disapproval.
"It's a very delicate subject," Michael said, pussyfooting around.
"I think Michael just means we should get reacquainted before having such a serious discussion," Stuart intervened. The key issues of Stuart and Michael's relationship and James's sexuality were still being carefully avoided.
"So are you two a couple then?" James asked, then without giving anyone a chance to speak he continued with, "I mean, after you cheated on Joshua I'm surprised you've stayed together all this time. You don't seem like the type to stay with one lad." Stuart immediately retaliated by pointing out,
"You're hardly Snow White yourself. You ruined Joshua's 18th party for a

start…" "Please don't do this!" Joshua begged.
"He's right," Michael butted in, offering the voice of reason.
"Just for the record, Joshua and I are a very happy couple and he's forgiven me for everything," James announced calmly.
"I can't believe you turned out to be gay," Stuart laughed, now maintaining the calmness of the situation. Michael was at this point struggling to with-hold his own giggles.
"So are you two a couple now?" Joshua asked with genuine interest.
"Yes," Stuart replied with a smile, "We have been ever since…" He interrupted himself before finishing the sentence with, "we split up."
"It's ok," Joshua assured him.
"Don't want to rub your nose in it," Stuart continued. Joshua was himself surprised by how relaxed he felt in the present company.
"James and I may be an unlikely couple but we're very happy," he announced. This declaration gave James a sense of confidence in what had been an awkward situation. Even James was loosening up. The conversation became more light- hearted as the meal went on and the former friends caught up with each other's lives. It was almost beginning to slip people's minds as to why they were there. They talked of mutual friends from days passed and quirky events of their lives.
"Is anyone having a dessert?" Michael asked as the table at this point was covered with empty plates. It was all so casual. Joshua began to realise at this point that all the bitterness had vanished. He'd forgiven Stuart and Michael for their betrayal. Perhaps it was because Joshua himself was so happy and content with his new life that the grudge didn't seem worth holding on to. Everyone agreed that they were suitably stuffed and couldn't possibly find space for a dessert.
"I'll ask for the bill next time the waiter passes then," Stuart added.
"Is this all we came here for, to make small talk?" James asked. Michael and Stuart were speechless as they glared at him.
"James," Joshua said in his most nagging tone.
"No he's right," Stuart interrupted, "We asked to meet you for a reason. I'm really sorry that I have to tell you this, considering how nice this meal has been. It's felt just like old times for me."
"Me too," Michael added. Joshua was beginning to feel uncomfortable about what was about to be revealed. "We got in touch because we felt it was only fair to tell you," Michael said. It was obvious that this was a painful topic for Stuart and Michael to discuss as they seemed to be avoiding making this statement for as long as possible. However, the delay was angering James.
"Will you get to the point," he blurted out.
"James please, this is obviously difficult for them," Joshua said in his

usual mature, understanding way.
"No, it's ok, we should tell you immediately. It's very important. Time is of the essence," Stuart replied. A look of concern passed between James and Joshua. "Joshua, I'm really really sorry…." Stuart began, tears filling his eyes. Michael placed his hand on Stuart's.
"Would you like me to tell them?" he asked.
"No," Stuart insisted, "Joshua, If I've ruined your life I'll never forgive myself, I mean that."
"You haven't Stuart; I forgive you for what you did. I'm happy now," Joshua said as he missed Stuart's point entirely.
"You don't understand Joshua. I'm HIV positive," Stuart announced, "and you could be infected too." HIV, the 3 most feared acronym for any gay man to hear. Joshua had always been so cautious and had had so few sexual partners that he'd never even considered the possibility of being infected. And now here he was looking the virus directly in the eyes, looking Stuart directly in the eyes. His eyes were filled with sorrow and regret, he was like a lost soul. "I'm so sorry," Stuart apologised again. James immediately stood and reacted with anger, but Joshua remained silent and stared at Stuart, unintentionally causing him to feel uncomfortable. James's yelling was just a background noise to Joshua, he wasn't concentrating enough to hear the words. It was simply noise. He turned his attention to Michael who looked ghostly white with concern as his partner was being yelled at. His eyes met Joshua's and he froze for a moment. Eventually a tear reached the surface and slowly trickled down Michael's face. He made no attempt to stop it. James halted his screaming and glanced at Michael. At this point they were all oblivious to the stares coming from around the restaurant.
"Do you have it too Michael?" James asked calmly. Michael nodded his head and more tears flowed from his eyes. He couldn't bring himself to answer the question verbally. "So you two both have it and now we probably do too," James clarified, his voice increasing in volume again. Joshua slowly stood. He looked at everyone in turn, first James, then Stuart and finally a distressed Michael.
"James is right. It looks like we're all going to pay for your promiscuity," Joshua said, aiming the comment at Stuart. He couldn't deny that his actions were the cause of this potential epidemic, not even to himself. "I need to be alone for a while," Joshua declared and left the restaurant.
"It's a shame we couldn't have all got together for a nicer reason since we got on so well," Michael said with genuine disappointment. With Joshua no longer present, there was nothing left to say. James was the last person that Michael and Stuart had expected to be spending the afternoon with and they had little time for the former homophobic bully. The feeling was

mutual. James slammed a twenty pound note on the table and departed without a gesture of goodbye.

Outside, James looked left and right but Joshua was nowhere in sight. He attempted to call him on his mobile phone but it had been switched off. His next move was to immediately light a cigarette, but even that didn't calm his nerves. The words spoken by Michael and Stuart were spinning around in James's head; over and over they repeated themselves. He needed Joshua but he had disappeared.

"James is gay!" exclaimed Stuart to an equally shocked Michael.
"I didn't see that one coming either," Michael commented. They were both questioning his intentions towards Joshua.
"Do you think he's genuine about Joshua?" Stuart asked.
"Seems a bit of a turnaround from outing him at his eighteenth party," Michael added. Although they both felt terrible about the news they'd had to deliver to Joshua, the surprise of James's sexuality was clouding the issue.
"I'm going to send a text message to Joshua," Stuart announced. He typed, 'Hi Joshua. We're so sorry. If you need us please call.'

Greg answered the door to a distressed Joshua drowning in an ocean of tears. "Is Megan in?" he asked, vaguely attempting to conceal his upset.
"Yes, come in. Joshua what on earth's the matter?" Greg asked as Joshua entered the house. Janice approached them and immediately asked the same question. The last thing Joshua wanted at this moment in time was a sea of concerned faces all asking what was wrong. All he wanted was a moment alone with Megan, the one he always turned to in times of crisis.

"What on earth's the matter? Megan asked with concern as Joshua entered her room looking like an emotional wreck. She threw her arms around him without hesitation. "Tell me what it is." Her voice was soft and compassionate.
"It's Stuart and Michael…" Joshua blurted out. Megan let go of Joshua and glared at him in shock.
"Stuart and Michael! What have they got to do with anything?" she asked. Joshua fell back on to the bed and held his head in his hands. Megan seated herself beside him and placed her hand on his leg. Joshua explained the situation.
"I don't believe it. They both have HIV! You must get a test!" Megan insisted. "Yes you must," Greg agreed as he revealed himself in the doorway, closely followed by Janice. Joshua passed a slightly annoyed glance to them, although his irritation over the eavesdropping was quickly forgotten when he received a concerned hug from what he considered to be his family. "We'll get you tested as soon as possible,"

Greg said in his bedside manner. The doorbell rang and Janice excused herself to answer it. Both Megan and Greg attempted to re-assure Joshua that he may be perfectly healthy. They then began shooting questions at him such as, "Did you always use a condom?" Janice returned to the room.
"You've got a visitor Joshua," she said softly. James entered.
"I figured I'd find you here."
"He's with the people who love him," Greg remarked. He then followed it with, "I'm going to arrange for a HIV test for Joshua tomorrow. Shall I do the same for you?"
"Yes please," James replied, "After all, we're in this together, whatever the outcome." Joshua rushed into James's arms and cried.
"I'm so sorry. I could have infected you."
"I love you Joshua. That won't change no matter what happens," James assured him while clinging to him tightly. Observing the display of genuine love and concern put to rest any doubts Megan still had of James's sincerity. She had struggled to accept his change of personality, but her mind was now at ease.

"Do you want to stay at my place tonight?" James asked as he and Joshua wandered down the dark, silent street.
"I'd better go home to Dad. Besides I think I want to be alone tonight. I'll definitely be over tomorrow though, before we go for the tests," Joshua replied. "Will you tell your Dad?" James asked.
"I think so," Joshua said, pausing his steps as though it was the most important decision he'd ever made.
"Are you sure?" James asked looking puzzled. "He's been honest with me about his problems, perhaps I owe him the same courtesy," Joshua suggested. James's facial expression revealed his skepticism over the issue.
"Why don't I come with you for moral support?" James suggested. Joshua pondered this for a moment.
"Well he claims he can handle my sexuality and our relationship, let's do it," Joshua said boldly.

The smell of cigarettes and alcohol hit them as soon as they entered Joshua's house. They walked into the living room to find Neil snoring beside several empty liquor bottles. "I thought part of your anger management was supposed to be cutting down on the booze," Joshua commented loudly, causing Neil to stir.
"I'm trying," Neil said half asleep.
"I need to talk to you Dad," Joshua announced as he collected the empty bottles and headed for the litter bin.
"You don't need to do that son," Neil said as he struggled to stand. He

turned around and became aware of James's presence. Immediately he pulled down his jumper to conceal the area of his chest that had been on display. "Oh hello son," he said to James.

"Hi," James replied briefly.

"I think we should all sit down," Joshua suggested. James and Neil complied. "What is it....Only Corrie's on in 5 minutes," Neil said light-heartedly.

"I decided we should tell you this because we've been so honest with each other lately and we've become close. I trust you Dad," Joshua began. Neil thanked him, he was obviously touched. "I'm still absorbing this myself...." Joshua continued, a tear departing his eye. James put his arm around him. Neil struggled to contain his reaction to this.

"An ex-partner contacted me and we met up. He had some important news..." Joshua was stalling with the information, unsure of what reaction to expect.

"We don't have to tell him right now," James said lovingly.

"I think you should," Neil interrupted sternly, "Spit it out." He was attempting to conceal his slight anger toward James.

"To cut a very long story short, my ex is HIV positive and so is his current partner," Joshua blurted out.

"And....have you shagged this boy?" Neil asked. The bluntness of this statement surprised both Joshua and James. Joshua hesitated for a moment, then nodded. James held his hand.

"So this means you have it too.....this disease," Neil said. Joshua nodded again. Neil stood and walked towards the kitchen. He then slammed his fist into the door causing a dint. James held Joshua's hand more tightly. Neil turned to once again face his son and gave him a look of contempt.

"You fucking dirty pervert!" he yelled. James leaped off his seat and screamed,

"Don't you talk to him like that!" Neil pushed James back on to his seat and pinned him down.

"I'll talk to my son any way I like," he said aggressively. Joshua stood and pulled Neil away from James.

"No you fuckin' well won't," he cried, "and you leave my boyfriend alone."

"It's boyfriends that got you into this. Fags like him!" Neil shouted.

"How dare you?" asked an outraged James as he stood behind Joshua.

"All I ever wanted was for you to be a man, get a girlfriend, have kids like normal people. If you'd done that you'd be healthy instead of fearing for your life right now," Neil said more calmly.

"I can't help the way I am, and I'm not a pervert," Joshua retaliated. He could feel the anger bubbling up inside him. He was about to explode.

"You're both perverts, sick perverts. Maybe if you are ill it'll teach you a lesson," bellowed Neil. Joshua could no longer control his anger. He thumped Neil on the nose, causing him to fall back into the kitchen door.
"Well what do you know, you can fight like a man, even if you are a big girls blouse," Neil said sarcastically.
"Calm down Joshua, he's not worth it," James intervened. "You're right, let's go," Joshua said and he and James headed for the front door.
"Must have been your mother's influence that made you this way," Neil remarked behind Joshua's back, "She always was pathetic." Joshua slowly turned to face his father, the demon of his life.
"My mother was a damned good woman and she didn't deserve the treatment you gave her, so don't you dare speak ill of her now!" Joshua demanded.
"Just get out," Neil said, using tissue to catch the blood from his nose. James patted Joshua's shoulder encouraging him to leave. They slowly turned and walked further away towards the door. Joshua stopped sharply and turned once again to face Neil.
"You killed her you bastard! It's all your fault," he yelled. Years of penned up anger were reaching Joshua's surface. He slowly walked towards Neil. "Did you think I didn't know what was going on? She was a nervous wreck. Did you think I didn't hear the beatings? You ruined her life, and you have the nerve to judge me! You killed my mother! You might as well have put a gun to her head!"
"Oh no, that's where you're wrong," Neil protested, "You were being a little shit as usual and your mother couldn't concentrate on her driving, that's what caused her death."
"You had me believing that for years, but not now, I know the truth. She was in a state that day because you'd been laying into her again. It was not my fault. It was you Dad, and I hope you get what's coming to you, the sooner the better," Joshua said in a manner that was so calm that it sent a shiver down Neil's spine.
"Let's go Joshua, leave him to it," James said. Joshua agreed and they headed for the door. Neil sat on the arm of his chair in a slight state of shock. Joshua faced him one final time as he closed the door.
"Damn you father, damn you to hell."

"I'm proud of you Joshua," James said as they walked down the driveway. "I'll go and collect my things tomorrow before we go to the hospital. You don't mind me moving in do you?" Joshua asked.
"Nothing would make me happier," James replied, offering a smile in spite of the events of the day. James held Joshua tightly for several minutes before they walked any further. Neither of them cared who was around to see it.

Chapter 11

Joshua was lying awake following a sleepless night. He held James tightly in his arms and listened as he breathed gently in his sleep. The wicked statements Neil had made the evening before had been spinning around in Joshua's head. "Pervert. Pervert. Fagot. Your mother always was pathetic…" He glanced at the clock; it displayed the time as nine o'clock. Joshua gently removed himself from James, attempting not to disturb his sleep. He stood and walked toward the door.

"Come back babe," James said as he awoke. Joshua sat beside James on the bed.

"Sorry, I didn't mean to wake you," he apologised. James opened the bed covers inviting Joshua to return. He lay back down and received a passionate kiss closely followed by a hug. His grip was so tight, as though he never wanted to let go.

"I love you babe," James said and kissed him on the forehead. "Did you sleep at all?"

"No," Joshua replied honestly. Joshua's mobile phone began to ring.

"Ignore it," James said. Joshua glanced at the phone and noted that the caller was Greg.

"It's Greg, I'd better get it." He reached for the phone and answered it.

"Hi Josh, it's Greg. I've booked your HIV tests for two o'clock this afternoon. Is that ok?" Greg asked from the other end of the line.

"We'll be there," Joshua replied.

"Good luck. I'll make sure I'm around when you arrive at the hospital," Greg said. Joshua thanked him and ended the call.

"Greg's got us in for the tests at two. He'll be waiting at the hospital for us," Joshua said to James.

"He's good to you," James commented.

"He's been more of a father to me than my dad ever was," Joshua said. James smiled and placed his arms around Joshua once again. "We'd better get ready. We have to collect my things from dad's house before we go to the hospital," Joshua said as he removed himself once again from James's grip.

"I'll be here for you no matter what," James assured him.

They arrived at Neil's house and were confused by the presence of his car in the driveway. "He should be at work, shouldn't he?" James asked.

"The bastard! He knew I'd come to collect my things today and he's waited in on purpose," Joshua replied angrily.

"Let's come back another day," James suggested. Joshua pondered this idea for a moment, then glanced at Neil's front door and insisted on proceeding with his plans. "Shall I come in with you?" James asked.

"No, you'll just aggravate him. Wait here. I won't be long," Joshua replied as he affectionately caressed James's arm. He slowly entered the house. The door was unlocked which surprised him because Neil had always kept his door locked whether home or not. "Dad, are you here?" Joshua asked loudly, but received no response. The house was silent. Joshua wondered if Neil had left the house on foot. He walked into the kitchen where an empty paracetamol bottle was acting as a paperweight on top of a folded note. Joshua picked up the bottle to confirm it's emptiness. He opened the note and began to read it. From only a brief glance, it was obvious what the rest of the note would go on to say. In a state of panic, Joshua dashed into the living room where he discovered Neil lying completely still on the floor. He was so pale and lifeless. He screamed and stood glaring at his father as though he'd been frozen and couldn't move. James barged in, reacting to Joshua's scream and halted immediately at the sight of Neil.
"Oh my god! …. Is he…?" James began. Joshua didn't respond. He simply stared at his father in a state of bewilderment. James kneeled down beside Neil and felt his neck in search of a pulse. He stood and faced Joshua. "We're too late," he uttered. A tear rolled down Joshua's face. "I'm so sorry babe," James said sympathetically.
"Why?" Joshua asked coldly. "He was a bastard, why be sorry? Look at me. I must be pathetic. I'm crying over him."
"He was your dad," James reminded him.
"Well he wasn't much of one," Joshua added and he slowly walked into the kitchen. James followed him. He picked up the empty paracetamol bottle. "I bet he took them last night after our argument. They'll have been slowly killing him all night long." James picked up the suicide note. "I think you'd better read this."
"I don't care what he has to say," Joshua said as though trying to prove he didn't possess a heart. James skimmed the note and his face went ghostly white. He passed the note to Joshua and insisted he read it.
"Seriously, you're going to want to read this." Joshua began to read.

Hello Joshua

If you're reading this then that means by now you must be rid of me for good. I'd like to think that this may sadden you a little but I'd understand if you were glad I'm gone. I made your life and your mother's life a misery and I realise that now. It hadn't quite dawned on me until you gave me some much-needed home truths tonight.

You were right. Lynne's death was my fault. I was out of control and my behaviour was inexcusable. What a shame I had to be sitting here while a paracetamol overdose slowly kills me before I realised it. As hard as this may be for you to believe, in my own way I truly did love you and your mother. I realise now that I only blamed you for Lynne's death to conceal my own feelings of guilt and regret. Deep down I always knew it was my fault, I just didn't want to face it.

I am truly sorry for all the pain I've caused. All of my possessions are yours Joshua. I'm not a rich man, but this house will be a good start for you and James.

There is something else you ought to be aware of. Lynne and I always said you'd never learn the truth, but now that you're without us both it seems only fair for you to know, you were adopted. I'm not sure who your real parents were, a young couple I think. If I knew any more I'd tell you.

I wish you happiness for the rest of your life.

Love Dad xx

Joshua's heart sank almost without a trace. He placed the suicide note back on the kitchen table and slowly walked back to the lounge. James stayed close to him.

"All these years I've tolerated him, and he's not my real father," Joshua said softly as he glared at Neil's body. "What a coward. He couldn't admit it to me could he? He doesn't deserve my pity." James grabbed Joshua and held him tightly.

"It'll be ok," James promised. "Why don't you go and lay down upstairs? I'll call the police." Joshua nodded and slowly headed upstairs. He lay on his bed and experienced a feeling that was difficult to fathom. He felt freedom; it was as though discovering that Neil wasn't his real father had freed him from the nightmare, none of it mattered anymore.

Several hours later he stirred and glared at the clock. For a few precious seconds he was blissfully unaware of the situation, until reality set in and what had happened came flooding back to his mind. He leapt out of his bed and walked down the stairs. When he reached the bottom the first thing he saw was the sight of Neil being carried outside in a body bag. Greg was reading the suicide note as he stood beside Megan, James and Janice.

"What does it say?" Janice asked. Greg was about to respond but was interrupted by James.

"He was adopted," James announced. "The bastard wasn't even his dad." Megan and Janice appeared shocked and yet Greg didn't seem to have reacted in any way to the note. Megan became aware of Joshua's presence and hurried over to him.

"Are you ok?" she asked. Joshua gave a look of uncertainty and Megan flung her arms around him. The body was now gone and Joshua was left with only a selection of sympathetic ears. It's at times like these one realises who their real friends are. "You'll look after him won't you?" Janice asked, directing her question at James.

"Of course." Megan, Janice and Greg respectfully departed, sensing that company wasn't what Joshua required. They all went through the motions of offering support of any kind while knowing that in reality there was little they could do to aid Joshua's pain at this time. With the threat of HIV looming, the death of Neil and the discovery of his adoption it was difficult for Joshua to prioritise which issue to emotionally deal with first. The following week Joshua spent in solitude with the exception of James's company.

Joshua was straightening his tie in front of James's mirror. James entered the room and commented, "You look fabulous." Joshua thanked him and turned to inspect his attire.

"You don't scrub up so badly yourself," Joshua complemented him. "We don't have to go to the funeral you know, nobody would blame you if you didn't," James said. Joshua considered this for a moment.
"I made the arrangements and if I don't turn up I doubt anyone else will. I at least owe him this."
"You owe him nothing," James insisted.
"You must think I'm pathetic, still wanting to please him after all that's happened," Joshua commented.
"Not at all, I think you're the sweet caring man I fell in love with," James replied. Joshua smiled and put his arms firmly around James. His grip was so tight and protective and made Joshua feel completely safe, as though at this moment in time nothing and nobody in the world could harm him.
"I don't want to ruin your suit," Joshua said as he pulled away slightly, sensing his tears were landing on James's shoulder.
"I don't care," James said almost aggressively and pulled Joshua back into his clutches. Joshua wept wildly for so long, he wondered if his eyes would ever stop watering.
"Why couldn't he have said the things he wrote in the letter to me, instead of making sure he was dead before realising how sorry he was?"
"He was a coward," James replied.
All of a sudden weeks, perhaps months, or even years of penned up anger, hurt and frustration was being released. Joshua had tried so hard to be strong but recent events had taken their toll on his emotions.

The journey to the church was silent. James drove the car slowly with a pre-occupied Joshua in the passenger seat. He was gazing out of the window, not looking at anything specific, his mind filled with thoughts and memories. He didn't quite understand himself why he was making such effort for a man who'd done very little for him besides cause him pain. Perhaps it was some sort of misplaced loyalty, especially as he wasn't a blood relation. It hurt James to watch Joshua in so much pain and he felt so useless himself. At times when he had a free hand he'd touch Joshua's leg, but Joshua didn't seem to notice. He parked the car on arrival at the church and switched off the engine. Joshua continued to glare through the window, seemingly oblivious to his surroundings.
"We're here," James said, but received no response. "We're here," he repeated slightly more loudly but not angrily. Joshua turned his head and left his trance. "Are you ready?" James asked. Joshua nodded his head.

The graveyard was a picture of tranquillity. There was barely a sound to be heard. "Looks like we're early," James pointed out as they approached the hole in which Neil was about to be buried. They stopped walking and Joshua glared at the ground.

"Hard to believe he's going to be down there for all eternity," Joshua said as he gazed at the soil. The vicar approached them and offered his speech of condolence that he'd already reeled off twice that day.
"When are the other guests arriving?" the vicar asked.
"There aren't any others; he wasn't well liked," Joshua announced slowly.
"I see," the vicar replied awkwardly. "Ok then, we'll get started." A figure dressed in black appeared behind them. As she walked closer Joshua began to recognise her.
"Karen!" he said in shock, and immediately reached for a hug. "I can't believe you're here." Karen embraced him and commented,
"It's been a while."
"I didn't mean for it to happen," Joshua defended himself.
"I know; and I understand how he could be. It would be very easy for a fight to have got out of control," Karen empathised, still holding Joshua tightly. Joshua thanked Karen for her attendance. "He loved me," she replied, then hesitated for a moment before continuing with, "In his own way he cared very deeply, he was just a very mixed up man."
"He wasn't my real father you know," Joshua revealed.
"I know, he told me some time ago," Karen replied. Joshua was startled by Karen's knowledge. "He didn't disown you when Lynne died; you've got to give him some credit. He knew you weren't his son but he did care for you to some degree." It was so typical of Karen to see the best in someone, and in Neil's case there were a lot of negative aspects of his personality to wade through before any goodness was visible. Joshua hadn't looked at the situation from this angle before and it was certainly food for thought. If Neil really didn't care for him at all he would have deserted him a lot sooner. Joshua felt a tap on his shoulder and released himself from Karen's arms to investigate. Megan, Janice and Greg were all standing behind him.
"We thought you could use some support," Megan said as she smiled as sweetly and innocently as ever.
"Thank you so much," Joshua said with a tear in his eye.

All of the guests stood in silence as Neil's casket was lowered into the ground. James held Joshua's hand; although he wasn't entirely sure his gesture had been noticed. Similarly to the state he'd been in in the car, Joshua simply glared at the ground, only passively listening to the vicar's speeches.

"It's a beautiful day isn't it?" Megan asked rhetorically as the guests stood awkwardly in the street, each mentally assessing Joshua's state of mind. Greg eventually changed the subject.
"Have you had the results yet of the HIV tests? I hate to ask, I

just want to know you're ok." Joshua glared at Greg, seemingly speechless. James quickly jumped in.
"We haven't actually had the tests yet." Greg instigated a short walk for he and James.
"Listen James, I know the timing's really bad, but you need to take those tests. It's vital that we catch this virus if you have it," Greg said with genuine concern.
"Thanks Greg, I'll talk to Joshua when we get home," James replied. Greg affectionately placed his arm around Joshua's shoulder and said, "Thanks for looking after him, we appreciate it." It briefly occurred to James that Greg was going beyond the call of duty, but this was no time for judging relationships. As they rejoined the group, it seemed their absence had been unnoticed. Joshua was firmly wrapped around Megan.
"Would you like to go home babe?" James asked softly. Joshua slowly released himself and nodded. His face was teary and ghostly white. James placed his arm around him and they slowly walked to the car.

The return journey was almost as awkward as the last. James contemplated raising the subject of the HIV tests but struggled to find the right moment. Joshua was so distant. "Are you ok?" James asked, unsure of how to approach a conversation.
"Yeah, I'm ok," Joshua replied in the most convincing tone of voice he'd used so far that day.
"I spoke to Greg earlier …" James began evasively.
"About what?" Joshua asked bluntly.
"I know this might not be the best time to discuss this…." Joshua gave a look of concern. "Greg asked me about HIV tests," James mentioned daringly. Joshua's look became more of a stare, although James had to devote at least a portion of his attention to the road. A silence loomed again for several moments and it became obvious that Joshua wasn't going to offer his views on the subject of the tests without further effort from James. "We really ought to be going for those tests," James added.
"You're right," Joshua agreed. He then turned his head towards the window as though the conversation was over.
"How about we go to the clinic now?" James asked spontaneously. Joshua's attention quickly returned to James. "I know the timing isn't ideal but we need to do this," James insisted.
"OK," Joshua replied without argument. His face gave no clues to what he was feeling.
"Are you sure you're up to this?" James asked with concern.
"Let's just go," Joshua said firmly. James turned the car around at the next opportunity and headed for the clinic. Not a word was spoken for the remainder of the journey.

On arrival at the clinic, Joshua immediately sat in the reception area, leaving the talking to James. He picked up a newspaper but the words were all rolling into one. His mind couldn't focus on anything but Neil's death, the question of his paternity and now his health. James seated himself beside Joshua.

"They won't keep us waiting too long." Joshua vaguely attempted a smile but it was clear he was anything but happy. James took his hand and assured him that whatever was to happen they'd stay together. A tear trickled down Joshua's face. He turned to look James directly in the eye and said, "Thank you."

"I love you," James reminded him. Joshua offered a slightly more convincing smile.

Within minutes they were all called through to a small, dull room where a middle-aged female was seated. Joshua and James were left alone with the woman who introduced herself as Mary.

"I'm a counsellor," Mary said. James quickly halted her in her tracks, "We don't need counselling, we just want to take the tests, get the results and be off."

"I'm afraid it's not that simple. The procedure is that you receive some counselling first, then we take a blood sample and within a fortnight we'll be able to tell whether or not you have the virus," Mary explained matter-of-factly.

"Two weeks!" James screamed with shock.

"I thought we'd be done and dusted in an hour or so."

"I'm sorry, it just doesn't work like that," Mary said firmly.

"Well can we just do the blood tests and go then?" James asked, attempting a compromise.

"No, you have to talk to me for a little while first, besides your partner looks like he needs some counselling. I'm here to help," Mary said, looking at Joshua who was seated and completely silent. He looked as though he wasn't paying attention to what was being discussed. "Please relax and let's talk for a little bit," Mary said using her nurturing tone she'd spent years perfecting with her worried patients. James could sense he was fighting a losing battle and sat beside Joshua. "So what makes you think you might have the HIV virus?" Mary asked using her daily script.

"It's a former partner of Joshua's that contacted us to tell us he had the virus. We then became concerned for our own health," James replied. Joshua stood and walked towards the door. "Joshua wait," James pleaded as he stood himself. Joshua briefly turned back.

"I can't face this right now."

Without a moment's hesitation Joshua was out of the door. James was about to apologise but was immediately interrupted by Mary.

"It's ok, you go and take care of him," she said. James smiled at the obvious kind nature of this stranger.

James arrived back at his car where he found Joshua in the passenger seat. He opened the door on the driver's side and entered.
"Please, let's just go home," Joshua requested. James nodded, pecked Joshua on the cheek and started the motor.

"I'm going for a nap," Joshua said before he'd removed his shoes. He dashed upstairs obviously attempting to avoid the outside world. James landed on the sofa; the events of late were taking their toll on him as well. His eyes closed briefly but his attempt at napping was quickly interrupted by the sound of his mobile phone ringing. He glanced at the screen and noted that Greg was calling. He contemplated ignoring the call for a moment but realised that Greg was more than likely feeling as unsettled as he was.
"Hi Greg."
"How did the tests go?" Greg asked abruptly. James hesitated for a moment before replying.
"Joshua didn't feel up to it."
"James you need to get these tests taken," Greg insisted slightly harshly.
"He couldn't….he's had a difficult time of it," James defended them.
"I'll be over in a few minutes," Greg said and abruptly ended the phone conversation. James wandered up the stairs and stood beside the bed in which Joshua lay.
"Everything ok?" Joshua asked without looking at him. James sat on the bed. Joshua continued to face the wall.
"Greg's coming over," James blurted out. Joshua turned his head to face him.
"I want to be alone. Can't people just leave me alone?" he cried.
"We care about you babe," James said softly.
"My head is spinning. I've just found out that my parents could be anybody……and now the man I thought was my dad is dead…..we might have HIV, it's all too much. I just need some time," Joshua screamed as he wiped away tears from his eyes. James couldn't stand seeing his lover this way but felt completely powerless to help. Joshua's spirit had completely faded away and he was almost unrecognisable as the man James had fallen in love with. "Please, just tell him to go away when he arrives," Joshua begged, and without awaiting a response returned to his original position facing the wall. James stood and walked towards the door. The sound of Joshua's wailing became louder; he couldn't hide his emotions any longer. James glanced at Joshua as he cried, then slowly walked up to the bed and climbed in. He lay beside Joshua for a moment, then put his arm around his chest. Joshua didn't react immediately but

several minutes later he placed his hand in James's. James wrapped his entire body tightly around Joshua's. Joshua continued to weep and tightened his grip on James's hand.
"It'll be ok," James promised. They lay silently in each other's arms for several minutes. Even without words this gesture gave Joshua a warm feeling of being loved and it soothed his pain a little. The calmness of the situation was disturbed by loud banging on the front door. Joshua continued his firm grip of James's hand signalling for him to ignore the interruption. The knocking continued and became increasingly louder.
"He knows we're here, he's not going to leave," James said apologetically as he released himself from Joshua's clutches and headed for the door.
"Get rid of him. I just want to lay here for a while," Joshua muttered.

As soon as the door was open, Greg barged his way into the house. He was carrying a plain white bag.
"Is Joshua here?" he asked as though his life depended on it.
"He's having a lay down, he doesn't want to be disturbed," James said defensively.
"Please, it's important." Greg looked deadly serious. It was obvious he was not going to be fobbed off.
"I really don't see what disturbing him will achieve," James argued. Greg emptied the bag revealing two small boxes similar to home pregnancy test kits. They were labelled 'Orgaquick Advance'.
"What are they?" James asked in confusion.
"These are HIV home test kits. If you and Joshua use these we'll know in 20 minutes whether or not you have the virus," Greg said assertively.
"I've never seen or heard of these before," James said. He was completely overwhelmed by this and the prospect of being just minutes away from discovering his HIV status. "Where did you get these?" he asked.
"They're not legal in the UK. They are sold in America though," Greg replied.
"How did you…." James began.
"Never mind that," Greg quickly interrupted him, "Let's just get Joshua down here and you can both take these tests."
"Why are they illegal here?" James asked, his intrigue taking over.
"It's believed that a HIV test should be accompanied by a counselling session. Don't worry though, I'll be here," Greg reassured him. There was a moments silence before he added, "Come on James, you know it makes sense."
"I'll ask him, but if he doesn't want to take the test I won't force him," James said. Greg could sense that this was non-negotiable and reluctantly

nodded and sat down. "Wish me luck," James said as he headed for Joshua's bedroom.

Joshua hadn't moved an inch since James had left him. He seated himself beside Joshua and stroked his hair for a moment.

"Did you get rid of him?" Joshua asked.

"No I didn't. He wants us to take the HIV tests now," James replied.

Joshua turned and sat up, startled by James's statement. James went on to explain what Greg had suggested. "So what do you think?" he asked.

Joshua pondered this for a moment. In spite of his emotional state he was still able to think with some degree of logic.

"20 minutes and this will all be over. We'd know for definite if we had HIV?"

"Yes," James re-iterated.

"Let's do it," Joshua said confidently. He pulled off his bedclothes and stood. James put his arm around him.

"You've made the right decision," Greg said from the doorway.

Downstairs, Joshua and James seated themselves whilst Greg fumbled around in his bag. They were both wondering what this ordeal would involve and dreading that in just minutes they'd discover whether or not they'd contracted a deadly virus. Greg opened the boxes and revealed what looked to be similar to lollipop sticks.

"What on earth are you going to do with those?"

"You lick it," Greg replied.

"Is that all?" Joshua asked in amazement, having expected a needle to be involved.

"Yes, the saliva will tell us all we need to know," Greg replied. "Ok, who's up first?" Greg asked as he held the sticks in the air.

"Wait," James said abruptly. Joshua and Greg both gazed at him awaiting an explanation for his outburst.

"There's something I really have to do first," James insisted and leaped out of his seat. He grabbed his car keys and headed for the door.

"I'm sure this can wait 20 minutes," Greg said in a tone of voice that failed to conceal his annoyance.

"Trust me, it can't. I won't be long. Don't do anything until I get back," James said and dashed out of the house before allowing anyone to argue.

"Where on earth has he gone?" Greg asked for the 13th time while running his hand through his own hair in a state of despair. Joshua glanced at him but was too emotionally drained to react in a way he normally would.

"Well if he's going to be out for a while I'll pop the kettle on," he said, and wandered into the kitchen. Greg sat down and remained silent until Joshua returned with the tea. "Makes everything better doesn't it? A

nice cup of tea," Joshua said, attempting humour as he passed Greg a cup.
"Even if you are HIV positive, it's not the end of your life you know. It can be controlled these days. You could live a long life," Greg said in an attempt to lighten the mood. It began to rain outside. Joshua walked over to the window.
"The weather outlook is as dreary as the outlook for the rest of my life."
"Please don't talk like that," Greg pleaded, "Whatever happens, we'll get through it together." Joshua turned to face Greg.
"Why?"
"Why what?" Greg appeared to be puzzled by the question.
"Why do you care so much? All I am to you is the friend of your partner's daughter," Joshua elaborated.
"You couldn't be more wrong," Greg replied.
"Do you think James is coming back?" Joshua asked, changing the subject.
"Of course. Maybe he just needed a little bit of alone time to digest everything," Greg suggested. A silence loomed as Joshua continued to stare out of the window, watching as people dashed around, attempting to escape the rain as though staying dry was the most important thing in the world. He wondered if that was their biggest problem in life. The passersby were drowning in the rain but Joshua was merely drowning in his own self-pity. He glanced at the clock on the wall, but the time had barely moved since his last look.
"Maybe I've been unfair to James. I've burdened him with all my problems when he's going through hell at the same time," Joshua said. Greg stood.
"Don't be so hard on yourself. Nobody blames you for being upset."

An hour passed before James returned looking as though he'd been running a marathon. Joshua and Greg glared at him as he dashed through the door.
"I came home as quickly as I could," he said as he gasped for breath. Before giving anyone else a chance to speak, he immediately followed with, "Shall we get on with it?" James appeared to be ready and raring to go. Greg and Joshua were intrigued by this fresh attitude that James had arrived back with; after all, it seemed he'd escaped a situation he'd felt uncomfortable in and yet now he was keen to proceed with the tests.
"Where have you been?" Joshua enquired, intrigued by James's eagerness to proceed with the tests.
"You'll find out," James replied with such a straight face that Joshua couldn't decide whether his absence had been for a positive or negative reason. Greg quickly took advantage of James's willingness and reached for the test sticks. He passed one each to James and Joshua.

"So we just lick them?" Joshua asked. Greg nodded.
"Then we leave them for the 20 minutes and the colour will tell us your HIV status." Everyone hesitated for a moment, all knowing what needed to be done but at the same time all unwilling to instigate it. Greg marked the sticks 'JA' and 'JO'. James and Joshua licked the sticks and returned them to Greg. Greg suggested placing them in the bathroom. Everyone agreed.
"We don't want to watch them change colour," Joshua added. Greg left the room with the test sticks firmly in his grasp. James and Joshua stood and glared at each other for a moment.
"No matter what happens, it won't change anything between us," James insisted. Joshua shed a tear and faced the floor. James grabbed him and held him in his arms. Greg returned and immediately gained everyone's attention. He glanced at his watch.
"It's four o'clock. At twenty past I'll go upstairs and check on them."

Each of the following twenty minutes felt like days. Every minute someone would glance at the clock, then at the others. "A watched clock doesn't move," Greg pointed out light-heartedly ten minutes into the wait. Joshua and James smiled vaguely, but clearly no-one was in the frame of mind for humour. "10 minutes to go," Greg said, desperate to break the silence. He didn't want to state the obvious but at the time what else was there to discuss? As twenty past four drew closer and closer Joshua began to pace the living room floor. "It's time," Greg declared. Joshua immediately returned to his seat and put his hands together between his legs; he began to tremble. James cautiously placed his arm around Joshua's shoulder. "I'll go and check the results," Greg said.
"Wait," James insisted sharply. "There's something I have to do first."
"What could you possibly want to do now?" Greg asked, he too now becoming agitated. James dashed over to his coat and pulled out a small bag from the pocket. He returned to his seat beside Joshua who was paying little attention and seemed to be lost in his own thoughts. Greg stood watching in amazement as James delayed the revelation they'd all waited so long for.
"Joshua, Joshua," James repeated, attempting to grab his attention. Joshua stared James directly in the eyes.
"Why don't we get the test results out of the way? I'm sure this can wait," Greg pleaded.
"It can't," James insisted. James opened the bag and revealed a small box. He opened the box, it contained a titanium diamond ring. "Joshua, will you be my civil partner?" James asked. A marriage proposal was the last thing Joshua had been expecting. He glared at the ring. He'd never been offered a gift of such elegance.

"I don't understand. Why now?" Joshua asked. Without giving James a chance to reply he continued, "Don't you want to see the test results before making a commitment?"
"No, that's exactly why I'm asking you now," James replied. Joshua continued to glare at him in disbelief. "I love you. No matter what happens I want us to be together. It's unconditional Joshua. Whether you have HIV or we both do, I want to be with you." Greg smiled.
"I think you're a lucky lad Joshua."
"I'm the lucky one," James said as he returned Greg's smile.
"I can't James. I can't agree to this," Joshua said, turning away.
"But why?" James asked, desperation in his voice. Joshua stood and once again faced James.
"We all know there's more chance that I'll have HIV. I'm the one who slept with Stuart, and since then we've always used protection. If I have HIV, I can't expect you to stay with me." James stood and took Joshua's hand in his own.
"Don't you see? This is why I'm asking you now." Joshua could see the sincerity in James's eyes. He wanted so badly to be James's civil partner; it was all he'd ever wanted, but he couldn't stand the thought of being a burden to James in the future. He wanted to grow old with James, but not if it meant ruining his life.
"I don't think you're going to get rid of him," Greg said playfully. In a sudden moment of spontaneity, Joshua reached out and grabbed what he wanted.
"Ok James, I'll be your civil partner." James threw his arms around Joshua with glee. They kissed passionately for several minutes. When they finally separated they noticed Greg was absent. "Where's Greg?" Joshua asked, still smiling.
"I guess he couldn't wait any longer," James replied. They could hear the sound of Greg's footsteps as he walked down the stairs on his way back to the living room. His steps were like a countdown as they awaited their fate.

They stood and gazed at the doorway for a moment awaiting Greg's return. He walked through the door, his face emotionless and unfathomable.
"Well Greg?" James asked nervously, "What are the results?"
"Congratulations. You're both HIV negative," Greg announced joyfully. They both glared at him in amazement. He held out his arms and quickly received a group hug.
"Are you sure? You are sure aren't you?" Joshua asked, being over-cautious.
"I'm positive, you're both fine. You can have your union and your

wonderful life together," Greg replied as he released them from the embrace.
"Greg, you've been such a good friend. I don't know how to thank you," Joshua said.
"Seeing you happy is all the thanks I need," Greg said boldly.

Later that evening, James and Joshua lay silently on the bed. The events of the day were still sinking in. Although he'd lost Neil, Joshua would have struggled to be unhappy at this moment in time; he had everything he wanted in life. After an hour of peaceful relaxing in each others arms, James's eyes slowly closed. Joshua gazed at him in his state of slumber. He was obviously dreaming of something sweet because his face was a picture of contentment. Joshua slowly caressed James as he slept; this seemed to be enhancing his dream. It was amazing how the sight of his lover sleeping could fascinate him so much. The only thing missing was James's beautiful eyes. As he continued to caress him he noticed a bulge had formed in his underpants; the only items of clothing either of them were wearing. Joshua began to fondle James's penis through the material. By this time Joshua's own penis was aching for attention. He began to tug gently and James lay back at ease. His eyes began to open and immediately locked on Joshua's activities. Joshua glanced at James's face and noticed he'd awoken.
"Nice way to wake up?" Joshua asked with a grin on his face. James smiled and grabbed hold of Joshua, forcing his tongue down his throat passionately.
"Are you sure you want this?" James asked, having not enjoyed any sexual activity recently. Joshua's smile answered the question without the need for speech. The kissing continued for several minutes, with the occasional pause to gaze into each other's eyes. Joshua's hand returned to James's genitalia and he furiously pulled down his underpants in a dramatic change to the mood. He pushed his knee firmly up against James's scrotum, below his testicles and pulled hard on his penis. James's head fell back against pillow; his eyes were firmly closed, he wasn't sure if he was able to open them or not. James reached a climax and ejaculated on to his chest. They collapsed on the bed together.
"Sorry you've waited so long," Joshua apologised.
"Don't worry, if I were only with you for that you'd know about it," James said in jest as he slowly caressed Joshua's nipple, his arm placed tightly around his neck.
"We ought to move in here together," Joshua suggested out of the blue. James tilted his head to glance at Joshua's expression to judge his seriousness.
"Are you sure?" he asked, once again relaxing.

"It's silly for you to keep paying rent on the flat when I own this house."
"But are you sure you can live here after all that's happened?" James asked. Logically it was a perfect solution; with James struggling to make ends meet and Joshua mainly living on student loans the prospect of not paying rent was rather appealing.
"I do have some fond memories of this place too you know. I lived here with my mother. She's given me some memories I'll treasure forever," Joshua replied. James reached over and kissed Joshua.
"If you're sure then I'd love to live here with you," said James.
"You can start moving your things in tomorrow."
"What about your father?" James asked.
"What about him? He's gone," Joshua replied stating the obvious.
"I mean your real father."
"What about him?" Joshua played dumb.
"Will you look for him?"
"No," Joshua replied; he then took James's hand in his own, "All I need is you James."

Chapter 12

"You look beautiful," Joshua said as Megan modeled the dress she was to wear to his civil union ceremony.

"I can't believe you're getting married tomorrow," Megan said excitedly as she twirled in her dress.

"How do you think I feel?" Joshua asked, a grin on his face.

"You can't wait!" exclaimed Megan. There was a faint knock on Megan's bedroom door.

"Can we come in?" Janice asked from the hallway.

"Yeah of course, come and see," Megan eagerly replied. Janice and Greg entered the room and gasped at the sight of Megan's beauty.

"Wow," Janice said.

"You look lovely," Greg said sincerely. Megan thanked them.

"My daughter's a bridesmaid!" Janice said giddily. She quickly dashed over and hugged her daughter.

"So is this ceremony to be like a traditional wedding?" Greg asked, aiming his question at Joshua.

"To some extent," Joshua replied, "Megan will be sort of a bridesmaid and I'd like to have a best man." Greg nodded. "So how about it Greg?"

"How about what?" Greg asked looking confused.

"Greg, you're the closest thing I have to a father. I want you as my best man," Joshua continued, pouring his heart out.

"I'm very touched Joshua….." Greg began. Having over-heard Joshua's proposal, Janice and Megan turned to join the conversation. "I didn't realise you saw me that way," Greg continued.

"Well I do….so how about it?" "I'd be honored," Greg replied, a tear falling from his eye. Janice touched Greg's arm, beaming with pride. "You'd better tell me what you want me to do. I've never been best man at a gay wedding before," Greg went on, unable to conceal the delight he was feeling. Greg dashed out in search of an outfit.

"It means a lot to him you know," Janice said and followed behind him.

Megan and Joshua were once again alone together. They seated themselves on Megan's bed.

"I can't believe it. I'm losing you tomorrow," Megan said, teary-eyed.

"Don't get emotional," Joshua pleaded, "You've not lost anything. You and I are like brother and sister. Think of this as gaining a brother in-law." Megan laughed and quickly received a warm embrace from Joshua. "I couldn't have done it without you," he uttered in a comforting manner.

"I love you," Megan said, unsure herself of in what context she meant it.

"I love you too," Joshua replied. In his own way he was being truthful. Joshua released Megan from his arms and looked her directly in the eyes.

"You will find someone. I promise," he told her. He was so definite. Until this moment Megan hadn't truly believed this herself, but now it was

difficult to deny.
"Thank you." Joshua stood.
"I'd better be going, my groom will be home soon."
"Will this do?" asked Greg from the doorway. Megan and Joshua turned to face him. His outfit was flawless.
"Perfect," Joshua replied.
"Shouldn't I be organising a stag party or something?" Greg asked.
"Nah, quiet night in with James," Joshua replied.
"Booooring," Megan yelled playfully.
"Good luck to you son. I'll see you at the registry office," Greg said and patted Joshua on his arm in a gesture of pride.

An hour later, Joshua was standing in the living room mentally planning a romantic evening. He lit two candles, poured two glasses of wine and dimmed the lights. There was a loud knock at the door.
"Don't tell me he's forgotten his keys again," Joshua muttered to himself. He opened the door. "You'd forget your head if…." he began, before realising Stuart was standing before him. "Stuart!" Joshua said in surprise.
"How's the bride?" Stuart asked in jest.
"I'm fine," Joshua replied, taken aback. Stuart invited himself into the house and immediately noticed the candles.
"You didn't need to go to all this trouble just for me," joked Stuart as he sprawled out on the sofa.
"I'm expecting James to be home any minute," Joshua pointed out, hinting for Stuart to leave.
"I know, I just wanted to chat a little," Stuart said as he sat up straight. "Sit beside me for a minute." Joshua complied, unsure of what this conversation was leading to.
"What did you want to talk about?" Joshua asked, harshness in his tone.
"I can't believe you're getting married first," Stuart began.
"This is becoming a bit of a cliché, you don't know how many times I've heard that today."
"Sorry," Stuart apologised.
"No, I'm sorry," Joshua said, realising his rudeness.
"I just wanted you to know….." Stuart began. He hesitated; it was almost as though he himself hadn't decided what point he was trying to reach. Joshua gazed at him, itching for him to end his statement so that he could begin the evening of romance he had ahead of him.
"My biggest regret is the way I treated you," Stuart confessed boldly.
"Thank you for saying that," said Joshua.
"I mean it," Stuart continued, "If I could turn back the clock back, I 'd do everything differently." His face looked nervous, almost child-like. It was

obvious he was being brutally honest; however this was a complication Joshua could do without on the eve of his civil partnership. "What I'm trying to say is…" Stuart went on.
"Maybe you should stop right there," Joshua suggested, interrupting Stuart's statement.
"I love you," Stuart blurted out. Joshua didn't react and remained silent anticipating Stuart would elaborate. "I'm so sorry for what I did, the way I treated you," Stuart apologised. Joshua took his hand into his own.
"You and Michael make a lovely couple," he said sounding almost patronising.
"I made a mistake," Stuart butted in.
"Yes, and it's too late to rectify it. I'm in love with James and you have Michael. Why don't you go home to him and let me get on with my evening," Joshua said softly. Stuart nodded and headed for the door. Joshua remained seated and quiet. As he was about to leave, Stuart turned to face his friend.
"We're still friends aren't we?" he asked.
"I want to see you at the union tomorrow with Michael by your side," Joshua said, offering a smile of reassurance. Stuart half-heartedly returned the gesture.
"I figured this would be what you'd say, which is why I got you these." Stuart rummaged around in his bag and pulled out 2 small pot bears, one was brown and the other blue, the blue bear was holding a heart with the gay pride flag colours. He passed them to Joshua. "I didn't make them, I wish I could! A friend of mine called Kieran made them. I showed him a photo of you and James and he made them specially with your eye colours. He hand crafted them with clay and painted them with acrylic paint"
"I don't know what to say."
"It's the least I could do considering the pain I've brought you in the past." Joshua chuckled for a moment as he examined the bear that represented him.
"My bear is holding the heart symbolising pride;10 years ago I would've been ashamed, it's funny how things change."
"People change too," said Stuart, "I'll see you tomorrow." Stuart closed his bag and departed.

Feeling a little dazed by what had just happened, Joshua gulped down his glass of wine and replenished it. He crashed on the chair, taking in the situation. "Stuart's still carrying a torch for me after all these years," he said to himself. He pondered for a moment how life would have turned out if things had been different. What if he'd never discovered Stuart's infidelity? What if he'd forgiven his indiscretions? He wondered whether or not their relationship would have survived. He quickly realised however, that everything had worked out for the best and he'd never been happier than the past few years he'd spent as James's significant other. In James's arms he felt safe and loved, he'd be a fool to even contemplate spending his life with anyone else and in a small way, the bears looking as though they belonged together symbolized that he'd made the right decision.

The doorbell sounded. "Who on earth this time?" Joshua asked himself out loud. It was obviously not James because the door was unlocked. "Coming!" he yelled.

"OK," came a voice from outside. Joshua recognised the voice.

"Surely not," he said to himself. He opened the door to find a well dressed Michael on the step. Joshua gazed at him, unsure of what to expect. Had Stuart left him before his confession?

"Are you going to ask me in?" Michael asked, breaking the silence.

"Yeh," Joshua said after a slight hesitation.

"It's looking nice in here," Michael complimented him. He noticed the wine on the table. "Are you planning a romantic evening? Usually a couple spends the night before their wedding apart," Michael pointed out.

"Well there's not much traditional about our wedding is there," Joshua replied, slightly annoyed at Michaels intrusiveness. "So what brings you here?" he asked immediately, taking a swig from his newly replenished wine glass as he dreaded what was about to be discussed.

"I was feeling nostalgic," Michael began as he walked towards the sofa, hinting for an invitation to sit.

"Sit down, please," Joshua said. Michael did so. Joshua took another gulp of wine and seated himself as far away from his friend as possible. He was treading on eggshells. It was impossible to know what to say to someone when their partner had just admitted their love for you.

"So you're feeling nostalgic," Joshua said, repeating Michael's words.

"Yes. It occurred to me how far you've come in your life. You've almost got your degree, you have your own home, and you're getting married to a guy that adores you…"

"Michael…" Joshua interrupted, but was immediately interrupted himself.

"Let me finish, please," Michael said. Joshua remained still and silent, "I was thinking about how differently things could have turned out if I'd lived my life differently." Joshua began to relax, realising that Michael had been completely unaware of Stuart's visit. It seemed Michael's visit was in fact for similar reasons as Stuart's.

"What are you trying to say?" Joshua asked bluntly.

"I love you, I've always loved you," Michael announced. He was being so brutally honest, in a way Joshua wasn't prepared to hear. Deep down he'd always had knowledge of Michael's feelings for him on some level, in the same way he knew how Megan felt, but it was almost inconceivable that all the years Stuart and Michael had been together they'd both independently harbored feelings for him. "Stop!" Joshua demanded. Michael was dumbfounded. "I appreciate your honesty and I want us to be friends...." Joshua began.

"Is it because of the HIV?" Michael asked randomly, clutching at straws.

"No," Joshua insisted, "I love James. We're going to have a great life together. I suggest you go home to Stuart. You make a nice couple," Joshua said firmly. Michael stared into Joshua's eyes for a moment.

"What a fool I've been," he said and briefly caressed Joshua's cheek as though he were taking his only chance to touch a pop star at the front row of a concert.

"I expect to see you and Stuart arrive together tomorrow. You need each other." Michael nodded and left without being shown out.

Joshua stood and once again reached for his wine glass. He glanced at the clock and realised how late James was. He studied the screen on his mobile phone in the hope that a text message or missed call from James would be awaiting his attention. The phone didn't display either of these so Joshua called his number. After several rings the call was diverted to voicemail. Joshua ended the call and placed his phone down on the table before returning to the sofa with his glass of wine. He glanced at the clock every few minutes, as though he were hoping that he'd previously read it wrongly. Nine o'clock arrived. It was the night before his civil union and his partner was nowhere to be seen. Joshua was unsure of whether to be angry, upset, or concerned. Was James with another man? Surely not, Joshua knew him better than that. The text message tone sounded and Joshua stubbed his toe rushing to the table to read it. It read, 'I'm really sorry, I'll be home in a couple of hours.' Joshua polished off his glass of wine. "Alone on the eve of my wedding," he said, feeling sorry for himself. He poured himself another glass of wine and gulped it down. "Fuck this!" he yelled, and stormed out, slamming the door behind him.

Greg was once again modeling his outfit in preparation for the following day.

"Are you sure I look ok?" he asked for the hundredth time.

"Yes!" Megan and Janice insisted simultaneously. He took another look at himself in the mirror, beaming with pride. It was obvious to Megan and Janice that Greg's appointment as 'Best man' meant the world to him. The doorbell rang.

"I'll get it," Megan said, trotting off to greet their guest.
"You're really looking forward to the union aren't you?" Janice asked, placing her arms around his waist from behind.
"It means so much that he asked me to be best man," Greg admitted.
"You're like a father to him," Janice said lovingly.
"Maybe even more so after tomorrow," Greg said evasively.

"Why aren't you having a romantic evening with James?" Megan asked Joshua in the doorway.
"He's been held up," Joshua replied, putting on a brave face to conceal his disappointment.
"Well come in then," Megan insisted, and they headed for the living room.

"Have you still got that outfit on?" Joshua asked as he entered the room. "Joshua; I didn't think we'd see you tonight," Greg said.
"I won't be staying long," Joshua replied.
"Sit down, I'll get us all some drinks," Janice offered and she scuttled off into the kitchen.
"I absolutely can't wait for tomorrow!" Megan said enthusiastically.
Janice returned holding a bottle of wine in one hand and balancing four glasses in the other.
"I think I've had enough for one night," exclaimed Joshua.
"Go on, just one glass," Janice coaxed him. Joshua reluctantly nodded and they all sat down. Megan proposed a toast.
"To Joshua and James…."
"To many happy years together," Janice added. The glasses clicked together and everyone took a sip.
"Joshua, I want to talk to you about something," Greg announced, bringing a serious tone to the mood in the room. Joshua was managing to maintain his falsely happy exterior so far, however he dreaded that what Greg was about to say may bring it to an end. "I'm so honored that you chose me as your best man and that you see me as a father figure. It's all I've ever wanted," Greg said seriously.
"Don't get all mushy on the lad," Janice interrupted.
"No love, it's important," Greg said. His tone was firm. Everyone was now listening attentively. "26 years ago I was a 17 year old boy, madly in love. Her name was Anne. She was a beautiful woman and I would have done anything for her. She was carrying my child and I was so proud. Even though we were young, we were determined that we'd be good parents…." Greg wiped a tear from his eye. Everyone present was intrigued. Previously Greg had been so evasive about his past and although nobody quite knew why he'd chosen this moment to bear his soul, they were eager to listen. "At the time I didn't know what career

path I wanted to take. All I was concerned with was providing for my fiancée and child." He paused for a moment.
"Go on," Janice encouraged him.
"Anne went into labor a month early. There were complications."
"Did the baby die?" Joshua asked.
"No, the baby survived, but Anne died. I think that's partly why I became a doctor," Greg replied.
"It must have been awful," Megan sympathised.
"He was such a beautiful little boy. He's 26 now mind," Greg continued.
"What happened to him?" Janice asked.
"He was adopted by a young couple. The woman was unable to have children of her own. At the time it seemed like it was for the best. I thought they'd be great parents; at least that's what I was told."
"Are you back in touch with him?" Joshua asked, intrigued by Greg's tale.
"Yes I am," Greg replied.
"What's his name?" Megan asked curiously.
"He has a lovely name; it's Joshua," Greg replied with slight hesitation.
Everything began to fall into place. Joshua glared at Greg in disbelief.
"You. You're my father?"
Greg nodded, almost unable to speak. A silence loomed for several moments.
"I couldn't keep you Joshua. I was seventeen, alone and heartbroken. I believed you were better with two adoptive parents. I didn't know Neil was such a bastard," Greg defended himself.
"When did you realise?" Joshua asked calmly and emotionless.
"After you were attacked and you came into hospital, I noticed your date of birth, then I looked at your medical records," Greg replied.
"So you've known for years, even before Neil died," Joshua said in amazement. Greg nodded, almost shamefully.
"I was going to tell you tomorrow, but I felt it only fair to give you the option of whether or not you still wanted me as your best man." Joshua took Greg's hand in his own.
"I'll be proud to have you, my father standing beside me as I say my vows. My only regret is that I didn't know sooner. You've been more of a father to me than Neil ever was," Joshua said tearfully.
"I love you Joshua.....son."
"I love you too Dad. You guys have been my family for years. I'm so glad that's truer than I ever imagined," Joshua replied, then put his arms around Greg. Megan and Janice quickly joined in with the embrace.

James arrived home before Joshua that night; he'd delayed himself by bombarding Greg with questions of his origin and staring at old photos of his birth mother. He entered the house, his smile beaming, high as though he'd been taking a wonderful drug. He glanced around for James but he was nowhere to be seen. He dashed up to the bedroom where he found James standing, facing the window.
"There you are!" exclaimed Joshua, "I don't even know where to start telling you what's happened today!"
"Joshua, we need to talk. I have something to tell you. I need to be honest with you," James said, still with his back facing Joshua.
"Please no, I can't take anyone else being honest with me tonight!" joked Joshua, "First Stuart, then Michael, then Greg…"
"Joshua please let me talk," James demanded. Joshua noticed two empty bottles of Corona on the floor.
"You've been drinking."
"I needed to. What I have to tell you isn't easy," he replied.
"You're scaring me James. Can't you at least face me?" Joshua asked.
"I can't Joshua. I don't want to see the expression on your face."
"I don't understand," Joshua said and he placed his hand on James's shoulder, "Nothing you could tell me would make me stop loving you."
James pushed Joshua's hand away. He sat on the bed. "Why are you being like this tonight?" he asked.
"Because I can't allow you to marry me until I'm honest with you. It already tears me up inside. I can't begin married life this way. I thought if I made you happy it would make up for it. I was so stupid. I was so wrong."
"James, whatever it is, you can tell me," Joshua said, his heart slowly sinking as he dreaded what was to come. The possibilities were running through his mind; however the only plausible explanation was that he'd been unfaithful. "Is it another guy?" he asked. James shook his head.
"What then!?" Joshua yelled.
"Remember when you turned eighteen, back then I was so homophobic, in denial a
bout myself, and I outed you. I was such a bastard…"
"Don't worry about all that. It's ancient history," Joshua interrupted.
"Listen to me please," James pleaded. A silence loomed as Joshua awaited an explanation. "I wish I could look you in the eye as I tell you this…..When you were attacked, not long after your 18th birthday…"
"What about it? Do you know who attacked me?" Joshua asked.
"Yes Joshua. It was me. I was the one who beat you up that night. I'm so sorry." His lips were trembling. Joshua could see his tears falling on to the window ledge. He couldn't believe what he'd just heard. James turned

to face Joshua who was gazing at him in disbelief. The sight of the disappointment in his eyes was too much for James. “Say something!” he demanded.

“I loved you,” Joshua said without feeling. It was as though with one sentence James had sucked out all of Joshua’s life, all of his sparkle. “How could you?” Joshua asked calmly, he didn’t have the energy to become angry. It had been such a trying day. James sat beside him on the bed.

“I love you. You have to believe that. I still want to be with you forever,” he said, desperately trying to salvage the situation. Joshua was still gazing in the direction of the window; it was as though he was in a trance, unaware that James had moved.

“Please Joshua, react in some way. Throw things around, shout at me……Just do something!” James yelled. Joshua finally faced him. He looked directly into his eyes, where he’d once seen his destiny, now all he saw was deceit and lies.

“I left Brad for you. He was the most decent and honest man I’ve ever known,” he uttered. He stood and walked to the door. James remained seated on the bed. “More fool me,” Joshua completed his sentence. James quickly turned to face him.

“I’m so sorry, we can still have a great life together; I know we can.”

“You’ve got one hour to gather your things together and leave my house forever.” Joshua’s words were so cold. James had never heard him sound so callus and unfeeling before. He truly knew he’d broken his heart. Joshua left the room and immediately James could hear his footsteps on the staircase. He dashed to the top. “What are you going to do?” he asked, “Go back to a life of one night stands? Circle the bars desperately searching for a man that will want you for more than a quick shag? You don’t want that. I know you don’t.” James was correct. What Joshua wanted wasn’t a life on the gay scene; it wasn’t meaningless sex. Joshua turned before reaching the bottom step.

“I wanted what I thought you were; now I know that doesn’t exist.” He looked at the bears on the bookshelf; everything they represented was a sham. He left the house, carefully closing the door behind him. Joshua’s calmness made James feel even guiltier. He walked down the stairs and noticed the table had been set with candles and wine for a romantic evening. He’d lost everything that truly mattered to him, and he’d nobody else to blame.

From the outside, Brad’s flat still looked exactly the same. Was it too much for Joshua to hope for that he’d take him back? He banged loudly on the door. A man in his early thirties wearing only a pair of shorts answered the door. He was obviously settled in for the evening.

“Hello.”

“Who are you?” Joshua asked, taken aback.

“My name is John,” he replied.

“Is Brad at home?” Joshua asked, his desperation obvious in his tone.

“No he’s not in right now. I’m his partner, can I help?” John said casually.

Joshua didn’t respond immediately. It took a few moments for the harsh reality of the situation to sink in. “Do you want to leave a message?” John asked.

“No….I made a mistake,” Joshua replied and slowly walked away.

Epilogue

Joshua and Megan clambered their way into the house, both weighed down with several bags. They immediately placed them on the floor on entry.
"I think that's the last of them," Megan said, breathing a sigh of relief.
"Come on Megan, let's sit down. All this can wait 'till the morning," Joshua suggested. They parked themselves on the sofa, drained of energy as a result of a day of lifting and carrying.
"I'm really sorry about all that's happened. You are sure you want a flat mate aren't you?" Megan asked.
"Of course I am. It'll be great to have you here," Joshua replied. It was late, and the light was minimal. Joshua's eyes were closing even as he spoke. Megan placed her arm around him and he quickly fell asleep on her shoulder.
"Don't worry," she said, "We'll find our perfect men someday."

About the author:

Brett Bradley-Howarth was born Brett Howarth in 1983 and has lived in Derbyshire, UK ever since. He is now in a civil union with his long term partner Colin. His main profession is working with disabled young people.

This book was inspired by events in the life of Brett and others close to him.

www.ingramcontent.com/pod-product-compliance
Ingram Content Group UK Ltd.
Pitfield, Milton Keynes, MK11 3LW, UK
UKHW020117200726
13856UKWH00002B/599

9 781446 184929